The Cost of Betrayal

David Dalglish

The Cost of Betrayal

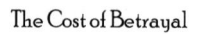

BOOKS BY DAVID DALGLISH

THE HALF-ORC SERIES

The Weight of Blood

The Cost of Betrayal

The Death of Promises

The Shadows of Grace (coming soon)

THE WORLD OF DEZREL

A Dance of Cloaks (August 2010)

The Cost of Betrayal

Part One

The Cost of Betrayal

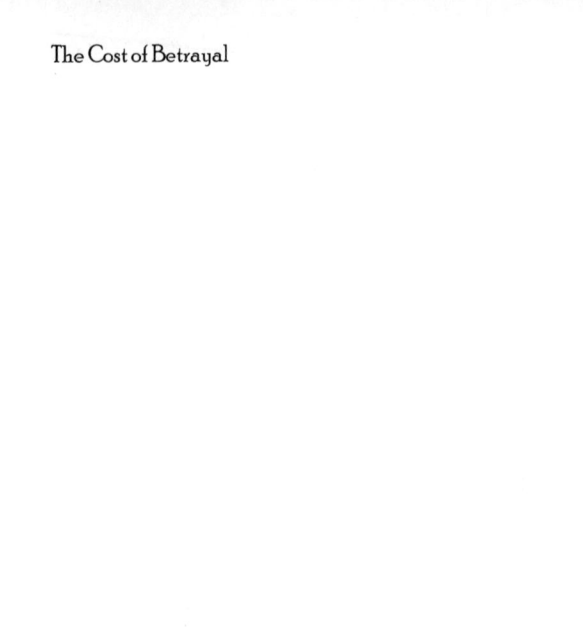

Prologue

The room was dark and plain, a strange combination for a supposed holy place.

"Take my hand, child," Aresh said. He stood inside the doorway, the noisy streets of Veldaren behind him. His polished armor shone bright, and the chainmail beneath the large sections of plate clinked from the movement of his outstretched arm.

"I'm no child," the woman said, refusing his hand but entering anyway. On either side of the wood walls were hard oak benches covered with thin blankets, stitched golden mountains across their lengths. There were no windows, and only the one door. She knew she should be worried, a girl trapped alone with a strange man. But he was a priest of Ashhur, and she was no normal girl.

She smiled at the priest. He was middle-aged, with thinning hair around his ears and a nose much too large for his face to be attractive. He smiled back, his lips parting to reveal clean, straight teeth.

"We use this room for confession and difficult talk," Aresh said as he closed the door. His voice sounded weak in the empty air, and a bit eager. "Many are not comfortable voicing their fears where others may hear. There are matters that demand privacy, even secrecy."

"Of course," she said.

"What about you, Tessanna? Is there anything you want to confess?"

She noticed he had taken off the bulkier part of his armor and set it aside. A part of her, deep in the back of her conscience, told her to be wary.

She wasn't.

"I've done plenty," she said, her voice still soft and shy, sounding much younger than her eighteen years. "But I wouldn't ever confess. That implies I think it was bad, or don't want to do it again. I like the bad stuff I've done. I liked it a lot."

Aresh's breathing had grown a bit louder, and Tessanna held in a laugh.

"That is because you are sick," he said. "Your mind is broken, Tessanna, shattered into pieces. I have discussed this with my fellow priests, even our high priest Calan, and we all agree. Your mind is like a puzzle. Someone must put the pieces back in the right order."

"And that someone is you?" she asked. The bench was cold and uncomfortable when she sat on it. She crossed her arms over her chest and gave him a knowing wink. "Can you put me back together?"

She noticed how smooth he was, even with her direct approach. He was not smooth enough, however, to hide the fact that he had loosened the belt at his waist.

"Ashhur's grace is something we must all receive," he said. "The glory of his light heals all wounds, and it would be blasphemous to believe that you are beyond healing, as some have said. You are a beautiful girl, Tess."

She lay on her back, her arms stretched over her head. She was slender, her skin milky white and smooth as polished stone. Her long black hair curled about her waist. Her eyes pierced Aresh's attraction, stirring a bit of guilt and worry. Her irises were solid black, so that her eyes were giant black orbs with hints of white at the edges, and under her gaze he felt naked. His smooth words seemed like childish lies, unneeded and unconvincing.

"Can you fix me?" she asked, a smirk touching the corners of her mouth.

"Close your eyes," he said. "And do not be afraid. I will give you my healing. Ashhur has blessed man and woman, and through his blessing, I will make you whole."

With her eyes closed, she listened as his armor and belt hit the floor. She felt a part of her retreating inward, toward the center, while the childish, frightened girl remained on the outside, passive and gullible. When he climbed on top of her, she dared believe it might work.

Because she wasn't whole. She was many, she was sick, and she had killed more people than Aresh would believe.

He grunted and moaned, and his jerky movements only elicited a tighter clenching of her eyes. His hands fumbled across her breasts. He tried to be gentle, but she didn't care. The pieces twirling in her mind waited and waited, but they felt nothing.

"Ashhur's salvation," Aresh said before kissing her.

Those words ignited something inside her, something opposite what he intended.

"Salvation," she said, opening her eyes and looking at him with a cold stare that shriveled his stomach. "This is your salvation? This is what Ashhur can offer me?"

He rolled off her, short of breath and seeming small and weak without his armor and white tunic. She giggled, and the sound froze him where he stood.

"I should have known," she said. "I didn't want to know, I tried not to know, but you lied to me. You shoved lies down my throat and kissed me to keep them down."

Aresh pulled up his pants, feeling a chill race up and down his spine. Tessanna slid off the bench and approached. All childishness had left her, vanishing as if it had never been. It seemed an entirely new creature stalked him, cruel and angry. He towered over her by a full foot, but still he felt terrified.

"I have made you whole," he said, his voice quivering.

"You filled a hole," she said. "And you did a poor job at that."

She grabbed his wrist. He couldn't tear away. She weighed next to nothing, she was so rail thin and bony. Why could he not pull away? The muscles in his arm tensed, then relaxed. He felt a strange presence, like a worm crawling in his brain. When she spoke, there was no trace of a smile, no hint of shyness.

"How many girls have you taken here?" she asked. Her hair lifted as if a strong wind blew through the room, but Aresh felt nothing, only the icy grip of her hand and the digging, squirming sensation behind his eyes.

"I've never…you don't…let go of me child. I have done Ashhur's work."

Tessanna laughed, but there was not a shred of joy in it.

"If you do Ashhur's work, then let me do Karak's," she said.

Aresh took a step back. Those eyes, he thought. Why can I not look away from those damn eyes?

"You don't want to do Karak's work," he said. "Karak is evil and darkness. Those who worship him will spend eternity in the fires of the abyss."

"Is that true?" Tessanna said. "Let's find out."

He had no chance to scream before fire burst from Tessanna's fingers. She bathed him in flame, and when he finally did scream, she laughed.

"Praise be to Ashhur," she shouted. "Bathe in his light!"

The light from her hands seared his flesh, and when he was nothing but ash and bone, a strong wind blew open the door and scattered his remains.

As the wind died, Tessanna knelt, her hands clasped against her chest.

"I'm sorry," she said. Her cold anger was gone. She was the shy, young girl once more. "You said you could fix me. You lied. You hurt me. I've been hurt enough. I won't let anyone hurt me anymore."

Mind still broken, she walked out into the streets of Veldaren, unworried about her hiked up dress and exposed left breast. When an old lady finally commented, Tessanna smiled, thanked her, and fixed her dress.

"Not a care in the world," the lady muttered as Tessanna walked on.

1

Qurrah was the last to awake. The sun was high in the air, dawn several hours past. He kept his eyes closed and his body still. Every muscle ached from the battle of Woodhaven the day before. He thought of his escape with his master...former master, he corrected mentally. Velixar had died, his body riddled with elven arrows tipped with blessed water. Abandoned and alone, Qurrah had staggered through the fire and corpses, bitter and angry at his brother Harruq for not being there in his time of need.

At the thought of his brother, Qurrah felt his stomach tighten. He could hear Harruq talking with Aurelia, an elf he had befriended over the past few months. He was smitten, though he seemed oblivious as to how badly. Their talk was of small things, purposefully avoiding the conflicts of the prior day.

A pleasant smell teased his nostrils. His stomach rumbled noisily. Qurrah finally coughed and stirred, alerting the two to his awakening. Noticing the movements, Harruq trudged over, food in hand.

"Morning," he said, handing him a plate full of sausage, lettuce, and buttered bread.

"Did you abduct a cook while I slept?" Qurrah asked.

"Courtesy of the elf," Aurelia said, walking over. "And finally you awake. Hurry and eat."

Qurrah took the plate and sampled a bit of sausage. The warm food stirred his stomach. He couldn't remember when he had last eaten. He rammed food into his mouth, not caring about any sort of manners. Aurelia watched him, a small frown tugging at the corners of her mouth. Qurrah seemed pale and drained, his muscles almost non-existent as they clung to his bones. He looked like a pathetic caricature of his brother, one drained of warmth, joy, and trust.

But not strength. Aurelia knew well the strength the half-orc hid, powerful necromancy honed to a fearful precision at the hands of his master, Velixar. Both brothers were half-orc, half-elf, and that mixture seemed to have unlocked a strange reservoir of power for the two of them. Many elves had fallen to them in battle, overwhelmed by blade and magic.

"Careful there," Aurelia said as Qurrah nearly choked on some lettuce. "I can make more if you're hungry. I never expected you to out-eat your brother."

A wave of her hand and the plate refilled. The brown sausage steamed as if just taken from a fire. Qurrah stared and shook his head.

"How?"

"A simple spell. I could teach you, if you wished."

The half-orc resumed eating, nodding as he did. "I would appreciate it."

Harruq sighed, remembering all the meager meals, many stolen, that he and Qurrah had shared over the many years.

"Too bad you never learned that spell ages ago," he grumbled.

After Qurrah finished, the three prepared for travel. It didn't take very long, considering their meager possessions. Qurrah had his magic whip, which he wrapped around his arm, and his pouch of bones and other components for his spells. Harruq buckled his swords to his belt, ran a hand through his hair, and then declared himself ready.

"So where are we to go?" she asked, her own few things tucked away in secret pockets of her dress.

"We know little of this world," Qurrah said. "We have been exiled twice. Once for our blood, and once for the blood we spilled."

Aurelia winced, still uncomfortable with mention of the battle. Harruq and Qurrah had fought against her elven kin and slaughtered many, but she had protected Harruq and even helped him escape. A day later, she still was not sure why. She just remembered the panicked, desperate look in Harruq's eyes when he thought she might die, murdered by his own hands.

"Mordan banished my kind," Aurelia said. "And it seems now Neldar has done the same. East or West, there is no home for me."

"You said yesterday you could get us into Veldaren," Harruq said. "Is that true?"

Veldaren was the capital of the kingdom of Neldar, and had been the brothers' previous home before they had been expelled.

"Only if you both play along," Aurelia said. "How we live once we're in, though, will depend on you."

"It might not be comfortable," Qurrah said. "My brother and I are used to the dark and the filth. Could you say the same?"

"Don't treat me like a prissy child princess," Aurelia said. "I've lived longer than the two of you combined. I can endure a bit of hardship. Now close your eyes, Harruq."

She placed her hands on his face as he stared at her with wide eyes.

"Um, what are you doing, Aurry?"

"Be quiet. Can you remember what Veldaren looks like from beyond the gates?"

"Yeah, but why?"

"I said close your eyes. Concentrate on that image. It'll be hard, knowing you, but try anyway."

Qurrah smirked as Harruq did as he was told. He remembered the great wall surrounding the city, made of stacked stones, each one taller and wider than several men. He remembered the great oak doors, lined with metal and steel. He remembered the castle proper, looming over the city with its great collection of towering spires and crenellated walls. It was an awesome sight, crafted by the hand of the dark god, Karak.

Aurelia focused on these images, lifting them from Harruq's akin to a ladle drawing water from a well. She focused on the fields of grass stretching from the front entrance on either side of a worn path. Perfect. Eyes still closed, she let go of Harruq and stepped back. Words of magic slipped through her lips. The air before her ripped open into a flat, whirling blue essence.

"And there we go," she said, opening her eyes. "Veldaren."

She stepped through the portal and vanished. The two half-orcs glanced at one another.

"You first, my brother," Qurrah said.

"I'd hate to leave you again. I'll follow after."

"Get in there, you child."

"Fine," Harruq grumbled. He took a deep breath, took another, and then stepped through. Qurrah followed.

Both felt the same sensation of flying over a great distance, yet to their minds they had taken a single step. The gentle hills north of Woodhaven were gone, replaced by the walls of Neldar, the city of stone.

"That was easy enough," Harruq said. He decided not to mention his insides felt like they were doing loops.

"We have been banished, as has your kind," Qurrah said. "How do you plan to sneak us in?"

"Through the front gate, of course," Aurelia said. "Just give me a moment."

She chanted again, the words far different than any spell Qurrah was used to hearing. This was no magic of destruction or death. No, it was a much subtler magic. Aurelia's dress changed from a simple green to an elegant mix of reds and violets. The gold of her skin faded pink. Her ears lost their upturned tips, enlarging and rounding out into human ears. After a quick snap of her fingers, white gloves appeared, covering up to her elbows.

"I look the definition of a rich noble of Mordeina, do you not agree, my servants?" she asked.

"Servants?" Qurrah said. "Surely you jest."

"Why else would you two accompany me? Keep your mouths shut, and agree with anything I say. Oh, and here."

Another snap of her fingers, and suddenly large leather bags, clipped together by gold and silver buckles, appeared at their feet. The elf winked.

"A noble doesn't travel empty handed."

"You mean a noble's servants," Harruq grumbled. He picked up two, grunting at their weight. "What is in here?"

"Rocks. And you forgot a bag."

He looked at the third, sitting in front of Qurrah.

"I am but an advisor and protector," the weaker half-orc said. "You would not think I would be forced into physical labor, would you?"

Aurelia laughed into her glove as Harruq shifted two bags to his right hand and grabbed the third with his left.

"Laugh all you want, I'm dropping these things the second we're inside."

"You poor dear. Now hurry, we don't want my delicate skin in the sun for too long."

They were far enough away from the entrance that Aurelia's shift in clothes and facial design went unnoticed. Harruq grunted and groaned with every step, his arms bulging with muscle. He felt they would pop out of their sockets if he travelled much farther. He dropped the bags as they halted before the two gate guards, who had barred the entrance with their crossed spears.

"I'm sorry, milady, but those things have been banned from the city," said one guard.

Aurelia scoffed at the two guards as if they were children.

"I don't know how, since I, and they, have never been here before."

"Only human blood is allowed entrance," said the other. "I suggest you leave them outside during your stay."

"I most certainly will not," Aurelia huffed. "You don't expect a frail thing such as myself to carry these bags on my own, do you?"

"I'm sure you could hire…"

She interrupted him by snapping her fingers in front of his nose.

"I have already hired my servants. And if I recall, you have banned elves, not orcs."

"Milady, we may turn away any we wish. I am telling you, those things behind you are not coming inside, servants or otherwise."

Qurrah put a hand on Harruq's arm, which was shaking with slowly building rage.

"Calm, brother," he whispered. "Save your anger for when it may do good."

Aurelia untied a coin purse from her sash, hoping neither of the gate guards heard Qurrah's words.

"Now then," she said, her mood brightening, "you say I can hire new servants? Well, how about I hire you two?"

The guards exchanged glances, and did so a second time with much wider eyes when the disguised elf opened the purse to reveal a pile of shiny gold coins.

"I'd say three a piece is fair, don't you?" she asked.

"More than fair," the first guard said.

"Oh yes," said the second.

"Good," she said, dropping the thick coins into each outstretched hand. She tied the purse back to her sash. A flick of her finger, and Harruq picked up the bags.

"Well, my servants, I could use such armed and competent men as yourselves. I've been afraid of thieves the past few days. Could you stare off that way and make sure none chase after me? I'll sleep better tonight if you do."

"Welcome to Veldaren," both guards said in unison. They uncrossed their spears and pointedly ignored the two half-orcs as they entered the city.

"Since when are you a rich little elf?" Harruq asked once they were beyond earshot.

"Since never," she laughed. "In about an hour, those two will find themselves three copper pieces richer. I hope it is enough to buy them a drink to drown their sorrow."

"And I thought I was the devious one," Qurrah said.

A few peddlers eagerly brought out their wares as the trio passed by. Aurelia waved them off without slowing. For the most part, however, they were ignored. The southern districts of Veldaren were filled with homes of the poorer inhabitants. It wasn't until the center of the city that the real merchants set up shop. A beautiful fountain carved as a statue of a crowned man wielding a sword marked where the roads leading from the southern and western gates met. Aurelia paused before the statue, reading aloud the writing beneath.

"Valius Kren, first great King of Neldar…"

She chuckled at the blurred writing underneath, knowing full well what it originally said.

"…to be appointed by the hand of glorious Karak himself," she finished. Harruq gave her a funny look, but Qurrah seemed far more intrigued.

"How is it you know this?" he asked.

"About sixty years ago some priests of Ashhur demanded the statue be destroyed, or the words below erased. Karak founded this entire nation, and placed the stones with his hands, yet it seems many would like to forget such an allegiance. It was all the talk among the elves, many fearing the humans would soon forget, and then repeat, the mistakes of their past."

"I would not have expected empathy for Karak from one such as you," Qurrah said.

Aurelia frowned at him in her foreign face.

"It is not empathy. I just wonder at the foolishness of humans. Before Karak and Ashhur warred, both were loving, benevolent deities. If anything, mankind should remember that all may fall."

"Fascinating, but my arms are really starting to hurt," Harruq said from behind them. "Where the abyss are we going?"

"Didn't you two used to have a home here?" she asked him.

"Yeah, but you don't want to live there. It was just a small shed, we hardly fit inside."

"Milady of Mordan, may I interest you in the finest silks this side of the rivers?" interrupted a shouting voice.

"Oh Celestia help us," Aurelia moaned as a chubby man with a mustache waddled over, purple cloth in his hand.

"Not interested, buddy," Harruq growled, intercepting the merchant. "Go bug someone else."

"Do I know you?" the merchant asked, giving both brothers an inquisitive look.

"They're my pets, and you know all orcs look the same," Aurelia said, gently pushing Harruq aside. "And forgive us, but I would like to delay until I have rented my room."

"Of course," he said, bowing deeply. Qurrah crossed his arms, his mouth locked in a frown.

"What is it?" the elf asked him once the merchant marched back to his stand propped against the side of a building. Qurrah dipped his hand into the fountain and drank.

"His eyes never left me and my brother," he said once finished. "Any merchant worth his wares knows to never break contact with the buyer." He nodded again, his eyes darting to the side. "And he watches us even now."

"A thief, perhaps?" Aurelia asked.

"There are no thieves," Harruq said, shifting a bag from his right hand to his left. "Guess you don't know about the guilds here, do you?"

"Another time," Qurrah said. "Someone else is watching us. We need to leave."

"Well," Harruq said, taking the initiative. "Nowhere else to go but home, if it still stands. Anyone follows us, we'll know."

Harruq led the way, following the western road for a quarter mile before darting south. Fewer and fewer people traveled the streets, and those that did stared openly at Aurelia. It wasn't often a noble of worth came anywhere near their homes. Harruq led them deeper south, into the old, decaying part of the city.

"Is anyone still following us?" Aurelia asked.

"Not that I see," Qurrah said. "But I feel it still, eyes watching from afar."

"Come on, we're almost there," Harruq said. "I'd say we already look suspicious enough. Think I can dump the bags?"

"No need." A wave of her hand and the bags vanished into nothing. Harruq stretched his arms, moaning with approval.

"Much better." His hands fell to his swords. "Follow me."

With Harruq no longer carrying the bags, they made a faster pace. Aurelia took in as much as she could as they weaved through homes and back alleys. They were so close to the prosperous northern districts, yet here it seemed the sun shone less, the faces bore little happiness, and no sign of wealth dared let itself show. With each turn Harruq led them on, things grew worse.

"There are no places such as these in Woodhaven," Aurelia said softly.

"Welcome to the dark parts of mankind," Qurrah muttered with strange amusement. Drunk men wandered the street in daytime. A few whores catcalled to them. The air stank of feces and urine, for the thin sewers on each side of the street were clogged and overflowing. Lying beside a ditch, crowned with a halo of flies, was a blood-spattered corpse. No one seemed to notice.

Qurrah glanced back, barely catching sight of a yellow robe.

"Find us a building," he said to Harruq. "Make it large and empty."

The big half-orc approached what had once been a storehouse. A shove of his arm, and the weathered door collapsed. Dust erupted as it hit the ground. Harruq led the way, Aurelia and Qurrah following after.

"Cheerful place," Harruq said as he looked about the mostly empty building. Dust covered the floor, and splintered boards hung from the windows. Feces and dried urine filled one corner, and stacked hay filled another. A few crates and some rotting wood decorated the place.

"Who chases us?" Aurelia asked, frowning at the sight around her.

"Are your spells ready?" Qurrah asked her.

"I'm a sorceress. My spells are always ready."

"Good. Because I fear we have a mage nearby."

As he said those words, Aurelia's robe faded back to its deep green, her ears returned to their sharp points, and her face, back to its exotic beauty.

"Uh oh," she said.

It was then that a wide blanket of interlaced webs fell on top of all three.

2

"Now I'm pissed," Harruq said, yanking at the web surrounding his body. He yanked one of his swords out from its sheathed. The black blade easily cut him free. Aurelia remained perfectly still, her eyes closed. Qurrah let his whip drop, the fire burning away all webbing that it touched.

"Just stay put, you durn idiots," a voice cried out. A short, stocky human dressed in full platemail stood at the door, his chest nearly covered by his black beard. Each hand held a nasty looking punch dagger.

"Aren't your swords a little tiny to be calling us idiots?" the half-orc shouted, tearing loose from the web and storming toward him. "Now what in blazes do you want?"

"Harruq, look out!" Qurrah shouted. Harruq glanced back, but was too late. A figure leapt from atop a pile of crates and crashed down on the burly warrior. The butts of two sabers smacked his skull, dropping him like a sack of grain. The attacker landed without a sound, his entire figure shrouded by swirling gray cloaks.

"Enough of this," Aurelia said, still shrouded in webs. Twin lightning bolts arced out from her hands, tearing through webbing as they streaked toward the ambushers. The man in gray cloaks whirled, dodging the blast. The shorter fellow did not fare as well. The lightning hit him square in the chest, lifted him off his feet, and deposited him outside in a gasping lump of metal, dirt and flesh. Aurelia followed with two more bolts of lightning. The man in gray dodged back and forth, leaping off walls and crates so that each strike just barely missed.

Qurrah lashed his whip, burning away more of the webs. He heard soft chanting from within the darkness high above his head, and he recognized it for what it was: a wizard casting a spell.

"Darkness is no haven here," he said. Invisible forces gripped his arms and legs, slowing their movements. Qurrah ignored them, knowing they were mental illusions. He kept his hands looping through the semantic motions for his spell. The darkness covering the ceiling suddenly recoiled and fled as if it were a living thing.

The Cost of Betrayal

Standing there, illuminated in no light but still clearly visible, was a middle-aged wizard dressed in yellow robes, a yellow cloak, and a tall yellow hat. In his left hand he held a long, knotted staff.

"Hello there," he said, realizing his cover was gone. "Clever fellow, aren't you?"

A ball of fire leapt from his hands to convey his appreciation.

"Aurelia!" Qurrah cried as the fire approached. The elf stopped her barrage of lightning just long enough to place a warding spell around them. The fireball hit the ground and detonated. The flame swirled about Aurelia and Qurrah, held at bay by Aurelia's spell.

When the fire dissipated, the half-orc laughed at the wizard in yellow.

"Surely you can do better than that," Qurrah said.

"Aye, that I can, but why should I?" asked the wizard.

"Because you gave me one mother of a headache, and that makes me cranky," Harruq said. He staggered to his feet, his swords drawn but flailing wildly as he tried to gain his balance. Before he could move, the points of two blades pressed against his back.

"Move, and you're gonna get more than just a headache," a rough voice said from behind.

"You're a short little guy, aren't you?" Harruq asked. He shifted his hips slightly, tightening the grips on his swords as he did.

"What's that got to do with anything?"

"Nothing."

The half-orc leapt forward and away. Qurrah covered his flight with a sharp burst of cold air. Aurelia whirled on the yellow wizard, red light on her fingertips. Several bolts of pure magic flew outward, fizzling into smoke as they struck an invisible shield.

Harruq found little reprieve, for the man in the gray cloaks assaulted him with a wicked barrage of double-stabs and feints. He batted away what he could, furious and confused as he watched what should have been killing cuts repeatedly deflect off his armor, or cut no deeper than a scratch.

"You're gonna pay for that one, ya pansy caster," the short warrior said, a bit of frost sticking to his beard. He charged across the warehouse with his punch daggers pumping the air. Qurrah laughed. A snap of his whip took out his attacker's feet. He crashed across the floor, a rolling, jumbling mess of armor.

"I'm a pansy caster too, don't forget," the wizard in yellow said, smiling down at Aurelia even as she launched a swirling blue cone of ice back up at him. He pointed his staff toward her, summoning a clear shield of pure magic. The cold swarmed about him, doing no harm.

She opened her mouth to cast again, only to feel the curved tip of a sword press against her lower lip.

"Do not give me cause to harm such beauty," the cloaked man whispered. He shifted, using the elf as a shield between him and Harruq.

"Don't you dare touch her," Harruq said.

"Lower your weapons," the wizard said. "We have no desire to hurt you."

The fire left Qurrah's whip. Harruq sheathed his swords, glaring at the cloaked man with open hatred.

"God-damned pansy-tripping cowardly weaselwhip-using orc-kisser!"

The short warrior jumped to his feet, fuming.

"Don't worry, Brug," the wizard said. "Being useless in this battle doesn't make you useless as a whole."

Harruq raised an eyebrow at the yellow-garbed wizard, who was levitating down to join them. A nod from him, and the cloaked man removed the sword from Aurelia's face.

"Is there a reason you attacked us?" Aurelia asked. "Or did you just feel like a little fun?"

"One could have a lot of fun with you," the wizard said, blatantly examining her lithe and firm body. "But, it would be impolite without first knowing my name. I am Tarlak Eschaton, at your service."

"Did I miss something here?" Harruq asked.

"You missed a few of Haern's swings, by the looks of your face," Tarlak said. "Don't worry. We'll get you a healer, if you want."

Qurrah joined his brother's side, his whip dragging along the ground. He put another hand on the burly half-orc's arm, hoping for patience, but not expecting it.

"State your purpose," Qurrah said.

"It's simple, really. The King has banned elves from Veldaren. Elves also happen to be a sneaky bunch. They can disguise themselves, as, say, a noble woman from a far off country. So our little gang of mercenaries was hired to flush out and remove any such sneaky elves."

He bowed again to Aurelia.

"My apologies, but you must leave."

The Cost of Betrayal

A woman entered through the doorway, dressed in the white robes of Ashhur. Red hair fell down past her shoulders. Her face had soft, curved features, and she bore a strong resemblance to Tarlak.

"Should I attend to Brug first as usual, Tarlak?" the priestess asked. Tarlak glanced back to her, a smile flashing across his face.

"Do you have to ask, Delysia? Brug got himself--"

And then a whip wrapped around his neck. Haern drew his sabers, but Qurrah glared at him, prepared for his speed.

"With but a thought I can surround my whip with fire," he told him. "Move, and I burn him alive."

"I'd greatly prefer you stay still for now, Haern," Tarlak said, the muscles in his neck taut.

Haern sheathed his swords. "Of course," he whispered, his voice barely audible. "Let me know when you want them dead."

"Qurrah, release him, he intends us no harm," Aurelia said.

"He means to order us around," Qurrah said. "I do not appreciate that. Besides, if you go, we go, and I happen to like this city."

"Touching," Brug grumbled, his knuckles white as they gripped his punch daggers. "But you're a fool thinking you got yourself a bargaining chip. I'll gut any who cause him harm."

Delysia slowly approached, standing at Brug's side with her arms crossed.

"I do not like stalemates," Qurrah said, his eyes jumping from one to the other. "So I propose that you four pretend you never saw us, and no one will be the wiser."

"Bad idea," Tarlak replied, wincing slightly, half-expecting fire to engulf his neck. None did, so he continued. "We let you go, and someone finds out, or even worse, you go off and kill someone, our heads would find themselves a nice new spike for a home. Personally, my head likes my neck, so we need a solution that addresses that particular worry."

"Don't sound like there is one," Harruq said, drawing his swords. "Because we're not leaving."

The cloaked man drifted around so fluidly that Qurrah did not realize he had moved until he was almost gone.

"Order him where I can see him," Qurrah said. "I need no assassins at my back."

"Well, that is what you have, my friend," Tarlak replied. "And quite frankly, I can't order him to do anything. You're the one with the fiery whip, after all."

"Qurrah, I'm not liking this," Harruq said, shifting attention back and forth from the short warrior and the cloaked man.

"Nice to know," his brother said.

"I believe I have a solution," Delysia said. All eyes turned to her. "Let them join the Eschaton."

Harruq, Qurrah, and Aurelia all glanced about in confusion at this, but this hardly matched the confusion of their counterparts.

"Join us?" Brug roared. "By Ashhur, I'll join 'em in a grave before I join 'em in Eschaton!"

"May I ask what the Eschaton is?" Aurelia said.

"The Eschaton Mercenaries," Tarlak answered. "Named after my sister and I. The four of us in front of you would be the Eschaton. We do a few jobs, kill a few people, and get paid outrageous sums for it."

"They are skilled," Haern whispered from behind, startling all three. The sharp end of a saber curled around Qurrah's neck. "Skilled enough to be trained."

"How does this solve the problem with my elven blood?" Aurelia asked.

"Vaelor's edict ordered the Veldaren Guard, and the Eschaton Mercenaries, to remove all elves from his city," Delysia replied. "It did not order elves to be removed from the Eschaton itself. Our home is not located within Veldaren's walls."

"It is a weak argument," Qurrah said, his eyes locked with Tarlak's. "And a tough decision to make at the point of a blade."

"Well I have to decide at the point of a, well, whip. So go ahead. You three seem more than capable. Feel like becoming part of the happy family?"

"More like the black sheep of the family," Brug grumbled. Delysia swatted him on the head.

"I will trust your judgment, Qurrah," Aurelia said softly. Qurrah nodded. A flick of his wrist and the whip returned, slithering underneath the arm of his robe. Haern's sword vanished just as quickly.

"Well," Tarlak said, rubbing his neck, "glad that is over with. So, I guess I should be the first to welcome you."

"Honored," Harruq muttered. He looked about, seeing an angry man storming out of the warehouse, the priestess following him in mid-argument, and no sign of the cloaked one. "Odd mess of a family."

"Well, we just added two half-orcs and an elf. It seems diversity is now our strong suit. By the way, do you three have names? It helps with the bonding process."

"I'm Harruq Tun," the half-orc said. "This here is my brother, Qurrah Tun."

"And I am Aurelia Thyne," the elf said, offering a tiny curtsey.

"Wonderful!" Tarlak said. "Follow me. I'll show you your new home." He followed Brug and Delysia out the warehouse, not stopping to see if the three followed.

"We really gonna do this?" Harruq asked.

"We have no home, and no lawful standing to be here," Aurelia said. "Don't forget, you two have elven blood as well. I see no reason not to give this a try."

"I can think of plenty," Qurrah said. He offered none when Aurelia gave him a look.

"Well, off we go then," Harruq said with a shrug.

The road leading from the west gate of Neldaren forked north and south less than a hundred yards from the city. The southern road followed the banks of the Kinel river, leading to a multitude of farming villages beyond. While the southern road traveled for hundreds of miles, the north road was far shorter. The King's forest surrounded all of northern Veldaren, and built against the southwest curve loomed an old sentry tower. Back when orc armies could still cross the bone ditch, the small stone structure housed a powerful scrying device permanently aimed west. Years ago, the magic of the scrying device had failed, the sentry tower was abandoned, and when an enterprising mage in curious yellow robes offered to purchase the structure, King Vaelor had been more than receptive.

"Welcome to your new home," Tarlak said, gesturing grandly before the stone edifice.

"It's, well, a little better than our last home," Harruq said, staring at the tower in surprise. The building rose far above the tops of the trees, looking like a cylindrical piece of stone growing out of the earth. Twin doors barred entrance inside. Windows marked each floor, which Qurrah counted to be more than six.

Tarlak continued talking, clearly proud of his tower.

"It's a little drafty come the winter months, but a brilliant man designed the heating, and an even more brilliant man, me, decorated the place and made it livable. By the way, can you all share a room?"

Aurelia's frown was by far the biggest of the three.

"Excuse me, Tarlak, but if you haven't noticed, I have some important differences from these fine gentlemen here."

The wizard laughed. "Yes. Two stand out immediately."

Aurelia glared. "Do you know any polymorph spells, Tarlak?"

"No, why?"

"Because I do. Another comment like that, and you will have to admire my figure through the eyes of a mudskipper."

For a long moment, the wizard paused, mulling over the concept with a blank stare.

"Moving on!" he said when finished, marching toward the oak doors. Harruq shook his head.

"Odd guy."

"He would most likely prefer eccentric," Qurrah said.

"I'll go with lecherous," Aurelia chipped in. The doors creaked open with a rustic sound, and then the three followed the wizard in.

Beautiful, isn't she?" Tarlak said, smiling as he led them through the large bottom floor. Filling nearly half of it was a giant wood fireplace, a myriad of pipes stretching out from the top, entering the higher levels of the tower through snug holes in the ceiling. Still in the early stages of summer, there was no need for a fire yet, but Harruq smiled at the thought of spending his first winter warm and cozy, instead of miserably shivering in some rundown home.

On their left, stone stairs wound upward. On the right, split logs were stacked neatly. Two old but sturdy couches faced the fireplace. Next to the couches, a long table stretched from wall to wall. The couches, the drapes over two windows, and the carpet were all a deep, luxurious red. The contrast with the dark stone was sharp, to say the least. Still, the place had an undeniable, simplistic charm. To Harruq and Qurrah, who had lived in total squalor, the place seemed a castle.

"What are all the pipes for?" Aurelia asked, gesturing to the fireplace.

"That is my wonderful brilliance put into action," Tarlak said, beaming as if the furnace were his own son. "When I first moved in, one large pipe acted as a chimney for the smoke. Now, however, each of the pipes leads to the different levels, heating them all."

"Where does the smoke go?" asked Harruq.

"Gotta use this," Tarlak said, tapping his forehead. "I have a few magic spells in me. The heat goes through all the pipes except that big one in the center, which funnels cold air in and smoke out.

Trust me, come winter, you'll be ready to worship me for how toasty my home stays."

"Your home?" asked Delysia as she came down the stairs. "I do believe it was my money you purchased this place with, dear brother."

"Our home," Tarlak said, duly corrected. "After the nasty business with the Citadel, I needed a new place to start. My dear sister here was kind enough to lend a hand."

Qurrah's eyes narrowed at mention of the Citadel, but he kept his questions to himself.

"Giving the grand tour?" Delysia asked.

"Of course. I need to show them where they'll be living. Speaking of, do you think you can share a room with lovely Aurelia here?"

Delysia glanced around Tarlak to look at Aurelia.

"Is that fine with you?" she asked.

The elf shrugged. "Better than rooming with these two lugs."

"Excellent," she said, still smiling. "Follow me upstairs. We'll make room for you while Tarlak gives the boys the rest of the tour."

"You're gonna leave us?" Harruq asked as Aurelia stepped around a frowning Tarlak.

"I'm sure you'll be just fine," she replied.

"I would prefer she stay with me, sis," Tarlak said. A tiny pout crossed his face.

"Oh, I don't want to be a bother," Aurelia said, locking her arm in Delysia's, a huge grin on her face. The priestess laughed and batted her eyelashes at her brother.

"Bye-bye, Oh Great and Wise Eschaton!"

The two dashed up the stairs, leaving an unhappy Tarlak and Harruq watching after them. Qurrah, amused by the whole ordeal, could not keep silent.

"So who exactly is in charge here, the women or the men?"

"The women, just like everywhere else in the civilized world," Tarlak sighed. "Oh well. Let's get on with it."

They followed him up the stairs, which slowly curled about the wall. Tarlak stopped on the first floor, which appeared to be nothing more than a wall and a door less than two feet from the stairs.

"I added walls and doors to give every room some privacy," he explained. "This is my sister's, and now your elf girl's, room. Don't expect to be inside there much."

"Same goes for you, I would say," Qurrah said.

"Quiet you!" Tarlak said, although his voice hardly carried any conviction. "Let's go to a more interesting floor, shall we?"

The second floor's door was wide open. When they peered inside, they saw a mess of a place, with pieces of armor littering the floor. Buried underneath a particular deep pile was what appeared to be a bed. Various weapons, axes, swords, and daggers lined the walls. In front of a large grinding wheel in the corner, grumbling to himself, sat Brug.

"Afternoon Brug," Tarlak shouted. Brug, in the middle of sharpening one of his daggers, startled so badly he fell off his chair and onto his rump.

"Dadgum idjit wizard! I told you not to do that!"

"Precisely why I do," the wizard beamed. "I want you to meet the newest members of the Eschaton."

Brug glared over before returning to his stool. "I already met 'em."

"Yes, but I would prefer you meet them *without* trying to kill them."

"Don't care to."

"You'll win him over," Tarlak semi-whispered to the other two. "He's always cranky after he gets his ass handed to him in a fight."

"What did you say?" Brug roared, spinning in his seat so fast it sent him toppling, this time on his head.

"Next floor!" Tarlak said, slamming the door shut and dashing up the stairs.

The next door was shut tight.

"This is my room," the wizard said. "Nothing exciting here. Next floor!"

When Tarlak stopped at the fifth floor, he turned to the other two, his face serious.

"This is Haern's floor," he said. "As a bit of warning, do not enter unless you want an attempt on your life."

"Say again?" Harruq asked.

"That guy is an assassin, through and through. He likes to sneak up on anyone entering his room. I've tried catching him sleeping, eating, practicing. No luck. Had plenty of sabers poked into my back and neck, though."

He pushed the door open a crack and gestured for them to enter.

"Guests first," he said.

"How kind," Qurrah said, shoving the door the rest of the way open. Harruq followed, his eyes searching the corners for the cloaked man. The entire room was barren but for a small chest and a simple bed at one side. There was no sign of Haern.

"Let me know how it goes," Tarlak said before banging the door shut. Harruq turned and shoved, but could not make it budge.

"I hate this place," he said. He joined his brother's side. Other than the bed and the thick curtains over the window, there appeared no place for the man to hide.

"You sure he's here?" Harruq yelled.

"I'm sure," came Tarlak's muffled reply.

"He hones his skills at all times to remain ready," Qurrah said, methodically searching the room with his eyes. "This is a test. Draw your blades, brother. If he does not obtain the kill with his first strike, he will have failed."

"You certain?" the half-orc asked as he drew Condemnation and Salvation.

"Very."

They slowly left the door. Shadows blanketed the walls, but none looked deep enough to hide a man. Harruq knelt and checked under the bed. Nothing.

"Hate to have to let this guy know breakfast is ready," he grumbled. He looked back to his brother, and then paused. Something was wrong. He could see the door closed behind Qurrah, could see the blank walls, but his gut knew different.

"Brother," he said, and that was all it took. Qurrah spun as Haern charged. A few words dashed off his tongue as he completed the turn. A saber lashed out, resting on his throat in the blink of an eye.

"You could be dead," Haern whispered, all but his mouth and chin hidden behind the low cowl of his cloak.

"As could you," Qurrah said, drawing the man's attention to a piece of bone hovering in the air an inch from his chest. "Stalemate."

The saber slipped beneath the multitude of cloaks as the bone dropped into Qurrah's hand. Haern abandoned his battle posture and stood erect. The cowl remained low, but his eyes shone through its shadow, a piercing blue color that reminded Qurrah of deep waters.

"I welcome you to the Eschaton," Haern said, his voice never above a whisper. His gaze shifted to Harruq. "I have fought you in battle, and I find you lacking."

The half-orc's eyes bulged.

"My life may one day depend upon your skill. Meet me behind the tower at sunrise. Bring your blades and armor."

Harruq was so flustered and angry he didn't know what to say. So he said a whole bunch at once. "How dare you…I could…you never beat me!"

Haern pointed to the many cuts lining Harruq's face and arms. "Every one of those could have been lethal."

"Stop lying, you never…!"

"My brother agrees," Qurrah interrupted, stepping between the two. "I thank you for the offer to train him."

"Qurrah!" Harruq gasped. Qurrah whirled on him.

"Shut up you fool. Now let's go."

When they tried to open the door, it swung in easily. Tarlak grinned at them as he leaned against the back wall.

"So how'd you do?" he asked as a furious Harruq followed his brother out, slamming the door shut behind him.

"A draw," Qurrah said. "To the final floor?"

"To the final floor!"

The final floor was a bit different from the others. There were no beds, no chests, no drawers, and no current occupants. Instead, piles upon piles of boxes and crates were stacked everywhere.

"Yeah, this is where we store most of our potions, armor, stuff like that," Tarlak explained.

"Where will we sleep?" Harruq asked.

"Will the floor do for now? I can purchase some beds tomorrow. I'll just loan it out from your next cut."

"Next cut?" Qurrah asked.

"Of your payment, of course. We are mercenaries."

Harruq rubbed his lower lip, a few things connecting correctly into place. "So we're going to make some gold here?"

"Not enough to be rich, but we carry a decent reputation here in Veldaren," Tarlak explained. "We have little competition, we're dependable, and now more than ever, we're incredibly versatile. A tenth of all our contracts go to fund the organization, and the rest we split evenly. Sound fair?"

"More than fair," Qurrah said. "I thank you for taking us in. It is more than we had hoped for."

"Well, you might have hoped for beds," Tarlak said, gesturing to the crates. "But we'll see what we can do."

Harruq waved an arm at all the miscellaneous things. "Where's this going to go?"

"Good question. Ever seen a portable hole?"

Both shook their heads.

"Well, neither have I, but I plan on buying one tomorrow. I'll consider it a one-time cost to hire you into our fold. For now, just shove aside all our crap and make yourselves at home."

"I doubt this place will ever feel like home," Harruq said.

"Yes, the roof doesn't leak," Qurrah muttered.

"Give it a shot," Tarlak said. "We might surprise you. Probably already have."

"Given our past few days, it's just one surprise of many," Harruq said, surveying the junk that filled his room. His room. Of his home. Surprising didn't begin to describe it all.

Tarlak sat on one of the couches before the fireplace, a much-needed drink in hand. His hat lay next to him, his shoes kicked off.

"About time you poked your head out," he said when his sister appeared, her priestess robes switched out for a more simple and comfortable tunic. "So many lonely hours down here eagerly awaiting feminine company."

"I doubt it is my company you were hoping for," Delysia teased. She scooted his hat over and sat down next to him.

"Is that necessary?" she asked, nodding at the drink.

"Absolutely," he said. "I just invited a whole collection of freaks into my little home, and on what grounds?"

"You know why," Delysia said.

"Do I?" Tarlak asked before draining the rest of the glass. "Are you sure that's them? Maybe Ashhur wanted some other group."

"I'm sure," Delysia said. "I don't know about the elf, but the two men are damaged. We do them much good by giving them a home."

"Yeah," Tarlak said, still not convinced. "You're probably right, at least about the damaged part, mentally and physically. But we're acting on a dream."

Delysia frowned, and her small face curled up in a clear expression of hurt.

"No dream," she said. "And no hallucination. Prayer, quiet and certain. They're the ones we were to help, and help them we will. It is not my fault Ashhur is more comfortable talking to me than you."

Tarlak laughed.

"Ashhur's just scared that if he says hello to me, he'll find himself missing a few lovely angels."

"Speaking of lovely angels," Delysia said. "You should go check on your new friends."

"As you wish, milady," Tarlak said.

When Tarlak returned to the upstairs room, he was pleasantly surprised by the half-orcs' progress. Qurrah had supervised while Harruq did the grunt work, as was common between them. Crates originally stacked against the wall they piled twice as high, and any empty crack did not remain empty. After about an hour of pushing and stacking, they had cleared a small space in the heart of the tangled jungle.

"I'd say it's about suppertime, wouldn't you?" Tarlak said, whistling at the sight. "By the way, remind me to have you two do my heavy lifting from now on."

"What's to eat?" Harruq asked.

"Come and see," the wizard said with a mischievous look. The two were more than willing to comply.

Supper was a feast that put many feasts before it to shame. Evidently Aurelia and Delysia, both skilled in forms of magic, had spent a good half hour conjuring up the most exotic, rare, and mouthwatering cakes, meats, crumpets, pastries, bread, and fruits, most of which the half-orcs had never seen before.

"Great leapfrogging Karak," Harruq said when seeing the food splayed out on the table.

"We eat well here in my tower," Tarlak said with a huge grin on his face. "Impressed?"

Harruq did not have chance to answer. His mouth was already full.

Aurelia joined the half-orcs as they were preparing to bunk for the night.

"You two busy?" she asked, poking her head through their door.

"Come on in," Harruq said. "Here to see our lovely living conditions?"

"Whiners. I'll be sleeping on the floor as well."

"Don't you mean hovering above it?" Qurrah asked. The elf shrugged.

"Same thing. I just wanted to make sure this was fine with you two."

Qurrah tilted his head and gave her a funny look. "We would not have joined if we did not so wish."

The elf shook her head and poked Harruq.

"You might not have, but I get the distinct impression this big lug would follow me around wherever I go. And I don't see you abandoning your brother either, Qurrah. So, humor me. Is all of this good?"

Harruq walked over, put his arms on her shoulders, and very, very slowly, spoke down to her.

"We…are…good."

"Good," Aurelia said with a smile before zapping him with electricity from her forefinger. She kissed his forehead as he lay on the ground, tiny bits of smoke trailing from his skin.

"Ni-ni Harruq, ni-ni Qurrah."

"Sleep well, lady Thyne."

"Nighters," Harruq groaned from the floor.

"You certainly have an interesting way with women, brother," Qurrah said as he closed the door.

"You think I insulted her?" he asked.

"Seems likely. By the way, you need another haircut."

"Very funny."

That night, as the two lay on bedrolls and stared at the ceiling, Harruq broke the silence.

"Hey, brother?"

"Yes, Harruq?"

"This whole thing…things are gonna be different now, aren't they?"

"Yes," Qurrah said softly. "I think they will be."

Harruq rolled onto his side and stared at the floor. Yes, things were different now. He wasn't sure how, he wasn't sure why, but a new chapter had begun. The question was, what awaited him in those unwritten pages. And more importantly, why was he so troubled by it?

Qurrah fidgeted, remembering the death of Velixar, and remembering the dust his master had become, nothing but a swirl of gray and white piled underneath garbs of black. It was the fate of all things to become ash and earth, he knew, but what fate lay beyond? He remembered Velixar's haunting words, and the thought of meeting him again did little to warm his heart. A soft voice, tiny and often ignored, dared speak up in his mind. All men turned to dust. Perhaps his life determined whether his soul, if it existed, would also turn to dust. The path he walked, dark and distant from so many, could it turn him to where the road faded into lightless forests of thorns and graves?

    Neither slept well that night, despite their full bellies and warm blankets.

3

A swift kick stirred Harruq from his dreams. He grunted, forced open a single eye, and then shut it when he saw Qurrah frowning down at him.

"What do you want?" he asked, the phrase coming out as a single, drowsy word.

"Sunrise nears. Get up."

Then Qurrah dropped Harruq's heavy leather armor onto his head. The warrior groaned in response.

"Why should…"

"My life depends on you," Qurrah said. "You've never been trained before. Here is your chance. Now get up."

"Fine. Fine. Fine." The bleary half-orc rolled the armor off his face and glared up at his brother. "Remember, I'm doing this for you."

"I doubt you will let me forget," Qurrah said, vanishing down the stairs.

"No games," Harruq said. He stood behind the tower, his armor buckled tight and his blades in hand. Dew covered his boots. A soft breeze sifted through his hair, the scent of morning awakening his mind. It was still cold in the shadow of the tower, the grass short and thick. The King's Forest stretched out before him, the woods wide, their branches intertwined along the top canopy.

"This is no game," Haern whispered, his body an inch behind Harruq's. The half-orc startled, then blushed red with anger and embarrassment.

"You said you'd be waiting for me out here," he said.

"Do you always expect people to be where they say they will?"

"Only those not trying to kill me," he grumbled.

Haern approached the forest, pulling his hood lower on his face. "The most deadly are the ones you think wish you no harm," he whispered.

"Yeah, yeah," Harruq said, motioning with his two swords. "Aren't you all smart. So we going to fight or what?"

The assassin's hands emerged from within his cloaks, his sabers drawn and ready.

"Have you ever been beaten before?" he asked.

"Of course not. Would I still be alive if I had?"

Haern's saber was on his throat before he could move.

"Yes," the assassin whispered, his breath warm on the half-orc's ear. "Because I have beaten you, yet you still live."

He turned away, blatantly putting his back to the furious half-orc. Harruq's temper flared. Roaring, he charged. Condemnation and Salvation hungered in his hands. Haern waited until the half-orc was almost to him before leaping into the air, high above Harruq's head. His knees curled to his chest as he looped around. When he landed, both his sabers stabbed forward, jabbing into armor without penetrating.

"Your hatred gives you strength, but it renders you stupid," he whispered from underneath his hood. An elbow shot back, trying to smash the assassin's nose. It caught air instead. Haern ducked underneath, spun on his feet, and froze, his sabers once again resting on Harruq's throat.

"When I ask you something, I want a real answer, not some cocky bullshit," he said through clenched teeth. "Do you understand me? Now have you ever been beaten?"

"Yeah," Harruq said, his hate still churning like a trapped fire. "Just once, to an elf."

"What was his name?"

"I don't know! He had the strangest weapon I ever saw. It was a bow with blades along every which way."

Haern stepped back, his sabers vanishing beneath his cloaks once more.

"Dieredon? You fought Dieredon and lived?"

Harruq shrugged. "Guess I have."

A soft chuckle escaped the assassin. "You have fought one of the very best there is, half-orc. Your swords never came close, did they?"

"He ambushed me," the half-orc countered. "Wasn't a fair fight."

"Of course he ambushed you," Haern whispered, slowly shifting his body left and right, his cloaks swaying. "An intelligent fighter doesn't give his opponent a fair chance. You think it fair you have the muscles of an ox while your other foes are mere mortals?"

His movements picked up speed. Haern's cloaks whipped back and forth through the air.

"What the abyss is your problem?" Harruq shouted.

"You!"

Haern leapt, his body rotating at blinding speed. Cloaks whipped up and down. Harruq brought up his swords to block but had no clue where the assassin's sabers were. Instinctively, he crossed them and braced his legs. One saber slid over the top, nicking his chin. When the mass of gray landed, the other saber cut upward, separating the two swords. The first, still high in the air, sliced straight back down, between the small opening the other had created, then thrust forward, unblocked.

Harruq stood there, swords shaking in his hands, as the tip pressed against his throat. A drop of blood trickled down his neck.

"Why did you bring me out here?" he asked. "To humiliate me?"

"So you may survive," Haern replied. "Your strength is great, and your speed decent, but you are reckless. All your attacks are obvious, beginner routines."

"I don't need to listen to this."

"You will listen!" The assassin's leg snapped forward, smashing his foot against Harruq's groin. The half-orc dropped to his knees. Haern bent down, grabbed him by the hair, and yanked his head back so that he stared straight into his burning blue eyes.

"We are to be a team," he whispered. "We must trust each other. You've seen, and felt, what I can do. I have fought impossible odds, and I have escaped without a scratch. You possess greater strength than most alive, and ancient blades from a time long past, and you act as if these alone will grant you victory. It is arrogance, Harruq Tun, nothing more."

"Go burn in the abyss," Harruq spat. Haern's kick broke his nose. He continued whispering as the half-orc moaned.

"I consider my point proven. I am the greater fighter, half-orc. I do not possess greater strength. My blades do not contain the magic yours do. I have spent a lifetime in training, and I have learned from those better than me." He chuckled softly. "My very first master broke my nose on our opening day of practice. I guess I have passed on that tradition."

Harruq struggled into a sitting position, glaring at the assassin as blood ran down his lips and neck. Haern tossed him a white rag.

Neither spoke as he cleaned himself, then held the rag to his nose. The morning dew vanished as the sun climbed higher in the sky.

"Are you ready to listen?" Haern asked. The half-orc nodded. "Good. I hold no anger against you, so hold none against me. It will simply lengthen things. Go inside and ask Delysia for a healing spell. Then, if you are willing, come back outside. I'll be here."

"In the open?" Harruq asked.

"Yes," he replied, his smile hidden. "Right here in the open."

Harruq stood and sheathed his blades. He dropped Haern's rag as blood continued to drip down his face.

"You're a bastard, you know that?" Harruq said.

Haern nodded. "Yeah. I know."

With that, the half-orc went in search of Delysia.

※

"Something's not right, Brug," Tarlak said, staring at a map of Veldaren divided into several colored districts.

"What you mean, Tar?" Brug asked. He was dressed in his bed robes, and his eyes were still dark from sleep. Before the wizard answered, there was a knock at the door.

"Come on in, we're decent," Tarlak answered. Qurrah stuck his head inside, his robes clean and his hair straightened.

"I will be in Veldaren for a bit," he said.

"Oh, alright, well you better take this then." The wizard pulled open a drawer, closed it, pulled open another, and then took out a metallic pendant, which he tossed to Qurrah. A quick examination showed it to be a rectangle with a small yellow square in the center.

"What is this?" Qurrah asked.

"That'll let people know you're one of us," Tarlak explained. "It'll also get you in and out the gates without too much hassle from the guards."

Qurrah bowed in thanks, and then slipped back out. When the door shut, the wizard turned back to his map.

"Lola's not sent word to me since spring," he said, continuing where he left off. "The Muggly brothers haven't contacted me since summer, and Jerend's offered no useful information for months now."

"Perhaps because things are quiet," Brug said from his seat in a comfortable padded chair.

"Thief guilds don't stay quiet," Tarlak said with a shake of his head. "Not even the neutered ones the nobles have created here in Veldaren."

"Then what are you thinking?"

"I'm thinking," the wizard said, tapping his red goatee, "that somehow my contacts are expecting more money by not talking to me."

"You think they're being bribed?"

Tarlak glanced at Brug, who seemed disgusted with the prospect.

"I hope that is the case. If it is, Haern can get us new contacts. I've got a more worrisome idea, though."

"Which is?"

Tarlak frowned at the multicolored districts, representing the territory of Veldaren's thief guilds. "That somehow the guilds have developed plans that make feeding me information no longer worth the copper."

Brug scratched at his beard, thinking over the idea.

"Can't be planning something that big without us knowing," he said. "Besides, Haern's the Watcher. Any one of them guilds gets out of line, and he'll come and set things right. A scary thought, though, the guilds working together."

"I hate thieves," Tarlak moaned, pulling his tall yellow hat down past his eyes.

"Half our business is keeping them in line," Brug said, hopping from the chair. "You're like a miner saying he hates the mountain but loves the gold inside."

"That's why I prefer to pay others to mine for me," Tarlak said with a grin. "Have you finished the pendants for our new members?"

Brug shook his head.

"Had trouble deciding the animal. Figured Harruq's would be a scorpion. Saw that one on his chest, so that makes sense. What about Qurrah, though?"

"Make it a scorpion, as well," Tarlak said. "They're brothers."

"And the elf?"

The wizard shrugged. "Go ask her. She seems a bit friendlier."

Brug half-saluted, then left. Tarlak leaned over the map, pondering schemes that might simultaneous earn every thief guild higher profits. Any that came to mind were either too farfetched, or too frightening. Brug popped his head back in five minutes later.

"Strange girl, that elfie is," he said.

"What animal did she pick?"

Brug made a go-figure motion with his hands. "She wants a spider as well as a kitten."

"As in one creature, or both?"

"Never heard of a spiderkitty before, so yeah, both."

Tarlak chuckled. "Compromise. Make one, but have it be both a spider and a kitten."

"How am I supposed to do that?"

"You'll figure it out."

Brug rolled his eyes and slammed the door.

※

Qurrah wandered through the streets of Veldaren, blessedly silent in the early hour. No merchants hawked their wares, and the few men and women that wandered about were busy with whatever task forced them from their beds. Qurrah preferred the company and secrecy of cities to the green of the forests. He always felt uneasy amid the tall trees, as if part of his blood recognized them as home, but the other half rejected all their comforts. It was in the dust, dirt, and stone of a city that he felt he could go about unnoticed. More importantly, he could let his mind wander.

His path led him straight to the fountain in the center of town. He stared at the great king of old, whose loyalty to Karak had been unfailing.

"What purpose do you have in my life now?" he asked that statue. The stone gave no answer, which was no surprise. It was a relic of an era many seemed desperate to forget. What if the stone could talk, Qurrah wondered. What if its mouth opened and words of a god came through? He stared, wondering, until he thought he saw the lips of the statue begin to crack, as if desperate to open. He stepped back, frightened, and that was when he saw the girl.

She sat atop the edge of the fountain, one leg dipping in and out of the water. Her black hair hung over one shoulder, trailing down to her waist. His eyes took in her soft face and pale skin. She hunched over her legs, which were exposed below the knee by a fairly common skirt cut uncommonly high. Her right arm extended outward. She clenched her fist, and the veins in her arm swelled. In her left hand, she held a dagger.

Qurrah's reaction was a mixture of shock and curiosity as he watched her cut the flesh of her arm. The movements of her dagger were not random. She turned the blade this way and that, forming separate runes. She showed no sign of pain or pleasure. The girl seemed completely apathetic to her mutilations as her bright blood dripped into the fountain, staining the water scarlet.

The half-orc glanced around, realizing he had been staring. He was intrigued by how the few people passing by showed no surprise at what the girl did. A few frowned as they went on their way, but most ignored her. Qurrah walked away, then turned about, resting his back against a small shop facing the fountain. His curiosity awakened, he patiently waited. For what, he did not know.

As time passed, and more and more people filled the center, the girl ceased her cutting. She raised her arm to the sky, turning it so she could better see the runes she had carved. A smile creased her face, and she giggled. She put the dagger into her pocket, not caring her sleeve and dress were soaked with her own blood.

The girl hopped down, turned to the fountain, and splashed the statue king. Qurrah's stomach twisted as she drank the waters. A man swore at her as he walked past, but this only elicited another giggle as faint red water dripped down her lips and neck.

"Staring at Tess, eh?" asked a voice behind Qurrah. The half-orc glanced back at a powder-covered baker standing next to him. Both watched as she left the fountain and traveled south, drops of blood trickling off the end of her fingers.

"Is that her name?" Qurrah asked.

"Tessanna, actually. Tess rolls off the tongue easier. I take it you've never seen her before?"

"No, I have not," Qurrah said.

"She's a weird one," the baker said. "Guards keep telling her to stop, but she keeps on, anyway. She scares me, and I'm not too easily spooked, if you know what I'm saying."

"Bloodletting has been done in your apothecaries for centuries, why should that frighten you so?"

The baker chuckled and cracked his knuckles.

"You seen her eyes?" he asked.

"What of them?"

"No good telling you, then. Greet her sometime. Look her in the eye, and if you don't get shivers, then Ashhur made you of sterner stuff than I."

Qurrah smirked at the final comment but gave no reply. He started toward home, but then stopped.

"That girl," he asked the baker. "Tessanna, does she come here every morning?"

"Certain as the sun," the man replied. "By the time I get here, the fountain's always colored red, and she's dancing off like a little princess."

"Thank you," Qurrah said, dipping his head in respect. He wandered the rundown parts of southern Veldaren, lost in thought. He had come to Veldaren to think of his future, but Tessanna had given him far more immediate concerns. With the sun high in the sky, he returned to the tower, his mind decided. That next day, he would not miss Tessanna's arrival. When the blood began to flow, he would be there to watch.

The sound of sword hitting sword was clear and loud from behind the tower, so Qurrah circled around, remaining quiet and pressed against the stone in hopes of catching the battle unseen. He succeeded, and the sight was a worthy reward.

Harruq stood panting before Haern, his arms low and dragging as if the weight of his swords was too great to bear. Sweat dripped off his face. His entire body shuddered with each breath. Haern faced him, his face and body covered with an elaborate combination of cloaks. The tips of his sabers poked out from the folds.

"…movements have slowed with your exhaustion," the assassin was saying as Qurrah neared. "You were not fast enough when we started, what hope have you now?"

"You should be sucking air yourself, assuming you're human," Harruq said. "We've been out here since sunrise!"

"Do you see my movements slowing?" Haern asked. He struck, his sabers a blur. Harruq blocked the first couple before a desperate parry missed its mark. Steel pressed against his throat.

"Not possible," the half-orc said. "You can't be less tired than me. You just can't!"

"When was the last time you were fully exhausted?" Haern asked, pulling back his blade. Without warning, he thrust it straight at his chest. Harruq slapped the thrust wide. He countered with his other hand, only to have it brutally blocked, pushed aside, and then ignored. Metal thwacked against Harruq's chest armor. Haern did not halt, though, instead repeatedly slashing that exact same spot. All the while he spoke.

"When was the last time you were beaten? The last time you felt no chance of victory? Tell me half-orc, when was the last time you were a coward and surrendered?"

"Never!" Harruq screamed, slashing with all his remaining strength. Haern rolled, the powerful swords smashing the dirt.

"Exactly," Haern whispered, his voice soft yet still heard in the commotion. His foot shot upward, nailing Harruq's kidney. The follow up kick mashed his already sensitive nose. Qurrah winced as blood ran freely. "I will exhaust you. I will defeat you. I will make you collapse in surrender, convinced you cannot win."

The butts of the sabers cracked against Harruq's thick skull. Condemnation and Salvation remained stiff in the dirt as the half-orc fell onto his side, silent but for his gasps of air. In this silence, Haern's words were clear and powerful, yet still soft and quiet. Despite his distance, Qurrah heard every word, convincing him there was magic involved with Haern's constant whisper.

"You will learn to fight me," Haern said. "Even after defeat. After exhaustion. After hurt and humiliation. When you can stand against me, to the very limit of your body, then we may truly begin. Your speed, your strength, your mind: they will all grow these coming days, if you are willing. That is the one thing I cannot help you with."

He left Harruq lying there, dazed, exhausted, and furious.

"Tell Delysia your brother needs more healing," the assassin said as he walked past Qurrah, not at all surprised by his presence.

"Will he learn, or will you merely increase his scars?" Qurrah asked, his words dripping with sarcasm.

"You know him better than I," Haern said, gesturing back to his protégé. "Why ask me?"

Qurrah glanced at his brother, who was an ugly mess. A grin spread over his face.

"Because you're conscious and he's not," he said before retrieving the priestess.

4

Throughout the rest of the day, Harruq nursed his injuries and sulked in silence. Even Aurelia's attempts to cheer him up were ineffective.

"I have never seen him like this," she said to Qurrah, who, in an uncharacteristically kind act, had asked the elf to cheer him up in the first place.

"His pride has been broken more than his face," Qurrah said. "He's never lost a fight, not that I know of. He will meet this challenge. I trust him."

There were no contracts or assignments so the day passed uneventful. Dinner was quiet. Qurrah expected a fight when Brug made a joke about Harruq's nose, yet his brother let it pass. They exchanged no words as they settled in their bedrolls, Tarlak promising them beds by the following night.

Qurrah looked over Harruq, who lay with his back to him. Several bruises lined his bare skin. A few inexperienced words of comfort died in his ruined throat. He rolled the other way, closed his eyes, and dreamt of the girl with the black hair, and of a knife dripping with the lifeblood that flowed through her veins.

That next morning, Harruq woke Qurrah with his stirrings.

"It is not yet dawn," Qurrah said.

"Yeah, I know. He likes games. I do too."

He stormed down the stairs, his armor shining and his swords already drawn. The necromancer watched him go, a smile on his face.

"Don't get yourself killed," he whispered before rising.

Harruq slowed his breathing as he pressed against Haern's door. It felt loose against his shoulder. His muscles tensed. Several deep breaths later, he kicked it open and rushed in, weapons drawn.

The bed was empty, as was the room. The half-orc scanned everywhere, continually turning so his back never faced one direction for too long. Still, no sign of Haern.

"Already out there waiting for me, aren't you?" he said. As he shut the door, he felt the sharp point of a blade touch the back of his neck.

"Did you really think I would sleep with the door unbarred?" Haern whispered into his ear.

"Will my nose get broken if I say yes?" he asked. He braced for pain, but instead received laughter. The tip left his neck. The half-orc faced his teacher, who grinned at him from underneath his hood.

"Much better, Harruq. Much better. Perhaps Delysia will not be required for today's sparring."

"Says you. I plan on breaking the first thing I get a hold of."

"As I said," Haern whispered, urging the half-orc down the stairs with a shove. "Delysia will not be required."

Qurrah watched them spar before leaving. Much of their combat was similar to the day before. Haern repeatedly batted aside his brother's best attack combinations, his sabers invariably touching gray flesh. Harruq's anger grew, but something was different. He no longer aimed his anger at Haern. He aimed it at himself.

"Very good, brother," Qurrah said quietly.

He left for Veldaren.

The moon still shone dim in the red sky when Qurrah arrived at the center of Veldaren. The place was barren but for an early shopkeeper and two women hurrying down the street. Fear rolled off the women in tangible waves. Qurrah closed his eyes and let his mind touch their fear.

"The loss of a brother," he said, opening his eyes. The women, young and dressed in cheap clothes, were gone. "Such cowardly feelings toward death. You two shame your deceased."

A thorn pierced his mind. The half-orc reeled backward, smacking his head against hard stone. He was hidden between two buildings. No one should have known he was there. Someone did, though, and someone was curious as to why.

"You want in?" he asked aloud. "Very well. Come to my dark corners."

He grabbed the thorn and pulled it deep inside. He swarmed it with memories of his childhood, sitting hungry and cold as Master's experiments snarled, gagged, and shrieked in the cages all about him. He altered the memory, replacing it with his nightmares. The unseen cage doors opened. The creatures bellowed their joy in fearful howls. They would feed, and the feast would be bloody, painful, and eternal.

Qurrah expected this to drive away the intruding mental presence, but instead the image twisted. His unseen nightmare creatures walked into visible light, revealing each one as a large man with belly heavy from a life of drink. Their mouths were sewn shut. The men tore at the thread with their hands. Flesh ripped, and shards of bloody glass spewed from their mouths.

"You killed mommy," the men said in unison as lungs and intestines followed, each punctured with glass. Qurrah tried to run, but instead his hands moved of their own accord, for he was hungry, so hungry, and in his lap was food. The taste was phenomenal.

"So you'll be quiet," the men continued. "You'll be good, and you can replace mommy. Now shut up. I don't want to hear crying."

Qurrah glanced down to see a female arm in his hands, cold and pale. Blood filled his mouth. The thorn seemed to shudder, and from it, infinite sadness and anger poured into his mind. He tried to pull away as rough hands seized his shoulders. The thorn dug deeper, and the half-orc curled into a ball as he felt the hands of the men tear away his clothes. He was powerless. His past, his choices, his sins, it all seeped into that thorn, now grown into a great root sucking out the wretched parts of his soul.

❈

Qurrah stirred in the alley, waking from a sleep he never remembered entering. The city was still peaceful, and the sun remained low above the horizon, so it appeared his slumber had been no longer than several minutes. The only change he could see was that Tessanna now sat upon the edge of the fountain. Her right arm, scarred from the day before, traced the dagger along her left, drawing thin lines of blood across her pale white skin.

"It couldn't have been you," he said from within the alley. The girl glanced up and stared straight at him, as if she had heard. Then she laughed. Her smile lit up her face. She looked eighteen, nineteen at the most, and she was beautiful. Beautiful, even as she drew the dagger back down to let the blood flow. Beautiful, even as she watched, mesmerized, at the drops staining the clear water below.

She carved four runes before the guards appeared.

"This is the last time, Tessanna," he heard one of them say. "We've warned you enough. Get off."

No guard touched her, even though they towered over her small, thin form. Qurrah's curiosity grew.

Tessanna stood, licked the back of her hand, and then gave one of the guards a flirty smile. When he made no movement, she flicked her wrist, spraying his armor with her blood. Still no guards moved. She waved and blew each one a kiss. She headed south, blood flecked across her lips and face. The guards shook their heads and murmured amongst themselves. One looked to the water, his disapproval visible. When they left, they were edgy, and in foul moods.

"Those images are of a madman," Qurrah said, remembering the man with his mouth sewn shut. "Or madwoman. Was that your childhood?"

The necromancer had always thought the cruelty and depravity of his early years was unmatched, but it appeared someone else had a tale darker than his own.

He stood, brushed the dust of his robes, and returned to the tower, fresh determination in his heart. He would speak with the girl the following morning. Part of him could not endure the wait. And part of him would gladly wait forever.

"You look well," Aurelia said when Harruq poked his head into their room.

"Better than yesterday?" he asked.

"Yes, but not by much."

The half-orc laughed, and then collapsed onto the elf's floor.

"Delysia!" she called, glancing back to where the priestess reclined on a bed reading a book.

"The big boy needs a spell?" she asked, not looking up.

"Or three." Aurelia cast a levitation spell on the passed out half-orc. He floated into the air, traveled across the two beds, and stopped beside the priestess. She reached up and touched the floating half-orc. White light surrounded her hand. Healing magic flowed out from her. Delysia withdrew her hand, having not once stopped her reading. Aurelia gently lowered Harruq next to her. Seconds later, he stirred.

"Eh? Where, oh, hello Aurry."

"Hello, Harruq," she smiled. "Care to stay awhile?"

"Sure thing."

"Good," the elf said, backing away and giving an exaggerated wave in front of her nose. "But bathe first, so we may stay together in the same room."

Harruq groaned. "Where can I do that?"

Aurelia glanced back to Delysia, who looked up from her book with an evil smile.

"Oh this is going to be bad, isn't it?" he asked as both began shoving him down the stairs.

"You have no idea," Aurelia laughed.

They took him to a tiny stone structure jutting out the eastern side of the tower. Harruq had to duck to get inside. The two girls stayed outside, the smiles on their faces only increasing his worry.

"What is so funny?" he asked.

"Nothing," Aurelia said. "Now take off your armor and clothes."

"Excuse me?" His face blushed. "Not sure you two want the whole show, do you?"

"Of course not," Aurelia said with fake indignation.

"Such a pervert," Delysia added.

Aurelia reached inside and swung a small, hinged door shut. It was high enough to reach the half-orc's chest.

"Now get naked," Aurelia said. "We won't peek in, we promise. Just slide your armor over the top of the door."

Harruq mumbled a few choice comments but made sure none were loud enough for Aurelia's sharp ears. He stripped down and tossed his belongings outside.

"Now what?" he asked.

"Say the word, 'water'," Delysia said.

The half-orc shrugged.

"Water."

Water fell from the ceiling, as if a tiny rainstorm were trapped inside. Harruq jumped, but the water was warm, and the rain, soft. There was no drain, instead the water faded away without ever pooling higher than his toes.

"This isn't too bad," he said, shaking his hair back and forth and staring at the ceiling. "Kind of soft, though."

"Say more," Delysia ordered.

"More."

The rain increased in intensity.

"Oh yeah, much better." Harruq began washing himself under the water.

"Thought you'd like it," Aurelia said. "By the way, just don't say much more."

"What happens if I say much more?"

One might as well have dumped seven buckets of water on him at once. The room roared with a downpour mightier than nature could ever muster.

"Aaah, make it stop!" the half-orc screamed. Both girls were too busy laughing, however, to tell him how. "Daah, stupid rain! Less, less!" The rain softened back to a tolerable level. He shook water out of his ears while the girls continued laughing.

"Think you're soooo funny," he grumbled.

"Of course." Delysia drummed her fingers against the door, smiling at Harruq. "You can say cold and warm to change the temperature."

"I'm fine, thanks."

Aurelia jabbed Delysia in the ribs, her grin still mischievous. "Think he's done in there already?"

"I'd say so," the priestess replied. "We did soak him pretty good, didn't we?"

"What're you two up to now?" the wary half-orc asked.

"Say 'dry' Harruq," Aurelia ordered.

"No. I don't trust you."

"Fine, I will." The elf hoisted herself up and stuck her neck through the top of the door. Harruq spun around, blushing furiously. The elf laughed and said, "dry very hard."

Massive winds slammed Harruq from one side of the room. He struggled against it, but eventually flew back, the impact with the wall taking away his breath.

"I hate you, Aurry!" he shouted when his senses returned.

"I love you!" she shouted back. She poked her head in once more, took a good look at the half-orc while Delysia opened her mouth in shock, and then said the word 'done.'

The wind stopped. All was quiet in the room. Aurelia stepped back while the priestess mouthed a question.

"It'll do," Aurelia said. Both burst out laughing.

"Can I have my clothes now?" a humbled and embarrassed Harruq asked from inside.

"Here you go," Delysia said, tossing the dirty clothes over the top of the door. "Although you really should keep those in there with you when you wash."

Both decided the curses coming from inside were not appropriate for female ears, so they left. Qurrah met them at the door to the tower.

"What's so amusing?" he asked.

"Your brother is just so *cute*," Aurelia said.

"Especially when he's all wet and grumpy," Delysia added. Qurrah remained outside as they left. He shook his head, honestly bewildered.

"Dezrel will rue the day those two met," he said. Harruq showed up, his armor in his arms. He was completely dry.

"Have fun with the girls, I guess?" Qurrah asked.

"Shut up," Harruq said. "And I'm never bathing again."

Still clueless, Qurrah could only laugh at his brother's anger as Harruq stomped upstairs in a huff.

Haern slipped inside Tarlak's room, shutting the door silently. The wizard sat as his desk, pouring over maps of Dezrel.

"Thanks for coming, Haern," Tarlak said without looking up.

"You've become more perceptive."

Tarlak chuckled. "Nope. Aurelia cast a few spells on my room at my request. Clever girl, really. I'll know when someone enters, or is listening, watching, or scrying. We're safe here. You can take that hood off if you want."

"Do you trust her?"

The wizard looked up from his notes. "Of course I do. Don't you?"

Haern shrugged. "I don't know yet."

"Then don't take your hood off yet," was the wizard's reply. "Not too complicated." He gestured to the seat before his desk. "Sit down. We need to talk."

The assassin crossed the room and sat. He glanced around, sighed, and then removed the hood. Long, curly gold hair danced with a shake of his head. Tarlak glanced at the face of his friend and sighed. He would die to have Haern's looks, yet all the assassin did was keep his features hidden underneath his hood, all so he could go unnoticed whenever he wished.

"You really don't have your priorities straight," Tarlak muttered.

"How so?" Haern asked. His voice was clear and firm, the whisper vanishing along with the hood.

"Never mind. We have a problem."

Haern leaned forward, scanning the documents and maps littering Tarlak's desk. "What is it?"

The wizard sighed and collapsed in his chair. "I don't know what it is, and that's the problem. Something big is going on. When was the last time any of our contacts gave you information worth a damn?"

A hand ran through the golden hair as he thought. "Two months at least. Maybe three. Are you worried my network has been compromised?"

"In a way, yes."

Tarlak leaned forward, propping his chin on his fists. "The guilds are planning something, something that makes our bribes weak by comparison. Our contacts have suddenly grown stupid. What could all five guilds be working on that benefits everyone from top to bottom?"

"Nothing," Haern said. "Only a return to the days of old would carry such charm."

"So who stands in the way of returning back to the days of fleecing the rich and robbing the merchants?"

"The heads of all the guilds are owned mind and soul by the nobles," Haern said. "They wouldn't dare risk losing the protection money they earn."

"Even if they could earn more by taking it?"

Haern shrugged. "There'd be the risk of being caught, having the other guilds cannibalize and destroy them, and of course, there's me. Any chance would require complete cooperation of four guild masters, possibly all five."

Tarlak nodded. He had come to the same conclusion.

"And that is the problem, Haern. One of your guys, Hensley, has passed us word that an attempt on guildmaster Thren will be made in two days."

"Why, to replace him with his second in command?"

Tarlak picked up a glass full of violet liquid and drank. Smacking his lips, he put it back down and spoke.

"Perhaps. It fits, doesn't it? Cooperation is needed, so the lower underlings, thinking a tougher leader might get them more money, arrange to have their current guildmaster killed. He is owned by the nobles, after all."

"You think this is a trap," Haern stated.

"I do. Hensley is the lowest rung on a ladder two feet deep in dung. No way would he know about such a plan."

The assassin leaned back in his chair, his eyes distant as he lost himself in thought. "Why the trap, though?" he wondered.

"You said it yourself," Tarlak said with a shrug. "If all the guilds cooperate, they won't be caught, and no one will cannibalize the other. So what is left that threatens them?"

"Me," Haern said, pulling the hood back over his face. A shadow immediately engulfed his face, born of magic. Only his blue eyes and his firm chin pierced out from his hood.

"Yes, the Watcher of the King, paid handsomely to ensure peace among the thief guilds by removing all who would turn our streets to anarchy. Well, it appears your efforts have earned you many enemies."

"I must visit my contacts," he whispered, turning to go.

"No," Tarlak said. His voice gave no room for argument. "You kill them and they'll know we see their bait for what it is. We're going to willingly spring this trap."

"Why?" Haern asked.

"Because someone organized all this, and I want to know who. Besides, a lesson to the underworld not to mess with the Eschaton could make our lives much easier in the coming months."

"If you insist."

He opened the door and was about to leave when Tarlak halted him again.

"Oh, by the way, will the half-orc be ready by then?"

Haern shrugged. "He is ready now. All that is left is years of polishing."

"Well, try not to beat him too badly that morning. We'll need him healthy for the assassination trap."

"Whatever you say," Haern said, offering a mock bow. He shut the door as quietly as he had entered. Minutes later, a loud banging startled the wizard from his task of copying spell scrolls.

"Come on in," he shouted. "I'm never doing anything important in here, just picking my nose and scratching my bum."

"Sounds important to me," Brug grinned, shoving open the door. "A whole lot better than your pansy spell crap."

"My pansy spell crap can make you a pansy mudskipper," Tarlak threatened.

"Mudskipper?" Brug asked, raising an eyebrow.

"Just came to me. What is it you need?"

"Wondering if you finished the scrolls I asked you for."

Tarlak grabbed two capped cylindrical containers and tossed them to Brug. "I take it those are for the ox?" he asked.

"Actually, no. I've been talking to the elf, and she says she's not too bad with that staff of hers. Figure if she plans on whacking things with it, it'd be nice if things noticed."

"Explains the first scroll. And the illusion?"

Brug chuckled, tucking both tubes underneath his arm.

"She's got nothing but a stick. Maybe it's just me, but I'm thinking there's more to things than just function. You gotta look good at what you do."

Tarlak chuckled.

"Fine. I'll give you free reign. Just don't spend too much of my money."

Brug winked. "Of course."

The door shut with a resounding thud. Tarlak sighed, his fingers rubbing his temples.

"Paranoid antisocial assassin with a secret identity, a bipolar blacksmith, and half-orc brothers hanging out with a girlie elf, and I've got to use them to keep chaos off the streets. Lathaar old buddy, I sure hope you're having a better time than I am."

At that time, Lathaar was deep in a haunted forest, battling against an ancient demon composed of pure darkness. If asked, the paladin would have shaken his head and refused to switch places. There are worse things in life than demons.

"Hey, Qurrah?" Harruq asked that night.

"Are these late-night conversations going to become common?" his brother muttered into his pillow. They finally slept in beds, although crates and supplies still surrounded them. Tarlak had said the portable hole would be longer acquiring than he thought, given his underestimation of their rarity. The beds, however, he had carted up the stairs with a few tricks of shrink and enlarge magic. The sheets, pillows, and blankets were all white, courtesy of Delysia. Stitched across their lengths was a golden mountain.

"What's that?" Harruq had asked her.

"The symbol for Ashhur. It'll help you sleep better, I promise."

The symbol didn't seem to be working, so instead he stared at the ceiling and talked to his brother.

"Do you…do you like it here?" Harruq asked.

Qurrah sighed, and his weak voice grew greater in volume and tone.

"Let's address this right now, shall we?" he said. Harruq squirmed uncomfortably. "You are happy, and enjoy this place, but since happiness is a rarity for us, you worry something is wrong, and if it is not you, then it must be me. I don't fit in well, brother, but the people are mostly kind, the food is grand, and our beds are padded and warm. What better accommodations have we ever had? None. So stop worrying about my happiness. And that goes for Aurelia as well."

"Not sure if Aurry is worrying too much about you," he said, trying to lighten the mood.

"Don't be stupid. You know what I mean, or will, given time."

Again Harruq squirmed. Yes, he knew what his brother meant.

"I love her, Qurrah," he whispered into the quiet. It seemed an eternity before Qurrah responded.

"I know. Go to sleep."

He did. Qurrah followed him into slumber, but only after kicking the blanket with the golden mountain to the floor. Only then could he sleep peacefully, the black-haired girl returning to his dreams.

5

Both were awake before the dawn. They spoke little. Qurrah assumed, correctly, that his brother prepared for practice. Harruq assumed, incorrectly, that his brother did the same. They parted, the warrior circling north around the tower, the necromancer heading southeast.

The center of Veldaren was blessedly empty. Qurrah sat on the edge of the fountain, dabbing a hand in the water. Nervousness gnawed at his heart. She had power, how much he didn't know, but for her to dive into his mind and twist his own defenses against him showed a mind sharper than the blades his brother carried. Time passed, and the sun crawled its way above the walls of the town.

"Why do you delay?" Qurrah muttered. "Surely by no fear of me."

More and more people passed by, giving him curious glances as they did. Still no Tessanna.

After an hour, he felt a very familiar thorn enter his mind.

You wait for me, he heard inside his skull, the voice delicate and shy.

I wish to speak with you, he replied silently.

It is more than that. You border on obsession.

His anger flared. *Do not say what you know is untrue.*

A resolve hard as iron overtook the delicate voice in his head, banishing any trace of weakness.

I have drunk from your mind, Qurrah Tun. I know what you are, but I will come. I, too, am curious.

Tessanna stepped into view, walking slowly up the southern road. She had cut her ragged dress even higher than before, exposing much of her thighs. For the first time, she and Qurrah met face to face, and the chill running up his back gave credence to the words of the baker. Only a shred of white encircled the outer edges of her eyes. The rest was completely black, both her irises and pupils. Her stare was blatant and powerful. She could see through him, and he knew it.

She approached, her dagger in her right hand. Qurrah could not move, could not even speak, as she stopped less than a foot in front of him. He felt like an old, lumbering giant compared to her. Her forehead only came up to his chin.

"Hello. I am Tessanna Delone," she said, her voice cruel and hard. "You wished to speak with me?"

Qurrah wondered where the soft, giggling girl of the day before had gone.

"My thoughts refuse to waiver," he said. "I had to see your face, lest I lose my mind forever."

"You should let it go then," she said. "I did years ago. The freedom is a thrill."

She outstretched her left arm over the fountain. The dagger pressed the underside, just above her elbow.

"Why do you bleed yourself?" he asked her. "Why the runes? Why the pain?"

"You ever ask people why they fuck?" she shot back. "Feels good. Feels normal. Anyone ever ask you why the scent of the dead riles your blood?"

Red anger filled his pale face. "How dare you…"

"You want to speak to me? Fine. Let's see how obsessed you really are."

The dagger slashed, quick and vicious. This was not like her previous days of carving, instead she cut one long, open wound that poured blood like a crimson rain into the fountain. Tessanna closed her eyes and inhaled deeply. She clenched her muscles, and then the flow grew in power. Qurrah stared, his mouth agape. When she reopened her eyes, her entire countenance had changed. She giggled.

"I'm sorry. I'm having too much fun. Here come the guards."

Several armored men bullied themselves past Qurrah, the necromancer unaware of their approach. They surrounded the girl, their swords drawn.

"Enough's enough," the lead guard said. "You won't make a fuss, right?"

"Of course not," he heard her say. "But you might have to grab me. I won't fight too much." She giggled again. Something carnal underneath the sound made Qurrah tremble. Unlike the cold shiver when he had seen her eyes, this one was one of fire.

The guards, ignoring Qurrah completely, marched Tessanna toward the castle. He watched them depart, slowly realizing what it was the girl had just done.

The Cost of Betrayal

"I do not take kindly to being tested," he said. The whip tightened around his arm, sensing bloodshed to come.

In the northwestern corner of Veldaren, tucked against the giant beauty of the stone castle like a swollen, mutated foot, was the prison. The construction was simple and practical. It looked like a giant box, with barred windows, half below ground, half above. Inside, however, was far more twisted and complicated than any rational mind could devise. Qurrah wasn't known for his rational mind. He arrived at nightfall.

The moon was a thin sliver of light in the darkness. For this, Qurrah was grateful, for his mixed blood would grant him sight in the darkness. Two bored soldiers guarded the locked iron doors leading into the prison. Another guard looped around the compound, his gait slow and his eyes dull. A single spell put him to the ground. A second put out his torch. Qurrah made no pretense of hiding the body. In a minute or two, the front guards would notice. Still, he did not hurry.

Qurrah felt her presence as a physical pull on his chest, one he could see when he closed his eyes. He approached her window and pressed his face against the cold bars. Tessanna sat on an aged bench, her wrists bound together by rusted metal and chained to shackles around her ankles. A second chain ran up her chest, around her neck, and then attached to a metal plate bolted into the stone.

"Tessanna," he whispered.

"Why are you here?" she asked. Her voice was devoid of all emotion, the sound of perfect apathy.

"Do you wish to be freed?" he asked, ignoring her question. She never moved her head to look at him.

"No. I am fine. Go your own way."

The half-orc ignored her again. He shifted next to the window and placed his hands against the wall. His body turned translucent, and like a ghost he slipped through. Grunting in pain, he absorbed the landing on his shoulder. When he stood, he wiped dirt from his robes and glared at her.

"Do not play games with me," he said. "I should let you rot."

Tessanna's eyes remained cast to the floor, her long black hair hiding her face.

"Yes," she said. "I should rot down here, so leave me be. You don't know why you came, so why should I feel glad you did?"

In answer, Qurrah slapped her across the face. The sharp sound stirred the lone occupant in an adjacent cell.

"Whatcha doin' over there girl? Found yourself a buddy?" A tanned man with dirty hair pressed against the bars.

"Hold your tongue, or I will kill you," Qurrah said. The other man laughed.

"You can't even touch me. How about you let me free, or I start screaming for guards?"

Qurrah started to cast a spell, but stopped when hands grabbed his robes. He startled when he glanced back at Tessanna. Her face had changed. Life burned in her eyes. Angry life. Before he could respond, she released his robes, pointed her shackled hands at the nuisance, and whispered a word of magic in a dark tongue of old.

"*Relnka,*" Qurrah heard. The prisoner gargled and coughed. Blood spilled out his lips, as well as his nose, his eyes, his ears, and every other orifice. He collapsed. Dark liquid pooled underneath his body as he silently died.

"I should bleed you as well," she snarled at Qurrah.

"Try and you will die," he shot back, wishing he felt as confident as he sounded. "I come as your savior. I will leave as your murderer."

Tessanna held up her constricted hands.

"Release me."

He touched the metal shackles and pondered. Unsure, he tried the same spell he had used to enter the cell. The metal swarmed with shadow, nearly glowing with its darkness, and then slipped to the ground, the flesh like air to it. When he started to cast the spell on her legs, she waved him off.

"Open," she commanded, hooking her fingers in strange, fluid formations. The locks around her feet clicked and fell. She stood, tossing her hair off her face.

"How do we get out?" she asked. Not a bit of gratitude revealed its presence in her voice.

"You did not need me to free yourself. Why do you need me now?" Already he felt foolish. He was no savior to this girl. At any time, she could have cast aside the chains that held her.

"I cannot walk through walls," she replied. "Locks are a different matter. We can leave through the front entrance, but people will die."

"They will hunt you if we do," Qurrah said. "Give me your hand."

"No."

He took it anyway. She glared at him, her eyes bulging with anger, but the anger melted away. He held her hand so gently. Qurrah closed his eyes to think, and when he opened them again, Tessanna was blushing. He raised an eyebrow.

"Your hand is soft," she said in a quiet, shy voice. Qurrah pretended not to notice.

"Follow me. My former master taught me this spell, but I have never used it before."

"You'll do fine," she said. "I know it."

He cast the spell. A black door formed against the wall, constructed of shadows and magic. They stepped inside, the door vanished, and then they were far away.

The shadow door reopened inside a tiny, decrepit building. The two stepped out, the entrance scattering into nothingness behind them. Tessanna looked around, her arms wrapped across her chest. There was barely room for them to stand side by side.

"Where are we?" she asked.

"Still in Veldaren," Qurrah said. "This is where my brother and I used to live, before we were evicted and forced to travel to Woodhaven. It has long been abandoned."

She looked away, her arms still wrapped tight about her body. "Why did you come? Good does not come from me, Qurrah Tun. It never has."

"That does not mean it never will."

Before going to the prison, he had stashed blankets and a pillow in the corner. He picked them up and offered them to her.

"Thank you," she said, gripping the cloth as if her life were at stake. "Please, how can I repay you?"

He shook his head. "We are kindred, Tessanna. We both sense it."

"But I want to thank you," she said. She put the blankets down and stepped closer. "Don't you want me to thank you?"

She reached for the sash around his waist. He grabbed her arm. "What are you doing?" he asked.

"Thanking you," she said. Her voice was so soft, so child-like, it hurt him. "Please. It'll be okay."

Her other hand slid through the tight cloth. She felt his knee, caressed it with the back of her fingers, and then slid her hand higher.

"Enough!" he shouted, shoving her away. She fell, and the look of pain on her face would haunt his dreams for nights to come. Curled up on her knees, she looked at him, tears in her eyes. His breath was heavy, and he did his best to calm as he spoke.

"I desire your company, Tessanna, but not in that way. I do not even know you. Tomorrow morning, I will come with food. Please, sleep well this night."

She nodded. A hand wiped away her tears. When they were gone, so too was her emotion. The girl of apathy had returned.

"I will await you here," she said. She took the blankets and spread them out in the corner. Without another word, she nestled in, pressed her head against the pillow, and tried to sleep. Qurrah stared at her, his skin hot and his mind blurred.

"Tessanna," he said, his voice full of fear.

"Go home," she interrupted. "My dreams are dark. I do not want you hurt. Go home."

He did, cursing himself every step of the way.

"Qurrah," Harruq grumbled in a drowsy voice. "That you?"

"I had trouble sleeping," his brother said, sliding into bed.

"You sure nothing-"

"I am fine," he said, sharper than he meant. His throat throbbed, his head ached, and his heart thumped as if it were to explode.

"Brother?" Harruq asked, rising from his bed. "What's wrong?"

"Go to bed, Harruq," Qurrah said. "I will explain in time."

The big half-orc shrugged. "If you say so."

Qurrah put his back to him and stared at the wall. His thoughts never left Tessanna, even when he slipped into the world of dreams.

"My dear Eschaton, we have ourselves a beauty of a task," Tarlak said to the collected mercenaries of the tower. They grouped together on the first floor, the two females sprawled across the couches, the men sitting unhappily on the floor, except for Haern, who haunted the stairs leading upward.

"How's the pay?" asked Brug.

"No pay for this one. Charity stuff here." Tarlak scratched his goatee, his eyes glancing over to Haern. "We do this one for the Watcher."

"Not to sound dumb, but who is this Watcher?" Aurelia asked. The yellow wizard turned to her and beamed.

"I would gladly tell you, my dear-"

"I am," Haern whispered, interrupting him. "I keep the thief guilds in line."

Both half-orcs glanced at him with shocked faces.

"You're the Watcher?" Harruq said. "Holy orcbutt, no wonder you beat me so bad."

"Holy orcbutt?" Delysia asked, raising an eyebrow at him. Harruq shrugged.

"Got the point across."

"So now I know who the Watcher is," Aurelia said. "But how exactly do you keep the thief guilds in line?"

"Lovely Aurelia, do you have no knowledge of how the guilds operate in Veldaren?" Tarlak asked.

She shook her head.

"Who wants to inform the girl?" Tarlak asked the crowd.

"Fifty years ago," Haern began, "the noble families in Veldaren declared war on the thief guilds. After five years of mercenaries roaming the streets and nobles bleeding out in the night, they made a truce. The nobles would pay the thief guilds what they were paying the mercenaries. In return, they gained protection, and not just for their homes, but the entire city. Five guilds accepted, and the rest were eradicated. Odd as it sounds, the thief guilds protect their territory, and only the poorest of streets are left to a few vagabond burglars."

"So you have no crime here?" Aurelia asked. "A miracle."

"We have crime, my lady elf," Haern whispered, "just no robbery. Murder and rape are another matter."

"Many thieves want to return to the days of old," Tarlak added. "They feel like bodyguards now, bottom rate sentries. The number of members in each guild has doubled and tripled, with each member getting a smaller and smaller cut. Only guildmasters make a luxurious living. This leads me into our wonderful surprise for tonight."

He cleared his throat and grinned at everyone.

"Guildmaster Thren Felhorn of the Spider Guild is to supposedly be assassinated tonight."

"Supposedly?" Brug said.

"I say supposedly for I believe it a trap. All of you need to be on your toes. The largest obstacle to returning to the days of old is not the guildmasters. It is our dear friend, Haern. Those who speak out against the current system have a way of not waking up. Isn't that right, oh wise and all-knowing Watcher?"

"Get on with it," Haern said.

"Right. My informant claimed that Thren is meeting a higher up of the Shadow Guild, about what is irrelevant, inside an old warehouse owned by the Spider Guild. I want half of you inside that building, the other half out and around. We'll hide best we can. If it is a trap, leave one or two of them alive. It's hard to make dead people talk."

"But not impossible," Qurrah said. All eyes went to him. He had seemed mentally absent the whole meeting, and had not previously spoken.

"I take it conversing with dead is a hobby of yours?" Tarlak asked.

"I consider it a profession. The dead talk same as the living, and the dead can't lie."

Brug made a show of throwing up his hands and rolling his eyes. "Wonderful people you brought into our fold, Tar."

"Shut up, Brug. I'll leave it up to you all, then. Kill if you want, but let's not be sloppy or stupid." Tarlaked started packing his maps. "Meet in this room by nightfall. And come prepared. Tonight, we're going to have some fun!"

✠

Qurrah spent the day meeting with Tessanna. He brought food wrapped in another small blanket for her to use during the chilly nights. She was sitting outside when he arrived, staring at the sky.

"I almost took a quick trip to the fountain," she said, her voice distant and emotionless. "But I figured I am too popular with certain men right now."

"Are you hungry?" he asked. He unwrapped the pieces of bread, bacon, and hard cheese. She blinked at it and shook her head.

"I don't need to eat, at least, not often," she said. "Bring me something three mornings from now." She held up her right hand, showing him a simple wooden band around her ring finger. "It looks plain," she said, her voice almost bored. "My family handed it down for generations. It helped them survive famine. I only have to eat once every six days."

Qurrah sat down opposite her. He awkwardly fumbled for words, for he had many questions, and he wished to ask them all at once.

The Cost of Betrayal

"Where is your family?" he finally asked.

Her black eyes grew darker, the white at the edges deepening to gray.

"I have no family," she said. The apathy slowly faded into anger. An animalistic being controlled the girl's voice. "My mother died giving birth to me. My father died later, along with my stepmother. I have no family."

His body shivered at the sound of her voice, but he pressed on. She had pried into his mind. It was his turn to do the same.

"Tell me, Tessanna. What happened to them?"

She brought her gaze down from the sky. "You want to know? Fine. I didn't kill my stepmother, but he thought so. He drank a lot because of it. I can't blame him though, considering what he came home to." As she talked, Qurrah watched as the angry girl seamlessly turned shy and quiet. "We lived in the King's forest. Daddy owed lots of people money, so we hid out there in our tiny cabin. Daddy gambled. He came back here, though, said he was going to make lots of money. Lots and lots of money!"

"Well," she continued, clutching her hands together and batting her eyelashes at him. "Daddy didn't make enough, so bad people took him, made him work real hard. He couldn't come home and see me and mommy! He needed to, because mommy got sick. I was still young, and she was too sick to leave and buy food for us. So she gave me this ring. She starved to death after a few weeks."

She giggled.

"I didn't have to eat often because of the ring, but when I did, I was famished. But we had nothing! So-" another giggle, "-I ate what I had to."

The vision Tessanna had shown him, of a female arm in his lap, and the taste of blood on his lips, darted across Qurrah's mind. He shuddered. It seemed he was not the only one who had been forced to eat the scraps of the dead.

"Daddy came home and saw me eating," she said. "He thought I killed mommy. He was finally free, and he came home wanting mommy, but mommy was gone. He told me there was stuff I could do for him, though, stuff mommy used to do."

Another image, the rough man tearing at his clothes, sank Qurrah's stomach. Hatred burned in his heart.

"What happened to him?" he asked.

Tessanna crawled closer and whispered as if telling a great secret.

"He liked humping me. He drank all the time, probably because if he wasn't drinking he'd realize how bad it was to take your thirteen-year-old daughter to bed. I did it, though. Maybe I liked it. It feels awfully good inside you." She laughed at Qurrah's blush. "He never even bothered to tell me he loved me. He hated me. I knew it, so he never lied. I think sometime over those two years he broke my mind."

Again that insane laugh. Qurrah's heart tore at the sound. Part of it was adorable. The other part was pure madness, and it frightened him beyond words. She continued, her voice dropping into an even quieter whisper.

"One night I had a plan. I made it seem like I wanted it, even liked it. Aren't I such a horrible liar? He got really, really drunk that night. When he was done with me, he drank even more, and fell asleep in a chair. I took some rope and I tied his hands and feet. He couldn't get out. I tied his neck, too. I didn't want him moving, because that would ruin the fun."

"Fun?" Qurrah asked. "Torture is what that man deserved."

"Torture *is* fun," she said. She didn't smile that time. Qurrah considered fleeing then, but he didn't. He wanted to hear the end of the story.

"I crushed some glass into tiny pieces and shoved them in his mouth. He woke up choking, but I didn't stop. I sewed his mouth shut. I had practiced, but with flesh you have to be forceful. Once he couldn't spit out the glass, the real fun started. Lots of fun. Two years worth of fun."

She looked to the ground, her face suddenly blushing.

"I kissed his neck just before he tried swallowing the glass. I'm not sure why."

"He died choking on his own blood," Qurrah said more than asked. The final image took its turn before his eyes, that of the rough man vomiting intestines filled with shards of glass.

"Shhhh," Tessanna said through clenched teeth. "It's a secret." She leaned back, smiling into her hand. "And don't you tell anybody."

"I promise I will not," Qurrah said. He stood and stretched his arms. "I must go. Will you be fine spending a few more days here?"

"Will you come visit me?" she asked. She curled her legs to her chest and peered over her knees. Qurrah would have done anything she asked, she was so beautiful.

"Of course. Every day. I promise."

She lowered her head, as if in hiding.

"Thank you," she said.

"For what?" Qurrah asked.

"You know what. If you don't, you're dumber than I thought."

The half-orc chuckled, glad to hear the edge of sarcasm. She seemed sanest when she was being sarcastic. He bid her farewell and returned to the tower.

6

"Why do I have to be stuck with the orcs?" Brug grumbled in the quietest tone he could manage, which was not very quiet at all. They hid near where the assassination was to take place, and Tarlak had just outlined the groups. Naturally, the wizard was to be alone with Aurelia.

"Because you're so short," Tarlak said. "And all short people must suffer. It is the Eschaton way." Tarlak's grin faded when he realized Brug was not amused. "Listen, Haern stays on his own, because he works best that way. Delysia remains safe until it is all over and done, and she can heal whoever needs it. Aurelia and I will sneak in through the roof, and that leaves you three watching from the streets."

"How come I can't be with Aurelia?" Brug whined. "She needs a melee fighter in case something goes wrong."

"It appears you have competition, brother," Qurrah said, an amused expression on his face.

"Bah," Harruq said. "With the mage or the short guy? Either way, I'm not too worried." Both turned and glared. He grinned back. "Hello! Aurry's going without you, so one of you better go."

He pointed to the elf, who was twenty feet in the air and climbing, courtesy of a levitation spell. Tarlak patted Brug on the head. "Looks like you can't follow. Good luck. Save our asses if we screw up."

He cast a spell, his feet bumped an inch off the ground, and then he followed Aurelia. Harruq put his hand on Brug's shoulder as the three stared.

"A shame," he said. "Look on the bright side, though. You can almost see up Aurry's dress from here."

Brug's face turned beet red. "One day," he snarled. "Just…one day…you'll see."

Tarlak landed on the roof, beside Aurelia.

"Gorgeous night," he said. "A perfect time to spend with a beautiful woman."

"Hope you have enough coin on you," she said.

"I said with, not on," Tarlak corrected. Aurelia shrugged.

"Whatever. I take it the three mummers are guarding the southern entrance?"

Tarlak nodded.

"Haern should be watching the other, which leaves the roof to us."

"Time to vanish," Aurelia said.

The two faded from view as they cast their invisibility spells. The roof was flat and bare, leaving them no other options for hiding. With all ways into the building covered, there was nothing to do but wait. Twenty minutes later, a lone man appeared, circled the building, and then dashed away.

"A scout," Tarlak explained. Aurelia glanced down the alley, and from her vantage point, noticed Harruq's shoulders peeking out from behind a few conveniently placed crates.

"I think Haern needs to teach Harruq a thing or two about stealth," she said. Tarlak laughed.

"Stealth? If he isn't screaming and wrecking stuff before the fight, I'll be thrilled."

She tried to jab him with her finger but missed. "Next time I see you, you are getting such a hard poking."

"Be gentle, I am a delicate creature."

Tarlak suddenly stiffened. The elf could not see his posture change, but the abrupt silence quieted her as well.

"The Shadow Guild," the wizard whispered a moment later. Down the street walked a man, flanked by ruffians dressed in black leather. Blue scarves covered their faces. The man wore a suit of polished leather armor with silver runes shining across his sleeves and neck. His scarred face showed the price of his position. They marched to the northern door, opened it, and went inside.

"Odd," Tarlak murmured. "No checking. No searches."

"More come from the south," Aurelia said. Another group, this time adorned in pure gray clothes and armor, the black spider emblazoned on their clothing, traveled up the street. In their center walked a young man, his face covered by a hood pulled low.

"They look so much like Haern," she said.

"He was to be their prized assassin," Tarlak whispered. "Reared from birth to be silent and unseen. The Spider Guild planned complete conquest of the other guilds, and then dominion over Veldaren's streets."

Aurelia observed their silent movements shrouded by their long gray cloaks. They did not move like men. She shivered. "What stopped them?"

"They underestimated Haern. They thought his mind enslaved to their dogma. A certain red-headed girl saved him."

"Delysia?"

A soft chuckle escaped the invisible wizard's throat.

"Aye. He may not look it, but a small gold emblem of the mountain hangs from his neck. Ashhur saved him. In turn, Haern has saved us a hundred times over."

The group of men reached the warehouse, opened the door, and marched inside. The door slammed shut behind them.

"Fun time. Do you know pass-wall?"

Aurelia shook her head, and then laughed when she realized the wizard would not be able to see. "No, I don't," she said.

"Very well, I was prepared for that. Um, hrm. Say something, I need to grab your hand."

"Over here."

She reached out her hands and slowly searched the air.

"Here?" he asked.

"To your left."

"You mean here?"

"Other left. My left, wait, never mind, that won't work will it?"

"Here you are." A hand suddenly wrapped around her waist. "Found you."

"Unfind me right now, mister wizard."

"Why should I do that?" was his flirty reply.

"Mudskipper."

The hand vanished. Fingers wrapped around her arm, then slid to her wrist. From her left, she heard spellcasting. A tingling sensation flowed all the way to her toes. Suddenly, it felt like the ground beneath her feet vanished. She started to fall, but the firm grip on her wrist held her steady.

"Levitate for Ashhur's sake, woman!" Tarlak said loud as he dared.

She closed her eyes and did the semantic components with her right hand. When the final words left her tongue, she floated up and off the ceiling.

"You have about a minute left," Tarlak said. "Float on down and stay at the top of the room. I'll be beside you."

"No more whispering," Aurelia said before dipping down. "They might hear."

Then she was falling through the ceiling.

"Time to go?" Harruq asked.

"That's just one group, no clue when others are showing up," Brug argued from behind his barrel. "We wait until we get ourselves a signal."

"What kind of signal is that?"

"Fire, screams, writing in the sky," said Qurrah.

"Funny," Brug grumbled.

"You're not laughing."

"Because it ain't funny!"

"Stop lying then, and you're being far too loud," Harruq said. "How about we wait five more minutes?"

If anyone was bothering to count, and Qurrah was, it was the fifth time Brug's face turned beet red from anger, embarrassment, or both.

"Both parties have arrived," a voice whispered from behind them. "And I know of two-year-olds that make less noise than you three."

Brug jumped, Harruq spun, and Qurrah laughed.

"Can one really expect a quiet conversation between a half-orc who thinks with his muscles and a human who doesn't think at all?" Qurrah asked.

"Yes, if both are dead," Haern replied. "Guard the door. The other side is mine. Enter at the sound of combat."

The assassin dashed to the warehouse, cut around the corner, and vanished, all without making the slightest sound.

"Showoff," Harruq grumbled. They made their way to the warehouse, armor creaking and footsteps aplenty.

The sensation was unique, and to Aurelia, entirely unpleasant. Her eyes saw the inside of wood rafters, as if they had been chopped in half. Then darkness, followed by more wood, and suddenly she hovered above a large building stacked full of barrels. More than thirty men stood in the center, some dressed in black, some dressed in gray. The two leaders stood face to face, discussing some matter in hushed tones.

"What do you think they are going to do?" Tarlak whispered into her ear.

"I thought I said no more speaking," she whispered back.

"Can't help it. I'm a nervous talker."

Aurelia rolled her unseen eyes. "They want Haern, right?" she asked.

"Right."

"What will bring Haern rushing in?"

"I'm going to say someone dying."

The elf chuckled. "So what do you think is about to happen?"

Tarlak pointed, knowing Aurelia would not see the gesture. "That."

The members of the two opposing guilds had drawn their blades. Aurelia ran through a litany of her spells, pondering her course of action. She preferred not killing anyone, but if things turned rough, she would not risk the lives of her friends.

"You think all this is rehearsed?" Tarlak asked. The two leaders appeared to be arguing vehemently, while their cronies twirled their daggers and prepared their swords.

"Tarlak," she said, ignoring his question. "If someone is plotting Haern's death, do you think it probable that one of the men down there knows about it?"

"I'd say it's a safe assumption."

"Good."

The sound of spellcasting filled his ears.

"What in blazes are you doing?" he asked none-too-quietly.

"It's all an act," Aurelia said, "and the prelude bores me."

A thick blue ray of swirling dust hit the floor underneath the two leaders, freezing the ground with a thin, clear layer of ice. Her invisibility spell ended, broken by her casting of an offensive spell. The rogues looked up, easily maintaining their balance on the ice.

"Oh dear," Tarlak said beside her. "You just have to have things exciting, don't you?"

Several of the thieves shouted warnings as others rushed to the doors. Then five of the Spider Guild members pulled out throwing knives and flung them into the air.

⋈

"You hear that shouting?" Harruq asked.

Brug nodded as the half-orc drew his blades.

"Should we make our entrance loud or sneaky?" he asked.

"Allow me," Qurrah said. He approached the door, placed his hand upon it, and cast his spell. The aged wood splintered and shook with power, and then with a tremendous explosion, the door shattered into a hundred shards, blasting inward as if blown by the winds of a hurricane. The pieces clacked and broke against the far interior wall.

"One abyss of a knock," Brug said, clanging his punch daggers together. He led the way, followed by Harruq and Qurrah. They managed a brief glance about before a pack of gray thieves assaulted them. A large group of both guilds stood in the center, dodging and weaving around spells. Harruq's heart jumped as he saw dagger after dagger fly toward Aurelia, but she evaded all with ease, spinning her body or dropping up and down with her levitation spell. On the far side of the building, a large collection of black-leathered rogues battled against a whirling gray mass that could only be Haern. Despite being outnumbered seven to one, he seemed to be on the offensive.

"Bring it on ya pansies!" Brug shouted, barreling his way into the thieves that rushed to them. "My daggers are bigger, harder, and pack a whole lot more thrust!"

Harruq followed, bellowing out his war cry. Condemnation and Salvation drank in the blood of the closest attacker. Brug smacked away a couple quick thrusts before letting a third purposefully slip through. The dagger struck his hardened platemail and deflected off, making hardly a dent. Brug's stab, however, had only weak leather to slow it. The wide blade left a gaping hole in the rogue's chest. Brug punched repeatedly, perforating the thief's ribcage.

A second attacker snuck around, eyeing a crease in Brug's armor near the shoulder blade. Brug ducked low when he saw the man circling, and then whirled to face him. He rammed his head into the thief's groan, then grabbed his legs and lifted him into the air. With a hearty bellow, he slammed them both to the ground, the collision again ramming Brug's forehead against his groin. Brug scrambled to his feet, inadvertently kneeing him a third time. When his punch daggers stabbed for the throat, there was no resistance.

Qurrah stayed back, watching the fight. The two warriors provided a wall between him and the rogues, one he planned to use well. A rogue slipped past their attack and dashed toward the apparently unarmed half-orc.

"Idiot," Qurrah said. "*Hemorrhage!*"

The thief felt a tingle in his belly, a tingle that rapidly grew into a raging fire. His skin ruptured, and blood poured forth. The shock of it sent him staggering right into Qurrah's arms. The half-orc caught him, unafraid of the dagger he still held tight. His pale gray hand clutched the rogue's throat. His eyes were blue. His hair was blond. They would not stay so. Qurrah hissed the words to a spell. His hand turned vampiric, draining the essence of life. The man's hair was gray. His eyes were dead.

Qurrah dropped the body to the floor. Power surged through him, eager for use. He closed his eyes, tendrils floating out from his body. They were extensions of his power, black and deadly. One thief, deep in combat with Brug, was touched mid-swing by one such tendril. He shrieked, his dagger dropping from his hand. Images of the abyss to come swirled before his eyes. Clawing things with bloody fingernails gnawed at his mind. Brug buried his punch daggers into the rogue's throat to silence his shrieking.

Another thief, fleeing from Harruq's rage, felt a tendril snake around his ankle. The madness came quick, fueling his already burning fear. He shrieked, seeing nameless fiends sinking teeth into his ankle. He stopped his retreat, dropped to one knee, and began sawing off his ankle with his own dagger. Harruq halted above him, stunned by the sight.

"Kill him," Qurrah said, smoke drifting from his eyes. "Save him from his madness."

Harruq felt a pang of guilt, but knew his brother's words were true. He buried his sword deep between collarbone and neck.

"This all ya got?" Brug shouted, stabbing his dagger into the side of the lone thief that fought the three. The thief hobbled back, grimacing at the pain of his wound. Qurrah narrowed his eyes, remembering the spell Tessanna had cast in the prison. He had prepared earlier in the day, practicing those same words the girl had used.

"*Bleed,*" he hissed in the arcane tongue. Blood poured from every opening on the man's body. Brug spat on the corpse.

"You got some creepy spells, half-orc, but they're effective."

Harruq looked up to Aurelia, relieved by the sight of her unharmed. Bodies of the dead littered the icy floor. Haern approached from the other side, a trail of defeated rogues in his wake.

"Well that was easy!" Harruq shouted to the others.

"Too easy," Qurrah said. "If this was a trap, it was a poor one."

The two casters floated down, Tarlak eyeing the corpse of Thren in particular.

"He fell to a single lightning bolt," Tarlak said, stroking his beard. "Something smells fishy, and it's not Brug. Aurry, do you know any dispel magic?"

Harruq felt a pang of jealousy.

"Yes," she said. "And don't call me Aurry."

The jealousy quickly faded.

Aurelia swung her hands about and cast her spell. A wave of white magic washed over the entire building. Harruq felt his armor and weapons sizzle in protest.

"Your equipment should be fine," the elf told him when she noticed Harruq's puzzled expression. "If I focused the spell entirely on your weapons, I might manage to destroy their magic, but I doubt it."

"It wasn't Thren," Haern said, pointing to the body. "Illusions. A trap, for sure." The guildmaster's body had changed, now no different from any other common thief who lay dead around them.

"You three leave any alive?" Tarlak asked Brug and the half-orcs.

"Not thinking so," Harruq said. "Did you?"

Tarlak shook his head.

"I like fire and lightning. It appears they didn't. Haern?"

"One still breaths, yes," Haern whispered. "Shall we have a talk?"

"Oh yes," Tarlak beamed, cracking his knuckles. "Most definitely, yes."

The rogue was a young man, with not even a scrap of hair on his chin. He lay on his back, wheezing with each breath. His hands clutched a bleeding wound in his side.

"Will he be alive for much longer?" Tarlak asked, peering down at him.

"No," Haern said. "Call in Delysia."

"Will do."

Tarlak reached into his shirt and pulled out a gold medallion shaped like a tower.

"Come on over, sis," he whispered to it. The gold flared a brilliant white before returning to its soft shine. Standing in front of Tarlak, her hands on her hips, appeared Delysia.

"I wish I didn't have to stay behind so often," she complained.

"We've gone over this," Tarlak said. "I would be an awful brother to risk you being hurt in a melee."

Delysia rolled her eyes. When she caught sight of the wounded rogue, she winced. "Oh, you poor dear. What'd you do to him?"

"I might have stabbed him," Haern whispered.

"Might?" the rogue gasped before falling unconscious. Delysia knelt beside him, her hands on his chest and her eyes closed in prayer. Qurrah slid beside Tarlak and said softly to him, "He would talk easier if he was dead."

"All men have a chance to be redeemed," Tarlak said back. "Killing in combat is one thing, but I will not finish off a helpless man I can save. Delysia would furious, otherwise."

White light surrounded Delysia's hands and then poured into the dying man. The wound closed, ending the flow of blood. Strength poured into him, stirring him back to consciousness.

"Wakey-wakey," Brug greeted. "Care to answer a few questions?"

"I'd rather die," the rogue said.

"You almost did," Delysia said, frowning at him. "Glad to know my aid is appreciated."

He sneered at her but said nothing.

"Haern, we need an attitude adjustment," Tarlak said. He snapped his fingers. The assassin walked over, knelt down, and then buried a saber into the thief's right wrist. He screamed and struggled, but the location of the saber was perfect, in between the bones so the blade could not tear free. Finally, the man calmed, wincing against the pain. Delysia pointedly turned away, her face disgusted.

"You do not approve?" Qurrah asked her.

"There are always better ways," she said. "Violence is rarely the best."

The half-orc laughed. Aurelia glared at him.

"Silence, Qurrah, or I will quiet you myself."

He grinned at her but obeyed.

"Care to talk now?" Tarlak asked once the thief regained his composure. The man nodded. "Good, tell me your name."

"Terrence."

"Alright Terrence, who orchestrated this whole farce? All I want is a name and I will let you live."

"They will kill me if I talk," Terrence said.

"You will die if you don't," Haern whispered. "Besides, all will think you dead. Now give us a name."

Tarlak stood watching and stroking his goatee. The man appeared to be greatly troubled, and when Haern yanked his blade free, it did not help his confused mind.

"I will tell," Terrance said at last. "But I want you to promise."

Tarlak clapped the man on the shoulder, ignoring the wince of pain on his face. "I speak for the Eschaton. You will not be harmed, nor persecuted for any crimes you might have committed in your guild."

Terrence glanced about before his eyes settled on a vacant area of the floor.

"What they've told us," he said, "is that all of the guildmasters wish the Watcher dead. The guilds are united. They prepare for war."

Haern's face darkened. He pulled his hood lower. "Who initiated it?" he asked.

"I don't know," Terrence said. "The Spider Guild seems the most eager. Thren has spoken with our representatives every night. Now may I go?"

The mercenaries let him stand. He winced, clutching his tender chest. Delysia turned back around and grabbed his hand in hers.

"Go with the peace of Ashhur," she told him, light swirling about her hands. When she released, there was no trace of the wound. He nodded to each of them, pilfered coins from his dead comrades, and then ran.

"Why did you let that one live?" Tarlak asked, watching him go.

"He was the least bloodthirsty, and had some measure of skill. I thought he might be the most tempted by a new life."

The wizard shrugged. "Makes sense to-"

"Look out!" Aurelia shouted. She dove in front of Haern and then screamed as an arrow pierced through the flesh of her breast. Haern spun, seeing just the trace of a gray cloak at the door Qurrah had shattered. Tarlak caught Aurelia in his arms and helped her to the floor. Haern knelt beside her, eyeing the wound.

"Poison," he whispered. "Lady Thyne, please forgive me."

He yanked the arrow out.

Harruq rushed to the door, his swords drawn and ready. He ran out into the street, spun one way, then the other. No one was in sight.

"Move Haern, I must help her," Delysia said. She knelt down, her hands upon the wound. She prayed for healing, and white light shone about her. Suddenly, her face contorted in pain, and a black light poured out of the wound and into her fingers.

"Sis, stop it!" Tarlak screamed, trying to pull her away.

"I have to…I have to…" she said before shrieking. More and more darkness poured into her, pushing away the white. As the rest stood helpless, Qurrah walked over, knelt beside Delysia, and put his hands atop of hers.

"*Delrn rel thun yaer,*" he hissed. The black magic poured into his hands, but did no harm to him. Instead, it swirled above his palms, held captive by the necromancer.

"Let your death go elsewhere," he said. He flung his hand as if throwing a spear straight into the ground. A dark, ethereal arrow flew through the dirt and vanished. For a brief moment, healing light flowed into the pale and dying Aurelia. Then Delysia fell back, unable to keep her balance. Tarlak caught her gently in his arms.

"I think I helped her," Delysia said, her voice barely a whisper. "I don't think it'll kill her. I don't think…"

She slipped into sleep in her brother's arms. Harruq returned then, and looked down at his precious Aurelia.

"Will she be alright?" he asked.

"The arrow was cursed," Qurrah said, his eyes looking not to his brother but to Haern. "They wished you to die of poison, and they wished death upon any that tried healing you. Aurelia saved your life."

"Who did this to her," Harruq said, the whole world turning red in his eyes. "Was it the Spider Guild?"

"Don't do anything foolish," Haern whispered. "They are many and powerful."

"And they'll soon be many and dead."

Qurrah put his hand on his brother's shoulder.

"I will await you at the tower. I will be of no use to you now. I have not the strength. If you wish any to speak, however, I will be ready."

Harruq turned to Tarlak. "Can you get her to the tower?"

The wizard nodded. "I'll open a portal. Haern and Brug'll help me carry Aurelia and Delysia. What is it you plan on doing?"

Harruq's grip tightened on his swords, and the rage in his eyes was visible fire.

"Killing everyone responsible," he growled.

Tarlak glanced to his sister, weak and sleeping in his arms.

"Kill them twice for me," he said.

With a nod, Harruq stormed out of the warehouse and into the dark streets of Veldaren.

He did not get far before Haern fell from the top of a building and blocked his path.

"Out of my way, Haern. This is something I have to do."

Haern's cold voice showed no sign of backing down. "I will aid you. The Spider Guild is strong. You cannot do this alone."

"I can, and I will."

He tried to shove his way past. Haern hooked his foot behind Harruq's ankle and kicked. The half-orc fell, Haern holding an arm so that his landing was not too painful.

"Do not be foolish," Haern whispered into his ear. "They meant to kill *me*. Aurelia saved my life. I will repay such a debt."

Harruq snorted, blowing dirt away from his face. "Fine. Do you know where we should start?"

Haern released his hold on the half-orc. Harruq brushed himself off, got to his feet, and glared at his teacher. Haern's glare back showed he cared little for his pupil's attitude.

"Follow me," the Watcher said.

7

The Black Mug Bar was a dank, crowded building made of old plaster and uneven walls. Its drinks were often watered down and always overpriced, but despite this, it remained fully stocked with customers. Most were not there for the ale. In the back of the building was its real purpose. A guarded door led to an expansive and well-lit basement filled with the finest luxuries available. To enter, one needed a password, which changed every month, and to show a sigil proving membership. Harruq and Haern needed neither.

"What you say?" a burly man asked as they approached.

"Pissed off half-orc," Harruq said. The guard shook his head.

"You two should leave. Nothing down there you want."

"Oh yeah, there is," the half-orc said, grabbing the man's head and slamming it against the door. The guard slumped to the floor. The few patrons jumped to their feet, drawing weapons. Most were members of the Spider Guild, and donned gray cloaks similar to Haern's.

The assassin whirled upon them, drawing his sabers.

"I have killed more men than all of you have combined," he said, his blue eyes blazing. "Those wishing to live, leave now. Those who dare face the wrath of the Watcher, come now, and die."

Uncertain glances were followed by disappearing cloaks. Soon only the barkeep remained. Harruq kicked the door, splintering the meager lock.

"There was a key on the guy you just clobbered," the barkeep said, pouring himself a drink.

"Keys. Bah."

Haern tossed the barkeep a silver coin.

"To cover your losses," he whispered before following Harruq down into the depths of the Spider Guild.

As they descended the stairs, two thieves ambushed from either side. Harruq jumped, landing hard at the bottom. Haern smashed his feet into his attacker's face. The man staggered back, blood pouring from his nose. Haern took his feet out from underneath with a sweeping kick. Twin sabers buried into his heart as he fell.

Harruq drew his blades, relishing the surge of power they offered. His attacker rushed him, his dagger thrusting. The half-orc smacked it aside like a toy. The longer reach of his swords was too much an advantage. The thief fell before him, several gaping wounds in his chest.

"You ever been down here?" Harruq asked, glancing around. They were in a tiny room filled with dusty barrels and crates.

"Yes, a long time ago."

The assassin approached what appeared to be a bare stone wall. He traced the subtle indents of the bricks with his fingers.

"Here," he whispered. He stepped back and pointed at a particular section. "We need a new door."

"With pleasure," Harruq said. He tucked his shoulder and ran right through the false wall, showering rock and stone everywhere. Haern dashed in as dust clouded the air, his swords drawn and his eyes searching. All about were plush cushions, silver platters of food, exquisite dining tables lined with black and scarlet patterns, and several private rooms adjacent the main floor. There should have been lords and nobles, scantily clad women and wealthy merchants, trading, dealing, and bribing one another with pleasures of flesh, powder, and coin. Instead, the room was dark and empty.

"Everyone go home for the night?" Harruq asked.

Haern shook his head, his eyes still darting. "The pleasures are partaken here night and day. I fear we made a great error, Harruq."

"I'd say so," called the barkeep from the top of the stairs. "Thanks for the coin, by the way."

Haern flew back through the busted wall and up the stairs, only to find a wall of magical origin blocking his way. Harruq came rushing after, his swords still in hand.

"What the abyss is going on?" he asked.

"The meeting wasn't the trap," Haern whispered, turning back around to face the half-orc. "This is."

The deep grinding of stone rolling against stone came from the far room.

"I'm scared to ask what that was," Harruq said.

"They are called the Spider Guild for a reason," the assassin said. He knelt in front of Harruq, pulled out a golden medallion shaped like a mountain, and then, as the half-orc stared incredulously, whispered a quick prayer. When finished, he slipped the medallion back underneath his tunic and stood.

"Come," Haern whispered. "I have no intentions of dying this night."

"You got that right," Harruq said. The two re-entered the plush room. On the far side, surrounded by rubble, was a newly created hole. From within came loud skittering sounds that made the half-orc's skin crawl.

"Oh, that better not be what I think that is," Harruq said.

"Go for the soft underbelly," Haern whispered. "And don't get bitten."

Loud thumping sounds joined the skittering. After a few quick motions by Haern, they ran to either side of the entrance in hope of an ambush. The sounds grew louder, and then out crawled a giant tarantula, enlarged to the size of small house. Of all the things Harruq had seen in his life, nothing prepared him for legs the size of pine trees, giant mandibles beneath eight huge eyes, and that loud, constant shriek.

"Don't get bitten," he mumbled, staring at the fangs protruding out from the bottom of its head, each one bigger than his hand. "No kidding."

When it was halfway out, Harruq used every bit of his courage to swing at one of the legs. His sword thudded as if hitting a tree, and clear blue ichor spewed across his hand. The spider shrieked in fury. Harruq hacked two more times as it spun about, focusing all eight eyes squarely on him.

"Hello!" he said, then flung Condemnation end over end. The blade pierced one of the eyes, embedding up to the hilt in green and black gunk. The spider rushed forward, horrifying Harruq with its speed. It slammed him backward with the top of its head. He flung across the room, thankfully landing on a pile of pillows. He struggled to his feet, throwing a couple as he did. Then Haern came diving in.

The assassin rolled underneath the spider, his sabers slashing in a silver flurry. It shrieked and smashed its belly down, but Haern was already gone. He slashed its legs, spilling ichor to the ground. When it spun, giant fangs biting, he dove back underneath with a sideways roll. With every revolution, he sliced his sabers into its belly, soaking his cloaks with the discharge.

The bulbous back to him, Harruq gripped Salvation in both hands and struck. The spider reared onto its back legs, its forelegs pounding great dents in the ceiling. When it landed, it slammed backward, smashing its abdomen against Harruq and the wall. The red hairs on its back were like thorns, shredding his exposed skin. The legs turned, flinging Harruq across the room. This time he missed the pile of pillows.

"That hurt," he said, getting to his knees. His gaze settled on the tarantula hissing at him from only a few feet away.

"Ah, shit."

The thing spun around, whipping its legs at him. Long spikes protruded from its back two legs, each the size of a broadsword. The first caught his forehead, tearing open a bright red gash. The other deflected off his armor, the blow stealing his breath and jolting him back. The tarantula continued spinning, its back legs arching out just above its body.

"A little help!" Harruq shouted. Haern weaved outside the range of the spider's legs, studying. He stepped closer, and then retreated just as quickly. A spike nearly took off his head. He repeated this, pulling back seconds before acquiring an impaled skull. The spider continued its spin. The third time, Haern did not pull away. He ducked down, his sabers slashing. The spider screeched as the end of one of its back legs flew across the room, trailing fluids.

Harruq swung Salvation wildly, hoping for similar results. Instead, a great impact sent his sword flying from his hand. Unarmed, the half-orc had no option but to crawl away on his back.

"I so hate spiders, I so hate spiders," he said repeatedly.

Haern watched the shifted pattern in the tarantula's spinning. It was incredibly quick, the spikes on its legs deadly, but it was still just an enlarged version of an unintelligent animal. The spin, which worked against all enemies it encountered in the natural world, was all it knew. The only change was the equivalent of a limp due to Haern's cut. The assassin danced in and out, his sabers slashing. Another chunk of leg flew across the room. The giant tarantula was vulnerable.

He leapt high into the air and landed atop the spider's abdomen. Both sabers pierced through the tough exoskeleton and into the slender heart tube that ran through its center. The spider rocked back and forth in its dying throes. Haern flipped away. Harruq rolled and crawled, desperate to evade the flailing legs. The spider's loud screech rose higher and higher. Still spinning, it charged at random, smashing into walls until in one sudden convulsion it shriveled its legs underneath itself and died.

Harruq stood, frowning at the gunk covering his armor.

"That has to be the most disgusting thing I have ever seen," he said. Haern, also covered with ichor, chuckled and pointed at the half-orc.

"I have to agree, but where did you find a mirror?"

"Ha ha ha. Shaddup you."

Harruq approached the spider, still feeling queasy at the sight of it curled up in death.

"Stupid thing," he said. "Probably smashed my sword further in when it ran into the wall." He looked around, trying to see Condemnation, but could not.

"Guess you will have to dig for it," Haern said. He clapped the half-orc on the back. "Good luck."

Harruq's heart sank. "Can you go get it for me? You're a whole lot more nimble."

"It's your sword," Haern replied. Harruq grumbled, and then climbed up a leg, shuddering with each touch of the hard, bristly hairs. He found the ruptured eye, and sure enough, the sword was nowhere visible. Closing his eyes and keeping his nose as far away as possible, Harruq pushed his hand inside. The slurping noise nearly made him vomit. He slipped in further and further, until his hand touched metal. He grabbed it and pulled. Condemnation ripped free, its red glow dimmed by the gunk covering it.

"Hope I never have to do that again," he said, shaking as much of the nasty stuff off his hand as he could. He hopped off, preferring the jolt to his legs over climbing down the dead spider's leg.

"Any ideas how to get out of here?" Haern asked him.

Harruq gave him a funny look.

"Aren't you supposed to be the smart one?"

The assassin shrugged. "And you're supposed to be the strong one. So if I can't figure a way out, you need to punch us a hole."

"What is blocking the top of the stairs?"

"A magical wall."

Harruq chuckled. He retrieved Salvation and then clanged both swords together.

"You know, I do have an idea."

The barkeep downed his fifth glass, showing no signs of it affecting him. He had listened to the muffled sounds of battle, his neck hairs standing on end every time the spider screeched, but now all was quiet. His customers were gone, and it was too late for more to arrive. Perhaps it was time to call it a night.

A tapping against his magical wall interrupted his drink.

"Who's there?" he asked.

"Please, help me," said a weak voice on the other side. "The spider is dead, but I've been bitten. Please, the poison…"

"I'm sorry, but you're supposed to die," the barkeep told the wall. "Nothing personal, of course."

"A drink then," the voice whispered. "Please, a drink before I die. I have gold."

The barkeep's greed kindled. If he left the bodies down there for Thren and the rest to return, he would get nothing. If he could loot the bodies first, however…

"Very well," he said. "I can't refuse a dying man his drink."

He picked up a silver wand resting atop the counter. Thren had given it to him, along with instructions of when and how to use it. He poured a drink, tapped the wand twice, and then said the correct words. The wall dissipated into dust, revealing Haern lying on his stomach, his hands shaking and his voice weak.

"Here you go," the barkeep said. He reached out the cup to Haern. To his horror, a strong, healthy hand grabbed his wrist.

"That's alright," Haern whispered, his eyes full of life. "I'll help myself."

He twisted the wrist into a painful lock. The barkeep's eyes bulged, and he turned his body to prevent the bone from snapping. Haern rose and shoved the man into the bar. Another hand slammed his face against the counter. Bottles of ale scattered, breaking and pouring everywhere.

"Where are they?" Haern asked.

"I don't know anything," the barkeep said. "They paid me to lock you in, that's all."

Harruq pounded up the stairs, his swords ready. He swung one next to the man's head and left it there, embedded deep in the wood.

"Care to answer that one again?" he asked.

"I said I don't know!" the barkeep shouted. "I serve drinks. That's it!"

"These drinks?" Harruq asked, glancing at some of the bottles lining the shelves. He grabbed one at random, popped it open, and took a swig. "Aaah, good stuff." Then he knocked the entire shelf to the floor. The barkeep winced with each shattered bottle, pondering the prices he had paid. Haern grabbed the barkeep's head and forced him to watch the half-orc tear his place apart.

"Mmmm, brandy," the half-orc said, guzzling a bit from a barrel. He used his other sword to split the barrel and spill its contents to the floor. He did the same for three more, sampling each one before destroying it.

"Gonna get trashed before all this stuff is gone," he laughed, booze dripping down his chin.

"Do not forget the private stash," Haern whispered. He pointed down below the bar, where a few small bottles were hidden. Harruq marched over as the barkeep's eyes bulged in horror. He took one, popped the cork, and drank.

"Woooweee, that is good," he said. He tossed another to Haern, who flicked it open with his thumb and drank a bit. He poured the rest onto the barkeep's head.

"I don't know how much they paid you," Haern whispered, "but I doubt it was even half the price of that bottle. Or that blue one there. Toss me that, Harruq. Thank you." He smashed the bottle and smeared the barkeep's face in it. "Go ahead and lick it up. Someone might as well drink. My patience is ended, barkeep. Where are they hiding? Who paid you?"

"Thren and his boys," the barkeep muttered. "They gave good gold to lock you in. They said they would return tomorrow morning. I swear, I don't know where they are now!"

Haern let him up. Harruq downed half of another expensive bottle, then dropped it to the soaked floor. The barkeep glared.

"Nothing personal," the half-orc said. The two exited into the night.

8

"Where to next?" Harruq asked. The two stood outside the bar, still trying to clean off spider fluids from their clothes and armor. "We only have a few more hours until morning."

"We will finish before the stars fade," Haern whispered, pulling his hood down tighter. "And I have no idea."

"Aren't you the best of leaders," the half-orc grumbled. "Why am I following you, anyway? Aurry's hurt, and you can't find the one who did it."

"Aurelia may very well be dead, Harruq."

"She's not!" he shouted. They halted in the dark alley, Harruq grabbing Haern's shoulders and shoving him against a wall. "How can you be so heartless? Never say that. Never!"

Haern smiled when he saw tears forming in the half-orc's eyes.

"No, she is not dead, but it is good to see your rage and sorrow. Remember why we fight this night. Now come. I may not know where to go, but I will find someone who does."

A small, unshaven man stood outside the expansive mansion, glancing up and down the barren streets. The gray cloak of the Spider Guild was tied around his neck.

"Who is that?" Harruq asked, staring around the corner of a nearby building.

"I don't know, but he wears the correct colors. Stay here."

Haern looked up, judging the height. After a few seconds, he nodded, seeming pleased. Then, to the half-orc's amazement, he leapt into the air without even a running start, vaulting all the way onto the roof.

"How the abyss did you do that?" Harruq asked. Haern placed a finger over his lips and pointed to the thief. The half-orc threw up his arms in surrender, figuring some sort of magic involved. He leaned back and enjoyed the show. Haern stalked across the roof, his eyes locked on his prey. The man most likely waited for word that the Watcher was dead and theft could begin without fear of reprisal.

The mansion certainly had its treasures, but he would get no chance at them.

With the grace of a cat, Haern leapt again, his cloaks trailing behind him. He kept his sabers out and ready. His slender body descended, his cloaks somehow not making a sound despite the air whipping through them. Haern landed directly behind the thief, standing back to back. The assassin spun, the butts of his sabers smacking skull. The thief dropped like a stone.

Harruq helped drag the body into the alley. Haern propped him up, and then reached into a pocket beneath his cloaks. He pulled out a small green vial barely larger than his pinkie. He popped the cork and splashed a little inside the man's mouth. Coughing and sputtering, he jolted back to life.

"Welcome back," Haern whispered, pocketing the vial. "Stay silent, or things will have to turn brutal."

The thief realized who it was and paled. "You!" he exclaimed. "I haven't done nothing, I swear."

"Quiet." Haern glanced to Harruq. "Do you wish to torture him, or should I?"

"I doubt I'm as neat as you," Harruq said. "Think we got the time?"

"No, please, what do you want, I'll help you," the thief cried.

Haern yanked him close. His eyes, looming out from a deep shadow that surrounded them, pierced into the thief's soul. "Where is Thren hiding?"

"Oh come on, you can't go asking me that. It'll be my head."

"It'll be your tongue, your fingers, and your manhood if you don't," Haern said. "Now answer me."

"I can't!"

Haern placed the edges of his sabers against the man's neck, and then slowly moved one downward until it pointed directly at his groin.

"Then there will be many other things you can't do."

"Wonder what it'd be like peeing through three holes," Harruq said.

Haern faked a thrust, and that was all the man could take.

"They moved the headquarters!" he shouted. Haern smacked him across the face.

"Quieter, and calmer. Where did they move it to?"

"The Swine's Pearls," he said.

"Sounds like a nice place," Harruq said. "New to me, though."

"Just opened last month," Haern whispered. "Your boss plays a dangerous game, little thief. Run home. Tell Thren I'm coming, and by tonight's end, he will bleed at my feet."

Haern removed his saber, and the thief fled. When he turned out of sight, the assassin gave chase, leaving the surprised Harruq standing far behind.

"What are you doing?" he shouted, sprinting after. Haern's glare silenced any further shouts. Rounding about a corner, the half-orc grumbled as he watched Haern leap into air, grab a jagged brick halfway up a building, and then use it to propel himself to the roof.

"How am I supposed to follow you now?" he asked. He ran after, the fleeting image of gray cloak upon the rooftops as his only guide. They crisscrossed southwest, deep into the heart of the city. Harruq caught glimpses of Haern and their thief, who did not appear to realize he was followed. The half-orc ran on until he lost sight of both.

"Forget it," he said, slowing to a walk. He gasped for air, his many bruises crying out in fresh pain. The gash on his forehead trickled blood atop his eyebrows, and he wiped it with the back of his hand. The hairs on his neck stood. He whirled about, his swords drawn. Haern stood there, grinning.

"You have gotten better," he whispered.

"Don't have much choice, do I?" he shot back. "What's with the running? Where is the Pearl's Swine place?"

"The Swine's Pearls, and it is in the northwestern corner of Veldaren."

Harruq sighed in surrender. "Alright, so why are we here?"

"Because the new headquarters is not the Swine's Pearls. That fool had the audacity to lie to me. Come. Our friend has just arrived, and we must not let them prepare for our appearance."

The half-orc smashed his swords together. He felt his adrenaline surge yet again, and he desperately hoped it would be enough. It had been a long night, after all.

"Let's go make them pay for Aurry and Delysia," he said.

The assassin drew his own sabers and flashed a wicked smile.

"The Watcher has come to collect."

<hr>

On the outside, the new headquarters for the Spider Guild looked far from extravagant. To the passing eye, it appeared to be a small, poorly lit store offering vague, unsorted items, with only the hanging sign of a barrel and smith hammer offering any idea of what services might be appropriated inside. The two approached the door from either side. With a nod from Haern, Harruq kicked the door open, the half-orc following Haern in.

A few poor quality weapons lined some racks. Smithing and fletchery tools covered the others. Foul smelling barrels of ale filled an entire corner. Behind a rotted counter was a single unguarded door. Haern crossed the room silently. Harruq, on the other hand, stretched and popped his neck and back without worry for the sound. When his part of their impromptu plan arrived, he would do as expected, except he would do it loud and nasty.

Haern pushed the door open with the side of a saber. He put an ear to the crack and listened. He heard voices, one in particular loud and panicked. Perfect. Their thief friend had just arrived. The assassin nodded to Harruq, who cracked his knuckles.

"Disgusting habit," Haern whispered across the room.

The half-orc chuckled.

"Let's go already," he said, spurring the man into action. Haern kicked the door all the way open and entered as a whirlwind of cutting steel. The room was a small, well-decorated entryway leading to a larger door. Their thief was in conversation with two guards blocking the way. They never had a chance to move. Haern buried one saber in the left guard's eye, the other slicing the right guard's stomach, spilling intestines to the floor.

The thief drew his dagger as the two guards fell dead to either side of him.

"You lied to me," Haern whispered. He hit the dagger with a savage combination of chops. It flew to the floor. "You could have lived." The thief turned to flee. Haern felled him before he took a single step. He twisted the blades when he pulled them free. Voices shouted from the other side of the door, their quick exchange having alerted those within.

"Ready, Harruq?" Haern shouted.

Before Harruq could answer, the door swung open, and armed guards rushed out. They wore little armor, and wielded shortswords and clubs. Outnumbering Haern six to one, they had little chance. The assassin dashed to the left, parrying away everything that came near him. The guards formed a semicircle, blocking any chance to retreat. Undaunted, Haern spun, whipping his multiple cloaks into a frenzy. The gray cloth twirled about, hiding the actions of the assassin's blades. The first guard who tried a thrust watched his severed hand fly to the floor in a great spurt of blood.

The guards stared, unsure of what to do, and then Harruq barreled into the fight, his swords held high. The closest two died without a fight. Another tried to block Harruq's double-chop, only to have his blade, and bones, shatter under the magical power of the twin blades. Haern leapt out of his cloak dance, running between two fleeing guards making for the larger door leading further into the complex. His curved blades sliced soft flesh. When he reached the far side of the room, he somersaulted off a wall and landed atop the guard whose hand he had severed. A vicious stab ended his life.

The remaining two, wounded by Haern's pass, threw down their weapons and fled for the street. Harruq snarled at their cowardice.

"Let them go," Haern shouted. "Thren is the one who must pay."

The half-orc ignored him, charging after the fleeing guards. He flung Condemnation through the air. The sword blasted the nearest guard off his feet, the blade piercing through his back. Harruq yanked his sword free as he ran past. The final guard grabbed a sword from a rack and faced his attacker.

Haern shook his head. Such foolish anger had no place in battle. Focused anger, perhaps, but never uncontrolled idiocy. The half-orc still had much to learn. The killing was far from done.

Beyond the entryway was a much grander lounge. Red and blue pillows covered the floor. Thick red curtains sectioned off parts of the room for privacy. On the far side stood guildmaster Thren, a near perfect image of Haern, barring the aged look of his hands and his bulkier stature. Twenty members of the spider guild formed a shield between them.

"It is time to die, Watcher," Thren said, his voice calm, unwavering. "The honor of thieves must be restored."

He snapped his fingers. In one single mass, the twenty charged. Haern saluted their deaths with one saber, and then stunned them all by pulling his hood from his face.

"Halt!" Thren shouted. "By the gods, put down your weapons!"

Haern chuckled, shaking his gold hair loose.

"I have kept my face hidden for a long time," he said, his voice no longer a whisper but strong and firm. "I feel it right you know the truth before you die."

The members of the spider guild halted and glared. Many more spat and gestured obscenely, especially those that had grown up training with the guildmaster's long lost son.

"You were to be our savior," Thren said, pulling back his own hood. His hair was gold, and his eyes an ocean blue. "Every man and woman would have quaked at the sound of your name."

"I am Haern, Watcher of the King. Men do quake at my name, but only those who deal in shadows and death." He bowed to his father. "You have hurt those I love and I will not risk their harm for my sake again. Look upon my face, all of you. Those who see my face must die. May Ashhur take pity on your souls before casting you to Karak's abyss."

Thren sighed. "You have been dead to me for seven years. Nothing has changed. Those loyal to my name, slay this man, and receive the highest honor I may bestow. I will call you son, and my heir, to replace he whom you slay."

Haern let his cloaks fall forward, hiding his arms and blades. The twenty resumed their charge, a wave of dagger and muscle. The assassin spun, a whirling disarray of cloth, blade, arm, and foot. Those that neared, died. Still they came.

Haern ducked his arm underneath a thrust, rotated a hundred and eighty degrees, and then slammed his foot into his attacker's neck. His foot looped around, connecting with the chin of another. Two thieves attempted to flank him, timing their strikes in near perfect precision. Near perfect, however, was still not enough to draw blood. Haern halted the spinning of his body and leapt straight up. Stabs struck his cloaks trailing beneath him. As he fell, he sliced open one thief's neck. His foot kicked backward after landing, crushing the other's windpipe. Gasping for air, the man staggered away. Haern descend upon him, his twin sabers ending his suffering.

Seven lay dead at Haern's feet, but more remained ready to strike. The thieves swarmed, surrounding him in a ring of biting daggers. Haern resumed his cloak dance, for no other purpose than to buy time. A few seconds later, Harruq arrived, having finished with the thief above.

"Which one of you shot Aurry?" he roared, decking the closest thief before trampling over his body to reach the others. "Was it you?" he asked, lopping off a thief's arm. "Or was it you?" Condemnation took another man's dagger, Salvation, his throat. "Or were you the coward?" That particular thief offered no resistance, instead turning tail and fleeing. Harruq was the faster. He cut him down, picked up his body, and threw it at two more. Haern needed no better distraction. He pulled out of his cloak dance and lunged, batting away several daggers to slip his sabers in between ribs.

The remaining guards backed away, their numbers advantage gone.

"Such a shame, my son," Thren said from the far side of the room. He pulled out a small metal object from his pocket. "You are a beauty to behold, a beauty that must be broken beneath my heel." He blew on the metal object, which emitted a high-pitched whistle. Curtains fell from the sides of the rooms, and in came the entire Spider Guild, more than a hundred men dressed in gray cloaks and armor.

"Crush them," Thren shouted to his minions. "Bring forth the time of the thief once more!"

"That all you got?" Harruq roared, smashing his swords together so sparks flew for several feet in all directions. "Bring 'em on!"

"To me," Haern shouted. Harruq obeyed, joining his teacher. The two put their backs to a corner and faced their attackers.

"Any ideas?" Harruq asked, just before the multitude hit.

"Yes. Whoever kills more marries Aurelia."

"What?"

The first wave hit, and freely the blood flowed.

"To the other side!" Haern screamed, charging into the throng. He spun and whirled with the grace of a dancer, his sabers blurry whirls about his body, with red specks flicking in all directions. He weaved his way through ten, leaving a bloody swath in his wake. Harruq bellowed, choosing a strategy more suitable to him. He used his greater reach and swung side to side, his strength and power massacring any who attempted to block. Daggers bit into his arms and chest, and the blood of him and his foes soaked his armor. As the pain of his cuts grew deeper, he lowered his head and charged right through a group of twelve. Bodies flew, bones broke, and Condemnation and Salvation drank in the death of others.

Harruq and Haern linked up on the other side of the room, corpses strewn in their wake. Still, a great many remained, although their tactic had changed. Instead of charging forward, they pulled back. To the front came several men, each armed with throwing daggers.

"How many you got?" Harruq asked.

"Nine."

"Eleven."

"I have plenty of time."

They prepared another charge. Before they could, a blue portal ripped open in front of them, and out stepped a wizard in yellow robes. Daggers whirled toward his throat and chest only to ricochet off, unable to penetrate the magic enchantment surrounding his skin.

"How rude," Tarlak said, glaring at the crowd. "Those could have hurt." Electricity crackled across his hands. "Just like you hurt my sister."

A great bolt of lightning sundered the opposite wall, charring the luckless souls caught in its way. The thieves rushed the wizard, but twin blades halted their attack. The two fighters, teacher and student, formed a shield before Tarlak, shredding the life from any who neared. Slowly a wall of the dead built before them. Tarlak shouted the words of a spell. His hands lunged, his fingers hooked in dual circles. A small ball of flame shot between Harruq and Haern, under the legs of a thief, and then hit the ground. A great rush of expanding fire filled the room, followed by screams.

The curtains on one wall caught fire, billowing red smoke. Haern swore when he saw it, knowing that it would not be long before the entire room was at a loss for air.

"No more fire!" he shouted to the wizard.

"Sure thing! Where's your hat?"

"They deserve to see the face of their executioner."

Tarlak shrugged, the words of another spell on his lips. A bolt of lightning leapt from his hands, struck a nearby thief, and then bounced to the next closest target. It continued until seven thieves lay dead on the ground, smoke wafting from their mouths and noses.

Haern looked about the room. His eyes narrowed as he spotted Thren still on the far side. A great bow was in his arms.

"Look out," the assassin shouted, lunging for Tarlak. An arrow flew across the room, its aim straight for the wizard's heart. Haern lashed out with his sword, but he knew his timing would be too slow. The arrow sank deep into flesh, but not that of the wizard. Harruq stood between Tarlak and Thren, his hand clutching the arrow embedded deep in his chest. With a shriek of pain, he tore it free.

"The poison..." Haern said.

"Won't be able to take me down," Harruq said. "You humans. Either cut off my head or rip out my heart." He tossed the arrow to the ground, his eyes glaring into Thren's. "And I'm guessing that you're the one who shot Aurry."

Biting cold air swirled out from Tarlak's hands, freezing several men into stiff corpses. Some of the rogues fled, while those remaining readied their daggers and tensed in preparation for the onslaught.

"He is mine, Harruq," Haern shouted. The half-orc ignored him. He charged the wall of daggers, uncaring for any wounds he might take. Their thrusts came in, fast and deadly, but compared to the speed of his teacher, they were nothing. Harruq parried them away, shoved aside one thief, butchered another, and then continued on to Thren, who stood alone. The guildmaster drew two shortswords from his belt.

"Come, orc," he said. "I yearn to kill this night."

"Then yearn for this!" Harruq shouted, slamming down with both his swords.

"Out of my way," Haern yelled, scattering the remaining few thieves with brutal cuts of his sabers.

The fire cast a red hue across the room, and smoke covered the roof. Sweat and blood clung to them like honey in the rapidly heating area. Tarlak slaughtered a few more with a bouncing ball of lightning.

"Help him!" he shouted, his back to Harruq and Thren. "I'll guard your back."

Haern nodded his appreciation, and then raced to his pupil. Harruq and Thren were deep in combat, slashing and parrying in a dance only the most skilled of blade wielders could create. Blood ran down the half-orc's face and arms. Fresh blood. He was losing.

Thren lashed out twice with his sword, pulled back, and then feinted with the other. Harruq fell for the feint, Salvation swinging wide to block. The guildmaster stepped forward, his foot snapping out. His heel crushed cartilage as it connected with Harruq's nose. He gasped in pain as blood exploded across his face and neck. He collapsed to his knees, his vision blurry and his arms limp.

"Miserable," Thren muttered. He thrust his sword for Harruq's eye.

Haern parried away the fatal thrust, giving his father a brutal kick. His foot smashed against the left side of his neck. The wise old fighter rolled with the blow, fell to one knee, and then slashed blind. Haern was already in the air before the swing. He landed with both knees on Thren's shoulders, blasting the air from his lungs. Both sabers curled around his throat.

"You abandoned us," Thren gasped, feeling the sharp edge cutting into his skin. "Now you come to murder us, murder your own father. I would not have tried killing the Watcher if I had known it was you."

"You were a wretched father," Haern whispered into Thren's ear. "And I was not your son. I was your assassin, nothing more. Now, I am your better."

He yanked both blades viciously to either side. Blood flowed. Thren died. The assassin stood, his cloaks wrapping about his body in the red haze. He pulled his hood back over his head, letting the comforting shadow hide all but the blue of his eyes…the eyes that shed tears despite the words he had spoken.

"Time to go," Tarlak said, putting a hand on Haern's shoulder. "Come on. I need help with the big guy."

"I'll be fine," Harruq said, staggering to his feet. The movements jostled his face, and he clutched his shattered nose. "Damn it, always my nose."

Tarlak hurried through a spell. A blue portal ripped open before him. Without another word, Harruq took two shaky steps and vanished through.

"He lied to me," Haern whispered, staring at the body of his father.

"What are you talking about?" Tarlak asked. He put his arm around his good friend, trying to sound calm as he watched the spreading fire he had created.

"He knew I was his son. Perhaps for all these years, he knew. Yet he still tried to kill me."

"It's all over now," Tarlak said, stepping toward his portal. "You have a better family now. You have us. Let's go home. This smoke is killing me."

Haern nodded. He gave one last look at his father, face down in a pool of his own drying blood, and then followed Tarlak home.

<hr />

Brug greeted them at the door, his face sullen.

"Good to see you three alive," he said, his normally boisterous voice subdued.

"How is Aurry," Harruq asked, one hand still clutching his face.

"We'll get that fixed up, and then you can go and see the elf," Brug replied. Harruq nodded, stepped past him, and then collapsed. Brug caught his chest and held him steady.

"I'll be alright," Harruq mumbled. "I just need to…" His words trailed off as his body went limp.

"Just follow me," Brug said. "Bedtime for you. You can say hi to your girl tomorrow." He nodded to Tarlak and Haern before helping the half-orc up the stairs.

"Any wounds on yourself?" Tarlak asked, glancing over the assassin.

"None that will not heal in a few days. But I could greatly use a drink."

Tarlak beamed.

"That, my friend, is something I can help you with."

9

Harruq awoke sprawled on his chest, still dressed. He tossed his blanket aside. Sweat drenched his body. His entire head throbbed, his nose especially. It felt as if someone had rammed a tree branch up one nostril and down the other.

Gradually, the previous night came back to him, and he lurched to his feet. Fighting off an initial wave of nausea, he staggered downstairs, placing both feet firm on a step before lowering to the next one.

"Morning, sunshine," greeted Tarlak, who sat at the table on the bottom floor. "Although morning is hardly appropriate, considering I just finished lunch."

"Slept too long," Harruq muttered. "Where's Qurrah?"

"Beats me." The wizard shrugged. "I could spy on him to find out, but that's not what I do."

The half-orc nodded, rubbing his eyes with one hand. The huge fingers paused, though, when he spotted a large sausage link uneaten on Tarlak's plate.

"Take it," Tarlak said. "I'm stuffed to the brim."

Harruq wolfed it down, even though the chewing ignited pain in his nose.

"How's Aurry?" he asked, suddenly remembering her grievous wound. His heart shuddered at the look Tarlak gave him.

"Follow me, Harruq. I'll explain on the way."

The two climbed the stairs to the second floor, Tarlak talking as they walked.

"She's been unconscious for hours. Her breath and heart are weak. Our hope is that she holds on long enough for Delysia to heal her."

"Can't you find another healer?" Harruq asked. The wizard opened the girls' door, shaking his head as he did.

"That's another thing we need to discuss. Your little elf has managed to attract some considerable attention." He did not elaborate, instead beckoning inside. Both Delysia and Aurelia lay in their beds, tucked underneath several blankets. Delysia seemed to be only sleeping. Aurelia, however, appeared much worse. Her skin was pale, and her hair was dull and lifeless. Her breath was slow, the rise and fall of her chest almost invisible.

"Your brother said Delysia should awake in a couple more hours. As for Aurelia, well…"

Tarlak shrugged his shoulders. "Del managed to get a tiny bit of healing magic into her before she collapsed. Perhaps it was enough to combat the poison."

"Yeah," Harruq said. His eyes lingered on Aurelia, and in his breast stirred fears he had never felt before. He pondered thoughts of her death, each one tearing his heart to pieces. He walked over, slowly, as if not to wake her, and then knelt beside her bed.

"You wake up soon, alright?" he whispered into her ear. He stroked her hair with one hand, unaware he was doing so. "Don't do anything dumb like dying on me." A surge of fear shook his chest, and he wiped away tears, hoping Tarlak did not see. A glance behind revealed him long gone. Harruq smiled. Despite his oddities, the wizard could read people brilliantly.

Harruq turned back to Aurelia and stroked her face. He felt almost criminal. Never before had he touched her, and now, while she lay helpless, he felt the gentle curve of her chin, the gradual slope of her nose, and the soft brush of her eyelashes. Finally, he pulled his hand away, unable to bear the guilt. He pressed his forehead against her arm.

"Not yet," he said. "I haven't told you yet. You can't die without me telling you." He looked back up, overtaken by the beauty of her face. He leaned forward without thinking and gently kissed her lips. Despite the paleness of her skin, a trickle of warmth remained, and he relished its feel. The half-orc backed away, his throat constricted.

He left without saying another word.

"Greetings, Tessanna," Qurrah said as he climbed into the dilapidated building.

The girl glanced up from her drawing and smiled.

"Hello, Qurrah. Care to play a game?" The half-orc eyed the strange lines and circles she had drawn in the dirt.

"What is it?" he asked.

"Find and Seek. It is a scrying game, that's all."

"Another time," Qurrah said, sitting opposite of her. "I come to ask a question."

"Sure." She sent a hand dancing back and forth, ruining the symbols. Qurrah spotted a fresh set of markings on her arm, but said nothing about them.

"Can you heal someone?" Qurrah asked. Tessanna gave him a funny look.

"I kill people, Qurrah, not heal them."

"But can you?" he asked, more forcefully. "I have learned my spells from my masters, and from my experiments, yet you control power without ever having had a teacher. You are special, and we both know it. Now answer me. Can you heal someone?"

Tessanna crossed her arms and looked away.

"I don't feel like answering."

"You will," Qurrah said. "I have no time for games. A loved one of my brother is dying."

"Why do I care?"

Qurrah stood, and the whip uncoiled, its tip slapping the ground. Tessanna stared at him, showing no hint of fear.

"He is my brother," Qurrah said. "If she suffers, then he suffers, and I will do whatever I can to stop it. Now answer me!"

Tessanna stood, anger swirling behind her eyes. She drew closer, ignoring his threatening glare. Her arms lunged out, grabbing each of his wrists. She shoved him against a wall and forced her lips to his. For one agonizing second, they shared the same breath, and all time became a frozen river. Then the thaw as she pulled back her lips and giggled.

"I think I can, Qurrah. Do you want me to? Because I will. I'll do what you want."

Qurrah nodded, holding in a gasp for air. His heart thundered in his chest, and he wished it to stop.

"Come with me to the Eschaton tower. Help me, and I might find you a home."

"I don't want a home," she said, letting her hair fall before her eyes as she batted them shyly.

"What is it you want?" he asked.

"You."

She laughed. Qurrah felt a stirring throughout his body. He did his best to ignore it. He offered his hand, and she accepted it with a smile.

"Follow me," he said.

"You weren't at practice this morning," Haern said when he found Harruq hunched over on a couch.

"It'd be dumb of me to practice without a healer ready," the half-orc countered. "Besides, my nose is already broken. Nothing left for you to do until it gets fixed."

The assassin took a seat opposite him, handing him a mug of ale.

"There's plenty more for me to break. I will make up for it tomorrow. Here, this will help with the pain."

Harruq took a few gulps, set the cup on his lap, and stared into the liquid.

"She's dying, isn't she?" he asked. Haern drank from his own cup, thought for a moment, and then nodded.

"Yes. Delysia delayed the poison, but did not cure it. I know much of poisons, and Aurelia seems unable to combat the one destroying her. She will waste away before our eyes."

Harruq nodded. He took another drink. "I hope you're wrong, more than I have ever hoped for anything in my life."

Haern patted the half-orc's shoulder. "Don't worry, Tarlak won't let her die. We know people who can help her, but someone else has complicated matters."

The door cracked open, and both glanced to the entrance. Their reactions were of confusion as Qurrah walked in, a young woman at his side. She looked at them with her deep black eyes, the sight of her raising the hairs on their necks.

"We must see Aurelia," Qurrah said. "Now."

"Who's the girl?" Haern asked, rising from the table. "I will let no stranger near Delysia or Aurelia in their states."

"I'm Tessanna," she said, her voice so quiet that both struggled to hear. "I want to help."

Harruq stood, raising an eyebrow. Qurrah nodded back, and his look was all the convincing Harruq needed.

"Let them go. We'll follow. If she's dying, we have nothing to lose."

Haern let his cloaks fall forward, and his hands rest on the hilts of his blades. "Very well. Tessanna, follow me."

He led them up the stairs and to Aurelia.

Tarlak was kneeling by his sister's bed when they arrived. He glanced up, his face hiding any surprise upon seeing Tessanna.

"A visitor to our tower?" he asked, standing. "I was not informed. I would have swept first."

"She is here to help," Qurrah said. He placed his hands on Tessanna's shoulders and whispered into her ear. She glanced back, her eyes afraid. Qurrah merely nodded and gestured to Aurelia.

"Very well," she said. She approached the bed, all eyes upon her.

"What is her name?" Tessanna asked.

"Aurelia Thyne," Haern whispered.

Tessanna nodded. She knelt, curling her slender fingers around Aurelia's wrist. Her head lowered, and long black hair fell across the bed. Silence filled the room as she meditated there.

"Who is she?" Harruq whispered to his brother.

"No different than us," Qurrah whispered back. "Her life, her childhood, rivals that of our own. But her power…"

He stopped, for light had begun to fill the dimly lit room. Tessanna's lips quivered with healing words that felt foreign to her tongue. The flesh of her hands shone white, gradually growing in power. Her hair floated in the air, as if blown by the softest of winds. She arched her head back, her face full of pain. Harruq shot a glance to Qurrah, but his brother's look ordered him not to move. Haern drew his blades, but a hand from Tarlak kept him still.

A sound like the shattering of a boulder accompanied the great surge of healing magic into Aurelia's body. The elf's chest lurched upward as she cried out in pain. Tears flowed down Tessanna's face, yet still she kept the magic flowing.

"I can't cure it," she cried, the light fading from her hands. "I'm not strong enough!"

"You are," Qurrah said. "You are, now try!"

A brief flash of anger overwhelmed her shy features, then retreated just as quickly.

"Fine," Tessanna said, her voice dead. "You want her saved. You want her to live. Then she will."

The white light darkened to gray. Aurelia gasped for air, seeming awake although her eyes remained shut. A new spell spilled from Tessanna's lips, whose words of power jolted Tarlak with recognition.

"No, don't!" he shouted. It was too late. The girl arched her entire body away from Aurelia, only her iron grip keeping her from falling. A scream of pain came from those beautiful lips. The paleness of Aurelia's skin retreated, pulled away like smoke in the wind. The death seeped into Tessanna, filling her veins. At last, the spell complete, she released her grip and collapsed.

"Tessanna!" Qurrah cried, rushing to her side. Harruq was not far behind, taking Aurelia's hand and feeling the warmth inside.

"She took the poison into herself," Tarlak said, staring at Tessanna with a look of both admiration and horror. "Harruq, pick her up. We must get her to the priests, immediately."

"Why can we take her but not Aurry?" the half-orc asked.

"I have my reasons, now do as I say!" Tarlak shouted. No longer was he the kindly wizard. The leader of the Eschaton stood in that room, and he would accept nothing short of perfect obedience. Harruq knelt down and scooped the thin girl into his arms. Tarlak stepped away from the others and opened a portal into the heart of Veldaren. He stepped inside, followed by the two half-orcs and the dying girl.

They exited in front of an ancient stone temple, lined with pillars and carved of rare alabaster stone. Tarlak leapt up the steps, and when a young man dressed in robes moved to stop them, the wizard waved his hand, completely paralyzing him.

"Sorry, young priest, I have no time." He shoved open the doors, the others following in his wake. Inside was grand and open. Huge columns lined the outer walls, and a painted ceiling of magically strengthened glass depicting the seven lessons loomed above them. Several priests milled about, the symbol of the golden mountain across their chests.

"I seek Calan, high priest of Ashhur," Tarlak shouted. A few priests turned to him, recognized the yellow robes, and rushed off in obedience. The two half-orcs glanced about, the praise to Ashhur echoing from every piece of stone unnerving their souls. They could not have been more uncomfortable if they had been naked.

A door opened, and out stepped an old man dressed in white, a symbol of the golden mountain hanging from a long silver chain around his neck. Not a single sharp edge existed on his entire face. Such a round, gentle look made it so that when he smiled, it was impossible not to warm one's heart to him.

"Tarlak Eschaton," the high priest said, his gentle voice disarming. "I trust there is good reason to interrupt my nap with such rude shouting?" His beady green eyes stared at Tarlak, unflinching.

"This girl is dying of poison. I need her healed."

Calan glanced behind the mage to see Tessanna curled in Harruq's arms. The high priest nodded. "Place her on the ground, half-elf."

Harruq glanced at the man, confused and angry.

"Do as he says," Tarlak ordered.

"Don't you need a bed, tonics, potions and such?" Harruq asked, gently placing her on the stone.

"The only bed she will need is back at your tower." Calan knelt down beside Tessanna, examining her with his eyes. "What a poor soul. Such beauty, even in a body so frail."

He bowed his head and laid his hands across Tessanna's forehead. He whispered a prayer to Ashhur. Healing light surrounded his own hands, but unlike Tessanna's, its glow was comforting, uplifting. Its shine was deeper, its light, purer. Gently, it flowed into the young woman, banishing the poison in her blood. Mere seconds later, Calan stood, the magic fading from his hands.

"She will be fine," Calan said, sighing. "Her wounds are many, and the worst are in her mind. I know this girl, Tarlak. Be careful with her."

Qurrah knelt beside Tessanna and held her. He stared at the high priest with his steeled gaze.

"How do you know of her?" he asked.

"Several of my priests have died because of her," Calan explained. "They sought to heal the chaos of her mind. A few thought a demon resided in her. Others, in their pride, felt their power sufficient to put the pieces back together."

"She killed them?" Tarlak asked.

"The madness they tried to exorcise engulfed them, instead. The pain they caused her, though..." He shook his head. "They thought themselves wise. She was to be proof of their faith. That is why they died."

"But can you heal her?" Qurrah asked.

Tarlak stood back, eyeing the two. Something odd was going on, but he didn't know what.

"No, I cannot heal her," the high priest said.

"Why not?"

"Only Ashhur can heal a mind that tortured and broken," Calan said, clearly unwilling to be convinced otherwise. The necromancer felt his chest tighten, and knew that the priest analyzed him with his stare.

"What is it you see?" Qurrah asked him.

"Tread carefully," the priest said, knowing that all stared at he and Qurrah. "The girl binds herself in darkness because she has never seen the light, while you cling to the dark like a babe in fear. You walk a path leading to ruinous things."

"Do not speak to me of fear," Qurrah said, his voice seething with anger. He turned to Tarlak. "May we go? This place makes my skin crawl."

Tarlak's look churned his stomach.

"Very well, Qurrah Tun. You need not express your gratitude for him saving her life."

Qurrah glared but said nothing. The wizard bowed to Calan, removing his hat as he did so.

"Many thanks, high priest. I'm sure we'll meet again."

"Hopefully not during my naps," the priest said, returning the bow. Tarlak opened a portal home and then gestured within. The two half-orcs entered first, Tessanna in Harruq's arms. Once they were gone, Tarlak turned back to the wise old man.

"What do you think of my new recruits?" he asked. Calan chuckled.

"Careful, young friend. Both their souls are strong. Do not preach. Example is all they will believe."

"May Ashhur guide your steps," Tarlak said, bowing one final time.

"Go with his blessing," Calan said. The wizard reached into his pocket and handed Calan several pieces of silver. Tipping his hat, he entered the portal and vanished.

※

That night, Qurrah hovered over the sleeping body of Tessanna. He watched every breath, yet never gave a single caress of her skin or hair. She slept in Delysia's bed, who had recovered several hours after their return from the temple. Aurelia remained unconscious, but her skin had regained its color, and her heartbeat was strong and steady.

Harruq entered the room, closing the door quietly behind him.

"How they doing?" he asked, his voice just above a whisper.

"Both sleep peacefully," Qurrah said. "Tessanna did not just take the poison. She took the very pain from Aurelia's body. Her body is weak, though. Too weak."

"Sounds like a certain half-orc I know," Harruq chuckled. "And he's survived through plenty worse than this."

Harruq stood by Aurelia's bed and ran a hand across her cheek. "Going to bed," he said. "I suggest you do the same."

Qurrah offered no reply. His eyes lingered on Tessanna's closed eyelids as his brother left. When he spoke, it was to himself as much as it was to her.

"The hardness of your life is over," he whispered. "You have earned your peace. I will give that to you, Tessanna. I promise."

He pulled the hood of his robe low over his face and left the tower.

Qurrah wandered Veldaren's empty streets in a trance. He had been to the temple of Ashhur, but there was no aid for him there. Instead, he searched for another temple hidden among the winding streets, one to a darker god, a hidden god. A simple spell guided his path. He could feel the pull of dark magic, leading him on like a thin thread. The closer he approached the luxurious areas of the city, the more it throbbed in his temples. One house in particular cried out to him in a voice only his mind could hear.

Our faith is stronger. Our way is truer. Our destiny is assured. Order cometh.

He halted at the black iron gates. At first glance, the home seemed perfectly normal. It was not fancy, but well kept. Its walls were painted a soft white and its roof a dull brown. His soul opened, and his eyes saw what normal sight could not. A new building towered before him. Several pillars lined the front, chiseled of dark marble, their sides scrawled with runes that glowed red in the darkness. A giant skull of a lion hung above the door, carved from the finest obsidian, its mouth open and dripping blood.

"Let me pass," Qurrah whispered to the gate, his fingers wrapping around the cold metal. "I will pass, I will enter, and I will speak with whoever is the strongest." The gate creaked open, yielding to his touch and his words. He slipped inside, flinching when it slammed shut behind him. In all those years he had grown up in Veldaren, he had never once visited the temple. The doings of the gods meant little to him, but there was something the priests of Karak might know more of than the priests of Ashhur, and that was madness.

He approached the door. Built of the thick strips of oak and bound together with long straps of iron, the monumental portal hummed with magic as his knuckles rapped the smooth front.

"I come seeking knowledge," Qurrah said to the door. "I bade thee let me enter, for willingly or not, I shall pass through."

The creaking of metal and groaning of wood broke the silence. The door swung inward, and waiting in greeting was a man dressed in robes a shade lighter than Qurrah's. A pendant shaped like a lion's skull hung from his neck. His low hood hid much of his face.

"What knowledge is it you seek," the man asked. "For many turn away at our truth, or yearn for false answers to the questions they ask."

"I seek chaos," Qurrah said. "And I seek a way to end to it."

The man nodded. "Come. We've been waiting for you."

10

"The fall of Karak's right hand was known to us from the moment it happened," the priest said, shutting the great door.

"You speak of Velixar," Qurrah said.

"That was one of his names, yes. Karak's sorrow was great, but even as we mourned, he gave us hope in visions. Velixar had an apprentice, one who could continue his legacy. We were told he would be a living heresy, an elf of blood both cursed and pure."

They passed through an expansive entry room, with purple curtains tied above portraits of long dead priests of Karak. These contrasted with the deep black of the stone, making their color all the more vibrant.

"I have the blood of orc and elf in me," Qurrah said, "but I have no desire to replace Velixar. I wish to aid one dear to me, and that is all."

The priest waved his hand as if this were no matter. "Velixar needs no replacing, as you will one day see. In time, you will accept your path. For now, we will aid in any way we can."

They reached a set of double doors made of stained wood. Gold runes marked the outer edge in a language unknown to Qurrah. The priest grabbed one of the ornate door handles, then paused

"Tell me, stranger, what is your name?"

"I am Qurrah Tun," he answered.

"Qurrah, have you ever bowed in prayer to Karak?"

The half-orc shook his head. "I have felt his presence, but never have I prayed. Prayer is naught but begging to a god. I do not beg."

The priest chuckled, his dark eyes gleaming.

"We shall see."

He swung open the doors. Standing tall was a statue to Karak, chiseled in stone older than the race of man, and sculpted by divine hands. Twenty feet into the air it towered, a handsome man dressed in armor scarred by war. Long hair fell down past his waist, blown by an eternal wind. In one hand, he held a sword with a serrated edge. In the other, he held high a clenched fist. In this ageless pose,

The Cost of Betrayal

he demanded all who looked upon him to tremble before his power. Twin altars churned violet flame at his feet, yet they produced no smoke.

"Behold the Lion," the priest said.

Qurrah gasped. His heart weakened, and he felt a pull on his chest like never before. Many bowed before the statue, crying out prayers, heartfelt and brutal in their honesty. The half-orc's guide knelt to one knee, his eyes diverted as if he were not worthy to look upon its beauty. Qurrah stared into the statue's eyes, mesmerized. How could this be the god condemned to eternal darkness and fire?

Qurrah knelt there at the door. He prayed, five words, and he wished for no reply. *Aid me in aiding her,* he prayed. He felt compassion encircle him, and a confidence fill him. There on his knees, Karak answered.

In all you do, I shall be there. Do not forget the words of my servant Velixar, or the desire of all that serve me.

When he opened his eyes, he discovered his vision blurred. Tears. He wiped them away, ashamed. His guide stood and smiled down at him.

"Never forget the power of prayer," the priest whispered, extending his hand. "Come, tell us how we may help."

Qurrah took his hand and stood.

"Her name is Tessanna," he began.

He finished his tale in the priest's private quarters. It was a small room, simply furnished with a cot, a desk, and a small window. Qurrah sat on the cot, facing the priest, who leaned back in his chair behind the desk.

"Our study into madness is extensive," the priest said. "We feel it a result of the chaos that has engulfed this world. To bring about a cure, one must study the disease."

"I wish to end the chaos in her mind," Qurrah said. "Many have failed, but they did not seek to understand, only bandage it like a wound."

"How will you study such a mind?" the priest asked, leaning his elbows on his desk. "She will resent all but the most casual observance. Anything deeper will risk permanent harm."

"I know," Qurrah said. "That is why I wish to study others with such madness."

The priest cradled his head on his palm.

"Where will you find so many with madness akin to hers?"

The half-orc's eyes hardened. "I will make them."

For a long time, the priest was quiet. He only stared, studying Qurrah with his gaze. It was the second time Qurrah had felt that type of stare, and it troubled him still.

"Few of our brotherhood ever hear this truth," the priest said. "Only in absolute emptiness is there order. To cleanse chaos, much must be sacrificed. You seek to kill others. Do you understand this?"

"I do," Qurrah said.

"Then know this: life is, by its definition, chaotic. Karak fought against all that represents this mortal life. We still do. Ashhur preaches against the nature of man, not the nature of life itself. His goal is smaller, his resolve, weaker. He seeks to end this chaos by instilling common beliefs inside every mind, with hopes of a world of puppets. We are above such nonsense. Let every breath halt in this realm. Let us end all that Celestia has coddled. Karak led you to Tessanna, and now to us. All is as it was meant to be, and now I shall aid you."

He reached into a cubby and pulled out a frayed collection of paper. He flipped through it, touching its pages like they were precious things, and then pulled out several he deemed useful. The priest handed the pages to Qurrah as he asked him if he could read.

"I can," the half-orc said, his eyes flicking over the words. "And these are spells."

"Not spells. These incantations represent perfect order. The chaotic mind tries to adhere to them and cannot, and so it shatters. There are many kinds of madness; with those words, you can create them all. Just make sure you do not hear them yourself. Do not memorize them, for there is risk in even that."

The priest took out a book bound with black leather, archaic runes inscribed with gold across the front.

"In this book are the spells from the most ancient of necromancers. Its knowledge is inferior only to Darakken's spellbook. Take it. Know we will do all we can to aid you in the path you walk."

"Thank you," Qurrah said, accepting the book. He bowed, his gifts wrapped tightly in his arms. "Before I go, may I know your name?"

"I forfeited my name to Karak. If you must, you may know me as Pelarak."

"Very well, Pelarak," he said. "I offer my gratitude. One day I may return."

"We will await you every dusk."

Qurrah went to the door, stopping only when Pelarak called out to him.

"Yes?" he asked, glancing back. A sly smile was on the priest's face.

"Do not forget to pray," he said. Qurrah nodded.

"I will consider it."

Back at the Eschaton tower, Qurrah knelt by Tessanna's bed and took her cold hand into his.

"Your salvation is now a matter of time," he whispered to her, the love in his voice sounding dangerous and foreign. "Even if a thousand must die, you will find peace."

He slept beside her, willing to suffer the hard floor to ensure he was there when she awoke. In the other bed, Aurelia stirred uneasily. She had awakened seconds after Qurrah's return, and with a chilled heart, listened to those heartfelt words and wondered.

When Harruq forced himself awake to spar with Haern, he found his teacher standing over him, lightly waving a saber above his neck.

"You're dead," he said, his face cold and dark. Then it brightened. "And Aurelia is awake. She wishes to see you."

The half-orc hurried down the stairs and barged into the girls' room. Sure enough, Aurelia was awake. She was also in the process of changing into cleaner clothes. Her back was to him, her dress spread out across the bed. A pair of brown pants lay at her feet, and in her arms she held a simple green shirt Delysia had loaned to her.

Aurelia heard his entrance, glanced over her shoulder, and glared. "You really should learn to knock."

Harruq stammered, his face flushed. His eyes traced down her long hair, her arched back, and all the way to her rear. When he realized she still glared at him, he turned around and faced the door.

"Um, I thought, um, sorry."

"It's fine," he heard Aurelia say. The half-orc shifted his weight uncomfortably as he heard the sound of fabric sliding across skin. Finally, he felt Aurelia's hand on his shoulder, and he turned around. She smiled at him, life returning to those twinkling eyes.

"You didn't worry about me, did you?" she asked, tossing her hair back with her hand.

"We all were. If it weren't for Tessanna, you might have, well…"

The elf gave him a funny look. "Tessanna?"

Harruq gestured to the bed next to hers, and then realized the girl was no longer there.

"Huh. She slept there next to you. Big black eyes, black hair, kind of creepy. Was she there when you woke up?"

The elf nodded. Her face grew troubled for a moment, drawing a frown from the half-orc.

"You alright?" he asked.

"Yes, I'm fine," she said. "Just a little weak, is all. And yes, I saw her. She left with your brother about an hour ago. Is she a priestess?"

Harruq shrugged. He stole a glance down the elf's shirt, which was too big for her and left quite a bit exposed.

"No. She's just, forget it, I don't know what she is. Qurrah found her somewhere, brought her here, and then she took that poison out of you and put it into herself."

Aurelia smiled. "Nice of her. Now come downstairs with me. Tarlak wants to talk to us."

"Yay. Everyone seems to want to see me today. You. Tarlak. Haern, but he doesn't count. He just wanted to pretend he killed me."

The elf slipped her arm in between Harruq's and looked up at him. "I'm still a little weak, so help me down the stairs, please."

His heart skipped at least two beats before time resumed normally.

"Sure. Yeah."

They walked down the stairs, Aurelia holding his arm and a goofy smile on his face. When Tarlak saw them, the half-orc immediately blushed.

"Aren't you two a cute couple," the wizard laughed. He took a bite from his plate of eggs and sausage. "So when can I expect to be a godfather?"

"I may be weak, but I think I can still muster a polymorph spell," Aurelia warned. Tarlak threw his hands up in a gesture of peace.

"Of course. Take a seat. Let me whip up some breakfast."

By whip up, he meant twirl his fingers so that two plates magically appeared, steaming with bacon, ham, potatoes, and eggs. Harruq's mouth watered at the sight. Aurelia released her grip on his arm when they reached the bottom floor, kissed his cheek, and took a seat next to Tarlak. Harruq sat opposite the two and started wolfing down his meal.

"I'm never good at bad news, so I'll tell you both straight." The wizard bit off a chunk of bacon, chewed it twice, and then stunned them both. "Aurelia, a bounty has been placed on your head."

Harruq nearly gagged.

"I feared as much," Aurelia said, sighing and pushing away her plate. "Who placed it?"

"I traced the official bounty back to the Quellan elves. I wanted to bring you to the priests of Ashhur, but as good a friend as Calan is, he's still a priest. He would have reported your whereabouts. Respect for law and nonsense like that. As for now, I believe your presence here is still unknown."

Harruq coughed, gaining the attention of the two. "Excuse me, but can one of you fill me in here. Why do the Quellan elves want her dead?"

"They don't want her dead," Tarlak said, chomping down on his final piece of bacon. "The bounty is null if she isn't alive. A thousand gold pieces for her capture. As for a reason, that was interesting, most interesting."

The wizard's expression hardened. He began quoting the bounty's details.

"A thousand gold pieces for the live capture of Aurelia Thyne, responsible for the escape of two murderers of elves and human children." He stopped and stared straight into Harruq's eyes. "I've heard many exaggerations, and there are times when people die, but it is the children that worry me. I would like to know what I am dealing with before every bounty hunter in the country comes knocking on our tower door."

Harruq started to reply, but Aurelia stood, leaning against the table on weak arms. There was nothing weak about her eyes or her voice when she spoke.

"The battle at Woodhaven was just that, a battle. I fought for my friends. Harruq and Qurrah fought for reasons that will remain unsaid. Those murders are nothing more than the deaths of elves in combat. Many died that day, but there is no bounty on every soldier that fought for Neldar."

"Then why the bounty on you?" he asked, his voice equally strong.

"Because I helped them escape. I am a traitor to elven kind, and so they wish me to explain myself."

"And then kill you afterwards?"

Aurelia shrugged. "Perhaps. I hope not."

"This is horseshit," Harruq said. He smashed his fist against the table, stood, and flung his plate across the room. It smashed against a wall, splattering egg. "They can't take Aurry. They can't!"

"Calm yourself," Tarlak said, the only one still seated. "I am not turning any of you over to some bounty hunter. Aurelia saved Haern's life, who is like a brother to me. There is much I owe her, and keeping her whereabouts secret is a small step I can take toward repayment."

Harruq's breath was heavy and heated through his nostrils as he fought to control his temper. "Then what do we do?" he asked.

"Nothing. We have Aurelia lay low in the tower, going out only in disguise, until we do something about that bounty."

"No," Aurelia said. She stood tall and shook her head. "No. That won't work."

"Why not?" Tarlak asked.

"Because I know who put the bounty on my head."

The two men glanced at each other.

"And who's that?" Tarlak asked.

"Dieredon," Aurelia said, her voice nearing a whisper. "And he will hunt for me until he knows my whereabouts. I will not live my life in hiding."

"Dieredon," Tarlak said, rubbing his eyes. "Why did you have to upset *that* elf?"

"Dieredon?" Harruq asked. "Wait, is he an elf that uses a crazy bow with spikes?"

"That would be him," Tarlak said, adding a bit of grandiose to his speech. "Scoutmaster of the Quellan elves, unbeatable in blade and bow, tracker of shadows, and master of the silent arrow in the night. Thank you, Aurelia, for all the wonderful fun you bring to my tower."

Harruq frowned, feeling his rage grow. His body ached, remembering wounds the skilled fighter had given him during their brief skirmish. Aurelia staggered a little, a dizzy spell overcoming her. Harruq rushed around the table and held her in his arms as she recovered.

"I'm fine, Harruq," she said, pushing him away. "Don't worry. And I know why he's looking for me. Crazy as it sounds, he's worried about me. Probably angry, too. That is why the bounty is so high, and only if I am unharmed. If I talk to him, the bounty will most likely be dropped."

"So how do we find him?" Tarlak asked.

"That is simple enough," said a voice from the stairs. The three turned to see Haern sitting on the lower steps, wrapped in his cloaks. His lowered hood exposed his golden hair and fair skin. Despite her weakness, Aurelia felt a tingle go through her at the sight of him.

"No disguise?" the wizard asked.

"No need, not in here. And you do not need to hunt down Dieredon."

"Why is that?" Harruq asked.

Haern chuckled.

"I will bring him to us." The assassin stood and pulled his hood over his face. His voice immediately shrank to a whisper. "I must ensure the other thief guilds learn from the ruination of the Spider Guild. Before I finish, I will send word to the elven lands that we stand ready to collect the bounty."

Tarlak scratched his beard. "Clever. We don't want her captured and turned in, so we just beat everyone to the punch by doing it ourselves?"

"Sure this is a good idea?" Harruq asked, looking to Aurelia for an answer. The elf nodded.

"Do it," she said. "Killing bounty hunters gets old after awhile. They make it so damn hard to get a good night's sleep."

The men in the room stared at her with inquisitive looks. She winked back to them.

"Don't ask."

They didn't.

Qurrah and Tessanna slipped out to the forest long before Harruq awoke. The half-orc carried Pelarak's papers with him cradled against his chest. Tessanna did not ask where they went, or why, and Qurrah did not say. They stopped at a stream. A fallen tree stretched across it. The two sat on one end and listened to the sound of birds filled their ears with a sweetness unfitting either of them. Qurrah had never learned to appreciate it, and Tessanna had long forgotten the peacefulness the sound used to impart her.

"I want to show you something," Qurrah said, handing her the papers. Tessanna glanced over them and shrugged.

"I cannot read," she said, handing them back.

"They are runic words of power. They can drive any living man insane just by hearing their recitation."

The girl smiled. "Sounds fun. Too bad I'll never try them."

Qurrah nodded, his eyes refusing to look at hers. "I wish to cure you, Tessanna. For everything you've done. I can decipher what happened to you. I can learn to undo it. Will you accept this from me?"

The girl's eyes flared with pain, and her entire body shriveled away from him.

"I just wish to help," he said.

She shook her head, pain bleeding out her eyes in the form of tears.

"As I am, Qurrah. Can't you be with me as I am? Can't anyone?" She stood, backing away as if he were a monster. "People have tried. It hurts so badly, Qurrah. My mind is broken glass, and all they do is shove the shards together and hope they stick. I've killed every one of them. I never mean to. Please, please, I don't want to kill you."

"This is different," Qurrah said, approaching her even though she cowered away. "I am no priest. I will not beg to a god who shall not listen. I will find what broke your mind, and I will remove it. You deserve this."

Tessanna felt a tree press against her back. She glanced about, but had no place to go. Qurrah blocked her path.

"I thought you loved me," she cried, sliding to the ground as the rough bark tore her skin. "I thought you were different."

Qurrah knelt and grabbed her hand. Anger flared, and her black eyes widened.

"I *am* different," he said. "I have suffered as you have. If I could undo my childhood I would, but no cure exists but death. I am beyond salvation. You…" He released her hand. "You deserve better than I. You are beautiful. You have life burning inside you. It is the least I can do."

The girl absently touched the black of his robes, rubbing the cloth in her fingers.

"You think I'm beautiful?"

"Yes. I do."

She stood, a visible change sweeping over her. Her eyes looked into his with strength and fire. "Take me. Now."

Qurrah felt his heart skip, and his nerves flare with fear and lust. "What? Why?"

She grabbed the front of his robes and pulled him to her. Their lips met, and for one long moment, they kissed. It ended when she bit down on his lip, tasting his blood across her tongue. He forced her back, gasping for air.

"You wish to cure me," Tessanna said, a wildness swirling within her eyes. "You love me. I know it. But if you love me, you must love me as I am now. Then you may change me. But love me now. Prove it."

"I can't," Qurrah said, rubbing his lip with his fingers and then staring at the blood upon them. "I don't know, I've never…"

He stopped, but he had already said too much. Tessanna laughed as she finished what it was he meant to say.

"Never done it before?" she asked. Her eyes burned with lust. "Take me. Or I will take you."

She pulled him closer once more, locking their lips together in a salty, bloody kiss. Qurrah felt his resistance drain away. The passion swirled across his tongue. Throughout his body kindled a virgin flame. When she removed the sash of his robe, he did not stop her. At the foot of that tree, he made love to her. She was fire underneath him, wild roaring fire, and never could he have imagined the pleasure of being burned.

When they finished, Tessanna cried.

"Please help me," she whispered into his ear. "You'll kill people, won't you? For me?"

"If I must," Qurrah whispered back. She pulled him close so that her tears wet his hair.

"Do it. I'll help you, if you want. Just promise you'll never leave me."

"Never," the half-orc said.

Tessanna stood, her bare skin shivering in the autumn air. She went to bathe in the stream.

"I've slept with many men," she said, turning back to him. Her tears were gone. Apathy had stolen over her. "But you were the first I've ever made love to." With that, she slipped into the water. As she bathed, Qurrah slept, the doubts and whispers in his own mind alleviated for one glorious moment.

Fallen angels rejoiced in black song as they watched. The promise of death had brought the two peace. Never before had Karak's truth shone so pure and so lovely.

11

In the back of the crowded bar sat a man with three empty tankards in front of him. He smoked in the shadows, only his eyes and the smoke of his pipe visible. A young boy entered the bar, glanced around, spotted him in the corner, and then approached.

"I have a message from Melhed, sir," he said.

"Out with it."

"He says the best purse is held in yellow clothes, to be bought by tomorrow's eve."

The man blew a ring of smoke and tossed the kid a dull coin through it. "Get on out of here."

The boy bowed and left.

"So Aurelia's in the hands of the Eschaton?" he muttered, filling the end of the pipe with more blackweed. "Puppets like them shouldn't be allowed such a fine catch."

If the message was true, someone from the elves would come to take Aurelia by tomorrow night. That left little time to plan an ambush, but he was confident his boys could get it done.

"Another mug," he shouted. A serving wench heard his demand and rushed a glass to him, fast enough that froth drifted down its sides.

"Good girl," he said, offering her a wink. She smiled, holding in her shudder until her back was to him. The man laughed, having seen that same reaction a hundred times before. Luckily for the wench, he was in a good mood. He might have killed her otherwise, if only to cheer himself up.

An hour later, he paid for his drinks and left.

"Come in," Aurelia said as she heard a knock on her door. She expected Harruq, but instead Brug entered, his face already in full blush.

"I have something for ya," he said, one of his hands hidden behind the door.

"Well let's see it," she said, leaning up against the pillows of her bed.

The Cost of Betrayal

Brug stammered a bit, sighed, and then brought his hand out. The elf gasped when she saw what he held. It was her staff, bearing little resemblance to the original plain stick of wood. The whole of it had been tarnished and darkened so it resembled a long, thin branch. Beautifully painted leaves spiraled down the length. Carved along the sides were spiders, frozen in the process of making a web that spanned from leaf to leaf. The webs thickened near the top, crisscrossing into a dizzying display. In Brug's hand, the staff radiated a soft green, highlighting only the leaves and bits of web that touched them.

"Brug," she gasped. "It's beautiful! Please, let me see it closer."

He handed the staff to her, his blushing reaching ripe tomato color.

"I try to make something for every member we get," he stammered. "I'll get ya that pendant, but for now, will the staff do?"

At first, Aurelia said nothing, too busy running a finger across the smooth webs and sensing the slight aura of magic.

"Yes," she said. "Yes, this will most definitely do." She pulled him close and kissed his forehead.

"None of that mushy stuff," he said, jerking away. The red of his face spread to his ears. "Anyway, Tarlak said to tell ya Dieredon is coming sometime tomorrow to claim your beauty…uh, bounty."

"I'll be ready," she said, grinning. "Thank you for the staff."

"Was nothing," he mumbled, beating a hasty retreat from her room.

⋈

When Qurrah and Tessanna returned, the half-orc went to find Tarlak.

"What's the matter?" Tarlak asked, shutting the door to his room behind Qurrah.

"I wish Tessanna to stay here," the half-orc said. "Not as a member of the Eschaton, but merely as a guest."

The wizard plopped into his chair and leaned back, his fingertips drumming the desk. "A guest? We usually don't do that type of thing here. But, who cares about what we normally do, eh?"

"Can she stay with Aurelia and Delysia?"

Tarlak shrugged. "I have no objection. You will need to ask them. Oh yeah, I finally got that portable hole. Harruq's been working upstairs the whole day. You have a room now, instead of a cubbyhole among boxes."

"Much appreciated," said Qurrah. "And I will ask the girls if they mind her staying. If you wish, you may take her rent out of my pay."

"Nonsense," the wizard said, emphasizing this with his hand. He stood and walked Qurrah to the door. "You're family now. You don't charge family rent. Not the members you like, anyway."

Qurrah chuckled. "Very well. I will speak to the girls."

"Don't go too far tomorrow," Tarlak said. "We might need you when Dieredon comes."

"I understand."

The half-orc told Tessanna the news. Aurelia and Delysia readily agreed to let her stay, albeit on a few bedrolls piled between their beds. The tower was getting crowded, but no one seemed to mind.

Melhed paced inside his small but luxurious home. His frame was scrawny and triangular, matching the shape from the top of his head down to his laboriously trimmed black goatee. Throwing daggers lined his belt, oiled and well cared for.

"They won't show," the man said, his voice sounding like a rat squeaking. "I knew they wouldn't. They drank themselves dumber than mules, and now I'm stuck."

A knock on his door ended his whining. He looked through a peephole to see a mammoth muscled chest covered with blue and black armor.

"About time," the spindly man said, throwing open his door. "You're late."

The floor creaked under the giant weight as the highest paid killer in all of Neldar stepped inside.

"Shut up, Melhed. I'm here, and that is all that matters."

"Where's your men," Melhed asked. The giant man chuckled. It was a deep, dangerous sound, and he knew he was treading on very thin ice.

"They are warriors of Karnryk!" the giant man shouted. "They will be here."

Melhed disappeared to get drinks ready. Karnryk picked at his teeth. He was a half-orc, his human mother raped by an orc. Karnryk had grown up an outcast, his large ears and chubby face earning him names like Dogface and the Pig. His enormous size and strength, however, had granted him a few perks. He had been educated. He had been trained. Nearly every guild in Neldar had seen his

The Cost of Betrayal

enormous potential, and the half-orc had milked training from every single one before abandoning them when their usefulness was at an end. Now he worked for himself. The pay was better, and his reputation had spread far and wide.

"You heard about the spider guild?" Karnryk shouted to Melhed, who was two rooms away.

"Someone told me it was no more. I assumed they were joking."

"It's no joke," the half-orc said. "The Watcher killed most of them, and the rest begged themselves into the other guilds. Sickening, really."

"How so?" Melhed asked, returning with huge pitchers full of ale. Karnryk downed one in two huge gulps.

"They quiver at the name of the Watcher," he roared. "They act as if he were a demon or a god. It is my name they should fear, not his!"

"To be fair, you approve of what the thief guilds do, while the Watcher, well, doesn't." Melhed sipped at his own, much smaller cup. "If you called a bounty on the heads of all thieves, people would cower at the thought of your approach."

The giant man leaned back in his chair, which creaked loudly in protest. He wore little armor, feeling no need for it. A sword the length of an average man hung from his back, notched and chipped from many battles. Scars ran down his face. His eyes were an ugly yellow. Still, he was stronger and meaner than a raging bull, and such attributes lent him many friends.

"Knock-knock," a voice shouted at the door. A group of men barged in, all carrying drinks. They were armed to the teeth, and beneath their ragged street clothes shone glimpses of old chainmail.

"Put your ale away," the half-orc said to Melhed. "They've already had enough."

"Of course, Karnryk."

The pitchers of ale vanished, to the groans of the small rabble.

"Hey, I'm thirsty," one in particular said, starting after the scrawny man. The half-orc grabbed him, wrenched his arm, and slammed his body to the ground. The man cried in pain, his hand pinned underneath him at an awkward angle.

"Shut up all of you," the half-orc roared. "This ain't the usual crap we go after, so I need all of you sharp. Now spill the beer and listen up. We finally get to do what I've always wanted to do."

"What's that?" asked one, sneering at the pinned man.

"The Eschaton tower. We're going to make it ours."

A cheer rose throughout the men crammed into Melhed's home.

"Don't the Watcher live there," one man dared ask. Karnryk grinned at him, his eyes filled with anticipation.

"Yeah, he does, and get ready to collect the hidden bounty. By tonight, every one of us is going to be stinking rich."

Another cheer. Karnryk didn't bother to say he would claim the bulk of the secret reward offered by the heads of the thief guilds. The others would be well off, but nothing six months of binging on ale and women wouldn't whittle away to nothing.

"Melhed, did you figure out a plan?" the half-orc asked.

"It's simple, but I think it will work," Melhed replied.

"Shut up, all of you!" Karnryk shouted. The room immediately quieted. After a gesture to start, Melhed explained the plan.

They covered themselves with the morning dew and crunched fallen leaves underneath their bodies, while the birds of the forest listened to their moans. When their flame burned out, Tessanna once again bathed in the chilly stream. Qurrah remained in the grass, dabbing a hand in the water.

"Qurrah?" Tessanna asked, the water up to her neck.

"Yes?"

The girl swam away, her eyes never leaving him. "How did you know I could heal the elf?"

The half-orc shrugged, not wanting to spoil the pleasant morning by thinking. "I didn't. And I did. I'm not sure I can explain."

"That won't do," the girl said. "You knew somehow, didn't you? Now tell me."

Qurrah glared. "I'm not lying. I don't know how I knew. You're different than me, though. I've practiced necromancy all my life. Have you?"

Tessanna lowered her face below the water so that only her eyes peered out. The half-orc sighed.

"Fine. You've been inside my mind. You know what I have done, what I have learned. Where did you first gain access to magic?"

The girl dove all the way under, turned, and then lunged to the surface, her long black hair flailing behind her, the scattered drops raining down all about.

"I don't remember," she said, her back to Qurrah. "I've always known."

"Nonsense," the half-orc said. "What was the first spell you cast?"

"I don't know," she lied. Under Qurrah's glare, she finally swore and told the truth. "I was four. A kitten died when my father stepped on it. He said it was an accident. I put my hands on it and I healed it."

"You brought it back as undead," Qurrah corrected.

"No, I healed it," she insisted. "My first spell was not necromancy. I didn't delve into that until…" A playful look overtook her face. "Until I had fun with daddy. People starting dying around me after that. After daddy. I hope you aren't one of them."

Qurrah joined her in the water then, taking her thin body into his arms. The girl nuzzled her face into his neck.

"I could stay with you all day," he told her.

"Then what's stopping you?"

The half-orc grinned at her, realizing she had asked an excellent question. What was stopping him?

"Nothing," he said. Tessanna bit into his neck, hard, yet he only felt pleasure. "Nothing at all."

⁂

"We're walking a long way to go a short trip," one of Karnryk's thugs grumbled. "You think this necessary?"

"From the forest we'll have free run of the tower's backside," their leader grumbled. "If we're taking on the Watcher, we give him as little time to prepare as possible. You don't think our rabble would get within half a mile if we stuck to the roads, do you?"

The same thug rubbed his arm, cut from passing through a line of thick brush, and spat.

"I don't know. Just hate this stupid forest is all."

"We'll be out soon. All of you stay sharp and close. Won't be too long, now."

The rest, numbering ten plus Karnryk and Melhed, shouted their approval. That communal roar woke the two lovers from their sleep.

"Are you awake?" Qurrah asked, his eyes snapping open.

"I hear it," the girl whispered into his neck. "They're close, and they're many."

They stood, Qurrah throwing on his robes, Tessanna watching him.

"Aren't you going to dress?" he asked her. She smirked in response.

"Don't you think I'm more intimidating as is?"

The half-orc looked up and down her body. She was thin, she was pale, but by the gods, she was beautiful.

"You'll steal their hearts, but only to draw them closer, not send them running."

She laughed. "I know. I'll put on clothes if you insist, though."

She donned her short, weathered dress, tracing her fingers across the stains of blood. Finished, the two slipped through the trees toward the source of the noise.

<hr>

"I count twelve," Qurrah said, hidden behind a collection of brush. Farther ahead marched the mercenaries, cutting and cursing their way through the forest toward the Eschaton tower.

"Who's the big one?" Tessanna asked, licking her lips. When she caught Qurrah watching, she laughed. "I'm not interested in that, at least, not while he's alive." She laughed again. Qurrah wasn't sure if she was joking or not, and that alone disturbed him.

"They move for our tower," the half-orc said. "For what reason, though?"

Tessanna shrugged. "You need subjects for your scrolls, right? Well, I see plenty. I'll leave you one breathing."

With that, she stripped off her dress and left their cover. Fully exposed, she shouted to the group.

"What's the hurry?"

The men turned, their eyes bulging at the sight of Tessanna approaching, her black hair falling down either side of her face, covering her shoulders and the sides of her breasts. The morning was cold, and her body showed it. Her face held no expression, for the being of apathy had come over her.

"What in Karak's name is going on?" Karnryk growled. All around him, his thugs glanced at each other, each one looking for the courage to go to her, despite what their half-orc boss might say.

"A nymph of the forest, perhaps?" Melhed offered. "I have heard rumors of such beauty, but I've never seen one."

"We can share her, can't we, Karnryk?" asked one. Several others echoed similar sentiments.

"Hold it!" he shouted, putting his arms out to stop them. "Something ain't right, boys, can't you feel it?"

They could feel something, but it felt right to them.

"Look upon me," Tessanna called, caressing her body with her hands as she walked. "Enjoy my beauty. Many already have."

Karnryk felt a tug to go to her, but the warrior in him shrieked in protest. A cool wind blew from her direction, even though the air had been still all morning. The forest darkened with her steps, as if clouds formed a permanent cover above her head. And her eyes... When she looked upon him with those huge black orbs, he felt naked, helpless, and doomed to die.

"Get your weapons ready, boys, this girl's no prize."

"Are you mad?" said one thug. "You want us to hurt a thing like that?"

"I want you to-"

He stopped, for Tessanna had begun to change. The shadows around her darkened. Cold air tossed her hair in all directions. A creeping mist seeped out from her, hiding her features. Step after step, the transformation continued, until she appeared a dark goddess walking the land of Dezrel. Her eyes were the darkest of all, tunnels to the abyss leering out at the living.

"I am alive," she said, her voice the shriek of a banshee, beautiful and deadly. "I am the angel. I am the nightmare. I have come."

Black tentacles shot from her outstretched fingers, curling around trees, slicing through bushes and low branches, and then piercing into the flesh of the nearest thug. He screamed until two tentacles ripped out his tongue. Black lightning swirled around his body. The tentacles finally drew back, leaving a bloody pile of flesh.

Karnryk drew his sword, fear palpable on his face.

"If you value your lives, she needs to die," he ordered. The others drew their daggers and swords, doing their best to ignore the carnage that had been their comrade.

"Come to the angel," Tessanna beckoned. Tentacles flared out her shoulders and swirled into great black wings that stretched higher than the trees. Power flared through her, and the courage of all men who looked upon her melted like ice before the sun.

If the display had lasted a bit longer, they would have fled, never to return. Tessanna's power, however, was not as absolute as she made it seem. The black wings dissipated, the tentacles faded as if they never were, and in one great silent implosion the darkness returned to her body. Now only a beautiful, naked girl, Tessanna fell to her knees, gasping for breath.

"Damn poison," she whispered, sensing traces still lingering in her veins.

"Kill her," Karnryk ordered. They charged, bolstered by her collapse. Then Qurrah stepped out from behind the brush let loose a crack of his fiery whip.

"I will drive mad any who dare touch her," he shouted, ignoring the horrid pain in his throat.

"Too late!" Karnryk bellowed, not slowing in the least. The rest of his thugs were not far behind. He saw Qurrah cast a spell, so he raised his sword in defense. The bones of the dead body animated and assaulted the group from behind. Men screamed and fell, bones cracking their spines, necks, and heads. A pelvic bone smacked Karnryk hard in the back. He stumbled to the ground in a great explosion of leaves and dirt.

"Kill him," he shouted, struggling back to his feet. "Kill him, quickly!" The first to approach tripped, his feet tangled and his pants aflame. Two more lunged, but Qurrah knelt beside Tessanna and cast a spell. A single, impenetrable wave of darkness rolled forth, rising higher than their heads. They flew back, pushed on by the wave. Karnryk jammed his sword into the dirt and braced himself. The magic slammed into his body like raging floodwaters. He felt his flesh peel away, yet he held his ground. When the wave passed, only he remained standing.

"Impressive," he said, spitting blood. "But it will take more than a few spells to kill me."

"I do not seek to kill you," Qurrah said, snapping his whip. "As I said, I will drive you mad."

"He is mine," Tessanna said, rising from her knees. "The others you can do with as you wish, but I want him alive."

Qurrah nodded, trusting her. Many of the thugs were getting to their feet, only dazed by his spell.

"Very well." He turned to Karnryk. "My pity to you."

The necromancer walked around the powerful warrior, giving him a safe distance considering the length of his two-handed sword. Karnryk let him go, only concerned with the dark angel.

"Do you want me?" she asked, displaying her body. The half-orc spat in response.

"Too skinny. A man like me would crush you."

Tessanna giggled. "I'm tougher than I look. Really, I am."

The half-orc roared, yanking his blade out of the dirt and charging. He swung with all his might, attempting to behead

Tessanna where she stood. In response, she whispered words of magic and raised her hand. The sword smashed against her fingers and stopped as if striking a mountain. The impact nearly shattered Karnryk's hands and elbows. She reached out and ran a hand across his chest. Karnryk pulled back his sword and struck, this time at her scrawny waist. Again he smacked against stone.

"My sword is enchanted," he said, the pain in his arms unbearable. "Why do you not die?"

In response, Tessanna flattened her hand against his skin and lowered it to his groin. He tensed, exhilarated and terrified.

"There's only one sword I want," she cooed. "I'll tell you if you want to know."

She groped and pressed. He held her with one hand and pressed his sword against her neck with the other.

"Stop it," he snarled.

"Don't you want to know?" she asked. "I'll whisper it to you." She leaned forward, unafraid of the blade at her exposed throat. The half-orc felt his heart skip as her hair and lips brushed the side of his face.

"Are you sure you want to know?" she whispered into his ear.

"Yes," he gasped as she resumed the motions of her hand.

"*Bleed,*" she whispered.

The black magic poured into him. The pain he felt was indescribable, an overwhelming sensation so great his mind immediately shut down in defense. He fell, unconscious, a giant red smear across the crotch of his pants.

"I hope you'll keep my secret," she giggled, licking the blood off her fingers.

"Let go!" screamed the man as Qurrah's flaming leather whip wrapped around his ankle. He hacked at it with his sword, showering sparks and ash, but causing no damage. The smell of burning flesh filled his nostrils, and his screams grew all the louder.

"You will die like the others," Qurrah said, releasing the leg. The thug charged, howling like a mad beast. Eager to test out a new spell, the half-orc whispered words of power and outstretched his hand. A gray, swirling funnel, like a tornado turned on its side, shrieked out from his palm. Flesh cracked and died as the rolling magic swarmed over him. The man inhaled to scream but the tornado swirled down his throat, shriveling his lungs and denying him his final death cry. The body fell, looking like a freshly unearthed corpse.

A dagger sliced through the air, only its clear whistle giving Qurrah warning. He cried out in anger as the blade cut across his cheek. He dropped to the ground as two more flew above his head. He sought out and found his attacker: Melhed, hiding behind a tree.

"If blood is what you want," the half-orc said, "then I will gladly grant it."

He wiped his face, smearing blood across his palm. Dark magic hardened it into a small stone. It vibrated in his hand, filled with power. The next time Melhed threw a dagger, Qurrah released his own projectile.

A blink of his eyes, and then Melhed felt the impact. The ball shattered, swarming him in a tremendous explosion of blood. Its stickiness wrapped around his face, his arms, and his legs. He collapsed, gasping for air. The blood thickened, pulsing as if still encapsulated in veins. Struggle as he might, the rope-like substance held firm.

Comparatively, Melhed's dagger had far less effect. It bit into Qurrah's shoulder, a deep wound that would take time to heal.

Qurrah had time. Melhed did not.

"You struck me twice," the half-orc said. "I shall save you for last."

Last would not be long, for only three men remained facing the necromancer, and all three were wounded.

"Do any of you dare strike against me?" he asked, snapping his whip to the ground. The men formed a triangle, eyeing him fearfully.

"Get him," one shouted, his dagger thrusting at the half-orc's back. The other two remained, cowardly at heart, and did not charge with him. Qurrah spun, shoving his hand forward with his fingers hooked in a bizarre way.

"*Nightmare,*" he hissed in the tongue of magic. The thrust faltered, all strength pulled out of it. Qurrah batted it aside with his free hand and then gripped the man's face with an open palm. The man stared with wide, unblinking eyes as Qurrah forced him to his knees. From his mouth came screams of sheer terror.

"Do you wish this man's fate?" Qurrah asked the other two, shoving the shrieking man to the dirt as if he were a pitiful child. "The things he sees are beyond description. Stay, and you may share them."

"You'll kill us if we turn to run," one said, glancing to his partner for support.

"That's right," Qurrah laughed, wrapping his whip about his arm. Beside him, the shrieking man gagged and shivered as his heart gave out. "Still, if I were you, I'd be running."

All light surrounding his fingers sucked in and vanished, leaving two voids where his hands should have been. Black lightning crackled between them, its thunder that of a wailing eagle. Where Qurrah's eyes had been were now doorways to the abyss, seething with the cold promise of death. The men dropped their swords and ran. They died like cowards, lightning bursting their hearts in their chests.

Qurrah turned to see Tessanna approach. She remained nude, her dress in hand.

"They are all dead," she said, a wonderful smile on her face. The smile did not flinch even when she yanked the dagger out of Qurrah's shoulder.

"I left one alive," Qurrah said, grunting as pain flooded him. Tessanna kissed his cheek, her pale hands gently pressed against the wound. Healing magic sank into him, ceasing the blood flow. Satisfied, Qurrah pulled out a few pieces of parchment from a large pocket within his robes.

"Stay back," he said. "You must not hear the words I say."

"But I want to see," she pouted.

"When I am done, you may see the results," he offered. She sighed but consented. He ran a hand through her hair, admiring the perfection of her body. Then went to Melhed, who was still bound by the blood curse.

"What do you want with me?" the scrawny man asked, his voice just below hysteria. "I have money. Lots of it! It's in my house. Let me get it for you."

"Where is your house, cretin?" Qurrah asked, yanking the man's hair so that they stared eye to eye.

"It's in southwestern Veldaren," he said. "Fourth down Copper lane."

"What does it look like?"

Qurrah took out his whip and draped it across the man's neck, chest, and abdomen.

"Small, brown, thick cedar. My name is etched above the door. Please, I have gold in there, you can take it, all of it, just let me live."

The half-orc pulled back his whip. It vanished underneath the arm of his cloak.

"Thank you, kind sir," Melhed said, thinking his life spared. "I have no quarrel with you, I was paid by Karnryk. Yes, paid, that's all."

"I never said you could live," Qurrah said, his voice vile. He unrolled the parchment, to the horror of the bound man.

"No! No spells, please no, anything, please, use my daggers!"

"These are not spells," he said. He pulled out two globs of wax and shoved them into his ears. "They are far worse." His voice was distant and muffled. He hoped it would be enough.

The man screamed when he recited the first line of words written across the page. He thought Qurrah was about to explode his head or turn him into some pitiful creature. The words, however, had a hypnotic affect. He quieted, listening intently.

Qurrah continued. To him, he had read only seven lines, but to Melhed, nearly a lifetime seemed to have passed. His eyes grew distant, his mouth slackened, but still he listened, deep in concentration. When Qurrah reached the end of the passage, he stopped, feeling dizzy and weak. Melhed's reaction was far worse.

"Nooo!" he shrieked, writhing against his bonds. "Noooo! Speak! Speak!"

Qurrah did not know, but to Melhed, the silence was more than deafening. His entire mind had ridden the magical words like a man caught in a stream. With the end of the water, though, he found passage upstream impossible.

Tessanna arrived as he pulled the wax from his ears.

"It looks as if he yearns for something," she said, staring at Melhed's fanatical eyes.

"I do not know what," Qurrah admitted. "But this is nothing like you. He has no control. His entire mind is shattered."

The girl nodded, laughing at the way the man flopped around.

"Are you going to leave him here?" she asked.

"There are more than two-hundred passages I must test. He, and the passage he represents, is incorrect. I have no use for him."

"You poor baby," Tessanna cooed, kneeling down beside the shrieking man. She put a hand across his head, holding him steady. She put the rest of her weight on his chest. She kissed him, plunging her tongue deep down his throat. She purred as the stink of madness filled her nostrils. Before she ended her kiss, she grabbed his tongue in her teeth and bit down. The tender flesh tore, and the man's screams down her throat were waves of pleasure. The taste of blood filled her, and she reveled in pure, sexual delight. She stood, flashing Qurrah a smile.

"He will choke soon," she told the stunned half-orc. "That, or he will swallow his own tongue. Want to stay and watch?"

"No," Qurrah said, holding in his shudder.

"Aww," she said, her lower lip pouting. She put her dress back on, flipped her hair over one shoulder, and then slowly licked the blood from her lips.

"No fun," she told him. "No fun at all."

12

"I hope your brother and that girl of his return soon," Tarlak said, pacing back and forth in the main floor of the tower. "If Dieredon decides to grab Aurelia and run, things could get nasty."

"Qurrah will show if he wants, not much else we can do," Harruq said.

"I could scry for his location," Aurelia said, sitting on the stairs, her staff on her lap. "But I'd rather save my strength for more important things, like making sure you all stay alive."

"Your concern for our safety is touching," the wizard said. "Especially since we're doing this for you."

"Oh, please. You'd hate not seeing my cute butt again, and you know it."

Tarlak shrugged. "So?"

"You all are idiots," Brug mumbled, munching on a thick chicken leg smeared with sauce. "He comes in, Aurelia wiggles her ass, and then he leaves, everyone happy. Since when are things gonna get crazy?"

Aurelia winked at him. "It's me. Things tend to go that way when I'm around."

"I'll agree to that," Harruq said.

"Just try to keep the damage to a minimum," Delysia said, coming down the stairs in her spotless white robes. "I'm still a little weak, so if you can do with some bandages, then you will."

The door to the tower swung open, revealing Haern, his face hidden by his hood. "Dieredon circles above," he whispered.

"Fun time," Harruq said, drawing his swords.

"Put those away," Aurelia ordered, glaring at the dark blades. "Wait until you absolutely must."

The half-orc frowned but obeyed. Tarlak slapped his back before taking command.

"Look sharp and smart, everybody. You're Eschatons. You have a reputation to uphold here, mainly mine. Don't blow it."

"Oh yes, great and wise leader," Brug said, dropping his chicken and grabbing his punch daggers. "Your speech of inspiration reveals a silver tongue, indeed."

"Shut up, shorty."

The two were still bickering when they exited the tower.

Dieredon remained high in the air as he looped around the tower, his bow still slung across his back. There was no reason to expect trouble, but he kept it loose just in case. With a couple soft commands, he landed his winged horse, Sonowin, a safe distance away.

"Stay safe," he whispered, patting her side. "Things get interesting, take off. Understand?" The white horse snorted, showing her opinion of fleeing.

"Fine," Dieredon laughed. "Then trample whoever you wish."

He slapped her rump before approaching the tower.

An interesting crowd awaited him. A yellow-robed wizard stood at the front, beaming at the elf. Beside him was a priestess of Ashhur, her hair the same shade of red as the wizard's. To the side lurked a short warrior, his beard covered with red sauce. A man garbed in cloaks guarded the other flank. The subtle placement of the man's feet and his sheer intensity in watching Dieredon's every move identified him as the Watcher, rumored to live at the Eschaton tower. Dieredon marked him as the primary threat. Behind them, he saw the bounty he had come to collect, Aurelia Thyne. Standing next to her...

He halted, the grip on his bow tightening.

"Hail Dieredon, Scoutmaster of the Quellan elves," the wizard said. "I am Tarlak Eschaton, leader of the Eschaton mercenaries. I welcome you to my tower."

"You have puzzled us all, Lady Thyne," Dieredon said in elvish, ignoring the wizard. "You train with a murderer, flee with him from battle, and now accompany this wretch into the city of the humans?"

"And who would this murderer be?" Tarlak asked in fluent elvish. The scoutmaster glanced over, his opinion of the man rising.

"Harruq Tun, traitor to the city of Woodhaven."

The half-orc heard his name. His hands tightened on the hilts of his blades. Things were not going smoothly. He didn't need to understand elvish to understand that.

"Murderer or not, he is none of your concern," Tarlak said, glancing at the half-orc. "No bounty is upon his head, at least, none I am aware of."

"Answer my question, Lady Thyne," Dieredon asked, switching to the human tongue. "Why did you betray us? He killed elves, Aurelia. How do you stay by his side?"

Aurelia slipped to the front of the group, ignoring Tarlak's attempts to hold her back.

"He is a good man," she said, staring down Dieredon. "The one who ordered him is dead. He is free of his oath. Besides, the actions he committed were in battle. We all killed men that day."

"I know his puppet master is dead. I killed him myself. Come with me, Aurelia. You will be tried for treason in Quellassar for aiding the escape of a murderer."

"Nonsense," Aurelia said. "Even if he was a traitor to Woodhaven, the town does not fall under elven rule. I am staying. I ask you, as a friend, to rescind this pointless bounty."

Dieredon glanced about the mercenaries. "That half-orc is a murderer," he said to them, daring each to meet his gaze. "But he didn't just kill elves. He killed children. You have invited the Forest Butcher into your home." He glared at Harruq when he spoke, nearly spitting out the words.

"You don't know that!" Aurelia insisted.

"Enough of this," Harruq said, drawing his blades. He shoved past Tarlak, pulled Aurelia back, and stood between her and the scoutmaster. "She's not going with you, elf, and that's final. So hop on your flying horsie and get out of here, and call off this dumb bounty after you do."

The bow was off his back before any could move. Blades shot out the front, top and bottom as a cold expression fell over Dieredon's face.

"Twelve children," he said, his voice almost a whisper. "Twelve."

Harruq remembered the last words a child had spoken to him, just before he had ended his life.

You're an orc, aren't you?

The guilt sent him charging, his blades lashing out. Dieredon ducked into a crouch. The two swords cut air. He flipped backward, one foot cracking the bottom of Harruq's chin. As he staggered, the elf lunged, the bottom blade of his bow leading.

Harruq jerked his head at the last second, the bow slicing a gash across his cheek instead of ramming out the back of his head. Blood poured down the side of his face, further igniting his rage. He batted the bow to one side, thrusting with his other sword, only to have the bow swing around and parry the attack away. Twice Dieredon slapped Harruq's face with the flat ends of his blades, stinging his pride.

The half-orc lunged, every nerve in his body on edge. He had seen the speed of Haern. The assassin had trained him rigorously, yet still he felt as he had that very first day, clearly outmatched. His next few attacks, the elf blocked with ease, and then he found himself on the receiving end of a brutal series of thrusts. He dodged side to side, his desperate blocks barely connecting.

"He's going to kill him," Tarlak said, preparing a spell. Haern shoved his hand over the wizard's mouth, halting any casting. Tarlak glanced at the assassin and raised an eyebrow.

"Dieredon does not aim to kill," Haern whispered. "Something more is at stake. It is not for us to intervene."

"If he is too wounded, you must stop them," Delysia said.

"I will surrender before it comes to that," Aurelia said, her staff clutched tightly between her fingers as she watched Harruq hammered repeatedly in the face by kicks.

"I thought you were a warrior," Dieredon shouted, countering a thrust with a stab that cut through Harruq's enchanted leather and into skin. He pulled back, drawing only a small amount of blood, and then blocked a dual chop by the half-orc. "I thought you skilled. How many elves fell to you? Did you stab them in the back?"

"I killed them in combat," Harruq snarled, shoving hard against the elf's bladed bow. "They fought me face to face and lost. How many have *you* killed?"

"Thousands," the elf said, matching the half-orc's strength. "Orcs, goblins, humans, hyena-men, even elves." He tilted the bow, hooking the two swords on the razors along the front, and then shoved to one side. Harruq's blades and arms went with it, exposing his entire left side to a series of kicks.

"Why does Aurelia stay with you?" he asked, spinning back and away. "What spell has convinced her good is in your heart?"

"You would never understand," Harruq said, clutching his side as best he could without dropping his sword. "And neither will I."

The blades snapped in, and a bowstring materialized from thin air. Dieredon readied an arrow before the half-orc could move.

"Then why is it you stay with her?" he asked. "Why do you fight for her?"

"I don't know!" he shouted. He stayed where he stood, knowing the slightest movement would send the arrow flying.

"Then why should I not kill you?" Dieredon shouted back. "Why should I not bury this arrow in your eye!"

"Enough of this!" Aurelia yelled. "Please, I will go."

"No!" Harruq roared, charging the elf. The arrow flew through the air, its aim true.

Aurelia screamed as the arrow pierced into the half-orc's flesh. Harruq bellowed out his pain, the arrow deep in his shoulder. He neared Dieredon, who remained completely still. When Harruq swung, the elf darted inward, grabbed his wrist, and flung him over his shoulder. The blades snapped out of his bow, and down came the spike, halting just above the half-orc's throat.

"Why is it you should live?" Dieredon shouted.

"Because I love her!" Harruq screamed, his voice echoing across the land. All was silent as Dieredon kept the blade hovering.

"How can you love her?" he whispered. "Do you even know what love is?"

"She was kind to me," he said, gasping from the pain of his many wounds. "When I didn't deserve it, she was still kind to me." His voice dropped quieter. "And I hurt her, and still I was forgiven. I owe her everything."

Dieredon pulled back the blades, which vanished into his bow. He knelt down and whispered to the half-orc.

"If you ever, ever hurt her again, you will answer to me, and I will kill you."

"I know," Harruq whispered back.

Dieredon left him laying there and approached Aurelia. He slung the bow over his back and opened his arms. The two embraced, Aurelia staring past him at the beaten, bleeding Harruq.

"I still don't trust him," he said to her in elvish.

"I do," she said. "Is that not enough?"

Dieredon pulled back and smiled. "I guess it is, for now," he said. "I'll tell Felewen you are well. She might even visit, she misses you so."

Aurelia smiled. "Tell her that would be nice."

The elf looked to Tarlak and gave him a nod.

"I will rescind the bounty. Will you release them from your capture?"

"Release?" Tarlak laughed. "They've become part of the family. You're more than welcome to join. I know a few dragons we could slay with your help."

"I must decline," the elf said, cracking a smile. "Dragons scare me."

Dieredon hugged Aurelia once more, and then trotted back to Sonowin, halting beside Harruq on the way.

"She loves you as well," he said. "Only Celestia knows why, but she does."

The half-orc offered no response. The rest of the Eschaton mercenaries watched until he mounted Sonowin and took flight.

"Dang that guy's good," Brug muttered once he was gone. Aurelia rushed to Harruq, who started to apologize. She ignored him, wrapped her arms around his bruised neck, and kissed him. The stunned half-orc dropped his swords and held her close. When the kiss ended, she smiled at him.

"You stupid half-orc," she said. "Got yourself beat up for silly little me."

"Anytime," he said, blushing through the bruises.

Brug rolled his eyes at the display and returned to his meal. Tarlak followed, pretending to throw up. Delysia and Haern moved to Harruq's side, both their expressions somber.

"Go to my room, Harruq," Delysia said. "Looks like my healing magic is going to be needed after all."

"Yeah," he said, glancing down at the arrow. "That's gonna hurt when you remove it, isn't it?"

"Of course. I'll be waiting."

With a flip of her red hair, she returned to the tower. Harruq grinned at Haern, unsure of what his teacher would say.

"You need a lot more practice," the assassin whispered. "Not even a single hit. When I fought him my first time, I scored two cuts."

"You've fought him before?" Harruq asked, trying to imagine the two in battle. Haern only shook his head and left.

"Come on, big lug," Aurelia said, smacking him playfully. "Let's get you healed so I can snuggle you without getting blood all over me."

"As you wish," he said, seeing no reason to argue.

If Karnryk lay perfectly still, the pain only throbbed. If he kept his breaths shallow enough, the throbs weakened to dull aching. If he moved, the dull ache exploded into a thousand piercing daggers.

"Melhed," he groaned, no louder than a whisper. "Melhed!" The wave of pain this caused nearly rendered him unconsciousness, but he was Karnryk the Slayer. Never before had pain bested him, and he would not let it do so now.

He stared at the light streaming through the forest canopy, wondering how much time had passed. The girl and the necromancer were gone. The only sound he heard was a constant sobbing to his right, broken by the occasional shriek. A third time he called out, and still he received no answer.

That whore, he thought, trying not to visualize the damage to his lower half. *Hits me like a coward and leaves me for dead. I'll kill her. I'll eat her beating heart!*

Anger gave him strength to move. He lifted his head, ignoring the cry of protest from the waist down. The pain was so great, his mind could not focus where it came from. His legs felt broken, his thighs throbbed as if stabbed, and his feet were all but numb. Where she struck him, however, was beyond pain.

"Melhed, what'd she do to you?" he asked, propping himself up on his elbows. He could see his friend lying there, rolling back and forth as he sobbed. The half-orc waited, gathering strength for the agony he knew to come. Taking a deep breath, he lifted to a crouch. The movement was salt on an open wound. Agony assaulted his mind. Stubbornness alone kept his legs moving. He roared, throwing away rational thought and pushing upward, slowly, horrifically, until he stood screaming at the top of his lungs.

When his mind was back under control, he inspected his injured self. It looked as if he had wet himself, except with blood instead of urine. He sensed, in a way, that was exactly what had happened.

"You'll pay," he muttered, taking one small, painful step toward Melhed. Dead bodies littered the forest floor. His friends, his pride, and even his manhood, were now reduced to a single ally sobbing incoherently in the leaves. He often dealt in retribution, but never before had he felt hatred as stark and naked as when he took another step. His stomach churned as he felt a bit more blood slide down his leg, warm and fresh.

"Long and brutal," he said. "Very long, and very brutal."

As he neared Melhed, he knew something was wrong. His skin was pale, his arms and legs bound, and blood covered his mouth. His sobbing turned to a strange sucking sound, one that turned Karnryk's already weak stomach.

"It's me, Karn," he said, hoping against hope. "Look at me. I said look at me!"

The sucking sound grew louder, louder, and then Melhed began choking. Karnryk watched, his entire heart and soul numbed. The wiry man gasped and rolled to his side, gagging and retching silently. After thirty seconds of this, he managed to spit out something wet and red. It was a large portion of Melhed's tongue.

"I'm sorry, Mel," the half-orc said, kneeling beside the man, who gasped in air. He took a throwing dagger from his belt, gripped it in his fist, and said goodbye to his friend. Down went the dagger, through his eye and into the shattered remnants of what had been a mind. Karnryk screamed out his rage. Another reason for vengeance.

He started heading south, step by agonizing step. If he reached the end of the forest, Veldaren would only be a mile or so east. The distance, while not far, felt like a thousand leagues to Karnryk. The first few hours he took childlike steps, using a ricocheting path from tree to tree to give him support. Eventually he collapsed against a sturdy trunk and slept.

When he awoke, stars filled the sky. He took to his feet, with no greater ease than the first time. The hours crawled by, broken only by brief moments of sleep or unconsciousness. His heart cried out for him to fall, to succumb to the pain, hunger, weakness, thirst, but mostly the pain. His desire for vengeance was stronger than all of them. He pushed on.

It was well into midday before he reached the city gates. He said only one word to the gate guards before he fell.

"Healer."

"Such horrible taste," Tessanna said, frowning at the ornate furniture designed to look worth far more than the craftsmanship warranted. Her grimace grew when she saw the curtains, the worst shade of orange she had ever seen. Without a word, she yanked them down and tossed them to the floor.

"There are many houses nearby," Qurrah said, glancing out a tiny window. "Each one a potential for a prying eye."

"Why would you fear prying eyes?" the girl asked, sneering at him. "Because you drove the former owner insane and left him for dead in the forest, screaming like a mad little puppy?"

The half-orc frowned.

"There is that, as well. Any screams shall be heard, possibly by many. We cannot live here."

Tessanna crossed the room, giving him a flirty look.

"I'm sure some screams can be heard from inside without causing too much alarm," she said. "What is it that *you* plan on doing in here?"

"Just casting a few spells," Qurrah said. "Nothing to concern yourself about."

"Nothing you do could concern me," said Tessanna, curling her arms around his neck and looking at him with the wild eyes of an animal. The half-orc pulled her down onto the couch, locking her in a violent kiss.

Later, as they lay silent in each other's arms, Tessanna whispered into her lover's ear.

"There is a home where there are no neighbors. No one for miles."

"Where?" Qurrah asked, tracing a finger from her belly button to her chin.

"In the King's Forest. Not too far from the tower."

The half-orc sat up on the cushion and looked down at her.

"You speak of your home as a child."

"Few know it is there," she said, her voice shy. "Any we bring will be miles from help. The screaming will not bother anyone. I can cut myself again, too. There is a stream nearby. I used to watch the blood drip into the water. I miss it."

"You ask me to leave my brother," Qurrah said, staring at the wall.

"He can come if he wishes."

"No. Not for this."

Tessanna sat up and leaned against the opposite side of the couch. All sense of warmth fled from her.

"You fear he will not agree."

"I fear he will overreact, nothing more," the half-orc said. "Besides, I could not separate him now."

"From who?"

"From her."

Tessanna nodded, her eyes cold and lifeless. "The elf."

"Yes. The elf. He is happy with her. I would give anything for him, so now I must give him this. We've never been separate, not since we were seven."

She bit her lip and huddled against the cushion.

"You're doing this for me, aren't you?"

Qurrah brought his eyes from the wall to her. He nodded. "Yes. I think I am."

Tessanna just nodded back.

"Our home will not be far. If you wish to see him, you can. We will find men and bring them there. There are ways. I know how. Do you wish to take me again?"

The half-orc looked at her thin, pale body, curled into a tight ball of arms and legs.

"Yes," he said. "Yes, I do."

He pulled her over to him, and again they made cold, determined love.

"You can't leave," Harruq said, blocking Qurrah's way to the door. "You just got here. Pay is good, beds are warm, and you've seen the food!"

"This is something I must do," Qurrah said, his arms crossed. At his feet were all his belongings in the world; a few spare coins, the spellbook and scrolls from the priests of Karak, some bed sheets, and his enchanted whip, all packed in one large rucksack.

"Why? What must you do? And why the abyss is she going?"

Tessanna cowered behind the necromancer, currently in one of her shy, fearful moods. Qurrah saw her so, and his heart was instantly angry.

"She is going because I wish her to go," he said. "We do not belong here. Our magic, our ways, are limited by these walls. Freely we entered, and now freely we leave. Move aside."

Harruq shook his head, shoving his arms harder against the doorframe so that his knuckles turned white. "No. No. And, um, NO!"

"Harruq!" Qurrah shouted, loud enough to send pain spiking down his throat. "Listen to me. We are brothers, and long you have looked out for me, but I do not need your guardianship. Not anymore. You are a fine warrior, and I am proud of you. Now let me go. Please."

Harruq's eyes danced back and forth from Tessanna to Qurrah, trying to make sense of the conflicting emotions of his heart.

"I don't want you to," he said at last. "Do you have to? Really have to?"

Qurrah pulled the rucksack over his shoulder. "I must. I will return, as often as I can."

The half-orc moved aside. Qurrah took up his things, nodded to Tessanna, and then moved for the door.

"Where will you live?" Harruq asked.

"Not far. Please, honor this wish, brother. Do not look for us. I will be fine, I assure you. If I am ever gone longer than two months, you may have the elf scry for our location."

Nodding, the burly half-orc motioned for the door. Qurrah patted him on the shoulder. He opened his mouth to speak, but found no words, only a soft trickle of blood down the back of his throat. He turned and hurried down the stairs, subtly pressing the sides of his hood against his face on the way. Tessanna paused before poor confused Harruq, pitying his turmoil. She was still a stranger to him, and in a few fleeting days, she had come and stolen away his only brother.

"Harruq," she said, her eyes locked on his toes. "I just…I want to thank you." She kissed his cheek, blushed, and then fled down the stairs. The half-orc stood there long after they left, hating and loving his brother and his girl with the deep black eyes.

Tarlak waited for them at the bottom, his arms crossed and his foot steadily tapping the floor.

"Going somewhere?" he asked.

"We are leaving the Eschaton," Qurrah said. "We have a new home, and wish to move on."

The wizard nodded, his expression dire. "Good. Then I have just one thing to say to you." He strode over to Qurrah, reached into his pocket, and then pulled out a small, silver scorpion. It was exquisitely carved and dangled from a chain of gold. He handed it to Qurrah, who held it close to his face and opened his mouth in wonder.

"You will always be an Eschaton, and so I give you a parting gift. It is a token, representing your ties to us. Brug spent many hours working on that one, and I'm not sure what all it does. Tell it to awake."

Qurrah glanced at the wizard, his confusion apparent. "Awake?"

"Not ask, order it."

The half-orc shrugged. He held the medallion higher, impressed with the life-like detail and size. The pinchers were sharp, and the tail curled and ready to strike. "Awake," he told it, his voice firm. At once, color flooded the silver. It crawled about to face its master, snapping its claws repeatedly.

"Many wizards have a familiar," Tarlak said, smiling at the scorpion. "Brug decided you should have one as well. You won't have many of the same connections that most mages do, but I do know you won't end up in a coma for a week if this little guy gets squashed."

Qurrah brought his hand back and clicked with his tongue. The scorpion crawled onto his shoulder and nestled down into the black cloth.

"It is a fine gift," the half-orc said. "Far better than I deserve."

"You saved my sister," Tarlak said. "It is far less than what you deserve, but take it as an effort to thank you, just the same."

Qurrah shifted the rucksack to his other shoulder. "We will return occasionally. Make sure my brother is well each time I do."

"Other than a few bruises and broken bones from Haern, he should be just fine."

Tarlak bowed, and Qurrah returned it. Tessanna joined his side, stroking the scorpion.

"Pretty," she said. "And creepy. I love it."

Her laughter still echoed when they shut the door and left the tower.

⚜

Harruq was miserable the rest of the day, not brightening up even when presented with another bountiful feast for dinner. He picked at the food, and then pushed the plate away. He left without a word.

"Someone needs to cheer that guy up," Tarlak said, shoving pieces of chicken into his mouth.

"He will be alright," Aurelia said. "Give him time."

"I'll set him straight tomorrow if he isn't," Haern said, smiling. His hood was nowhere in sight, and his smile a bright sun to the somber table.

⚜

"The stars shine well this night," Aurelia said, approaching the lone half-orc. They were a mile south of the tower. The Eschaton tower and its surrounding forest were far away. Only hills and stars blessed their eyes. "They do so to light your way, and the way of your brother."

"Don't feel like talking, Aurry," Harruq said. His back was to her, hunched over and his head low. His eyes looked to the ground as much as they looked to the sky.

"I know," she said, sitting beside him in the grass. "Do you know why he left? It's because he must, Harruq. You two are brothers, closer than most humans and elves ever become to their kin, but you are not the same. You cannot walk the same path forever."

Harruq remained silent, absently picking at the grass.

"It's normal to miss him," she continued. "Please don't dwell upon it, though. You have friends here, and your brother is not alone."

"He has her," he said.

"And you have me," Aurelia said. Her fingers touched his chin, turning his face to hers. "Did you mean what you said earlier?"

Harruq met her gaze, a bit of anger flaring into his eyes, but then he pulled away and looked to his feet. "Yeah. I did."

The elf slid closer and wrapped her arms around him. Her head rested on his shoulder. She felt his muscles stiffen, and she sensed the instinctive discomfort it caused him.

"Don't look at your feet, dummy. The stars are far prettier."

He chuckled, mumbling some sort of protest. He looked to the stars. Long moments passed, quiet and warm, as they gazed at the beacons of white locked into the black painting above. Finally, Aurelia stood, brushing off grass from her dress. She pulled a silver ring off her right hand and held it out to him.

"Take this."

"What's it for?" he asked, accepting it. The silver twinkled in the starlight. Such a beautiful token seemed out of place on his rough, dirty hands.

"One day you'll understand," she said. She knelt and kissed his forehead. "All you give me I will return," she whispered. "Anything, and everything."

With those words, she left him to his thoughts. He twirled the silver ring, mesmerized by the reflection. When he returned to the tower, he placed the ring underneath his pillow and did his best not to look at the vacant bed beside him.

13

A strange sickness claimed the trees as they neared the clearing, miles from any established path. Grass lay curled and limp, its color a dull brown. The sunlight brought no cheer, for it shone through dead branches. In the center, dilapidated and weatherworn, was the former home of Tessanna Delone. It was a small cottage, overrun with brown vines, with a single door, flat roof, and clogged chimney.

"Pretty, isn't it," Tessanna said. Her voice was sullen and inward. "Daddy said the land died at my birth." She approached the front door, Qurrah at her side. The grass crumpled weakly under their feet. When she yanked open the door, the dull noises of the forest silenced altogether.

Qurrah was familiar with death. He could sense its approach, harness its power, and touch the cold trail that lingered long after its passing. Corpses meant nothing to him. He should have handled seeing what he saw. He didn't. His breakfast rushed up his throat, and he lurched to one side, doubling over and vomiting.

"Hi, daddy," Tessanna said. "Did you miss me?"

Tied to a chair hunched the remains of Tessanna's father. His shriveled hands were bound behind him. The ropes had loosened over time as the flesh underneath shriveled and decayed. The house had been his tomb, and within, he had almost mummified. Stitches of red cloth hung stiff from the leathery nubs of flesh that had been his lips. Covering what remained of his clothes were great blotches of dried blood, mixed with shards of glass.

"I wonder how he died," she said, glancing back to Qurrah. "I hope it was lengthy."

Qurrah entered, hands sweating and his stomach still churning. He chastised himself for his weakness. It was just a dead body, after all. Never mind the horrific expression on the man's face, or the expelled blood and glass. He blamed his reaction on the smell. The air was remarkably stagnant, preserving the body in all its gory detail.

"If we are to live here, we'll need to greatly improve the natural aroma," he said, holding a side of his hood over his mouth. Tessanna looked at him, her eyes blank.

"Of course. Did you presume us to leave the body here?"

Qurrah shook his head. "Never mind what I presumed. Help me dispose of your father."

Using Tessanna's dagger, they cut the ropes. His body slumped forward, his head falling between his knees as if he were to vomit. The girl took a rope, wrapped it around his neck, and dragged him out of the chair. She showed no sign of emotion as she pulled the body across the floor. She acted as if she were removing a chamber pot. Qurrah propped open the door, took the sheets from the bed and wrapped them around the chair. He carried it around back, planning to toss it to ruin in some far away brush. He stopped, though, for Tessanna was already there.

The grotesque body sat propped against a tree. Tessanna knelt opposite it. She was staring, not blinking, not moving. Qurrah put down the chair and approached.

"Tess?"

"I never said goodbye," she said. "I wonder why I never said goodbye. It never bothered me until now." In perfect contrast to her words, her voice lacked any of emotion.

"He didn't deserve any comfort or sympathy. You knew that, then. You have forgotten it, now."

The girl shrugged. "Perhaps you're right. He didn't deserve it. He didn't deserve me. He didn't deserve my hugs. My kisses. Me."

Still no emotion. Qurrah placed a hand on her shoulder. She jerked her head around and saw him, and then the tears started to flow.

"Oh, Qurrah," she said. She sniffed. "Want to do me a favor?"

"Anything, my love," he said.

"Fuck me."

She pulled him down to her, assaulting him with her kiss. They made love in the dirt while the corpse of her father watched.

◆◆

Harruq paced outside their door, Aurelia's ring in hand. Two opposing thoughts clashed in his mind. When he came to a decision, he knocked his large knuckles against the door.

"Who is it?" he heard a female voice ask.

"Just open it, Delysia," said another.

The door cracked open, and Delysia looked out, smirking at the half-orc.

"Care to join me in my prayers?" she asked.

"Ha, ha. Can I talk to Aurry, please?"

"Sure thing, cutie. Aurelia, your suitor is here."

She danced past him, grinning at the fierce blush in Harruq's neck. He pushed open the door, stepped in, and crossed his arms. Aurelia lay on her bed, her hair braided into a long ponytail.

"Yes, Harruq?" she asked.

In answer, he walked over, opened her hand, and shoved her ring onto her palm before he lost his nerve.

"What are you doing?" she asked, staring down at the ring.

"I know what you want me to do with it," he said. "I can't. Ever."

She clenched her fist and met his steeled resolve. "Why is that?"

"You know why," he said.

"No, I don't. Why?"

"Because it can't work!" he shouted. Aurelia flinched, and the sight stung him deeply.

"Why, Harruq?" she asked, quieter. "Why can it not work?"

"I'm an orc. You're an elf. It's never happened."

The elf stood, shaking. She slapped him with her empty hand.

"You think me foolish?" she asked, not giving him a chance to speak. "You think I haven't thought of that? I have abandoned my forest, abandoned my home, and made enemies of my friends, all to be at your side. Just because you fear and loathe the blood in your veins doesn't mean I feel the same."

"That's not, I Mean I I don't think you…damn it Aurry, you think this is how I want it to be?"

"What is it you want then?"

"I want you," he screamed, his face glowing red. "I want you at my side for the rest of my life. And I want to stop being so damn scared to admit it!"

They stared at each other, anger and confusion pulsing through their hearts.

"Say you love me," she said.

"I love you," he said.

"Fine." Her voice quivered, a knife's edge from breaking. "Then take this ring back. If you want to be with me forever, then to the abyss with what anyone else might think. There may be orcish blood in you, but never would I wish it gone."

She extended her hand, the ring laying in her open palm. Harruq stared at it, both fearing and yearning for it. Rejecting her was a kindness, a blessing, a noble act from an ignoble man. How could he be so wrong?

He took the ring from her hand.

"I'm sorry," he said, putting it into his pocket. "I'll be going now."

"Wait."

She wrapped her arms around his neck and kissed him. At first, he was unresponsive, but as his shock faded, his arms circled her waist, holding her close. When the kiss ended, she pressed her forehead against his chest.

"I've given so much," she whispered. "But I'll give more."

He hugged her tight at this. "I don't deserve it."

"And that doesn't matter, dummy. You can spend the rest of your life trying to earn it, if you want."

"That sounds like a plan," he said.

Aurelia slipped from his arms and smiled at him.

"Good. I'll be in the rain room. Don't take forever to decide. I may be an elf, but I still don't live that long."

Together they left, only to find Delysia waiting outside their door.

"Lover's squabble?" she asked.

"Nosy little priestess," Aurelia said, poking her side. "I should turn you into a gnat."

"Well, looks like the fights over. If you want to continue kissing and making up, I'll stay out a little longer."

Aurelia only winked, abandoning Harruq and his brightly flushed face as she skipped down the stairs.

"No, uh, it's fine, we don't need the room," he said.

Delysia giggled. Having nothing else to say, the half-orc fled up the stairs.

"Those two need to get married," she laughed to herself.

Two weeks later, Harruq awoke to the soft rustle of cloth against floor. His room was dark, and the sun still in hiding. A quick glance around his room showed no visitors, but he knew better. Haern lurked nearby, testing him. He shifted his head, still searching.

Nothing. Again, he heard a soft rustle, and he spun, thinking it directly behind him. He found only wall.

He glanced up. Nothing there, either. Slowly, Harruq reached down next to his bed and grabbed his swords. He gripped Salvation by the handle and drew it free. Bare-chested and dressed in an old pair of brown pants, he scanned his room. Through the small window, he could still see faint stars. In the dim light, nothing seemed out of place.

"Maybe he's not here," he mumbled to himself. Grumbling, he put a foot down to get his chamber pot. When the cold touch of steel pressed against his calf, his entire body jerked in fright.

"It would be difficult to fight without a foot," he heard Haern whisper from underneath his bed.

"You scared the piss out of me," Harruq said to him. "Well, nearly. Care to give me a bit of privacy here? Nature's calling."

Haern crawled out and removed his hood.

"You should always look under the bed," he said, frowning. "Just when I thought you were improving. Oh, and your brother is here."

"Qurrah?" he asked. "Be right down. Where is he?"

"Enjoying breakfast with the others. It is an early morning for the tower. We can practice once you have talked."

Haern saluted with a saber before vanishing down the stairs. Harruq did his business, threw on some clothes, and rushed after.

The whole gang, even the late-sleeping Brug, was at the table feasting.

"Qurrah!" Harruq shouted, leaping down the last few steps and hugging his brother, who nearly gagged on some toasted bread.

"Good to see you, Harruq," Qurrah said, coughing throughout the entire sentence.

"Looks like we won't be rid of them after all," Tarlak said, grinning at the two visitors. "Turns out they can't pass up a free meal."

"Your gracious company will always prove most alluring," Qurrah said, each word drowned in sarcasm.

"Usually Tar's gift is sending people running the opposite direction," Brug said.

"What was that, tough guy?" the wizard asked.

"Nothing."

"That's right, nothing. I have a sex-change wand and I know how to use it, so no sassy comments."

"Not even from me?" Aurelia asked, batting her eyelashes.

"No, not you," he answered. "Besides, what fun is there in using the wand on you? I don't cast that way."

"Could have fooled me," Harruq said. Tarlak pulled a pink wand out from a pocket and waved it menacingly. The half-orc feigned terror, then sat down next to Aurelia and started wolfing down his food.

After breakfast, the two left the tower, Harruq eager to speak with his brother.

So are you going to be staying?" Harruq asked as they walked, the tower a fading image behind them.

"That is what I came to tell you, brother," Qurrah replied. "We have a home now, far from others. It is peaceful there. More than we deserve."

"What's going on?" Harruq said, crossing his arms. "What is with this girl? You barely know her, yet you're going to live with her in the middle of nowhere?"

Qurrah shrugged. "Yes, that is our plan. Does this bother you?"

"Of course it does! I've spoken to her, what, three times? I don't even know her!"

"I do," Qurrah said, a cold look entering his eyes. "And your opinion doesn't matter. I will be with her, regardless of what you say."

Taken aback, Harruq could not keep the hurt out of his voice.

"What's happened to you?" he asked. "Your opinion was all that ever mattered to me."

Qurrah felt guilt creeping in his heart, strange and unwelcome.

"You have found a new home, one I cannot be a part of. I dare not say I love Tessanna, but I will be with her until the day of her death. Please, try to understand."

"I'm going to marry Aurelia," Harruq blurted, immediately regretting it. He stood there, waiting like a man with his neck on the chopping block. When the axe fell, it was soft as a feather.

"Do as your heart wishes," Qurrah said. "As will I. She is a fine woman, elf or not."

The warrior bobbed his head up and down, wishing he didn't blush so easily.

"At least you'll come visit us here in the tower, right?"

"Yes, I will. This is not abandonment, only a mere separation. Our paths broke and split with the death of Velixar. We both know that."

Harruq gestured to the black cloth his brother wore. "Is that the path you took up?"

A bit of sadness flickered in Qurrah's eyes, like the glow of a firefly.

"I chose the only path before my feet," he said. "Goodbye, Harruq. Live well, and be happy. Nothing more could we ever have asked for."

He turned to leave, stopping only when Harruq called his name.

"Yes?" he asked.

"If you need anything, I'll be here for you," he said. "Anything at all."

"I know," Qurrah said. Pulling his hood up to guard against the increasingly cold wind, he returned to the tower. Harruq stared a long while after as he vanished behind one of many rolling hills.

Tessanna was waiting for Qurrah when he returned, sitting beside the front doors of the tower with a guilty expression on her face.

"I got in trouble," she said in response to his questioning look.

"Then all the wiser to return home," he said, offering her his hand. She took it and stood. Before he could leave, the door cracked open. Tarlak emerged, beckoning the necromancer with his hand.

"A moment, if you would, before you go," he said. Qurrah shrugged and stepped inside. Tarlak slammed the door shut after him, his face deathly serious. All the others were gone, except for Delysia, who sat at the table and stared at her hands.

"What is it, wizard?" Qurrah asked.

"I know I owe her for saving my sister," he began, "but I am begging you, reconsider what you are doing. She is not well!"

"I know better than you what has been wrought upon her," the half-orc said, his tone vile. "Do not dare tell me what to do."

"Right now you are in my tower, so I'll do as I damn well please," Tarlak said. "And you best listen. She hurt my sister, half-orc, and I don't take kindly to that type of thing."

"Hurt her? Why?"

"She knew," Delysia said, her voice shaking. "Somehow, she knew. She asked for my hand, and I gave it to her. She cut my palm and…"

She could not finish.

"Wanted to taste such aged purity," Tarlak finished, his voice a whisper. "It's like wine, she said. I don't care what you say has been done to her. Her mind is not right!"

"I know that," Qurrah shouted. "That is exactly what I wish to heal. She saved Delysia's life, so consider the debt repaid. She has suffered beyond what you can imagine, so before you impose your limited view, know that I have been inside the chaos that is her mind. I will fix it. I will put it right, and not a soul is going to stop me."

"Her mind cannot be fixed," Tarlak shouted back. "Even Calan and all the priests of Ashhur are not strong enough to heal her."

"Then I will become stronger than Ashhur!" Qurrah screamed before doubling over in a violent coughing fit. All was silent in the room except for his labored breathing.

"Leave my tower," Tarlak said, his voice eerily calm. "You are free to return, but Tessanna is not allowed within my walls until you pull off this miracle you delude yourself into searching for."

Tessanna leapt to her feet as Qurrah stormed out of the tower.

"What is it?" she asked.

"We're leaving," he said. "Let's go home."

The two slipped behind the cover of trees and were gone. Harruq returned much later, and with stones in his gut listened to what his brother's beloved had done.

❈

They were a sullen pair sitting around the fire, faces dark, mouths closed, and thoughts turned inward. Qurrah poured over Pelarak's spellbook while Tessanna traced her dagger across her skin. A soft giggle brought his attention to her smiling face.

"I've forgotten how good this feels," she said, tensing her arm so that the blood fell on the fire. "Qurrah, why did we not go to Veldaren and take someone for you to experiment upon?"

The half-orc closed the large book.

"I realized something as I read over the tome. Even if I can mimic the way your mind has become, I know little of how to affect it."

Tessanna licked her bloody arm, staining her lips. "So what do you plan to do?"

"Pelarak recorded all his knowledge on the darker side of magic within this tome. He also has many spells, but it will take time to study them. Until I have mastered these spells, we can delay the messier side of our undertaking."

"What am I to do while you study?" she asked, her eyes locked on a rune she carved across her arm.

"Cut. Sleep. Return to Veldaren. You are free to do as you wish."

"I wish to stay with you," she said. She ran her hand down her arm, smearing blood all across it.

"I wish you to stay with me as well," he said, opening his book. "I'm sure we will think of ways to pass the time."

Tessanna looked at the half-orc, smirking. "Oh, I bet we can."

"I wasn't thinking sex, but yes, that would be one of the more preferable ways to pass the time."

"More preferable than reading some old dusty book?" she asked, crawling around the fire like a cat.

"Much more preferable."

To his surprise, he didn't really mind the blood from her arm smeared across his naked skin.

14

Harruq's days began with Haern's training, and they ended with Aurelia and the stars. The half-orc tested the waters by holding her hand one night, and he found the lightness of his heart and the fierce tingling of his fingers quite addictive. Soon, they relegated the stars to only occasional viewing, as they found each other far more interesting.

Qurrah had been gone for a month when Harruq popped the question… to Haern.

"If I wanted to propose to someone, what should I say?" he asked after a rigorous morning of sparring. Haern removed his hood, shook his blond hair, and then raised an eyebrow.

"Shall I assume there is a certain elf you wish to propose to?"

Harruq shrugged. "Maybe. Any ideas?"

Haern rubbed his chin, amused.

"First, set up the scene. Flowers. Stars. Make sure you're alone. Oh yes, and make sure you bathed recently."

"Ha, ha. Be serious."

Haern laughed. "I am serious. No one wants to marry a smelly half-orc. Besides, there are other reasons, if you know what I mean."

The half-orc's reaction showed that he did. "Just shut up and go on," he said.

"Not sure how I can do both, but very well. Tell her how much you love her, want to be with her, and then present her with the ring. This is after you get down on one knee, of course."

"Why one knee?"

The assassin gave him an incredulous look. "You really don't know anything, do you?"

Harruq crossed his arms. "Now when would I have been taught all this? Tutors? My parents? We street urchins aren't known for playing dress up."

"My apologies. You get down on one knee, like this, and then take her hand when you tell her all the mushy stuff."

Tarlak came around the corner, a scroll in his hand, just as Haern was illustrating the proposal maneuver. He stopped, blinked twice, and then burst into laughter.

"Am I interrupting anything important?" he asked. Haern leapt to his feet, and for the first time ever, Harruq saw him blush.

"Helping out my dear half-orc friend, here," he said, trying, and failing, to act nonchalant. "What is it you need?"

Tarlak gestured with the scroll. "Got a message for the King's Watcher."

Haern took the scroll, unfurled it, and read. A smile grew on his face as he did.

"Excellent," he said, handing the scroll back to the wizard. "I'll retrieve it tomorrow morning."

"Retrieve what?" Harruq asked.

"The King doesn't pay Haern just in gold for his services," Tarlak explained. "He pays in magical items. This one is for five more years of loyalty."

"You didn't answer my question," the half-orc said.

"You'll see tomorrow," Haern said, winking. "By the way, do you have a ring to give Aurelia?"

"Aye."

"Where did you get it?" Haern asked.

"Ring?" Tarlak interrupted. "So you finally found the guts, eh?"

"Aurry gave it to me," Harruq said. "So she's not going to be too surprised."

"Proposing with the girl's own ring? Nonsense!" Tarlak wrapped an arm around the giant man. "Listen here, we have one of the finest metalworkers in all the realms right in this tower, and he's not too bad with jewelry, either. Find some way to pay him, and I'm sure Brug can make you a ring that'll knock the eyes out of Aurelia's head."

"Brug? He'd feed my manhood to a dog if I gave him a fork."

"All show. I'll come with you. Trust me, that guy is a softie at heart, and when he hears it's for love, he'll melt like a tub of lard."

"Alright," Harruq said, shooting Haern a worried glance as Tarlak led them into the tower.

"Not no bloody-abyssy-way!"

"Like lard?" Harruq muttered, jabbing Tarlak with his elbow.

"I know you have plenty of precious gems for all your little toys," the wizard said. "Are you telling me you can't spare one?"

"Not just my gems you want," he said, storming to the other side of his room, not bothering to step over the pieces of armor. Metal clanged and banged as they flew this way and that. "You want me to take the time to carve a ring, decorate it, and why not, even throw on a magical effect or two. No problem! I'll drop everything just for that."

"Harruq needs a ring to propose to Aurelia with, and you're the best for the job," Tarlak argued.

"Propose!" Brug's eyes bugged out of his head. "This lame-wit porridge-skin muscle-brained dog is going to marry HER? Go find a clump of dirt for your ring and propose to a pig somewhere, that'd be a more appropriate coupling."

Tarlak winced and waited for the half-orc to detonate. He didn't. Instead, Harruq said, "I'll make sure Aurry knows. I'm sure she'll be thankful, if she believes you made it."

"What do you mean by that?" Brug asked. He kicked his grinding wheel. "I can make any damn thing in all Dezrel. You telling me she won't believe I could craft a gorgeous ring?"

"Well, not unless your name was on it or something," he said with a shrug. "Come on, a pudgy-fingered roundbelly like you making rings? I'm surprised Tarlak thought you could."

"My fingers are not pudgy!" he shouted. "And I know what you're doing, making me all upset and proud so I'll prove you wrong. Well, what if I make a ring, give it to her, and you don't ever get to see it at all?"

"Brug," Tarlak said, his patience clearly ended. "Just shut up, do a good job, and accept my thanks, his thanks, and Aurelia's thanks. Understood?"

"Fine. I'll do it, but it won't be my best work or anything. And I'm only doing it for Aurelia. If she's going to be married to that idiot, at least she'll have something pretty to help endure her wedding day."

"Very funny," Harruq said, and then, quieter, "I'm gonna kill him, Tar, I swear, I'm gonna kill him."

"Thank you, Brug," Tarlak said, shoving Harruq out as fast as he could.

The next day, Harruq waited for Haern, running his hand across the dew-covered grass and dozing off. He awoke at the sound of approaching footsteps.

"Please forgive my tardiness," Haern said, pulling back his hood. Youthful joy sparkled in his eyes. "Ready to begin?"

Harruq drew his swords. "So what's your new toy?"

"It will be more fun just showing you," he said. He drew his sabers and tapped them together, a sign to begin. Harruq approached, lacking the reckless hurry he had shown in his earlier sessions. The two circled each other, each waiting for the first move. An obvious feint by the assassin sent Harruq in motion, one sword slashing high, his other kept back to block. Haern rushed forward, his swords high.

And then he was not there.

The half-orc slashed air, staggering forward as the expected block did not come. He whirled about to see Haern directly behind him, sporting a huge grin on his face.

"How in the abyss did you do that?" he asked.

"You mean this?" Haern asked. His entire body grew fuzzy and then he was gone. A finger tapped his shoulder. Harruq jumped. Haern stood behind him once more.

"You've got to be kidding me," he muttered.

"Short range magic," Haern explained, showing him a simple silver band on his right hand. "It places me seven feet directly ahead. It is but a parlor trick, one that you will grow accustomed to. Those who have not fought me before, however-" his grin was dark and mischievous, "-I only need to fool them once."

"Craziness," Harruq said. "Pure craziness. But just straight ahead?"

"Yes. Not up or down or backwards."

"Good. Ready to go?"

The assassin tapped his blades. Harruq charged, and even though he still batted his swords away with ease, Haern was pleased by the increased speed and skill his apprentice showed. A quick parry sent Salvation out of position, and a saber stabbed in to take advantage. Harruq, having purposefully given the opening, twisted to the side, the thrusting cutting wide. He slashed with both swords at the over-extended assassin.

When he struck air, the half-orc turned and swung, expecting his foe to be lunging from behind. Instead, he saw no one.

"Clever," Haern said, poking a saber into his back. "But predictable."

The half-orc turned around, his face the epitome of annoyance.

"You said you could only go forward," he said.

"I did," Haern said, his grin wide. "I never said I couldn't turn around and activate it immediately after."

"That's it. I'm not sparring you anymore."

"Alright, alright. I won't use it for the rest of the day. Happy?"

"Yup." Harruq clanged his blades together, their ring matched by another from Haern's. "Let's rumble."

And rumble they did, and for the first time Harruq scored four kills to Haern's ten. His previous best in a day was two.

A week later, Harruq heard loud grumbling coming up the stairs. He lay on his bed, recuperating after a rough assignment from Tarlak to show a coldhearted merchant that his wealth didn't make him immune to retribution and justice. The half-orc's ribs still hurt from a tumble with the merchant's guards.

"That you, cheerful?" he shouted to the stairs.

"Nah, it's the ogre patrol, here to take you back to your swamp." Brug was in a surlier mood than usual, and he stomped into the room wearing a scrunched frown.

"Ogre's out back on a chain," Harruq said, doing his best not to wince when he sat up.

"Shaddup you. Now take it and be grateful." He thrust out his hand, which held a tiny wooden jewelry box. The half-orc took it, popped open the top, and then felt his jaw drop and his eyes nearly fall from his head. Hand shaking, he took out the ring and held it for a closer look.

Brug had carved the ring from two pieces of interlocking silver, twirling them together in an eternal braid. Three inset diamonds shone across the top. Welded across the braids were the shapes of a scorpion and a spider, each facing the diamonds. Faint writing covered both sides.

"What's it mean?" he asked, turning it around in his hands.

"Mean? What does what mean?" Brug had his arms crossed and his back to the half-orc, although he kept peeking to see his reaction.

"The writing, I can't read it."

"Scorpion side is orcish. Other's is elvish. Aurry's got this thing with spiders, and you got that scorpion on your armor, so it made sense. Both say love. Well, the elvish side says love. Orcs don't really have a word for love, so I had to make it up. Eternal friend was the best I could do. Not too worried. I don't expect any orc to correct my butchering of their guttural pig squealings."

Harruq returned the ring to its box, his chest aflutter. He had a ring. He had everyone waiting for him. The gods help him, he was actually going to propose.

"Make sure you treat her good," Brug said, interrupting his thoughts. "Something like that's sturdy, but if she breaks, good luck ever fixing it."

"Didn't know you cared so much for Aurry," he said. Brug's face flushed.

"I meant the ring," he lied.

"Of course you did. Thank you. I'll never be able to repay you."

"Don't I know it."

He stormed out of the room and down the stairs, mumbling the whole way. Once he was gone, Harruq took out the ring and held it, mesmerized.

"So," he said, twisting the ring in the light. "Now I need stars, flowers." He sighed. "A bath."

Night came too slow for the half-orc. He found a hill close to the tower that still had a patch of late-blooming flowers. He placed a blanket atop it, covered it with petals, and then topped it off with a bottle of strange, bubbly stuff that Tarlak had promised the elf would love. When finished, he paced his bedroom, working over how he would propose.

"How's it going, loverboy?" Tarlak asked, entering his room without knocking. "Been pacing for two hours, I'm guessing. My poor floor."

"Can't figure out what to say," he said. "No clue. I got no clue."

"You'll be fine," Tarlak assured him. "Try to say something romantic, and if you bumble out nonsense, she'll just find it cute. Now come down. Dinnertime."

After dinner, Harruq did his best to nonchalantly invite Aurelia out to stargaze.

"Wanna go outside?" he asked.

"Outside?" she asked back.

"You know. Outside."

"Oh. Outside. Sure thing, cutie."

As the two left the tower, Tarlak shot him a wink. You'll be fine, he mouthed. Harruq rolled his eyes briefly to show his opinion of that assessment.

"Ooooh, someone was prepared tonight," Aurelia said when she spotted the blanket. "Is the grass too scratchy for my poor half-orcie's skin?"

"Just, you know, thought it'd be nice." He wrung his hands, his nervousness nearly immobilizing him. He had fought skilled elves in combat. He had witnessed the dead walk. He had spent countless nights in the presence of the dark prophet Velixar. Cake, all cake compared to this.

"It is nice," she said, sitting in the middle of the blanket. She picked up one of the flowers and inhaled.

"Fall roses," she said. "You're up to something."

"No, I'm not," he said, far too quickly.

"Then what is this for?" she asked, picking up the bottle he had left and tilting it side to side. "Did you think it would be nice, too?"

"Yes, I did. That a crime?"

"I'll have to check. Sit, before I get cold and lonely."

He sat down, wrapped an arm around her shoulder, and stared at the star-filled sky while she nestled her head against his neck.

Ask her now, he thought. *Just get up, ask her, and get this whole thing over with. No, that's too fast. Got to be all romantic, like Haern said. Or was it Tar? Besides, I can't kneel like this. Ah, screw kneeling. Just pop the question, give her the ring, let her say no, and then be done with.*

"You alright?" Aurelia asked, glancing at him. "You look rather troubled."

"Nothing," he said. "Just thinking."

Thinking. Yeah. She knows. She has to know. She's smart, you're dumb, and now there's no point. Do it later. Next week. Next year.

A stubborn part of him reared to life.

You will not *do it later, you spineless chicken. Now get up on one knee and propose you sissy!*

"I am not a sissy," he grumbled without realizing he spoke aloud.

"Course not," Aurelia said, jabbing him. "But what are you being a sissy about?"

Just do it now! a part of him shrieked.

Forget it! Time's wrong! You're not ready! Don't do it! shrieked another.

"Aurry..." He hesitated. She looked at him, her hair fallen to one side of her face. Moonlight bathed her soft cheeks and brown eyes. He brushed her hair behind her pointed ear, his eyes lingering on her full lips. His heart, and resistance, melted away. "Aurry, I got something I want to ask you."

"What is it, Harruq?" She tilted her head to one side. Harruq broke from her grasp and stood.

"Aurry, I think you know, but...do you know how much I love you?"

"Yes," she said. "I do."

He fumbled for the small box in his pocket, his fingers shaking.

"Then, will you do me the honor of, um, being...will you marry me?"

Off came the lid. The ring sparkled silver and white, tiny circles glowing and fading like an open field filled with fireflies. The three diamonds shone a smoky blue, powered by the light of the moon. When Harruq removed the ring and held it out to her, the color trailed behind it, an afterimage of the deep ocean in the night. Her slender fingers accepted the ring.

"Of course I will, Harruq," she said, tears streaming down her cheeks. "Of course I will."

His relief was indescribable, as was the joy that replaced all the fear, doubt, and worry he had built up the past few weeks. She slipped the ring on as Harruq wrapped her in his arms.

Forever, he thought. *I'll remember this forever.*

<hr>

They announced the news as the Eschaton broke their fast. Everyone cheered, including Brug, although his was limited to a few quick claps before diving into his meal with ferocious intensity.

"About time," Tarlak said. "I think I speak for everyone when I say the wait was driving us insane."

"Are you going to have a wedding?" Delysia asked, staring at the ring in awe.

"Are we, Harruq?" the elf asked, jabbing her fiancé with her elbow.

"Um, uh, yes?"

Aurelia smiled. "Good boy."

"You're a lucky man," Haern said, rising from his seat so he could shake both of their hands. "Did he kneel correctly?" he asked Aurelia as he kissed her wrist.

"He didn't kneel at all," she said.

"No kneeling? Egad, you're marrying a dimwit," Brug said. When all eyes turned to him, he pretended to have said nothing. Aurelia, though, did not let him off so easily.

"It was a lovely ring you made me," she said, gliding over to where he sat. "I don't think I can ever thank you enough for helping my dimwit."

"Was nothing," he mumbled.

"It was everything," she corrected. She kissed him on the forehead, drawing forth the red cheeks and ears that sent everyone into laughter.

"You're evil," he said.

"I know. I love it."

"You are one to be envied," Tarlak said to Harruq. He stood and grabbed his glass. "A toast for the groom and bride-to-be?"

Everyone joined in a toast for a long, healthy marriage. Except for Brug. His toast was for a decent meal after the wedding.

◆◆◆

They set a date for two weeks later, neither seeing reason for drawing out the engagement. Harruq had no clue what to do, about the wedding, preparation, dress, or even why they were not already married.

"She's got my ring, and she's wearing it," he argued. "Why aren't we married?"

"Because someone other than you two needs to say you are," Delysia explained. "Ashhur needs to accept the union of your souls."

"Ashhur? When did I start caring what he thought?"

The priestess winked. "Since now. I'll get you ready while Haern helps Aurelia with the wedding."

"Wait, if Haern's doing wedding stuff, what are you helping me with?"

Her evil, mocking laugh was far from comforting.

Minutes later, Harruq sat outside with a towel wrapped around his neck. His hair was dripping wet. Delysia sat behind him, a gleaming pair of scissors in her hand.

"When was the last time you had your hair cut?" she asked.

"Couple months at least. You'd have to ask Aurry."

"No need," she said, snipping away. "We need you dashing for your wedding. Long, homeless half-orc hair is not going to cut it."

"Me? Dashing?" he tried to glance back but she held his head in place. "How the abyss are you going to do that?"

"My life is devoted to miracles," she said.

"Ha, ha, ha," he said.

"Keep still, unless you want to lose an ear," she said.

"Wouldn't that ruin the whole dashing thing?"

A loud snip made him jump. "I'd heal them afterward."

The way she said it, without a hint of jest, terrified him. He sat still as a stone until she removed the towel. Unfinished, though, she examined his face, tapping her lips as she did.

"Do you shave?" she asked.

"Shave? Not really. I don't think elves are known for their facial hair."

She ran a slender finger across the brown stubble covering his jaw line.

"Obviously, it is time you learn." She pulled out a thin razor, which gleamed in the morning light.

"Is this going to hurt?" he asked.

"You've never shaved before, correct?" Delysia asked.

"Nope."

"Then no, it won't hurt," she said as she pressed the razor to the side of his face.

15

His face decorated with thin cuts, he sulked for the next two days, ignoring all pleas from Delysia to prepare for the wedding, caving only after Aurelia threatened to polymorph him into a caterpillar.

"So what do you plan on wearing?" Delysia asked him. They sat in Harruq's room, speaking for the first time since the shaving incident. The half-orc shrugged and gestured to his armor with a careless wave of his hand.

"That's the best I got, really."

The girl frowned at the black armor.

"Hardly elegant. What will you wear underneath?"

"What I'm wearing now."

Delysia's frown sank to a new level of disagreement. He wore brown pants and a weathered white shirt stained a wide variety of colors. The sleeves were frayed around the edges, and in many places the fabric had begun separating.

"Under no circumstances are you wearing that," she declared. "I'll see what we can do about getting you clothes. Put your armor on, and let me see how it looks. Perhaps if we polished it up a bit…"

He strapped on the various pieces of stained leather, muttering to himself. His appearance was one thing, but he spent hours each day making sure his swords sang when swung through the air, and that his armor shone clean and bright whenever worn.

"Look good?" he asked. He flexed his muscles and posed.

"It'll do," she said, pinching her lower lip with her fingers. "Maybe some red underneath, your shirt for instance, and then get you some nice pants. Something is missing, though."

"What?" he asked. Far as he could tell, he had every piece of armor strapped on. Delysia continued staring, deep in thought.

"Of course! Take off your pauldrons."

Harruq shrugged, unlaced his armor and handed them to her.

"Here," he said. "Ruin them and I'll kill you."

"So melodramatic," Delysia said, tucking them underneath her arm. "I'm heading to Veldaren to buy you some clothes." She pulled out a long strand of rope with markings all along the side. "Stand up straight so I can measure you."

The half-orc endured the seemingly hundreds of measurements with calm, quiet grumbling. Finished, Delysia mentally rehearsed numbers, eyeing him with a growing smile.

"What?" he asked.

"You're so cute. You're being domesticated."

She fled down the stairs, a barrage of pillows, bed sheets, and other non-lethal objects hurling after her.

Two days later, Delysia barged into Harruq's room with an armful of clothes.

"I need a door," he said.

"Don't worry, I won't peek," she said, tossing him pants and a shirt. She put a bundle of black cloth on his bed, not yet unfurling it. "Now put those on."

He did as commanded after the priestess turned around. She knew when to look by the half-orc's complaints.

"You must be pulling jokes, missy."

She beamed when she saw him. The black pants were a bit too loose, but she could fix that, and she was still proud of the exquisite stitching along their sides, so small and tight as to be invisible. The shirt was a bright red, with the sleeves and chest lined with tiny silver buttons.

"I look like an idiot," he said.

"You haven't finished yet," she said, rushing over to him. She buttoned his wrists and then his chest, all the while telling him how dashing he looked.

"You've lost your mind," was his response. "This is not me. What are these pants made of? They itch like a whore's..."

He wisely didn't finish the rest.

"Sorry," he said instead.

"Just put your armor on," she said, a bit of her good mood dampened. Harruq felt bad, so he buckled his armor without complaint. It gleamed brighter than usual, the result of extra attention by a half-orc determined to show Delysia he was trying.

"Where's my shoulders?" Harruq asked when he was almost done.

"Right here," she said, grabbing the wad of black cloth and unfurling it. The half-orc coughed at the sight. Attached by silver clasps to his shoulder guards was a long, flowing black cloak. She turned it back and forth for him to see. Across the back of the cape was a giant red scorpion, identical to the one across the chest of his armor.

"I'm wearing a cape?" he asked, staring as if it were dangerous. "Surely you're joking."

"I'm hurt," she said, her lower lip pouting. "I attached it myself, and stitched on the scorpion. Trust me, you'll love it. Now put these on."

She handed them to him, which he took without a word. He slid the shoulders on. The cloak billowed down his back and teased his elbows. He slid his arms across the fabric, pondering. Suddenly, he had a desperate urge to see himself.

"One sec, going to go look at myself in a stream," he said, marching to the door, a childlike thrill in his heart at the feel of his cloak trailing behind him.

"No need, I have a mirror right here." She pulled a small square object from her pocket and gave it to him. Harruq took it and held it as far back as he could.

"Can't really see too much," he said.

"Grow and show," Delysia said to the object. It squirmed in his hand. Startled, he let go. Instead of falling, it floated, grew many times its original size, and then hung suspended in air. Harruq grinned at the sight of himself in the floating mirror. His well-oiled armor perfectly matched the red and black clothes peeking out underneath, and as much as he hated to admit it, the cloak made him look a tiny bit dashing, like some noble rogue from fireside stories. Coupled with his long, well-cut hair, he had to admit. He looked good.

"You look like a prince," Delysia said, smiling.

"Prince of orcs, maybe," he said, twisting side to side. "Not sure who around here would follow a half-blood like me."

"Oh please. You look spectacular. I'll tell Aurelia to come up and see you."

"No!" he said. "Let her wait until the wedding."

The priestess laughed.

"Very well, then. That's not too far away. I can wait to see her reaction until then." She hugged him and gave him a quick peck on the cheek. "You're too fun, Har. Too bad the elf got you first."

A snap of her fingers returned the mirror to its original size. She caught it on its fall, slipped it into her pocket, and hugged him once more.

"Don't worry about the clothes," she said. "I'll have Tarlak pay for them from your wages."

"Out of my, hey, I thought these were gifts?"

Delysia stopped at the top of the stairs and glanced back. "That was silly. We're not that nice around here."

"Should have known," he grumbled. His grumpiness could not last, though, not when he could glance down at his enchanted armor, ancient swords, and swirling cloak, and know he was a truly awesome sight.

Even though winter neared, the weather was warm enough that a few blankets and each other's warmth kept the outside bearable. Together, the soon-to-be wed couple nuzzled and held each other close.

"I've solved our dilemma," Aurelia told him underneath the blanket of stars.

"What's that?"

"Your brother. Instead of scrying for him, I'll send him a message."

"How's that?"

She wiggled her fingers in loopy and exaggerated movements.

"There's power in these here fingers. Tarlak taught me a spell that sends my voice to anyone in Dezrel. Whatever I say, he will hear, given a few seconds or so."

Harruq grinned.

"Some neat stuff you mages know. All I do is swing a sword."

Aurelia nestled her head against his chest and purred.

"Yes, but you do it well."

"I guess that's all that matters, eh?"

"You bet. Now hug me."

He did as he was told.

It was during lunch that Harruq thought to ask Aurelia who she invited to their wedding.

"Just Dieredon and Felewen."

He hacked, and he did his best not to choke on his food.

"You want Dieredon to come? Are you insane?"

The elf tossed her hair over one shoulder.

"Possibly. I am marrying you, after all. Why, do you not want him here?"

"I don't know, wouldn't him wanting to kill me make things a little tense?"

She took her fork into her hand and pretended it was a bow. Imaginary arrows flew one after another across the table, each one accompanied by the joyful sound of her laughter.

"Har har har," he said. "Not funny."

"Of course it is," Tarlak said, plopping down in a seat next to Aurelia. "What are we laughing at?"

"Harruq's being a baby," Aurelia explained, popping a cherry tomato in her mouth.

"Am not!"

"Are too!" the wizard shouted. He turned back to the elf. "About what, anyway?"

"I invited Dieredon to our wedding. Turns out he disapproves."

The half-orc threw his hands up in surrender.

"Could make the part where we ask if anyone has objections interesting," Tarlak mused.

"What?" the half-orc asked, very much worried.

"Nothing, dear," Aurelia said, elbowing Tarlak in the side. "I'll tell him to behave, and besides, seeing you do something civil for once might do him good."

"Yes, the domesticated orc," the wizard chipped in. Harruq's glare was full of death promises.

"I'll have to remember that," she said, smiling at her fiancé. "You're my domesticated little orciepoo."

"Why do I put up with all of you?" he asked, pushing away his plate and standing.

"Because you love us," Tarlak said. "Well, you love me, anyway. Not sure about the lovely lady here."

"Now now, Tar, I don't need any competition for my Harruq's love."

"You guys are so…wrong," the half-orc said, storming out the door. When he left, their laughter followed him down the hall.

"Should I worry about you stealing my love from me?" she asked him.

"Not really," Tarlak replied, his grin spreading ear to ear. "His butt's cute, but not that cute."

They both lost control, laughing only harder when Haern came down the stairs with a most perplexed look on his face.

They would hold the wedding outside, cradled against the forest. Tarlak purchased a few extra chairs for seating, all at Harruq's expense, of course. What Aurelia would wear they kept hidden from Harruq, just as his cape and clothing were hidden from her. No word had come from Qurrah and Tessanna, something that gnawed at Harruq even more with his wedding so close.

Felewen arrived three days before the ceremony. Her reception of Harruq was quiet but warm. The two elves talked for hours in Aurelia's room. Many times Harruq stopped by the door, wishing to enter. Common decency held him at bay. Dieredon's arrival the day after was just as quiet, but far less warm.

"Greetings, orc," was all he said to Harruq. To the rest of the tower, he was charming, witty, and graceful. Time found ways to crawl ever slower, and come the eve of his wedding, Qurrah was yet to show.

"Think he'll be here?" he asked his fiancé, who was wrapped inside his arms, their backs pressed against a tree whose bark was smooth as pressed grass.

"You know him better than I. What do you think?"

He wrapped a blanket around them both, shivering in the cool air.

"I don't know anymore. I think that is why I worry."

Leaves rustled in the nearby forest as a soft wind blew through them. Aurelia kissed his cheek, and then settled right back down against his chest.

"He'll come. There's good in him somewhere, and I think he's fond of me."

"Hope you're right."

"So do I," she whispered.

The cold sensation of air against his legs pulled Harruq from his slumber. He groaned, tucking his knees to his chest for warmth. He lay there, halfway between sleep and consciousness, until the gnawing sensation of something missing forced his mind awake. The slender form in his arms was gone. Harruq sat up and looked around. Dew soaked his hands, back, and wetted the blanket that covered his waist. The sun was low on the horizon.

The sound of rustling grass alerted him to someone's arrival.

"Aurry?" he asked, squinting against the light.

"Have they evicted you on your final night of freedom?" asked a quiet, raspy voice. Harruq beamed as his adjusting eyes spotted a frail form dressed in black robes.

"Brother!"

He staggered to his feet and wrapped him in a hug. Qurrah chuckled, offering a meager squeeze back. "I didn't think you were coming," Harruq said, grinning at him. "Why'd you take so long?"

"The elf's spell told us to arrive by this morning. As far as I know, I am not late."

"Did you bring the girl?"

Qurrah chuckled. "She did not wish to attend."

Harruq was unsure of what to say that would not offend his brother, so he let the subject drop.

"Ah well. Come on, let's get something to eat."

Qurrah's eyes glinted at the thought of food.

"That sounds wonderful," he said.

Qurrah's entrance to the tower was a mixed thing. The members of the Eschaton smiled and welcomed him, including Tarlak, but Felewen and Dieredon both lurched to their feet.

"I killed you," Dieredon said, an arrow already drawn and ready. Qurrah pulled back his hood to reveal his face, and with his steeled eyes, he stared Dieredon down.

"I know, for I was there," the half-orc said.

A deathly silence filled the room as the two faced off, the arrow not wavering even though the string was pulled fully taut.

"I will not have bloodshed in my tower," Tarlak said.

"It is strange company you keep," Dieredon said to the wizard, his body not moving. "Why should this one be left to live?"

"Do you wish me dead?" Qurrah asked, a sneer spread across his face. "I have seen my master murdered at your hands. I know my doom. The question is not whether I wish to live, but whether you wish me to die. You have released my brother from your condemnation. What have I done that he has not?"

"His eyes held regret when I was ready to take his life," Dieredon said. "Yours openly invite it."

"Regret is naught but fear in a different dress," Qurrah said. "I do not know fear."

"Enough!" Tarlak shouted. "Dieredon, put down your bow. Qurrah, outside, now. We have to talk."

"No," Qurrah said. "This elf thinks he can threaten any without worry. The supreme executioner, but he is wrong. There are those better than you, Dieredon. Faster. Wiser. Smarter. You are known only because you have murdered more than they. What have I done that you have not?"

Dieredon's eyes narrowed. Tarlak grabbed his bag of spell components, expecting an arrow to let fly at any moment.

"You seek glory in death," Dieredon said.

"Do not lie to me," Qurrah said. "I am not alone in feeling the thrill of the kill. I fight with fire and darkness, you with steel and arrow. How are we different?"

"I value life!"

The whip slipped down Qurrah's shoulder into his hand. Dieredon's look was simple: try it and die.

Before he could, Aurelia stepped between them, her face calm as stone.

"Put down the bow," she said. "If you harm him, *I* will kill you. Fail or not, I doubt you will sleep well with *my* death on your hands."

The string relaxed, and the arrow slipped back into its quiver. Dieredon slung the bow across his back and gestured to the door.

"I wish to leave. Please do not block my way."

Qurrah and Harruq stepped aside, giving him more than a wide berth. The elf glared at both as he left the tower. The door slammed shut, vicious enough that wood splintered.

"My apologies," Tarlak said, greeting the half-orc with a handshake. "It seems you have a way with people."

"I am used to that," Qurrah said. "I will do my best to not agitate him further."

"The fewer headaches the better," the wizard agreed. "Besides, this is a happy day. A wedding day! Speaking of such, it is time I started preparing. Forgive me."

He dashed up the stairs, a mischievous grin on his face.

Delysia gave Harruq a kiss on the cheek.

"We'll start getting you prepared after lunch," she told him before following Tarlak. Haern, who had remained calm and seated throughout the whole affair, clapped. When the two brothers glanced over, he grinned at them.

"You must be insane," he said. "Few have stared down Dieredon and lived."

"Not many have an elf named Aurelia to bail them out," Aurelia said, kissing Harruq. "Time to put on my dress. You all behave."

She turned to Felewen. "Will you help me with my dress?"

"With pleasure," Felewen said. Arm and arm, they hurried up the stairs. When they were gone, Haern stood and crossed his arms.

"Awhile ago, we made a wager," he said. "He who killed the most thieves would take her hand in marriage."

"If I remember correctly, I had thirty-three," Harruq said, bumping the number up by a couple from what he honestly remembered.

"And I had thirty-seven," Haern said. "It appears we have a problem. You would not go back against your vow, would you?"

"You are such an idiot, brother," Qurrah said, fighting back a smile.

"Wait a minute, you can't marry her just because you got more kills than me!"

Tarlak came back down the stairs, two different over-extravagant hats in his hands.

"More kills when?" he asked.

"On the night Aurelia and your sister were injured," Haern explained.

"What did you two finish at?"

"Haern says he got thirty-seven, while I only have thirty-three," Harruq said.

"Really? I finished with thirty-nine. Who do I get to marry?"

Qurrah laughed at the look on his brother's face.

"Delysia," Haern said, not batting an eye. "Congratulations. When will the wedding be?"

Tarlak shook his head, taking the two hats back upstairs with him. "You all have problems."

Qurrah laughed all the harder. Haern joined him, slapping Harruq across the back.

"The elf is all yours, half-orc. My sincerest congratulations."

Haern left to speak with Dieredon. With Brug still upstairs snoring, that left just the two brothers standing in the entranceway. The mood fell silent, but it was not an awkward silence. The two shared it as brothers do, glad with their company, and knowing much of what the other thought.

"Never thought it'd come to this, eh?" Harruq finally asked.

"Never dared hope for it," Qurrah said. He smiled at his brother. "Your mother would be so disappointed by you, Karak rest her orcish soul."

"Amen to that," he laughed, the tension of the past moments melting away into joy.

16

Outside, the chairs were set up, a simple but elegant carpet unrolled between the rows, and all was ready to begin. Only Aurelia, Harruq, and Delysia remained in the tower. The others mingled, ate a bit of food, and shared their stories. Qurrah and Dieredon did their best to remain at opposite sides of the gathering at all times. Tarlak was grateful for small favors.

Harruq was the first to arrive. His armor was polished, his clothes were clean and crisp, and his cloak flapped behind him in the chill wind. He joined his brother's side and quietly accepted the compliments on his attire. Delysia followed, gushing about how beautiful Aurelia looked.

"You remember, this was all my doing," she told the groom, winking at him. She stood at the end of the carpet, beaming at everyone. She wore her white robes of Ashhur. Her braided hair hung down her back, shimmering with gold lace. She had a youthful beauty, and many eyes lingered on her, including Harruq's. Then Aurelia made her debut, and his eyes were only for her.

Around the corner she came, seeming to float across the grass. Rosemary blooms encircled her hair, forming a crown. Her hair hung loose behind her back, though a few braided strands ran down the sides of her face. Earrings of cut sapphires dangled from golden chains in her ears. Her eyes sparkled, highlighted with hints of blue powder.

A new pendant hung from her neck, thin silver threads looping through its clasp. From one direction, it seemed to be of a spider, yet from the other side, the playful shape of a kitten. The twin illusion was marvelous. The pendant rested just above the swell of her breasts, which were on prominent display due to the low cut of her dress. The dress itself was simple, white, and elegant. She wore a single sash, of a sky color, and no shoes.

"How do I look?" she asked. Harruq tried to answer, but his jaw refused to budge from its half-open position. Seeing this, Aurelia lifted her arms above her head and twirled.

The Cost of Betrayal

"Did I ever tell you how much I envied you?" Tarlak whispered to the half-orc.

"Touch her and die," Harruq whispered back.

"Harruq, Aurelia, are you ready to begin?" Delysia asked.

"Are you?" the elf asked Harruq.

"Sure," he said, his smile huge and contagious.

"Good." She pecked him on the cheek. "Let's get this over with."

Although Aurelia had been in charge of the wedding, she did not wish it to be traditional elvish. The fact that a priest of Ashhur, and not Celestia, presided over it spoke much to this fact. In truth, they retained only one element of an elvish wedding, and that was the opening song.

"The union of souls should always be a beautiful thing," Delysia said to all in attendance. The girl was gone, replaced by a proud and solemn woman. "So let this ceremony begin with a beauty to both the eye and the ear. Felewen Queneya, let us hear your song."

The elf stood, smoothed out the soft blue-white dress she wore, and began to sing. No music accompanied her. No hands clapped along. The only instrument was her powerful voice. Its smooth melody was like the waters of the ocean, rolling from her tongue with a sound that was constant and beautiful. Three hundred years before, she had been taught that song for the funeral of her youngest sibling. Those who heard the words and understood them nodded in understanding and approval. Those who did not, such as Harruq, did not need translation. Their hearts understood.

When Felewen's song ended, followed by a respectful silence. All gathered there looked upon Delysia as she sliced through the quiet with her voice, carrying with it power and authority.

"Harruq Tun. A mixed blood, carrying the race of Celestia's condemned, as well as the blood of her chosen. You have the potential to be everything we fear, and everything we may hope to be. Whatever path you walked before coming to us matters not. The path ahead, I tell all of you, is what matters, and to marry out of love, and to give devotion to a single soul, shows what path you have chosen. Harruq Tun, I offer you my blessing."

She smiled and bowed to him. Harruq shifted uncomfortably, glancing more than once at Aurelia. The elf merely smiled and squeezed his hand.

"Aurelia Thyne. Many would give all their worldly possessions for such beauty as yours. Many more would sacrifice for the powerful magic you wield. Well known is the elven hatred of the orcish. Every man and woman on Dezrel walks with the taint of sin, and the failure of mortality. Few wear the proof of this upon their face, their skin, and within their bloodline. Fewer still would see the gem beneath. While all here have come to see the worth of Harruq Tun, you have come to love him as only a soul mate can. Aurelia Thyne, I offer you my blessing."

The elf smiled as Delysia bowed to her.

"You make me sound too good to be true," she whispered.

The priestess smiled. "Lovers, your rings."

Harruq pulled out a small black box from his pocket, while Aurelia levitated a similar box from atop a nearby chair. As one, they opened them. Aurelia's held a simple silver band. Harruq's, which he had not opened under Brug's strict orders, held a much greater surprise. Light burst from the opened box, a soft eruption of colors. Seven orbs of light rose into the sky, sparkling in lavender, blue, gold, green, orange, white, and red. The orbs danced above their heads before taking orbit and bathing them in the colors of the rainbow.

"You outdid yourself there," Tarlak whispered to Brug, who sat with arms crossed next to him.

"Cheap trick's all it is," he whispered back. Still, his face held a smug satisfaction as he watched the orbs revolve in the sky, bathing them in waves of light.

Delysia gave no reaction to the orbs, even though she had been given no warning of the display.

"Harruq Tun. The ring you hold represents your heart, which you give to your lover for eternal safekeeping. Do you give such sacredness freely?"

"I do," he said.

"And Aurelia Thyne, do you willingly accept his love into safekeeping, for as long as you draw breath?"

"I do," she said. At those words, Harruq felt a soaring in his heart.

"Give your ring to her, Harruq Tun, and know Ashhur watches and blesses your love with his."

He took her outstretched hand and slid the ring on her finger. Whirlwinds of feathers tore through his chest. His head felt full of air.

"Aurelia Thyne. The ring you hold represents your heart, which you give to your lover for eternal safekeeping. Do you give such sacredness freely?"

"I do," she said.

"And Harruq Tun, do you willingly accept her love into safekeeping, for as long as you draw breath?"

"I do," he said.

"Give your ring to him, Aurelia Thyne, and know Ashhur blesses your love."

Harruq stared at the ring sliding across his finger, a foreign thing, one he never thought to possess. When finished, the two interlocked their hands and stared into each other's eyes as Delysia finished the ceremony.

"Each of you holds the love of the other in your heart. Keep it sacred, and keep it close. May Ashhur forever bless and protect these two lovers before us all. Aurelia, you now are a member of the Tun family. Harruq, you may kiss your wife."

To a round of applause, Harruq took the elf in his arms, dipped her to one side, and kissed her.

The feast was beyond anything the wizard had ever prepared. Roast quail, venison, boar, and mutton covered a single table, all seasoned with basil, sage, and rosemary. Another table was piled high with cheese, fish, ale-flavored bread, wild fruits, and assorted beers, meads, and wines. Covering all was a blended array of spices, some rare, some common. Each bite contained a hint of cloves, cinnamon, pepper, ginger, or nutmeg.

When the feast was done, and the toasts were over, the guests said their goodbyes.

"Come visit me some time," Felewen said, hugging both. "Make sure you let me know when the babies are coming."

"Ha, ha, ha," Harruq said, grinning at her. Dieredon left with her, bowing to Aurelia and offering only a quick word to Harruq.

"Break her heart, I break you," he said.

"Will remember," the half-orc replied. The two mounted Sonowin and soared off into the southern sky.

Qurrah was last, his mood strangely quiet and somber.

"You will come and visit again, won't you?" Aurelia asked, offering him a curtsey. The half-orc bowed.

"I will do my very best. To both of you, I offer my most sincere congratulations."

"You stay safe, brother," Harruq said, hugging him. Qurrah chuckled.

"Of course. You as well."

Another bow, and then he ventured into the forest, vanishing amid the trees. Harruq resumed eating a bit more, worried by that last troubled look on his brother's face.

"What are your plans for tonight?" Tarlak asked, sliding beside Harruq while Delysia distracted Aurelia.

"What you mean?"

"You know what I mean," the wizard said, winking. "You do know what I mean, right?"

Harruq flushed. "Of course I do. Just figured, you know, upstairs in my room and all."

Tarlak laughed and clapped his hands.

"As a personal favor, I am paying for all of us to stay in a nice inn in Veldaren. The tower is yours for the night. Enjoy."

Harruq beamed at the wizard. "I owe you a lot, Tar."

"And you'll pay me back one day. I have faith in you. But for now, the night is yours. It is time for us to go!"

He clapped three times, and the rest of the Eschaton heard the signal and obeyed. They politely bowed and wished them well, entered the tower, returned with travel packs of clothes, and gathered at the door. Before they left, Haern trudged over to Harruq and removed his hood.

"Just so you know, I am still expecting a sparring match tomorrow morning," he told him. "Don't overdo it."

"I'll hold him in check," Aurelia said, kissing the man on the cheek. "Now run off. Time for us to have a little quiet time, right Harruq?"

"Right, Aurelia Tun," he said, a dumb grin on his face. "Aurelia Tun. Sounds so funny."

The gang bounded off southeast. Harruq and Aurelia waved, standing in front of the door with arms intertwined.

"Come on upstairs, love," Aurelia said when they were gone. She kissed his cheek. Hand in hand, they hurried upstairs. When they arrived, they found flowers piled across their beds, a dizzying array of roses, tulips, and daisies, somehow alive even though winter was fast approaching.

"I feel Tarlak's hand in this," Aurelia said, picking up one and gently pressing it against her lips.

"Silly wizard, why would I…"

He stopped as he watched Aurelia slowly drift the soft petals down her neck, lower, lower, lower.

"Gods bless you, Tar," Harruq said.

<hr>

The moon was a curved sliver of light illuminating a cold forest when Qurrah returned home. Tessanna sat before a fire she had built in the clearing before the front door.

"How was it?" she asked, the red flame flickering off the black orbs that were her eyes.

"Bearable," he said, sitting opposite of her. "They love each other so very much."

"Some people are lucky enough to find and marry their love." She grabbed a long stick and tossed it upon the fire. "And others never do. And then there is me."

"You're no different," Qurrah said. His voice was vile water spewing from his heart. "Are you incapable of love?"

Tears ran down the sides of her face. Even so, her words carried no hint of the emotion she clearly felt.

"I am capable of loving a man," she said. "And men are capable of loving me. But death comes for all I love and claims them like a bitter thief."

Qurrah cast down his eyes, ashamed of his outburst. "Ignore my words. I have lost my brother."

Tessanna curled her legs against her chest and peered at him over her knees.

"Do you wish to have me? It might help."

"No," Qurrah said. "Let my brother do the taking tonight." She stood to return to the house, but the half-orc stopped her. "Do not go," he said. "Stay with me."

The girl smiled, beautiful amid the dreary night. Whether the smile was honest or false, Qurrah was too tired to care.

"I will be inside my home," she said. "Our home. Do not worry about what your brother does this night."

She entered the cabin, shutting the door softly behind her. He stared after her, the flickering fire popping and cracking. His mind ravaged itself. How dare he fall prey to weakness. His brother's actions and choices were of no concern to him. If he found happiness in forsaking his blood and marrying an elf, then so be it. Philosophy was for the rich and the bored. Feeling was all that mattered. His brother felt happiness with her. He would feel happiness with Tessanna.

He stood and kicked out the fire. Silent as a thief, he opened the door to their home. Upon the bed she waited, her clothes cast aside, as if she had known all along.

"It is what we both want," she said. "I care of nothing else."

"I know," he said. He went to her.

※

That night, both brothers slept with fire. One was bright and roaring, a controllable inferno that surrounded and engulfed. One was cold, a blue flame, burning without heat, turning to ash without the warmth of consumption. Blanketed by stars and separated by a great distance, both found peace in the fire.

Of the two, only one created life.

17

Qurrah nestled in the old chair, a fire roaring at his side. In his lap was the book of Pelarak. Three times he had read it, analyzing every word. He was halfway through his fourth read, and still he marveled at the knowledge the cleric of Karak possessed. Outside, a heavy rain fell. Tessanna looked up from the bed, her small head poking out from a multi-blanket cocoon.

"Shouldn't you go?" she asked.

The half-orc flipped a page, pretending not to hear.

"You've been quiet," she continued. "Impatient. Terrible in bed, even."

He flipped another page.

"I will visit their child in time."

She shrunk her head further into the blankets.

"Will you start taking people again?" she asked. "Try making them like me?"

Qurrah chuckled. He had decided over the winter that he preferred the child-like mentality of Tessanna best. The sarcastic, cynical form was next. Her angry side, her fearful side, and her apathetic side, well...

He planned to get rid of those.

"Yes. We have let enough time pass to safely take another. I have not forgotten my promise. In time, your mind will be healed."

"What about until then?"

He glanced over. "Until then, we will make do with what we have."

They did not speak the rest of the day. Silence was not a thing either feared, nor did it imply anger or frustration. They could each dwell within the confines of their minds. Silence. It was a blessed thing.

Her shrieking wail was horrible to hear. Harruq couldn't imagine the pain causing it. Inside their room, Delysia attended to

Aurelia, doing things he preferred to stay in the dark about. He crossed his arms, uncrossed them, paced back and forth, and muttered incoherently. Childbirth. Such a stressful thing.

"What are you doing out here?" Tarlak asked as he came up the stairs.

"Kicked me out," Harruq said.

"Making too much of a fuss, eh? Well, brawny men with more muscles than brains usually don't mix too well with such delicate matters. I'll see how things are going."

"Don't go in there," the half-orc said. Tarlak waved him off, opened the door, and slipped inside. Harruq counted to three on his fingers, timing it perfectly.

"GET OUT OF HERE, NOW!"

The door flung open, and out fled the wizard as if seven fire-breathing dragons chased him for supper. He slammed the door shut, straightened his hat, and then fixed his robes.

"Kicked me out," Tarlak said. Harruq rolled his eyes.

"Don't worry ol' buddy," the wizard said, clapping him on the shoulder. "I'm sure Del has everything under control. Your child will be fine."

Another cry came from inside, sharp and focused. Both shuddered.

"Something tells me we got the easy part," Harruq said.

"Amen to that."

Another cry came, soft and shrill. Both stood alert at the sound. No woman made that sound. It was the cry of a babe.

"Aurry!" Harruq shouted, yanking open the door. His heart froze, and all things of the world fell away to a single image. On a bed, her hair frazzled and her face soaked with sweat, was the most beautiful woman Harruq had ever seen. In her arms, wrapped with towels, was a newborn child. His mind fought to grasp what he witnessed. His wife was holding his child. His child.

"I'm a father," he said breathlessly.

"It's a healthy girl," Delysia said, towels in her hands covered with blood, fluid, and sweat. "What shall you name her?"

Harruq slid beside his wife, his eyes mesmerized by the scrunched red face, swollen shut eyes, and tiny mouth of his crying child.

"As we agreed. It's a girl, so you get to name her, Aurry."

"Aullienna," Aurelia said.

"Aullienna," Harruq repeated. "Gonna take some time before I can say that right."

"You'll have plenty of time to learn it," Tarlak said, smiling beside the door. "Think of how many times you'll be shouting it. 'Aullienna, stay away from my things. Aullienna, put down my sword. Aullienna, stop beating up Brug.'"

Chubby hands reached from behind the door, and then the wizard was gone. A few seconds later, Brug ducked his head inside.

"Good to hear you're alright, Aurelia," he said. He winked at the little babe. "Hope it's a long time before you try beating up little old me, Aullienna."

Aurelia smiled, too tired to laugh.

"I need to nurse her," she told her husband. Harruq nodded, realized what that meant, and then nodded again.

"Everybody out," he said. "Private time."

As they were leaving, Haern slipped inside. He wore no hood or cloak, only a simple pair of pants and a shirt.

"I come to pay my respects to the child," Haern said.

"Respects paid. My baby's hungry, so time to go."

"Hush, Harruq," Aurelia said, her voice distant and drowsy. She stroked a hand across Aullienna's soft forehead. "We are grateful, Haern."

The assassin opened his hand and held it out. Flat across his palm was a long green ribbon with gold writing.

"Tie it to her crib, for now," Haern explained. "And when she is older, may it adorn her hair."

"Pretty," Harruq said, not understanding the true importance. Aurelia, however, read the writing and smiled.

"It is a noble gift, and a thoughtful one. We thank you."

"What's it say?" the half-orc asked after Haern bowed and left.

"*May Ashhur's eyes forever watch over this child, even as we of the Eschaton do the same.* Such a token is given by men who pledge armies to ensure the safety of a child." The elf smiled at her daughter. "I'll take Haern over an army any day."

"Can't argue with you there."

◈

Down on the first floor, Harruq found Tarlak pacing.

"Did my brother...?" Harruq asked.

"No sign," the wizard said. "I'm sure he is very happy for you."

"I'm sure he is too," he said, none too convincingly. He grinned at Tarlak. "You realize I'm a dad now? A dad! I'm a father!"

"Aye, that you are," the wizard said. "Scary as the abyss, isn't it?"

"Scarier," Harruq said. "Far, far scarier."

They moved Aurelia and Aullienna into the Tun's room later that night. Harruq carried the little babe in his arms, beaming as if his face had been frozen that way.

"Welcome to your home," he said, opening their new door slowly, with an unrehearsed theatrical flair. Aurelia kissed his cheek as she carefully came in behind him.

Due to carefully cast spells, the room was transformed into something more akin to a forest. Illusions enchanted the walls so they appeared, in touch, taste, and smell, to be covered with ivy. The floor was a carpet of smooth, short grass. As for a ceiling, there was none, not to the naked eye. Puffy clouds floated above on a gentle breeze. A single tree marked the center of the room, winding upward with branches positioned as steps. At the top was a cradle, thick and sturdy. Near the tree was a bed, covered with a great blanket of flowers. The entire room felt open, natural, and above all else, like a private home.

"Kind of bright for nighttime, don't you think?" Harruq asked. In answer, Aurelia snapped her fingers twice. The blue sky turned purple, and a sparkling field of stars covered the ceiling. The soft breeze vanished, and in its absence came the constant drone of cicadas. Aullienna was fast asleep, so she failed to show her amazement. The half-orc grumbled.

"One day she'll be old enough to know how neat that is," he said.

"Shush, you'll wake her." Aurelia took her from his arms and glided up the tree-steps to the crib. She laid her inside and stroked her face.

"I never expected to have a child," she said, cooing as she felt Harruq's arms wrap around her. "Never expected any of this."

"If you expected to marry a bumbling half-orc when you were a youngling, then something was wrong with you."

Aurelia reached back, put a hand around her husband's head, and pulled him close so she could kiss him.

"She looks elven," she said when their lips parted. "Nearly full blood, even."

"Guess we can be thankful for that," he said. "It'll help her be accepted. No shame in my orc blood, I just know her life will be easier without it showing."

"It does show," Aurelia said. "She's bigger than most elven babes. She'll grow tall, like her father."

"Is she going to wield swords and beat people senseless, too?" he asked.

"Only if daddy wants to get his cute ass fireballed," Aurelia said with a wink.

Harruq kissed from her neck to her ear.

"A tradeoff I'll take any day," he whispered. "Just to watch it drive you crazy."

"Oh, but I am already there," she said, running a hand down his face. "I married you, didn't I?"

"That's right, you did. Why'd you do that?"

"Because I love you, dimwit."

He flipped her around and kissed her lips. "Don't you forget it, either."

"Never," she said, smiling up at him. "Never in a million years."

After waking three times to attend the crying child, Aurelia's eyes didn't even flutter when the half-orc slid off the bed. He crossed his arms as if cold, although a soft, phantasmal breeze blew from the walls, warm and comforting. Up the stairs he climbed, his steps surprisingly silent for his bulk. Aullienna was sound asleep on her back, her fat face turned away from him. He reached out to touch her. Halfway there, his hand froze, unable to move any closer.

"How many did we kill, Qurrah?" he asked, a lump in his throat. His voice was a raspy whisper among the cicadas. "You were wrong. This life is not suffering. We were wrong, brother. We did…"

His finger brushed her face. He recoiled as if touched by fire. His foot slipped on a stair. He went down, slamming his knee on the top step. A sharp intake of air marked his pain. Kneeling there, clutching his leg, he fought back the tears. The girl. He had seen the girl, the one clutching her stuffed doll in the village of Cornrows. Like an animal, he had butchered her, driven his blade through that pretty face and those blue eyes.

You're an orc, aren't you?

"We were wrong," he whispered. He smashed his fist against his thigh. He remembered the mother who had held the child in her arms when he took their lives. All those questions he had wondered, they came thrashing back, for now he had the answers. They were a vile blade in his gut. Unable to hold back the tears, he sobbed there, a broken man.

When hands touched his back, he turned and snarled like the beast he felt he was. Before the sight of his wife, tired and worried, he could not remain such a thing. When she extended her arms, he accepted. In her embrace, he cried until his sorrow subdued.

"All will be fine," she whispered to him.

"You don't know," he said to her.

"That changes nothing," she said, kissing his forehead. "Come to bed. Whatever it is, it can wait until morning. I only have an hour before she needs fed, and I would like to sleep as much as I can until then."

He nodded, stood erect, and did his best to smile.

"Alright, let's go to bed."

Harruq slept with his back pressed against her stomach, her arms wrapped under his arms and around his chest. The steady feel of her breath against his neck calmed many of his thoughts. Sleep came, coupled with nightmares. When light flooded the room from an illusionary sun rising at dawn, his eyes were bloodshot and heavy.

"Morning, love," Aurelia said, kissing his back. "You should go. Haern will be waiting for you."

Without a word he stood, dressed in his armor, and left to spar.

"The baby wake you often?" Haern asked, seeing the red in the half-orc's eyes.

"Nah. Just didn't sleep well." Harruq drew his blades. "Let's get this over with."

Instead of attacking, the assassin frowned. "This is hardly the competitive spirit I prefer. Is something amiss?"

"Nothing is amiss. I just need some damn sleep, now either swing a blade at me or let me go back to bed."

The half-orc tensed, ready for a lunge, but instead Haern sheathed his swords.

"Get out of here."

Harruq stepped out of his combat stance. "What?"

"You heard me. Get out of here. My training is a privilege. My apologies for your lack of sleep, but you and I have suffered far worse. It is your attitude that has soured."

"Nothing's wrong with my attitude."

Haern crossed his arms. "You were a beacon of happiness yesterday. Do you fear being a father?"

"I don't fear anything," Harruq snarled. "Say stuff like that again, and you'll find yourself fighting, and the cuts won't be fake."

Haern turned his back to the half-orc and walked back to the tower. Harruq watched him go, emotions swirling in his stomach, until he violently sheathed his blades and stormed off into the woods.

Aurelia found him several hours later, sitting beside a stream that ran through the forest not too far from the tower. Unknown to Harruq, it was the same spot Qurrah and Tessanna had made love before Karnryk and his thugs had arrived. Sitting on a log, he stared at the moving stream, tossing in stone after stone.

"What is wrong?" Aurelia asked as she neared. "Haern told me about this morning."

"I don't deserve her," he said.

"And you don't deserve me either, but you have both."

Harruq glanced back at her, chuckled, and then threw another stone.

"Cute. But you're right. I don't. I've done... Aurry, she's just a child. A helpless child." He dropped a handful of rocks and ran his fingers through his hair. "Just helpless," he mumbled.

"Harruq, I don't understand. Please, tell me what's wrong. You're my husband. Nothing you have done will change how I feel about you."

"I'm sure you think that," he said. "You might even believe it. But you're wrong."

Aurelia knelt in front of him, her eyes strong as iron. She put her hands on his face and forced him to look at her.

"Don't do this tortured-hero nonsense. And don't you dare assume you know how I feel about you. I love you, unquestioningly and unconditionally. You cheapen us both when you spew such filth. Now tell me what damns you, so we may be damned together."

"I killed the children!" he screamed, lunging to his feet. Aurelia flinched at his words, but did not falter her gaze.

"What children?" she asked.

"Woodhaven, Aurry! I'm the Forest Butcher. I killed them, all for Qurrah. Every single one, it was me. That is who you married. That is who you want raising that precious child. I won't raise her. I can't. There's too much blood."

The silence that followed seemed to confirm Harruq's worst fear. Pain washed over her face, and for a long while, she struggled to speak. Harruq tore from her grasp and started walking deeper into the forest.

"How dare you," she said, the shaking emotion in that quiet voice deeper and stronger than any raging river. "How dare you." He turned to her, his eyes pained and his face frozen. She crossed the distance between them and slapped him across the face. When she spoke again, the sheer will in her eyes kept him from looking away.

"That child, that life that lives in our room, is from our love, Harruq. It is our doing. It is our creation. How dare you try to abandon it because of your pain? Because of your sins. How dare you try to abandon me?"

"Aurry..."

"No," she said, nearly screaming the word. "There are no excuses, Harruq, no reasons. Condemned or not for what you did, I would never abandon you for your past, nor for mine. How would I explain why no father was there for her first steps? What would I tell her when she asks who you were? What would I tell her when she asks me if her father loved her?"

"Tell her he loved her with all his heart," Harruq said, tears filling his eyes. "Tell her that's why he left."

"Never," Aurelia said, wrapping her arms around his neck and pressing the side of her face against his. "That is why you stay. I will not do this without you, Harruq. I won't."

He tried to stay angry. He tried to convince himself he was doing the right thing. He tried, how he tried, but against Aurelia's tears he felt rolling down his neck, he was powerless. The guilt of his sins crushed him, and every face he had murdered rushed through his mind.

"I'm sorry," he said, wrapping his arms around her. "I'm so sorry. I should have told you."

"It's alright," Aurelia said back. "I've always known. I just never wanted to believe."

To this, he said nothing, only sniffing as he felt his own tears streak down his face. As they embraced, Aurelia spoke.

"Never again, Harruq. Please, swear it to me. We will kill. It is the nature of those with skills as ours. But never children. Swear it."

"I swear it," he said. "I can bear the guilt no more."

She kissed his lips. "Then let it be gone forever. Come. Your daughter is waiting."

Hand in hand, husband and wife, they walked back to the Eschaton tower.

It was two months before Qurrah saw his niece. Harruq greeted him warmly, and proudly led him up the stairs to where his daughter slept.

"What name did you give her?" Qurrah asked as he neared her crib.

"Aullienna," Harruq answered, leaning against an ivy-covered wall.

"Aullienna?" his brother said, rolling the word over his tongue. "An elvish name. Do you hold no care for our heritage?"

"We have no heritage," he said. "I like the name, and so does Aurry. That's all that matters."

Qurrah stooped before the crib and peered down. Aullienna was napping, sucking on her thumb as she did. She was dressed in clothes given to her by Delysia: a plain white dress that hung over her diaper-cloth. Trailing down the crib was the ribbon given to her by Haern. Qurrah looked at this foreign creature, unsure of how to feel.

"She looks elvish," he said. "And you give her an elvish name. Do you wish to hide the blood that flows within her?"

"We're hiding nothing," Harruq said, his tone hardening. "You of all people should know that."

"Do I?" he asked, turning his back to the child. "The orcish blood in your veins gives you strength. It helped you survive the streets of Veldaren. Would you wish it gone?"

"Never," Harruq said.

Their gazes met in silence, broken moments later by Qurrah's voice.

"She is beautiful," he said, not looking at her when he said it. He climbed down the stairs, not having once touched her. "Though I fear for her fostering. A wild elf and a burly half-orc are far from normal parents."

"We'll be doing what we can," Harruq said, fidgeting as he followed Qurrah. "I was hoping you would be around more often. Help us raise her."

Qurrah put his hand on his brother's shoulder. "You will do fine in raising her. Teach her strength, teach her pride, and she will grow up an honor to your name. Now I must be off. Business awaits me in Veldaren."

"When will you be back?" Harruq asked, opening the door.

"I don't know. It will depend, but I fear it several months at least."

Harruq's disappointment was obvious. "Are you sure?"

Qurrah bowed to his brother. "My congratulations on such a wonderful daughter."

He walked past his brother to the top of the stairs. He stopped, turned around, and gestured to the illusionary grass, ivy, and clouds.

"Did Aurelia do all this?" he asked. Harruq grinned.

"All of it. You like?"

Qurrah nodded, smiling at a small cloud floating across the ceiling-sky.

"Impressive," he said.

18

The black gates gave no feeling of home, and no comfort in their familiarity. Only the aura of certainty, of order, that permeated from the bars soothed his turmoil. They opened as he approached, needing no word or touch from him. Halfway across the obsidian walkway, the great doors creaked inward. The night was young, and the wise man who stepped out seemed almost youthful in the moonlight.

"Welcome home," said Pelarak.

"No home of mine," Qurrah said. "I do not worship your god. How may it be my home?"

"Because your family is here, waiting for the wayward prince to ascend his throne." The old man bowed. "I trust my meager knowledge was useful to you?"

"Some things should be discussed in quiet rooms," Qurrah said. "No matter how calm the night may seem."

"Indeed," Pelarak said, fully opening the door. "Come inside, Qurrah Tun."

Inside he went, fighting the newly awakened feeling that perhaps he had come home after all.

They headed straight for Pelarak's small room, pausing only to offer a prayer before the majestic statue of Karak. The two sat opposite each other. With reverence, Qurrah took the tome the priest had given him and placed it on his desk.

"Your wisdom on such matters is humbling," Qurrah said, gesturing to the book. "I have to ask, how did you obtain such knowledge?"

"Do you mean the spells?" the priest asked.

"No, your writings. You talk of madness, its causes and its effects, with authority that leaves me in awe."

The priest rested his chin on his knuckles.

"That first tome I gave you, with the words to drive men mad, proved helpful. I truly believe they can create every kind of madness. It took many years, but I have seen the effects of all two hundred."

"Tessanna's mind," Qurrah said, "could you remember which of them formed something similar to hers?"

The priest sighed and leaned back in his chair, uncrossing his fingers as he did.

"In truth, no. I have spoken to her before, although I doubt she remembers me. Regardless, the key to her does not lie in my findings."

"But why?" Qurrah asked. "Surely one resulted in a similar madness."

Pelarak raised a bushy white eyebrow at the half-orc.

"Are you so sure it is madness?" To this Qurrah had nothing to say, so the priest continued. "Madness is a loss of order in the mind. The worse the madness, the less the order. Tessanna's actions may seem chaotic, but I have sensed the winding weave that is her mind, and within I found order, frail as it may be."

"Then how may I cure her?" Qurrah asked.

"If she has obtained a semblance of order in her mind, then I dare say she might already be cured. Her current mental state may be salvation from the true madness she suffered earlier in life."

"No," Qurrah said, rising to his feet. "Her mind is shattered, broken. It can be put together again."

"I welcome you to try," Pelarak said, his voice tired and honest. "But she is not mad. I was reluctant to tell you earlier, but I feel she is more fractured than insane, each piece seperate and controlled. As for what controls them, I may have something for you to think over."

The half-orc stayed silent, his mind sifting through what Pelarak had said. The priest rose from his seat and pulled a small diary from a shelf. He flipped through the pages until he found a specific passage and then read it aloud.

"A man called out to me for coin. He lived off the pity of others, for he was blind since birth. When I declined, he at first accepted, but as I passed, he lunged like a rabid animal, biting for my leg. I threw him back, broken. The animal left him as he cried for forgiveness. He claimed a demon lived inside him. Curious, I touched his mind to see. I found the demon, but it was not what he thought. Instead, it was himself, or at least, a part of himself, isolated into a second being.

"This vile second-self wished nothing but death and pain upon others. It fought for control constantly, and though I sensed no strength in the beggar, he succeeded in holding it at bay for many an hour before each temporary escape. Curious as to how, I searched deeper, and there I found it. I viewed a vine growing out of both, yet at the same time, it seemed a wall, blocking one from the other. I sensed this entity had a full form deep inside, but I was unable to probe any farther. Sadly, the beggar died. Karak curse my carelessness. If I had been more patient, I might have followed the snaking tendrils from these two selves to the center..."

Pelarak closed the book and set it down next to his spellbook.

"Take both," he said. "You still have much to learn. Focus upon this wall that separates her selves, and yet also connects them as well. Ask her if she knows about it, for she might. If anything can bring the pieces back together it is that secret, hidden self."

Qurrah took the books and bowed. "I will consider what you have said," he promised. "Although you err in saying she cannot be cured."

"I know little about love," Pelarak said, showing Qurrah to the door. "My mind is too cynical to study such chaos. Good can come from love, however, for I love Karak with every beat of my heart. Love Tessanna as she is. If you fail to cure her, the sting will hurt that much less."

"I will not fail," Qurrah said. He held the books tight against his chest and bowed once more. "I never fail."

"Spare me the theatrics," the priest said, a smile creeping on the corners of his mouth. "We all have failed. Some are humble enough to learn from their failures. They are the wise."

Qurrah left the temple, having gained no answers but plenty of questions, as well as a gnawing fear that there was more to Tessanna's mind than he so far discerned.

※

Back at their cabin, they lay soaked in each other's sweat. In the calm afterward, Qurrah dared ask the question Pelarak had urged him to ask.

"Tessanna," he said, his eyes closed. He felt less awkward bringing up the subject when he wasn't looking at her. "Do you understand what I mean when I say there are many in your mind?"

"Yes," she said, her voice subdued. She usually fell into such a state after they made love, although how long the apathy lasted varied greatly. "I believe I understand."

Qurrah searched for a way to ask what he barely understood himself.

"These different…parts of you. Pieces of you. They are all separate, but there's one that isn't. Part of it connects to every piece. Do you understand?"

Tessanna giggled, fading out of the apathy smoother than a boat floating across still waters.

"Something is wrong with me," she said, her voice intolerably shy. "I've always known it. People die around me, and sometimes it feels like strangers sit behind my eyes, spitting at them."

"But what of my question?" he asked. Tessanna did not answer. She closed her eyes, appearing deep in thought. Her eyelids fluttered. A look of pain crossed her face. When she reopened her eyes, a new identity spoke, one he had never witnessed before.

"The girl is a maelstrom," she said. All emotion, all fear, all shred of anything human drained out of her. "Her selves swirl about the edges. I am the Center. I am Celestia's chosen. Speak!"

Qurrah felt a phantom presence pass over his body. Shadows stretched and crawled along the floor toward them. The wood creaked, the bed shook, and all about darkness formed where darkness should not have been. He stared at her face with detached horror. Her black eyes were aflame, consumed with purple fire. Swirling deep within, he saw the face of a woman glaring out, similar to Tessanna except older and wiser. The creeping darkness took corporeal form, wrapping around her naked body like a phantom dress.

"How may I cure the madness within?" he asked, his voice almost lost in a sudden roar of wind.

"Do not meddle, half-orc," Tessanna said as her hair danced wildly about her arms, back, and breasts. "Otherwise Time itself will protect her from you."

The darkness flared, washing over Qurrah with burning wave after wave. His skin crawled with vile sensations. His mind reeled against horrible images of a vast emptiness beyond comprehension. Mortal power could maim, could kill, but this was beyond that. This was the power of a goddess.

The final wave came and went. The shadows returned to their rightful positions. A fragile calm overtook the cabin. Tessanna's hair halted its writhing. She stared at Qurrah with a terrified look, tears running down her face.

The Cost of Betrayal

"I thought you would be dead," she said. She flung her arms around his frail body and cried against his neck. "I thought…"

He held her, his eyes staring into nowhere. After a few minutes, her crying ended, her sorrow and fear vanishing as if it had never been.

"You should be bleeding right now," she said, pulling away from him. "Everyone always is after that."

"After what?" he asked. In answer, she shrugged.

"I don't know. Be thankful you aren't dead. It seems someone favors you."

"Perhaps," he said, rising from the bed to seek fresh air. "But I intend to find out."

<hr />

For weeks, Qurrah poured over Pelarak's diary, learning all he could. His brief encounter with Tessanna's inner…well, whatever it was, had certainly proven Pelarak true. This strange Center did indeed exist, and apparently disapproved of his efforts. A part of him was afraid, but a larger part ached with curiosity. He thought he knew much about the mind, but this girl mocked him with her complexity.

"When will you try to change me?" she asked him one day. A small squirrel sat in her hand, amazingly docile in her presence.

"In time, Tessanna," he said. "But I have found a new obstacle, and must find a way to overcome it."

Nothing from a book helped him to his next revelation. One night, as he sat in his chair with his head aching, he watched Tessanna carve runes into her arm. Her precise, intricate movements entranced him. She scrawled seven runes before stopping. While she watched the blood flow, she licked her wrists.

"What is it you write?" he asked her, standing from his seat.

"I don't know," she said. "Whatever feels good."

"There is too much detail for that to be random," he said, crossing the room to grab her elbow. "Do you know what these say?"

"Does it have to say anything?" she asked, attempting to yank her arm away. Qurrah latched on, his knuckles white. His eyes scanned over the blood-soaked runes, attempting to discern any form or meaning.

"Let go," Tessanna said. A new cold had entered her voice. "Let go of me, now."

"Spell runes," he said, releasing her. "By Karak, they are spell runes!"

"You don't know that," she said.

"What else could they be?" Qurrah asked.

"Others have tried to speak them aloud. Nothing ever happened."

"Those that tried, did they die?" Qurrah asked. Tessanna shrugged. The half-orc tossed her a rag. "Clean off the blood. We will see if I am wrong."

A fire raged beside them as they stood underneath the stars. Already, the cuts on her arm had faded to angry red scars, the rate of her healing remarkable. Qurrah had studied them carefully, perusing his spellbooks and finding runes matching the ones Tessanna carved. Some were identical, while others had slight deviations that he hoped were insignificant.

"Give me your arm," he asked her. She obeyed, seeming indifferent about the whole situation. She expected little to happen. As much as she loved Qurrah, she did not think him correct.

He, however, was certain he had stumbled onto something significant. What that significance was, well, he hadn't a clue. He put away such worrisome thoughts and held her hand. One after another, read the names of the runes.

"*Delk Mord-thun, Vaeln Nelaquir, Tirug, Nolfwud, Xeudayascar!*"

He spoke them as he would a spell from a scroll, feeling the power reeling out his body. Wind swirled around him, blowing leaves and sending their clothes and hair dancing. The runes glowed as if the cut skin were embers of a lingering fire. All about, the night grew dead. When the final word was spoken, Qurrah looked to his beloved, taking pride in the lack of fear in her eyes. He held her hand and prepared for the storm.

"Qurrah, stay with me," she said, moments before lightning struck her from a cloudless sky. The bolt lifted her into the air, her lithe frame hovering a foot above the ground. Her hand clutched his, her nails piercing his flesh. He felt no pain.

"Let all those who endanger the balance wither away as dust," the girl said. Her tone was flat, all emotion gone. It was the voice of the Center. She pointed a finger at him. "Be gone from her."

"Qurrah!" he heard her cry, a second voice from one mouth. Black power collected at the end of her accusing finger. Walls of

The Cost of Betrayal

wind ripped from the ground, sealing the two in a gray prison. The half-orc did not think, only react. He flung his arms around her, holding her tight. As a small ball of emptiness shot from her finger, he kissed her lips and awaited death.

The magic hit him. He wished for death. When he opened his mouth to scream, no sound came forth. His soul shrieked in agony immeasurable. The two hovered higher and higher as his vision blurred. A song rose over the roar of the wind, one of longing and desire, sung by an unseen choir of thousands. The magic ripping through him intensified, adding a physical component to his torture. The pain crawled up his arm and into his lungs. All breath ended, and his lungs filled with fluid. His arm were aflame with the pain of a thousand burns.

"What have you done?" Tessanna asked. The Center was gone, yet still she felt no fear, only wonder at the chaos surrounding her. Qurrah tried to respond, but his jaw locked as his neck muscles pulled tight. A black fog poured from his throat, which she breathed in like smoke. Her dark eyes flared with color, and then all he knew turned white. Continuous the choir sang, a chorus whose line he did not understand, but knew within it there was reason.

On and on, the ebb and flow of time. Balance, the balance, it will come eternal.

Ghastly was the pain, shredded was his soul, and all else a pure, numbing shade of white. So white, all thought, all breath, all heartbeat, halted. Arm in arm, the two swirled ever higher, stretching into a vast space beyond the sky, beyond the stars, and beyond time itself.

Part Two

19

"How long you think they'll be like that?" asked the ruffian. His leader grunted an unintelligible response. The man drew his dagger and thrust it into the ground, accompanying it with a grunt of his own. "Come on, we've been here for weeks. Why don't we just gut them and get out of here?"

They were camped deep in the King's forest, living off hunted game and growing fouler of mood with every passing day. There were nine of them, plus their leader. The generous coin each of them had accepted eased their complaints a bit, but not their boredom. More than a few would have considered abandoning their job, but they knew Karnryk the Slayer would have their heads if they left. So they stayed, grumbled, and pushed for a quicker ending to their task.

The complaining man was Marv, a bucktoothed scoundrel who bragged often of the many women he had taken at knifepoint. He pulled that same knife out from the dirt and pointed to the strange sight that dominated their clearing. A man and woman hovered in the air, their arms entwined. Their eyes were open, but they did not move. Their mouths hung low, as if in the middle of a scream, but they drew no breath. The air around them was calm, yet still their clothes and hair blew about as if in a great windstorm. They were Qurrah Tun and Tessanna Delone, imprisoned in time by a force unknown.

"What's so important about them?" Marv dared asked.

Karnryk stood to his full height, the half-orc towering over the scrawny man.

"They dared cross me," he said, shifting the greatsword on his back so his right arm casually rest upon the hilt. "And they dared hurt me. But go ahead, try and kill them. You'll end up just like Stokham."

"Stokham was an idiot," Marv said. He glanced around, seeking approval from the rest. "Ain't that right?"

"I know caves less hollow than his head was," one man said.

"Two turds short of a pigsty," said another.

A couple more nodded.

"Then by all means," the huge man said, gesturing to the floating couple. "Kill them."

"With pleasure," Marv said, licking the edge of his knife. After an exaggerated time spent aiming, he hurled his weapon. Its aim was true, and had it gone undeterred, it would have pierced through Qurrah's back and into his heart.

Instead, the knife froze in mid-air. An ethereal shield swirling around the couple flared to life. White magic crackled around the spherical defense. The sound of thunder boomed throughout the clearing. Wind blew. Dust scattered. A bolt of lightning tore through the air. Into the forest flew Marv's body, charred and smoking. As his henchman landed with a cracking of brush and leaves, Karnryk cackled with laughter.

"What he gets for thinking," he said to the rest. The swirling sphere vanished, and all was quiet once more in that dead clearing with the gray grass, withered trees, and mysterious floating couple.

While the others slept, Karnryk stayed awake, glaring at the two frozen forms. The very sight of them sickened his stomach and awakened old pains where the foul demoness had cast her spell. Their embrace was one of fear and love, and while he had no idea the reason for their imprisonment, it did not appear willing. In truth, he didn't care why. All that mattered was that their freedom was met with his bloody, painful welcome.

The spherical shield was clearly visible in the moonlight, the pale glow reflecting off like flowing water. Tiny circles of light wafted like smoke from a doused fire, glowing a dull blue. Directly underneath lay the ash and bones of what had been Stokham. Karnryk removed his greatsword and scraped a whetstone across it, knowing he needed to keep his blade, and his mind, sharp.

"Don't sleep too long," he said. "It's only making me crankier."

As if in answer, a slow rumble shook the clearing. A second, louder rumble sent his eight minions scrambling out of the cottage. Some had weapons drawn; most did not. The half-orc swore. His original men, the ones he had personally trained and kept until the two crazed lovers had butchered them, would have made dog meat out of his current crew. No matter. Those he liked he would train. The others… whatever happened to them happened.

"Knock the sleep out of your eyes, something's wrong!" he roared. A rainbow of colors poured out the magical shield, flooding the clearing with an unnatural hue. Karnryk held his sword high above his head.

"About damn time," he shouted. Cracks appeared in the rainbow, akin to broken ice atop a frozen lake. Clean light shone from inside, as if it were daylight within the sphere. Larger and larger the cracks grew, until every man there had to look away. Thunder shook them all. Air blew in every direction. The light vanished. The tempest faded. The two lovers landed hard, both looking as if awakened from a dream.

"Grab their hands, now!" Karnryk shouted, leading the way. Qurrah staggered to his feet, his reactions slow and drunken. Tessanna remained still, her eyes distant and her mouth open.

"Tessanna!" Qurrah shouted. "Stand, thieves seek our lives!"

Out came his whip, wrapping around the closest man's neck. Fire roared. He screamed and clawed at his charred flesh as the whip closed tighter and tighter. With his other hand, Qurrah cast a spell. Blood shot out another's forehead, as if an invisible arrow had struck him. Qurrah reeled, overcome with waves of dizziness. When Karnryk rammed his hilt into Qurrah's gut, he vomited all over the blade. His hands flailed for something to grab. He felt a huge fist yank his robe and hold him steady.

"You dirtied my sword," Karnryk snarled into his ear. His breath stank of rot, and again Qurrah felt his insides churn. A shove sent him to the ground. The huge blade hovered before him, glistening red and pink from bits of food and vomit.

"Lick it clean," Karnryk ordered. "Lick it, or I'll cut your damn head off."

Qurrah spat on it instead. His reward was a monstrous fist to his face, coupled with a welcome return to unconsciousness.

◆◈◆

When he awoke, his hands were bound behind his back and tied to a rope that looped around his neck. Even a twitch of his hands tightened them, choking his weak throat. All around, he heard the mutterings and jokes of petty lowlifes. The heat of a fire warmed his face and chest. Summoning the courage, he opened his eyes.

Karnryk's minions surrounded him. A bonfire roared several feet away. Beside him lay Tessanna, bound in a similar manner. Her eyes were open, but she seemed sleepy and incoherent. On the opposite side of the fire stood Karnryk, his sword heating in the flame.

"Good, you're both awake," he said. "Now we can start the fun. I want to see the fear in your eyes as I cut you to pieces."

"Then you will never have your chance," Qurrah said. "You cannot scare me. A bully with a sword is all you are. The things I fear are beyond your abilities."

"Really?" the giant half-orc said. "That so? Well, you don't have to be afraid for me to have my fun. Pain's my true specialty."

He reached over and grabbed Tessanna. His giant fingers dwarfed her small neck. She made no struggle as he lifted her into the air, her body dangling.

"Strange to see you with clothes on," he said, lewdly examining her body. "Last time you didn't seem to mind being naked." He took her dress in hand and ripped it, exposing her chest. His henchmen murmured in approval. "Want some fun?" he asked her. She said nothing. With a shrug, he tossed her to the ground.

"Well you're getting some, anyway," he said. With a nod, the first of many came forward, undoing the button to his trousers. When Qurrah looked away, Karnryk knelt beside him, yanked his head by his hair.

"No, you look," he growled. "You watch. You killed my men. She nearly killed me, so you better enjoy your fucking reward."

Tessanna showed no emotion as the first pushed up her skirt and pulled down his trousers. Qurrah watched, a burning anger growing in his gut. His lover gave no sign of pleasure, or displeasure, instead remaining perfectly still, her eyes far, far away. Without any struggle or signs of life, the man raping her beat her face, then her chest, furious. She did not scream. She did not fight back. She did nothing. When he finished, the man was furious.

"You have fun with her," he told the next in line. The second lowered his pants, knelt down, and howled like a wolf as he entered her. Qurrah marked him for death first.

One after another, they took her like she was their slave, their property, their conquest. One after another, Qurrah had to watch. Bruises covered Tessanna's face and body. Blood trickled from her nose and ears. Only Karnryk refused to touch her, hating the agonizing throb in his pants. It was not until the very last one had finished that she moved. Her elbows flexed, her neck tilted, and her black eyes shimmered in a way that sent cold fear creeping through all who had touched her.

"You took me," she said, looking around without any sign of anger. No, it seemed to be curiosity, and that chilled the men even more. "You took me while I was away…all of you?"

The ropes that bound her neck and wrists blackened and smoked as if a fire burned them from within. A sharp edge entered her voice.

"Did you enjoy it?" she asked. The ropes fell to the ground, nothing but ash. She stood. None moved against her. An unseen wind blew her hair. "Because I am about to enjoy this."

Black lightning arced to the nearest man, into his crotch, and then throughout his body. He died instantly. Still none moved. Her eyes held them still.

"Did you watch, Qurrah?" she asked, bringing her gaze to him. The half-orc nodded.

"Seven have had their way," he said.

"Then in seven ways I will have mine," she said, smiling to those around her. "Your deaths will be painful, I promise."

Karnryk lifted his sword and screamed for them to attack. What happened next was a blur of blade and black magic, a chaotic mess in which only Tessanna thrived. Waves of power washed out from her, sticking to the eyes of those that did not look away. They stumbled around, blind. One thug launched himself at Tessanna, wild with fear. The girl laughed at his terror, then multiplied it tenfold. Poisonous magic leapt from her fingers and into his mind. He sailed past Tessanna, rolling onto his back. He scratched and clawed at his chest, finally flaying at it with his knife. The whole time he shrieked, "The maggots! The maggots!"

Karnryk lunged with his greatsword, determined to take his vengeance. Tessanna saw him coming. The corners of her mouth curled into a brief smile. A single step back and the sword cut the air where she had been. Before he could strike again, she lunged forward and touched his chest.

"*Kelakkao,*" she said, almost seductively.

The half-orc staggered, his entire insides seething like a pit of snakes. He fell to his knees as wave after wave of vomit poured from his mouth, continuing until blood and acid scorched his throat and splattered the ground below.

Tessanna watched him until the furious cries of those she had blinded changed in sound. Her spell had worn off. They could see again, and they sought death. She twirled, her arms swaying like an elegant dancer. With each finger, she beckoned them closer.

Amid the death cries, Qurrah struggled against the ropes that held his hands tight. Each movement sent horrible pain throughout his throat, until he gave up squirming free. He glanced about, searching for another way. A dagger lay nearby, but the rope was far too thick. Then he saw his whip, for whatever reason untouched from when he had dropped it. The half-orc crawled on his belly like a worm until he reached it. He put his back to it so that his hands could close around the handle. Instantly it sprang to life.

"Not yet," he said to it. "First, my freedom."

The leather wrapped around his wrists, and at his command, burst into flame. The initial fire did not harm his flesh, but when the rope itself started to burn, so did his skin. Qurrah closed his eyes and endured the pain, hoping something remained of his hands by the time the rope broke.

"Rise, pale moon, for I am alone," she sang, a haunting melody accompanied by an orchestra of wind, eruptions of blood, and the screams of men. "Hide, burning sun, day waits anon." Black flame roared out of her hands, scattering back any who approached. Only four remained alive, three terrified men and Karnryk. To each one she turned, singing a lyric.

"Sing, night birds, night needs beauty." An ethereal arrow struck the back of one man's head as he fled. Blood shot from his ears, and then he fell.

"Dig, grave man, then leave me be." The second one hurled his dagger. It struck her side, drawing blood. She dipped a hand in her own wound and let it soak red.

"Goodbye, pale moon, for I am alone," she sang, removing her hand and grinning at it. Magic poured out of her. The blood stiffened, took shape, and flew. Seven hardened balls shredded the dagger thrower's face and punched out the back of his skull. Only one left before she faced Karnryk.

"Goodbye, burning sun, see me no more." The final fell to his knees and begged for mercy. Tessanna tilted her head, as if confused. Tears ran down this man's face as he groveled like a dog, unable to bear the sight of his companion's brutal deaths. The girl answered him with another lyric.

"Goodbye, night birds, dirt fills my ears."

She cast her spell. His eyes blasted out his body by a great surge of blood, and his body shriveled and curled in obscene ways.

She ended her song, smiling at the beautiful sight of death she had created.

"Goodbye, grave man, cover me in the morn."

The sound of movement made her turn. She felt no worry. Pure euphoria swirled inside her head. She was a goddess among mortals. None would dare strike her.

Karnryk was a furious warrior, proud and arrogant. He had no respect for goddesses. As Tessanna stared incredulously, he shoved his greatsword through her stomach. The tip tore out her back, the blade soaked in gore. She gasped as her blood poured out.

"Where's your magical armor now, bitch?" he asked, spitting on her face.

"Gone, as is your life," Qurrah said from behind. Karnryk turned, his blood chilling. Surrounding the necromancer in strange orbits were the bones of his dead hirelings, numbering in the hundreds. With but a thought, they assaulted. His eyes cold, Qurrah watched as Karnryk staggered about, surrounded by a tornado of bone that shredded his flesh, stabbed his eyes, and bruised every bit of exposed skin. Down he fell, unable to withstand the torture. Still the bones struck, faster and faster, their chalky white turning red. Qurrah was not satisfied.

"You struck her," he said, his voice a low, seething sound. "Suffer for your sins!"

The pieces of bone dug deeper into his eyes. Sharp rib bones broke through his teeth and poured down his innards. When the necromancer approached, the remaining bones parted for him. He yanked Karnryk's bloody mess of a face by the hair and whispered into his ear.

"I will torture you, even after death," he said. "You will yearn for the abyss, and you will not be granted its reprieve."

He shoved his fingers deep into Karnryk's eye sockets. The bones lodged there pushed farther in, deep into nerve tissue. Spasms wracked his body, and for the only time he screamed.

"*Hemorrhage!*" Qurrah hissed. Dark magic poured into the remnants of the half-orc's body. Qurrah yanked his hand free as a great explosion of blood and brain burst from where Karnryk's face had been. When the body collapsed to the ground, Karnryk was already on his way to the abyss.

"Qurrah," Tessanna said, the sword still through her waist. She lay on her side, her legs paralyzed. The sword had shifted when its point touched dirt, grinding against her spine. Qurrah rushed to her, kneeling down and grabbing her hands.

"Tessanna, I'm so sorry," he said. "I should have acted sooner, I should have-"

"Shut up," Tessanna said, her face pale and cold. "I hear the singing again…"

Those were her only words. Overcome with grief, he placed his hands on the giant hilt and apologized before yanking the sword free. Holding in a sob, he wrapped his arms around the painfully light body of his lover.

"Don't die on me," he said. "You can't die."

The lack of breath and heartbeat insisted otherwise, but Qurrah would not accept it.

"Delysia can heal you," he said, staggering south with her in his arms. Each step sent more blood dribbling across his knees. Everything was strange. It seemed the stars had shifted and the warmth of summer seemed lost into autumn.

The trek south through the woods was the longest, darkest time Qurrah had ever experienced.

No cloud dimmed the light of a single star. The Eschaton mercenaries had just eliminated a troublesome band of thieves with delusions of creating a new guild. Haern had given them the choice of death or surrender. Their leader had drawn his weapons. The rest surrendered when they saw how quickly he died.

"Nothing like a job well done," Tarlak said after depositing the thieves at the prison.

"This place always depresses me," Delysia said, pulling her robe tight about her. "Let's go home."

All glanced to Aurelia, who frowned at them.

"What am I, your wagon?" she asked. "The night is peaceful. We can walk, unless someone else is capable of opening a portal home."

"What about your kid?" Brug asked. "You should get home, not safe and all… right?"

Another frown. "Nice try. Aullienna's fine. Bunch of whiners, all of you."

They left town, traveling across the beaten path west. Harruq and Aurelia walked hand in hand, smiling as the wind blew against their faces. Haern let down his hood, shaking free his golden hair.

Tarlak led the way, babbling to the assassin about the idiocy of common thuggery in Veldaren.

When they reached the tower, everything changed.

"Someone awaits us," Haern whispered, seeing a deviation in the shadows at the door. Aurelia's keener eyes widened as she saw what waited there.

"It's Qurrah," she said. When Harruq heard, he ran ahead, a smile spreading across his face.

"Qurrah!" he shouted as he neared. "Qurrah!"

His smile faded when he was close enough to see.

"Brother?" he asked. Qurrah looked up, and to Harruq's great surprise, he saw tears. He held the pale body of Tessanna in his arms. Her limbs hung limp, her eyes closed. Blood soaked her clothes, which were ripped and torn. Harruq took a shocked step forward as his brother spoke.

"Please," Qurrah said. "I need help. Please, help me."

More and more tears rolled, along his cheek, past his thin lips, down the gray of his chin, and then falling, falling, until breaking atop the dead face of the girl with blackest of eyes.

20

"What happened?" Harruq asked. He saw blood everywhere, and Tessanna's face was a deathly white.

"Just help me," Qurrah shrieked. Everything inside him broke. He buried his face in her hair and cried. The rest of the Eschaton mercenaries arrived, stunned and confused.

"Let me see her," Delysia said, rushing past the others. She put a hand on Qurrah, only to have him shove her away. When he looked up his eyes were a bloody red. The priestess saw the wound on Tessanna's stomach and gasped.

"Help her," Qurrah said, realizing who it was. "Please, I know you, what you do. Please, help her."

Delysia put her hand on Tessanna's neck, and another on her breast. For a quiet moment, she closed her eyes, and when she opened them again, her look contained only sorrow.

"She is dead, Qurrah," she said. "Her heart is still. Her breath is gone. I'm sorry."

"She's not dead," he cried, staggering to his feet. He held Tessanna's body close. "You have healing spells. Cast them on her!"

"Qurrah, it will do no good."

"Do it," Harruq said, his face solemn. "Please, just do it, anyway."

Delysia glanced to him, and then to her brother. Tarlak nodded his approval.

"Very well. Qurrah, give her body to Harruq. We need to get her inside."

Qurrah reluctantly obeyed. Harruq lifted her in his arms, grunting at how light she was, and he shuddered at the strange ways her tightened muscles resisted movement. He laid her body on the long table inside. Everyone gathered about, watching in silence, except Tarlak, who moved to Qurrah's side.

"Who did this?" he asked.

"A giant half-orc," Qurrah said. "He wielded a greatsword, and had many men with him."

"Karnryk," the wizard said. "He posted a bounty for your whereabouts months ago. What did you ever do to him?"

"About a year back," he said, watching Delysia preparing her healing rituals. "When Dieredon came to speak with Aurelia. They were sneaking through the forest toward the tower. Their intentions were ill, so we struck them. Only Karnryk survived, somehow…"

Tarlak nodded, stroking his beard in thought. Suddenly he stopped.

"A year ago?" he asked. Qurrah gave him a quizzical look, but Tarlak shook his head. He would inquire about it later. Pure white light enveloped Delysia's hands. She put them across Tessanna's chest, letting the healing magic flow into her body. Nothing happened. She cast another spell, plunging the light deep into her wounds. Nothing happened. She cast a third spell, a fourth. Nothing happened.

"She's not dead," Qurrah said, watching her. "Please, keep trying."

Delysia glanced up, her eyes filled with pity.

"I will try, for you," she said. Sweat covered her brow, and her head hung heavy. All were silent as she worked. Every spell of healing she could cast, she did. When finished, and still no change had taken place, she rest her arms on the table and gasped for air.

"I am sorry," she said. "I can do no more. She is gone, Qurrah, beyond all that I can do."

"No, you must, you must keep--"

"She is dead, Qurrah!" Delysia shouted, her exhaustion overruling her kindness. "You are no fool. You know this, just as well as I."

The two glared at one another, neither backing down.

"Um, guys," Harruq said, drawing their attention to the body. "What's going on?"

A tiny light hovered above Tessanna's breast, shining a myriad of faint colors. The room darkened, as if the tiny ball of color sucked in all available light. The seven were lost to bewilderment as feminine voices filled their ears, singing softly. Faster the colors changed, pulsing with an eerie power. Louder grew the singing, an ominous throng tinged with triumph and victory.

The singing ended. The light plunged into her chest. The darkness of the room faded.

Tessanna coughed.

"Tess," Qurrah said, rushing to her side. He latched onto her hand and kissed her face. Delysia stared at the woman's waist, where the vicious wound was all but gone.

"Thank you," the half-orc said, his face pressed against his lover's as tears streamed down his cheeks. Delysia turned to Tarlak, who stared at her in wonder.

"What did you do?" he asked.

"That was not me," she said. "Whatever that was, I do not understand. Not my work, Tar, not my miracle."

"We should find out," Tarlak said, wrapping an arm around his sister as he watched Tessanna stir as if from a long slumber. "Riddles are interesting only when people are not involved."

Tarlak placed a cot in his room, reluctantly agreeing to let Delysia sleep there. Their two guests slept in his sister's room.

"As long as she behaves, she can stay," the wizard told Qurrah. The half-orc stayed by Tessanna's side long after she sank into sleep. When he felt certain the rest of the tower slept, he crept down the stairs. Harruq, however, waited for him at the bottom, leaning against the door.

"Where you going?" he asked.

"Outside," Qurrah said. "What is it you want?"

"Just to talk to my brother," he said. "Haven't seen you in forever."

"I would hardly call a month forever," he replied. His voice ached with exhaustion, his ragged whisper painful to hear. Harruq crossed his arms and blocked the way when Qurrah tried to leave.

"A month?" he asked. "Try eighteen. Aullienna is almost two. You didn't even come to celebrate her birth."

Harruq was not ready for the shock that came over his brother's face.

"Eighteen months," he said. His eyes grew distant as he remembered the magic that had encapsulated them. What was it the Center had said? Even time itself would protect her. "Could it be that long?" he wondered aloud.

"What now?" Harruq asked.

"Time," Qurrah said, dismissing the thoughts with a shake of his head. "It is amazing how fast it moves when you least expect it. My apologies for our separation." He beckoned to the door. "May I leave, or am I held prisoner?"

"Only tonight," Harruq said. "You look like you can barely stand. Go to bed. Do whatever you want to do after a good night's rest."

"Ever the protector," Qurrah said, a smile growing against his will. "I guess I will submit, this time. Good night, Harruq."

"Nighters, Qurrah."

The half-orc slunk back up the stairs, into Delysia's room, and under the covers next to Tessanna. He wrapped his arms around her waist, relishing the soft feel of her flesh. Succumbing to sleep, his last parting thought was how he could still feel the blood drying on his hands.

When he awoke, the night was deep, and a single candle lit the room. His arms were empty.

"Tess?" he asked, rising on one elbow. The girl sat at the edge of the bed, blankets huddled about her.

"I hurt you, didn't I?" she asked. Her shoulders trembled, and Qurrah thought he heard crying. "I always do. Always."

Qurrah rubbed the sleep from his eyes and looked at the length of her hair. "You did not hurt me, Tessanna. You protected me. Come, lie down."

She glanced back, her eyes voids unfilled in the dark. Tears ran from them. "Are you sure? Really sure?"

The half-orc threw off his blanket and stepped on the cold stone floor. He groggily walked before Tessanna, who looked away. His hand took her chin and forced her to face him.

"I would go to the abyss and back for you," he said. "And then do it once more to ensure peace in your mind."

She smiled, briefly.

"I heard the singing again," she said, her tears continuing. "It was so beautiful. They were talking to me, and their voices so sweet, but the words, please, why did they have to say those words?"

"What words?" he asked, resting her face in the palm of his hand.

"They called me something. They called me daughter. They called me balance. And then…and then…"

She shrieked, tearing at her face with her fingernails. Qurrah grabbed her wrists, fighting her wild thrashing as blood flecked the white sheets. She clawed at her flesh, howling like an animal.

"Cease this!" Qurrah snarled. Thankfully, she did. She slumped into his arms and sobbed.

"They said I am broken so I may fix that which is breaking," she whispered in between sobs. "They said I am to kill...but my purpose...my purpose..."

"Don't talk, love," Qurrah said, holding her tight. "Not if it pains you this much."

"No," she said, shuddering. "Please, let me say it so I may forget it. You remember it for me, alright?"

The half-orc nodded. "I will."

"They kept singing, all these voices, did you hear them? Their voices were pretty, but they sang ugly things. *Forgive me, my daughter. Forgive me, my child. Your path was done before you were born. Forgive me, for you are to destroy. All that is beautiful, you will ruin. All that is golden, you will tarnish. Shatter your reflection. Let the balance go on eternal.*" Tears streamed down her face as she finished. *"Forgive me, for your time was unkind, but all is how your mother decreed it be."*

She fell into silence. Qurrah pondered over the words as he held his love tight.

"You are not meant for such things," he whispered to her. "You will not destroy. You will not bring ruin. The voices are wrong."

"I don't want to hurt people," she whispered back. "Not those who are kind to me. I never mean to. I hurt them, I never know why, but now maybe I do know. Mother wants me to hurt them. I shouldn't disappoint her." Mad giggles interrupted her crying. Qurrah felt the hair on the back of his neck stand erect as her body shook with laughter.

"Mommy wants me to kill. I should be a good daughter and obey. Who does she want dead, though? Good daughters should obey without question, but I'm not that good. Who to kill? Who to kill?"

"Snap out of it, Tess," the half-orc said.

"Perhaps, you? Perhaps, Tarlak? Your brother?"

She leapt from the bed and danced in the loose dress she wore. Dried blood still covered it, and there was a gaping hole in the cloth where Karnryk's greatsword had punched through. "Is it Delysia? Ooh, I just felt my skin shiver. Maybe it is her. But no, someone else, mommy says it's someone else. Someone just like me. Shatter my reflection, she said. I should obey. All good girls obey, right Qurrah?"

The Cost of Betrayal

Qurrah stood, his fists clenching. Tessanna ignored him, turning to the simple dresser carved from stained oak. A small circular mirror hovered above it, held by twin supports carved in the shape of doves. The girl pranced over, cackling. She smashed it with her forehead, showering the dresser with bleeding shards. She smiled back at Qurrah, blood rolling down her face and around the corners of her lips.

"I did it," she giggled. "And it felt good."

The half-orc said nothing as he crossed the room. He put his left hand on her shoulder and held her firm.

"I love you, Tessanna," he said.

"I love you too, Qurrah," she said.

Qurrah struck her across the face. Hard. The girl slumped to the ground, unconscious. For a long while, he stood there, taking in great, shuddering breaths, as he prayed for his heart to slow.

"Forgive me," he said to her, pulling her onto the bed. He covered her with blankets, tucked them in, and then retrieved a cloth and a bowl of water. Carefully, he removed the pieces of the mirror and cleaned the blood from her face. When finished, he kissed her forehead. Tired beyond reason, he sat on the bed, pondering what it meant for Tessanna to be a daughter of balance.

As all of Veldaren slept, a man slipped through the shadows. His torn clothes were stained and stunk of feces. He wore no shoes. His scabbed hands clutched the shutters of a window. His eyes gazed inside, seeing a small child. He smiled as he drew his dagger. In daylight, he was mocked and scorned. In daylight, his mind was a shattered, broken frailty. In the darkness, he was the reaper.

The child cried out only once before the dagger plunged. His father staggered in from the other room, a club in his hand.

"What's going on?" he shouted.

The bed was empty. The room was empty. The window was open.

Two hours later, a guard patrol found the body. Pieces of it were missing. Others were in the wrong place. So appalling were the remains that within the hour a bounty was already posted, offering two hundred gold pieces for the capture of the Veldaren Reaper.

Qurrah and Tessanna were the last to come down for breakfast. Aullienna ran about the room, playing with small wooden toys Brug had carved. As they took their seats, Qurrah held in his shock.

The last time he had seen her she had been a tiny thing in a cradle, yet now she jumped, stumbled, and prattled nonsense that could almost be words. Qurrah ate with the feeling of being a trespasser.

"How long will you be staying here?" Tarlak asked as the meal neared an end.

"We will be gone by tomorrow's eve," Qurrah said. "We would hate to be a bother."

"Nonsense," Harruq said. "You're more than welcome here. Can you at least stay another week?"

"You ask the wrong person," Qurrah said with a chuckle. "It is Delysia's room that we occupy."

"I don't mind at all," Delysia said, feeling multiple sets of eyes on her. "Stay as long as you wish. My brother is not as great a nuisance as he seems."

Brug let out a satisfied belch, leaned back in his chair, and looked at Qurrah.

"So, your scorpion working right?" he asked. In response, the half-orc reached into his cloak and retrieved the token. It immediately sprang to life and crawled up Qurrah's arm, snuggling into the cloth on his shoulder.

"I believe it is quite fond of me, if such emotion is possible for it," he said.

"It might be. Tried to make the thing lifelike as possible. Glad to know it ain't keeled off."

Harruq watched the scorpion, a slight grin on his face.

"So that was your pendant?" he asked. Qurrah nodded. Harruq pulled out a similar looking scorpion on a chain.

"You ever see mine?" he asked. He held it out for his brother, who briefly examined it. Like everything else of Brug's workmanship, the piece was perfectly and intricately carved. Just by touching it, Qurrah could sense the magic flowing within.

"What does it do?" he asked.

"Makes his swords stronger," Brug answered, obviously pleased. "He can cut through stone if he swings hard enough. Considering the magic inside those swords already, shoddy blades just shatter against his."

"Quite a gift," Qurrah said.

"Yeah, I thought you might…"

"Someone is coming," Tessanna interrupted, saying her first words of the day. She glanced about, her face ashen and her voice emotionless. "He won't like me. I know it. He kills people like me."

"Who?" Tarlak asked, rising from his chair. The rest of the mercenaries stood as well, preparing their weapons.

"He's here," she whispered. Two loud thumps came from the door, the sound of a fist smashing the wood.

"Aullienna, come here," Aurelia said. The girl sensed the urgency in her mother's voice and frowned. She dropped her toy and rushed over, taking her mother's hand into hers.

"Haern?" Tarlak asked.

"I will see," the assassin said, pulling his hood low. He drew his sabers and approached the door. Again, the stranger knocked twice. As the second knock ended, Haern flung open the doors. The stranger staggered back as the curve of Haern's blade pressed against his neck.

"Your name," Haern whispered.

"Lathaar of the Citadel," the man answered, bowing even though the sword remained against the soft skin of his throat. "May Ashhur grant you peace."

All the worry rapidly melted away from Tarlak's face, replaced with joy.

"Lathaar!" he exclaimed, rushing past Haern to embrace the man. Delysia was right behind him with a chaste kiss on each cheek. Tessanna slunk to the back of the room, even as the others warmly welcomed him. Brug pumped his arm, and Haern exchanged a bow.

"Everyone, I want you to meet my best friend," he said, letting the man into the tower. "May I present Lathaar, paladin of Ashhur."

The man bowed, deeply and gracefully. Long brown hair was carefully trimmed. His eyes twinkled, also a soft brown. His nose was a bit too large, and his cheeks, too thin, but his smile lit up his face as well as the room.

Qurrah felt his whip seethe and curl, itching for his hand to take its hilt. He fought it down with effort.

The paladin took Aurelia's free hand, extended his right leg, and then bowed deeply, kissing her hand at his lowest point. Aurelia blushed, immediately smitten. Harruq, seeing her swooning, had to resist his temptation to punch the man in the face.

"May I have your name, precious gem of the elves?" he asked.

"Aurelia Tun," she said.

"And the child?" he asked. Aullienna hid behind her mother's leg. She had a round face, and rounder cheeks. Her sharp nose was reminiscent of her father, while her tiny ears were clearly Aurelia's. Lathaar knelt down and reached into his pocket. With a disarming smile, he pulled out a small object wrapped in paper and offered it to the girl. When she did not take it, he removed the paper, revealing a hard piece of candy.

"Her name is Aullienna," Aurelia answered, gently urging her daughter forward. The shy girl reached out, took the gift, and then retreated, sucking noisily.

"Adorable child," Lathaar said, rising to his feet. "And the father?"

"That would be me," Harruq said, crossing his arms. The paladin did not miss a beat. Instead, he grinned, gesturing once more to Aullienna.

"Her shyness certainly did not come from you. Greetings, half-orc." He outstretched his hand. Harruq stared at it, then yielded after a fierce jab from Aurelia's elbow.

"I'm Harruq Tun," he said, using all his strength when they shook hands. To his surprise, the man's grip was just as strong, and his smile never wavered. He glanced about the entry room with a look of nostalgia. When his eyes swept across Qurrah and Tessanna, however, his smile faltered for the first time.

"By Ashhur," he whispered.

"Lathaar, meet the two newest additions to our little family," Tarlak said, sensing the atmosphere tighten. "The half-orc is Qurrah Tun, and the lovely lady, Tessanna Delone."

Lathaar did his best to recover. He extended his hand, but neither accepted it. He brought it back down with no sign of insult.

"You say you are of the Citadel," Qurrah said. "Yet I hear the Citadel has fallen."

"I am still of the Citadel," Lathaar said, his grin faltering. "Whether it has fallen or not."

"Anyway," Tarlak said, trying to change the subject. "Come on upstairs. We'll find a room for you, with Haern, perhaps. I haven't seen you in…well, how long has it been?"

"Three years," the paladin replied. The two approached the stairs, followed by a rather large procession. Only Qurrah, Tessanna, and Harruq stayed on the bottom floor.

"He won't hurt you, Tess" Harruq said to the girl, who remained at the corner of the room.

"His kind is the bane of what we are," Qurrah said. "You are quick to side with your friends, Harruq."

The warrior snorted. "You're just paranoid."

He joined his wife upstairs, feeling the cold stare of his brother as he went. When they were alone, Tessanna pulled her robe tight and peered at her lover with childlike eyes.

"I'll try to be good," she said, her voice just above a whisper. "While we're here. While he's here. I'll try to be good. Is that good, Qurrah? Is that what I should do?"

The necromancer sighed, feeling the whip slacken on his arm.

"Yes, Tessanna. For now, that is what must be done."

◈

That night, Lathaar sat with Tarlak by the fire, a glass of wine in Tarlak's hand, flavored water in Lathaar's. He looked much more relaxed without all his armor. With his hair brushed and his face cleaned, he looked all the more handsome. The rest of the Eschaton were in bed, at least, as far as they knew.

"So where have you been the past few years?" asked the wizard. "I was worried sick, especially with all those dark paladins crawling around. Vultures, they are."

"I never meant to be gone so long," Lathaar said, rolling the water across his tongue to guess the flavor. He had tasted grapes once, and intermixed with them in the water, he swore he detected a hint of peach. "I crossed the river into Mordan, seeking refuge in the Sanctuary. The priests there were kind, and I learned much from them, but their way is not mine. They focus on healing and prayer. The edge of my sword needs neither."

"Never been much for the softer side of your profession," Tarlak said with a grin.

"Blame Mornida. Lolathan was the strongest of our casters but he…" The Paladin sighed. "Tarlak, I have long meant to ask you. I have seen things in dreams, and they trouble me. I think it a memory I lost long ago. It is about your teacher."

Tarlak frowned, placing the wine down on a small table next to him. "You have your stories, and I have mine. Madral is dead now, Lathaar. He died by my hand."

Lathaar nodded, glad to know such a powerful servant of Karak had been eliminated. "He killed Lolathan," he said. "Right before my eyes, and then bid me forget it with his magic. Sorollos brought down the Citadel, but Madral helped him rise to power."

"Such things will be made right again." Tarlak sipped his wine. "Ashhur does not slumber. I am sure your path was set for a reason."

"A reason I have already seen," Lathaar said, chuckling. "By any chance have you heard of the mountain of gold?"

Tarlak nearly choked on his wine. "You found it?"

"Found it?" Lathaar laughed. "Aye, I did, and I walked through its tunnels, which glittered like the gates to the Golden Eternity. It was all a ruse, Tarlak, a ruse my friend Malik fell susceptible to. Do you know what is buried beneath?"

"The demon Darakken is supposedly sealed inside," Tarlak mused. "Please, tell me, where is this mountain?"

"It was Elfspire," Lathaar said. "Right there, deep in the Stonewood Forest."

"You jest!"

"There is too much to tell, but two protected the mountain. One was a mimic of a servant of Karak, a rather frightening creature. Mira told me the name of their kind… Doru'al?"

Tarlak nodded. "Creatures of purest dark. They cannot survive in the daylight. Claws like longswords, teeth sharp as knives. You fought one?"

"I did, and it is a battle I would prefer to never fight again." Lathaar leaned forward, and his voice dropped in volume. "But there was another with the creature, a girl named Mira. The one beside Qurrah, with the black eyes and hair. Does she have a sister?"

"A sister?" Tarlak shook his head. "I hope not. One is enough for Dezrel."

"But there is more than one," said the paladin. "Of that I am certain. Mira could be her twin. Even their voices are similar. This girl…"

"Tessanna."

"Tessanna… does she possess powerful magic?"

The wizard frowned, obviously troubled. "Yes, she does. Very powerful, from what I sense."

"Mira is the same," Lathaar said. "Almost like a goddess. I thank Ashhur that I now count her as a friend, for the darkness I sense from Tessanna worries me."

"Anyway, back to Darakken," Tarlak said, urging him on with his hand.

"Against my wishes, Malik obtained a small army from the King of Mordan, and they marched upon Elfspire. To fight them, Mira created more of the Doru'al, sacrificing elves to do so. The conflict was brutal. Many men died, most to Mira's magic. The mountain was spared."

"I take it Malik did not know what was in the mountain?" the wizard asked.

The Cost of Betrayal

"None of us did. I learned only after, when Mira showed me. The Council of Mages received word of the battle, and they came, seeking Darakken's spellbook."

"It's a powerful item," Tarlak said, gulping down the rest of his wine. "Rumored to be the oldest of magical tomes of all Dezrel."

"The Council released the demon," Lathaar continued. "A giant thing with charred flesh and ebony claws. It had these enormous wings stretching twenty feet to either side, I swear. The sword it wielded was longer than I am tall. The spells it cast…"

Lathaar stopped, drank some of his water, and pondered for a time.

"We banded together with the surviving Council members. I still am in awe of the spells, ice boulders, streams of fire bigger than houses, magical missiles by the hundreds. You should have seen it, Tarlak. The eldest of magics, it shrugged off."

"Too bad I wasn't there," the wizard chuckled. "A few of my spells and he'd go down like a baby."

"Sorry, Tar, but a few of your spells might have tickled it. Only Mira could match its power." His eyes twinkled with wonder. "She looked like a goddess then, Tarlak. When I saw her, that's what I thought. I was staring at the power of a goddess. Even still, she faltered, and Darakken nearly killed her."

"What happened then?"

"Ashhur granted me strength to fight it. My blade became an Elholad, and I battled it as best I could."

"Elholad?" Tarlak asked. "Come now, don't jest with a wizard. We dish out well, but are terrible on the receiving end."

Lathaar stood and drew his longsword. Bright light enveloped it, its strength mirroring the faith of its wielder. The paladin closed his eyes, whispered, and then held the blade high, calmly saying the word 'Elholad'. All traces of metal from the sword vanished in a great flare. The weapon became a perfect creation of light, shimmering with blue and gold. He cut the air twice, displaying its incredible lack of weight. The light vanished when Lathaar sheathed it and returned to his seat.

Tarlak whistled.

"That is a rare gift of Ashhur," the wizard said. "Few paladins in all history wielded such a blade."

"Ashhur knew I needed it," Lathaar said, his grin fading as he sat back and looked to the floor. "Even then, my strength was not enough. I faltered, in both heart and mind. By the grace of Ashhur, we were saved, for he answered my prayers with an angel. I've seen so much these past few years, but none surpasses its beauty. I can only remember it vaguely, as if in a dream, but there is no white on this land that matches the hue of its robes, and no armor made like that which adorned its chest and shoulders. It did not kill Darakken. I believe it waited for me. When I stabbed Darakken's leg, the creature reared back in pain, and then the angel beheaded it. The energy of its death knocked me unconscious for several hours."

"You killed Darakken?" Tarlak said, thoroughly amazed. "An army of elves could not strike it dead. You don't look stronger than an elven army."

"No disagreement here."

"The spellbook," Tarlak said, "I must hear of the spellbook. Did it remain upon the demon's death?"

Lathaar's face grew dark. "Aye. There is no way to destroy it. We debated what to do. I even considered bringing it to you."

The wizard visibly sickened. "The words in that tome would cry against my very being, Lathaar. Ashhur keep me from ever looking upon its pages. So what became of it?"

"I took it to the Sanctuary. You're one of few I have told of its existence. If we are lucky, the book will pass to myth and legend."

Tarlak poured himself another glass of wine and drained half of it in one gulp. "So why is it you come here? Did you miss me?"

"Actually, I did." Lathaar let out a hearty laugh. "Here is as much of a home as I have anywhere. I decided it had been too long, I would come here to visit. And propose an idea."

Tarlak grinned. "Knew there was a reason. Out with it, my friend."

"I want to rebuild the Citadel," Lathaar said. "I need money, I need men, and I need a designer up to the task."

The wizard sighed. "Far beyond me. Money I have, and I do know influential people, but not enough for such a grand undertaking. Can't the Priests of Ashhur help?"

"I am here to speak with them as well. I cannot let Karak claim victory. I refuse to be the last paladin of Ashhur."

"We'll discuss this more tomorrow," Tarlak said, finishing his glass. "Let me sleep on it, alright?"

"Many thanks," Lathaar said. The two stood and embraced. As they headed for bed, Qurrah dashed upstairs having heard every word.

21

Morning came. Tessanna refused to join everyone as they broke their fast. Qurrah said nothing of it, and no one asked. A few jokes were exchanged, mouths were stuffed, and Lathaar told a tale from his travels. Halfway through the meal, Aullienna's crying cascaded down the stairs.

"You gonna get that, hun?" Harruq asked, his mouth full of food. Her look was icy.

"She's just throwing a fit because she wants downstairs," Aurelia said. "And why is it I should go?"

Tarlak and Haern exchanged knowing glances.

"How it works. You're better at shutting her up."

Again the icy glare. Brug let out a choked chuckle.

"I'm not finished eating," she said, gesturing to her plate. Harruq shrugged, and gestured to his plate as well.

"Perhaps it is wrong for me to intrude," Haern said, jabbing Harruq in his side. "But you should go and get your blades, anyway. We shall be sparring soon."

The half-orc glanced to his friend, his face full of betrayal. "I can go get them later."

"You can go get them now," the assassin whispered, wondering how the half-orc could be so dense. When Harruq continued eating, Aurelia rolled her eyes and gave up.

"I'll get the swords while I'm up there," she said, rising from her seat. "But that will be the only thing gotten in there for the next few nights."

Brug roared with laughter, and Tarlak joined in. Harruq glanced about, looking like a surprised deer.

"What?" he blurted. "What...hey, shut up, all of you!"

Aurelia kissed him on the cheek and glided up the stairs. She rolled her eyes as she reached halfway, for her daughter's crying had ceased. She certainly did not miss the multiple feedings and the starvation of sleep, but she was starting to understand why so many told her it was the second year to fear. Not to make the trip pointless, she continued on, figuring she could get her thickheaded husband's swords.

Her skin chilled when she reached the top. Their door was wide open. Sitting on her knees with her back to the door was Tessanna.

"Run kitty-kitty," said the girl in a sing-song voice. "I see a big dog, yes I do. Climb, kitty-kitty, big dog's coming and he comes for you!"

Peals of laughter erupted from Aullienna's mouth as Tessanna tickled her, making funny growling sounds as she did.

"More!" the little elf girl cried.

"I see a kitty-kitty, yes I do. Black and brown and a bit of blue. Meow, kitty-kitty, hungry little lass. Chase the mice, chase the mice, aren't they fast!"

Aullienna smiled, mimicking gestures Tessanna made with her hands. Her tiny fingers fumbled the movements, but Tessanna would reach out and mold them correctly. She pretended her hand was a cat, and before Aullienna pulled away, the cat pounced.

"Nooo!" she shouted, her eyes wide as her smile. As she leaned forward, giggling, she saw her mother. "Mama, we're playing!"

Tessanna lurched to her feet and retreated away with downcast eyes.

"I'm sorry," she said. "She was crying, and I thought she was lonely. I'll go."

"No," Aurelia said, stopping her. "You may stay, if Aullienna wishes. Just promise me you won't…hurt her."

The sincerity in her black eyes was impossible to deny. "Never would I hurt a child," she said. "Never."

"Do you want Tessanna to stay with you a little while longer?" Aurelia asked her daughter. The girl bounced her head up and down.

"She's plays. She's a kitty! Kitty-kitty and a mouse."

"The mouse didn't do a good job running away," Tessanna said, sitting next to her on the illusionary grass. "She needs to learn. Mice are sneaky." She acted as if Aurelia were not even there. Her hand crouched and jerked about, accompanied by twitching noises.

Aurelia watched them play, torn. In the end, she did what felt right. She let them be.

※

"You wanted to see me, Tar?" Harruq asked, poking his head into the wizard's room. It had been three days since Lathaar moved in, and with Qurrah and Tessanna also staying in the tower, things had been chaotic. The half-orc frowned when he saw his wife standing next to him, a dark expression on her face. Tarlak looked equally serious.

"Can you read?" he asked.

"Long as the letters are big and the words are small," he said, flicking his eyes back and forth. Neither found this amusing. Aurelia handed him a small piece of parchment. He read it, struggling only occasionally to make out the words.

Tarlak Eschaton, leader of the Eschaton Mercenaries,

The formal bounty is already announced, but due to the increasing brutality of the murders, I, Antonil Copernus, Guard Captain of Veldaren and servant to our great King Vaelor, offer an additional seven hundred gold pieces above the current eight hundred if you bring me the culprit known as the Veldaren Reaper. This increase is only if he is alive. He has taken twelve children, cut their throats, and done atrocities improper to list in complete detail. This bounty shall diminish a hundred gold for every body henceforth found in such a manner. I am confident you may stop the loss of life, given the fine skill of your mercenaries.

Loyal servant of Neldar,

Antonil Copernus.

By the time he finished his hands were shaking and the final words were a blur.

"You think it's Qurrah," he said. It was no question. It was an accusation.

"The night they returned, that very same night, these murders began," Tarlak said. "And I have spoken with your wife. You and your brother were the Forest Butchers of Woodhaven. The details of the murders, as well as the targets…"

"Qurrah is killing children once more," Aurelia interrupted. "Without you, but he is."

Blood surged to Harruq's face, and a thousand thoughts jumbled his mind. He tried to say something, but nothing seemed right.

"It is without you, isn't it?" Aurelia asked, quieter.

"I made a promise," he said, pieces coming together in his mind. "And I haven't broken that promise. But Qurrah's made no such promise, to me or you. I'll talk with him." He tossed the paper to the wizard.

"We need more than talk," Tarlak said, rising from his chair as the paper fluttered to his desk. "We need guarantees. Perhaps it isn't him. We'll be patrolling the streets tonight, just in case. Do what you can. I do not take the death of children lightly, Harruq. I've seen what you are now, and any worshipper of Ashhur should know that a man can change. But some don't."

Harruq nodded, his eyes distant. Deep down, he felt a bitter sting. He had changed. He knew he had, and welcomed it as much as he feared it. But he was not his brother. He turned and marched out the door. Aurelia watched him go, sadness in her eyes.

"Can he stop him?" the wizard asked. When she said nothing, he wrapped his arms around her shoulders and held her much as a father might hold a child. "Things will turn out right in the end. But I will not harbor a man who commits such acts."

"He loves Qurrah so much," she said. "I don't want him hurt."

"Qurrah will hurt him, Aurry. We both know it. All that matters is when, and what becomes of the two afterward."

They both glared at the letter as if it were an intruder in their home, bringing only poison and pain. Aurelia flicked her fingers and burned it to ash.

"We will catch whoever is doing these things," she said. "And I pray to Celestia we catch a stranger."

※

Tessanna and Aullienna danced together in the grass, playing like neither held a care in the world. Qurrah quietly watched, feeling a tugging on his heart he was yet to decipher. It always hit hardest when Tessanna would scoop the little girl into her arms and share in her laughter.

A loud bang turned him about. Harruq stormed over, his face flushed. Qurrah stood, preparing for some sort of ill news.

"Why?" Harruq asked, his whole body trembling with rage. "Why'd you have to continue like this?"

"Like what, brother?" Qurrah said, his own cold anger growing at the sudden, unexpected attack.

"Don't lie to me. The children in Veldaren. It's you doing it."

The necromancer frowned. His eyes narrowed down to thin, serpentine slits.

"Do you accuse me out of proof or conjecture? I know nothing of what you speak, but your anger is enough. Children have died in the city." When Harruq said nothing, the half-orc smirked. "I take it their deaths were gruesome? Their entrails smeared across the streets? Any fool can desecrate a body, yet you come running, already judging me guilty?"

Tessanna halted her playing, watching the two with her black eyes. Aullienna sensed her seriousness and frowned. She tugged on the woman's dress.

"Up!" she cried. Tessanna scooped her into her arms, and with tears in her eyes, she held the little girl close.

"Did you do it or not?" Harruq asked.

"The question is, dear brother, why do you care?" Qurrah chuckled, the laughter hiding his fury. "Do you suddenly regret all that you have been? Are you now willing to wish death and judgment on one who must kill fifty more children to rival the blood that stains your hands?"

"It's not right killing them!" Harruq shouted, his face inches away from Qurrah's. "Don't you get it? They're someone's son, someone's daughter, no different from Aullienna! I'd kill any man a hundred times over for laying a finger on her. All that shit about saving them from life's tortures, and not a word was true. Life is not suffering!"

"Your life is not suffering," Qurrah said. "But there are a million others who live under the same sun who do not agree. You are but a flailing child in this realm, Harruq, and no prowess with blades will ever change that. Your wisdom is like a worm lodged in an oak. Do you dare tell me what is right and what is wrong?"

"Damn it, Qurrah, just listen!"

"No!" Qurrah shouted, throwing magical power into his voice. "I will not kneel to my own brother. There was a reason I left this tower, and now I remember why."

"I don't want to leave," Tessanna said, drawing both their ire. "I like it here. I like Aullienna."

"You're not leaving, Qurrah Tun," Tarlak said, exiting the tower. "Until I know who this Veldaren Reaper is, you may consider yourself a permanent guest. Surely you understand?" In case Qurrah didn't, his hand slipped into one of his deep pockets, fingering a sparkling wand etched with sapphires.

Tessanna sensed movement behind her as she watched.

"Should this turn ill, I would hate for Aullienna to be hurt," Haern whispered into her ear. "Let me take the child."

Aullienna, who had begun crying, saw Haern and reached for him. Tessanna relinquished the child.

"Why?" Aullienna asked, her shrieks turning to sniffles.

"They are hurt," Haern whispered to her. "For different reasons, perhaps, but the hurt is the same."

He took her into the tower.

"Tessanna," Qurrah said, drawing the woman's attention away from the child. "Do you mind the stay?"

"It is fine," she said, her voice quiet and uncertain. "I just want to play with Aullienna."

"Come inside, then," Tarlak insisted. "We'll figure all this out."

Qurrah ignored the squirming of the whip around his arm and accepted.

✥

The half-orc poured over his tome as the stars braved the darkening sky. Tessanna quietly watched him. She did not want to break his concentration, nor did she want his attention. She just wanted to feel his touch against her arm as he read next to her. That was all.

Harruq poked his head into the room as if he were a robber.

"We'll be back before morning," he said.

"I hold confidence in your abilities to catch such a madman," Qurrah said, not looking up from his reading. "Exonerate me quickly so I may leave in peace."

"Yeah. Sure thing."

He left. Qurrah showed no sign he cared. An hour passed, and like thieves in the night, the Eschaton mercenaries scoured the streets and rooftops of Veldaren, seeking its Reaper. As the hour ended, Qurrah abruptly shut his book and rose from the bed.

"Where are you going?" Tessanna asked, seeing him pull low his hood and wrap his whip about his arm.

"I will find this knave whose meddling has turned my brother against me," he said. "I will return before the others."

"Please come back soon," Tessanna said, her eyes wide. "I can be alone, but right now I don't want to be."

"Aullienna sleeps in the highest room," he said as he opened the door. "Go to her if you must."

He hurried down the stairs and into the deepening night. Tessanna sat on the bed, her knees curled against her chest. She gazed into nothing, for her mind was on the man she had grown to love, if love was indeed what she felt. Desperate for the emotion, she made her way up the stairs, slid open the door, and stepped inside. Stars mimicking the real location of the night sky covered the roof. A soft breeze blew across her skin. Her bare feet brushed the wooden steps to Aullienna's bed, but she did not go up. Knowing the child was nearby was enough. She lay on her side, her head on her arms, and did her best to stay awake.

"Where is it you hide, fledgling killer?" Qurrah asked as he searched the streets. He closed his eyes, reopening them with a sight known only to those who walked the darkest roads of life. What he saw shook his chest and made his heart stumble.

COME FIND ME CHOSEN OF KARAK
COME FIND YOUR SAVIOR
COME FIND YOUR KILLER
FOLLOW THE BLOOD FOOL
COME FIND ME

Across every wall, this message throbbed in a deep purple. To normal eyes it would be unseen, or glimpsed only in passing and then immediately forgotten. Qurrah saw it. It splattered buildings as if the previous night's rain had been of blood. More ran along the dirt, crisscrossing in tiny streams that clogged the gutters and merged into great rivers leading west.

"Fledgling you are not," Qurrah said. "But I am no fool."

He waved his hand and cast a spell. The blood faded, dissipating as if it had never been. The writing on the walls vanished. Only the river remained, for he wished it so. Some illusions did have purpose.

He dashed down the street, following the river. Haern, leaping from rooftop to rooftop, passed over the area Qurrah had been but a second too late, his eyes seeing only shadow where he would have seen the necromancer hurrying away.

"Seen anything unusual?" Tarlak asked the Tun couple.

"The time the bodies have been found varies greatly," Aurelia said. "We must be patient."

"Or perhaps he's just not killing tonight," Harruq grumbled, his meaning clear.

"A lack of killing this night does not prove him guilty," Tarlak told him. "Although it sure doesn't help him, either. Keep looking.

Stick to the poorer parts of town. It seems our killer prefers them as his hunting grounds."

They broke apart, Harruq and Aurelia south, Tarlak east. Traveling below them, a shield of darkness wrapped about his body, was Qurrah. He followed the blood river west.

Nothing marked the alley different from any other, not unless one looked with the hidden sight. Runes marred both buildings beside it. They were ancient symbols of death, hatred, and exile written in an archaic script. The entrance was blocked by a broken cart filled with rotted fruit. Only a tiny gap remained, and Qurrah knew it was made for him. He stared into the unnatural darkness within. Whoever this person was, he had done the killings with purpose, and his gut told him it was to bring them together.

"I am here," he said to the alley. "And I fear not who resides within."

He entered.

A waiting man sat before a dead fire. He looked nineteen, twenty at most. His skin was pale and thin. His eyes were the darkest shade of blue he had ever seen. Every feature on his body suggested hunger and suffering. On a healthy man, his nose would have seemed pointed, so in his emaciated state it was jagged and thin. The sagging of such a young face darkened every feature, and placed a visage about the eyes that shrieked hatred and anger.

"So many years," the man said. He remained seated, and did not welcome his guest. "Your name. I must know the name of Karak's chosen."

"You have not earned it, nor have you given me yours," Qurrah said, sensing the shadows swirling about him.

"I have no name," the man said, his smile vanishing. "I have lost the honor of Karak's title. For a time I was Xelrak, death bringer of our dark god."

The name turned Qurrah's stomach. He recognized the name. Velixar had spoken it in purest contempt.

"You are the one who brought low the Citadel," the half-orc said. "A puppet of Velixar."

The man who had been Xelrak chuckled at the name.

"I owe much to Velixar, both gratitude and suffering. He found me as an orphan, gave me life when I should have died, and then raised me as his student. Karak's blessing was greatest then, and I rivaled even Velixar in power." His shallow face smiled.

"Your power would have faded the second you turned upon the man," Qurrah said, enjoying the hurt and anger that flared in those horrific eyes. They looked like dams before a river of insanity, and the years had formed many cracks.

"What do you know of Velixar?" Xelrak asked. "Did he tell you of his past, of his creation?"

"I know he died to Ashhur's hand, and Karak brought him back to serve."

"That was hundreds of years ago," the other necromancer said. "So long he has walked this land. I have searched for him, but Karak's whispers are clear. I am not to meet him until I meet with you."

"You will never meet him, not until the abyss," Qurrah said. "Velixar is dead."

He expected the man to be shocked, or at least flustered, but instead he laughed.

"Dead? You think him dead? I dreamt of that battle, half-orc. I saw your cowardice and abandonment. It may take time, but he will return. Karak has sworn this to me."

Qurrah's unease only grew. Something was amiss, and the knowledge of Velixar returning did little to help. He had thought him dead. He had almost *wanted* him dead. His life with Tessanna happened only because of his passing. What would happen if he returned?

"Why did you bring me here?" Qurrah asked, wishing to remain no longer.

"Your name," the starved man snarled. "I will speak no more until I know your name."

"I am Qurrah Tun, now tell me your reason."

"Things are rumbling," Xelrak said. "Rumblings in the realm of gods. You are blind, even Karak's closest servants are blind, but I have been told. I was his chosen, but I lost my master's favor. I must regain it."

He stood. His robe was identical to Qurrah's, only faded and filthier. Dark magic crackled at his fingertips.

"Give me your power, master!" he shrieked and laughed and cried. "Long has been my exile, but let me prove my worth to you!"

Before Qurrah's eyes, Karak granted him that very wish. Lightning struck the ground, swarming through the frail form that was Xelrak. Blood and faith mixed, and from the deepest pits of the abyss, magic came forth. The blue eyes shone with power. His smile was of pure pleasure.

"I have no reason to kill you," Qurrah said, summoning his own magic in defense.

"The stalemate shall soon be ended," Xelrak shouted in triumph. "One of us will lead the world into darkness, Qurrah or Xelrak, and it must be the stronger!"

A blast of pure raw energy shot from his fingertips, its color deeper than the chasms beneath the world. An ethereal shield spread from Qurrah's hand. The two spells collided in a thundering clash, known well to spellcasters like the sound of steel on steel was to skilled swordfighters. Qurrah felt his mind bend under the pressure.

"You idiot," Qurrah said. He shoved the stream of power aside, where it shattered a wall of stone. His fingers danced, and the darkness turned into crawling globules that sank their teeth into Xelrak's feet and ankles. "You do not strike with your strongest spell first. You immobilize, you bleed, and you cause suffering."

When Xelrak tried to pull his legs back from the biting things, he found his feet held firm by teeth and shadow. His glare to the half-orc writhed with pain and hatred.

"*Hemorrhage!*" he shrieked.

The spell surged into the half-orc, setting fire to his blood and attempting to have it burst forth through the skin of his chest. Qurrah, however, focused his mind, calming the blood and denying the painful rupture the spell yearned for. He retaliated not with spell but with his whip. The flame lashed out, drawing blood and burning flesh.

"No wonder you failed Karak," Qurrah said. "You are rash. You try to overwhelm with power and instinct. But I am greater, I am wiser, and I do not rely upon your pathetic god for strength!"

Xelrak sent waves of bones flying from a bag at his side. Qurrah shattered them to chalk with a thought. Xelrak launched a ball of flame that detonated like a miniature sun. Qurrah wrapped his whip about himself, feeling strangely calm as the fire enveloped but did not burn. As the smoke wafted into the air, Qurrah lashed the whip to the ground. A wave of molten rock filled the alley. Xelrak snarled, his fingers curled, and ice smashed the wave.

"You do not deserve the strength Karak has given you," Xelrak roared.

"Enough," Qurrah said. He summoned all his strength into a barrage of seven circular balls of darkness. Fire trailed after them like the tails of comets. Each one sundered the magical shield the other necromancer brought up to block. The protection cracked, splintered, and finally collapsed against the final blow. Xelrak fell to one knee.

"I will tear the balance asunder," he said, gasping for breath. "I will free Karak from the whore's prison. I will lead his army to victory, not you."

"Then lead them," Qurrah spat. "I care not for some petty squabble between brother gods. I am not his chosen. I am not his avatar!"

"Then what is it you want?" Xelrak asked, curiosity overcoming his anger.

"I want her healed," he said, nearly a whisper. "I want what I have seen in my brother. But you know nothing of that."

The man chuckled, and he shook his head as if finally understanding some great riddle.

"You are the stronger," he said. The black power left his hands. Death and cunning lingered in his eyes. "But your will is not with Karak. That is why we meet. Karak has shown me the path that awaits you. Kill me."

"Why should I bother?" Qurrah asked.

"I said kill me," Xelrak said, "or I will kill the girl you call Tessanna."

Black tendrils encircled the half-orc's hands.

"You are mad," Qurrah said. "You seek me here, cannot match my power, and then beg for death so desperately you threaten to harm those close to me? Is this the dream of Karak? A groveling dog that will obey its master without thought, without will?"

"I will tell you the dream of Karak," Xelrak said. "It is order reigning in this chaos. It is peace replacing murder, death, and villainy. It is you leading this world to the serenity it has long yearned for."

"A dream it will forever be," Qurrah said. "And may you go share that dream with him. Never, ever, pretend to control me."

Black tendrils snaked out his palms like spearheaded tentacles. There were nine, and each one aimed for Xelrak's heart. With a visage of perfect calm, the man accepted the blows. They tore into his chest, covered the alley with his blood, and mutilated his inner organs in a splay of gore.

Then the smiling visage was gone. The man himself was gone. Instead, the massacred remains of a twelve-year-old boy lay before

Qurrah, torn apart by the tendrils. The boy's head was mostly intact, and his eyes peered to the night sky with a lifeless gaze. Several runes marked his forehead.

Laughter filled the alley as Qurrah seethed. He had been made a fool.

Fear not my child, said a voice in the half-orc's mind. Its sound was the coldest chill on a winter morning and the strongest thunder in a raging storm. *Do not despair my ways. My servant has done as he was ordered. Walk with courage. The true test approaches.*

"Qurrah," said a voice, quivering with rage and horror. It was deep, and nearly a growl.

"Yes," the half-orc said. He turned and faced his brother.

22

Harruq stood at the entranceway, his eyes locked on the butchered remains of the boy. Tears ran down his face, even as anger overwhelmed his sorrow.

"This was not my doing," Qurrah said. "Listen to me brother, it is all a ruse, a ploy…"

"Don't lie to me!" Harruq shouted. "You think I'm stupid? It's all for your magic, your sick, damned magic."

"Not so long ago you helped me, or have you forgotten?"

"Those days are gone. I will not let you guilt me forever. I've moved on. You haven't."

As they talked, Harruq slowly approached, his hands clutching the hilts of his blades. His fingers twitched, seeming eager to draw. Qurrah watched, remembering all the times those swords had taken lives with brutal efficiency. Killing was what he was. He remembered this. His brother did not.

"You have not moved on," Qurrah said, the grip on his whip tightening. "You have merely forgotten. Delusional fool. Killing is what defines you. It is your greatest ability. Now you threaten me for doing what you are the better at?"

"I'm going to stop it," Harruq said, drawing Condemnation and Salvation. "Now. Swear it. Swear you'll never kill again, and maybe we can make this out alright."

Qurrah chuckled as his world shattered. Rage clouded his mind, coupled with a sweeping sadness covering his rage like snow on a volcano.

"I cannot promise this," he said. "Because I will forever hold my promise, and a killer is what I am. We are murderers, Harruq."

"Not anymore."

"Forever," Qurrah shouted, ignoring the rupture in his throat.

"I said not anymore!" Their faces were inches apart, their wills locked in a desperate struggle.

"I will kill again," Qurrah yelled. "I will kill children, women, elders, elves, Tarlak, Brug, I'll kill any I wish, whenever I wish.

Aurelia, Aullienna, their lives are nothing to me, nothing to you, have you grown too blind to see it?"

Harruq smashed Qurrah's face with the back of his fist. There was no thought involved. No decision. He just struck. Qurrah reeled back, clutching his face. His complicated tangle of emotions cleared into one heated moment of fury.

"You would strike your brother," he said. "For all we have done, all we have survived, you would betray me?"

"You'll not lay a finger on them," Harruq said, shaking. "Their lives over yours. That's how it must be."

"So be it," Qurrah said. A black tendril shot from his hand, streaking for an exposed part of Harruq's armor. Condemnation smacked it aside as he charged, his bloodrage taking hold. Bones ripped out of the dead child's body and pelted his hands and face. He felt a burn on his ankle and knew it was the whip. He halted, tensed his legs, and then leapt backward.

Qurrah released the handle, knowing he could not match his brother's strength. The fire died when the handle left his touch. Harruq kicked it off, the sting of it driving his anger. He rushed again, his arms up to protect his face.

"See only darkness," Qurrah said, a curse leaving his hands. "May you be as blind as your heart has become."

All light vanished from Harruq's eyes. It was as if he were in a dark cave far from the grace of the sun. He kept his charge, hoping his orientation had not changed. When he heard spellcasting to his left, he ducked. Wet objects splattered onto the wall beside him.

Knowing he had little time, Harruq leapt toward the sound of his brother's voice, still deep in casting. He felt his shoulder connect, followed by a faint gasp. His momentum continued forward, and when he heard the sickening sound of bone smacking against wood, his heart stopped.

"Qurrah," he said, taking a step back.

Then the hemorrhage spell hit his arm. His right bicep tensed, tighter and tighter, until muscle broke. Blood exploded out, pouring down his arm, his leg, and across his brother's robes and face. His mind white with pain, he lashed out with his other arm.

The sound was faint, but he knew it for what it was. In his pain, he had forgotten he still held his swords, and that single lash had cut deep into flesh.

"Qurrah?" he asked again, dropping both his blades. "Get rid of this damn dark and let me see you!"

The sound of gurgling blood was his answer. The image filling his head mortified him. He had slit his brother's throat, his scarred, torn throat.

"Please, Delysia can help you," he said. He staggered forward, his good arm searching. He felt a hand wrap about his wrist.

"I didn't mean to," Harruq said. "I didn't…"

Dizziness flooded his head. His entire left arm went numb. The pain followed. Agonizing, shrieking, stealing pain. His life poured out his flesh, stolen into Qurrah's grasp. Harruq collapsed, colors of violet and red swarming across the darkness that was his vision.

"You cut me," he heard his brother gasp. "You dared cut me."

"Please," Harruq said. "Please, don't go."

"You fear me leaving you," said the hissing voice just above his head. "But you have left me long ago."

"Qurrah!"

The raspy breathing trailed down the alley and faded away. Harruq struggled to stand, but one arm was numb and weak and the other torn and bleeding. He managed a sitting position. Next, he slid his legs underneath, grimaced, and rose to his feet.

"Qurrah!" he shouted again. "Where are you!" No answer. "Aurelia!"

He staggered out of the alleyway. He brushed the shoulder of his numb arm against the wall to keep his orientation. His ankle smashed against a crate, sending him sprawling.

"Aurelia! Tarlak!"

"Who has done this to you?" asked a sudden whisper, startling the half-orc.

"Haern?" he asked.

"Who, Harruq?" the whisper asked again.

"I can't see," the half-orc said. "Help me, I can't see."

"I have already sent for Delysia. Now tell me who."

"It was Qurrah," Harruq said.

"I knew it," he whispered. "Stay here until you are healed, Harruq. I will find him."

"No!" Harruq screamed. "Don't hurt him!"

"Look what he has done to you," Haern said. The half-orc felt strong hands grab his shoulders and prop him against a wall. "You are blind and bleeding, and he has left you."

"I hit him first," he gasped. "Please. I hit him first."

The assassin's mind had been set, and he thought no argument would stop him. Still, those words kept him by the half-orc's side.

The pain in his voice was too great. He waited for Delysia and the others to arrive.

"Harruq!" a female voice called out. A soft hand stroked the side of his face. "Are you alright?"

"Never been better," he said. "Haern's beat me a lot worse before." He tried to smile, but the tears flowing from his blind eyes revealed the lie. "I'm so sorry, Aurry. I'm so sorry."

Qurrah traveled through shadows all the way to the tower, knowing his time was short. They had to know he would come for Tessanna. He slipped through the doors and rushed up the stairs, all the while clutching his throat. He needed to stop and rest, but he had no time.

Guilt still panged him for stealing life essence from his brother, but he had no choice. He was dying.

"Tessanna," he said, opening the door to their room. Not surprisingly, he found it empty. Further up the stairs he went. He did not knock at the top. He simply barged in.

"Tessanna," he said, startling her from sleep. She was curled tight upon the grass directly below Aullienna's bed. "Come. We must go."

"What happened," she asked, fully awake even though her slumber had been deep. "You have blood on you."

"I have no time to explain," he said. "The others will be coming, and they will kill me."

"They couldn't," she gasped. "Why? What have you done?"

"Nothing!"

He saw her cringe at his outburst, and his guilt calmed his temper.

"They feel me guilty for things I haven't done," he said. "I fought my brother. His wounds are not severe, but that won't matter. We must hurry. Come."

"But Aullienna..."

Tessanna glanced up to where the little girl slept. Qurrah turned his back to her.

"Go, or stay. Your choice."

He went down the stairs. The girl glanced back and forth, hating him. It was not her choice. There was no choice.

She followed him down.

The two were deep within the trees when a blue portal ripped open at the tower door. Haern led the way, followed by Aurelia. The assassin scanned every room, his eyes missing nothing. The elf went straight to the top floor. Her relief at finding her daughter sound asleep was indescribable. They placed Harruq on a few pillows beside the fireplace. Without a word, Delysia began her craft.

"He never enters this tower again," Tarlak declared, his eyes hard. "Never. And neither does the girl. Is that clear?"

"Don't hurt him," Harruq moaned from the floor. "Please, don't hurt him."

"He has a fever," Delysia said, glancing back to the wizard. "I think his left arm is rotting."

"Do what you can," Tarlak told her. "We'll take him to Calan if we must."

Brug mumbled constant streams of curses while healing light poured out of Delysia and into Harruq. Aurelia stroked her husband's head, taking in every moan he made and every flinch of skin. They were signs of life, and she needed their reassurance.

Haern slid next to the wizard, his sabers drawn underneath his cloaks.

"Should I hunt for them?" he whispered. Tarlak watched the healing, knowing the decision he gave would hold grave consequences either way. In the end, he sided with his gut. The two were trouble.

"Do what must be done," the wizard whispered back. "May Harruq forgive us when he wakes."

Haern bowed, his eyes aflame.

"Ashhur be with you," he whispered.

"Ashhur be with us all," said Tarlak.

◈

They ran until Qurrah's body could take no more. His lungs gasped for air and his chest racked with cough after cough. Blood covered his throat, lips, teeth and tongue. Tessanna held him as they walked. The forest was quiet, its calm in strong contrast to their emotions.

"Don't push yourself so hard," Tessanna said. "Please, stop for a moment."

When she pulled against his arm he had not the strength to fight. Mouth agape and spitting blood, he wished he was dead. The girl knelt down before him, tossed back her hair, and started to whisper. Her face was calm, and the half-orc knew he shouldn't be surprised. A maelstrom lived inside Tessanna's mind, so why would she worry now?

A faint blue light surrounded the girl's hand, grew in strength, and then dipped into his chest. Energy filled his body. The ache in his muscles faded, and the fog that had grown about his mind lifted. She smiled up at him, batting her eyelashes.

"Did I do good?" she asked.

"Very good," he said. He wrapped his arms about her shoulders and pulled her up to him. They embraced, long and silent in the cool, dark air.

"We can't return there anymore, can we?" she asked, the voice of a child.

"No. Not for a long time."

"I'll never see any of them," she said. "None."

"I will find a way," Qurrah said, knowing what troubled her. "I promise."

"Just like you promised to cure me?"

The comment stung even though she had meant no insult.

"Yes," he said. "The same."

She sighed. The crook of his shoulder became the perfect place to rest her neck, and a sound came from her throat almost like a purr.

"Qurrah?"

"Yes, Tessanna?"

"Someone is coming to kill us."

He shoved her away and then ducked as a flailing mass of cloaks sailed past. He felt a sting on his arm, but the wound was shallow. He lashed out with his whip, desperate as he staggered off balance. The flaming tip wrapped about Haern's wrist. Before the half-orc could pull it taut, the man was gone, the whip curled about air.

"Behind," he heard Tessanna say. He spun, his heart halting. The man was right on top of him, his sabers leading. Knowing death was but a breath away, he still attempted to cast a spell. If he would die, he would die with a spell of necromancy on his lips.

But the blades did not come, and the next breath he drew was not his last. A howl of wind slammed Haern away. His legs smacked against a tree, spinning him so that he cracked head first against another. For a moment, he struggled to stand.

Qurrah used that moment well. The words of a curse left his tongue, draining away some of the strength in Haern's muscles.

Black clouds grew from the earth, enveloping his body and pouring into his lungs. The assassin gagged, the air poisonous and vile.

"What harm have I done to you?" Qurrah asked him, drawing ready his whip. "Was it my brother that sent you here?" He lashed out, browning a spot on Haern's back and ruining the fabric. He lashed the same spot, this time burning all the way through to singe flesh. "Or have you always hated me, and now you have your excuse?"

"I need no excuse," Haern said, staggering to his feet. "And I need no hatred. You know what you have done."

With that, he clutched his wrist and enacted the magic of one of his rings. White light swarmed over his body, banishing the clouds and scattering darkness for hundreds of feet. Qurrah cried out, the sight burning his eyes. The jewel on the ring shattered, the last of its power flooding Haern with healing magic. When the darkness returned, Qurrah's eyes took a moment to readjust. A moment was all Haern needed. He charged for Tessanna.

Tessanna, however, had no trouble seeing when the light faded. Her skin glowed as if she had absorbed the illumination. Fire swarmed about her body, covering her exposed flesh. Her anger gave it fuel, and all the restraint she had held within the tower burned away.

"You won't keep me from her," she shouted, fire leaping from her hands. Haern ducked between the streams and rolled past, slashing her legs with both blades as he did. The metal clanged as if hitting stone. Fire leapt off her body, traveling down the metal and torching the skin of his hands. Haern held in a scream of pain. The stink of his own burnt flesh filled his nose.

A bolt of shadow struck his back. Pain overloaded his senses, doubling in strength as a second bolt smashed the base of his neck.

"Do not touch her!" Qurrah shouted, his hands outstretched and bleeding darkness. "You are a coward, a fool, and deserve not the breath in your lungs."

The third shadow bolt flew. Haern tucked his arms and twisted. It struck ground, instantly killing the grass it touched. Not wishing to try his luck with a fourth, Haern leapt into the air, kicked off a tree, and slammed into Tessanna. Over and over, he bit his blades into her flaming flesh. His skin, his clothes, his hair: it all erupted into fire and smoke. He felt like a miner hacking a rock with a broken pickaxe in the middle of a wildfire. His lungs cried out for air as the fire on his skin continued to grow. He had no choice.

"Damn you, girl," he said, shoving his foot into her face and leaping off, a living ember in the night. A whip took his foot out from underneath when he landed, smashing his face to the ground. He didn't mind, for it put out the fire that had blackened his cheeks and nearly scarred his eyes shut. He rolled over to see Qurrah hovering over him, a sick anger in his eyes.

"I'll send my brother to meet you soon," he said. *"Hemorrhage!"*

The spell was aimed for his face, and most certainly would have finished him. Haern activated the magic of the king's ring. The spell fizzled. Haern was gone. Qurrah spun, his eyes searching, but he did not look the correct way. He did not look up. Haern fell as he had lain, on his back. The heel of his foot cracked across the top of Qurrah's skull, sending him spinning. Knowing his time was short, Haern scrambled to one knee, used his ring to teleport further into the forest, and then fled with all his remaining strength. Fire streamed after him, torching tree and bush and grass. It was not long before everything behind him was a raging inferno, a power that mocked his own feeble blades.

He chugged a small healing potion as he ran. It did little to subdue the pain he felt as his flesh tightened, ripped, and peeled. Anger burned his gut, far worse than the fire that had burned his skin. Even with the element of surprise, he had lost.

"Tessanna, are you hurt?" Qurrah asked, gingerly touching the knot growing on the back of his head.

"I'm fine," the girl said, the fire on her flesh withering away. Scratches covered her body. They were long and thin, and they were bleeding. Qurrah hurried to her, catching her in his arms. She giggled, licking her lips as blood from a slash across her eye trickled into her mouth.

"I burned him good," she laughed. "He was fast, but I burned him, and he'll glow forever."

"We need to bandage these cuts," Qurrah said.

"No. Let them bleed. I'll be fine." She shoved him aside. Her body appeared weak, but the will in her eyes was healthy, and terrifying, as ever. "He deserves what happened. I knew what he was thinking. He was thinking I will never see Aullienna again, and that made him happy. He deserves to burn. I want to burn him again and again and again."

"We both need to rest," Qurrah said, taking her arm. "Please, we still have a long walk ahead."

"Then let's walk."

Arm in arm, they made their way home.

On the third knock, the tower door opened.

"Where the bloody abyss have you…" Brug caught Haern in his arms, grunting at the weight.

"Delysia!" he called back inside. "Hope you got a bit of magic still left in you." He turned his attention back to the assassin. "Did you dance in a funeral pyre?"

"Amusing," Haern said with a grimace. "And you're closer than you know."

Brug dragged him next to Harruq, who slept soundly. Aurelia slept with him, her slender frame nestled against his.

"I'll do what I can," Delysia said, giving him a faint smile. Her entire face sagged, and the dark circles underneath her eyes hid much of her beauty. Still, she placed one hand on Haern's chest, another on his face, and began praying to Ashhur.

Lathaar took her hands into his own and removed them.

"You have done enough," he said, brushing strands of hair away from her face. "Let me do what I can."

Tarlak wandered over, his own eyes bloodshot from exhaustion. He watched Lathaar place his hands on the assassin's chest and face, strong blue light flaring from his fingers.

"How could they do this to him," the wizard wondered aloud. Brug heard him and snorted.

"You sent him after them, didn't you?" A soft nod was his answer. "If they can do this to Haern, I'm sure glad they're dining with the worms now."

"They're not," Haern gasped. "I failed, Tarlak. I failed."

Soothing light flooded his being. As the pain faded, his body cried out stronger and stronger for sleep. He had not the strength to resist. Lathaar backed away, letting Delysia go to him.

"Sleep will help you heal faster," the priestess whispered, kissing his cheek as the man fell into slumber. Her back creaked, and her legs wobbled unsteadily when she tried to stand.

"Easy there," Tarlak said, taking her into his arms. "I couldn't have said it better myself. You must rest."

"Since when did you start acting like the big brother you are?" she asked, smiling despite her aches.

"Never. This is just a fluke. Now go to bed."

He helped her upstairs, leaving Brug and Lathaar with the three sleepers. When he returned, they had taken a seat at the table. A frothing mug was in Brug's hand. Tarlak sighed and sat next to him, declining the offer for a drink.

"What Haern said, you think it means what it sounds like?" Brug asked.

"Qurrah and the girl still live," Tarlak said. "Yeah, I think so."

Brug gulped down a third of the mug. "That's terrifying."

Tarlak laughed.

"I'm being serious here," Brug insisted. "Anyone who can do that to Haern, and look at him, he's a crispy critter, anyone who can do that is not someone I want to mess with. You sent him to kill 'em both, didn't you? They know that. They have to know that."

"You fear retaliation?" the wizard asked.

"Course not. Not for myself. They won't retaliate against us, not in a normal way. They'll hurt us differently. A deeper way." Another gulp of the mug. "Always said they was bad news."

"Never disagreed with you on that," Tarlak said, snapping his fingers so that a long glass appeared, filled with a sparkling orange drink. He took a sip, ignoring Brug's disgusted look.

"They are necromancers," Lathaar said. "At least, the half-orc is. The girl knows many necromantic spells, but she isn't one in the strictest sense. If they seek to harm any of you, they have the ability. When you sleep, when you walk underneath the stars, it is then they can find you."

"Sounds like you have experience," Tarlak said. "Stories I haven't heard yet?"

"Necromancers and followers of Karak are essentially the same thing," Lathaar said. "They may believe otherwise, but any follower of Karak is a follower of a death god. And trust me, Tarlak, I've fought many followers of Karak."

"We going after them, or do we wait like sitting ducks?" Brug asked.

"We wait," the wizard decided. "We have no choice. I'll let Antonil know we found the Veldaren Reaper. At least the killings will stop. I doubt Harruq will let me hunt down his brother. The two are sad souls, really. I hoped to show them kindness, bring them out of the pits they had sunken into, but…" He sighed. "No good deed goes unpunished, right Lathaar?"

The Cost of Betrayal

"No good man goes untested," Lathaar said, rising from the table. "All good deeds have their reward. Never confuse the two."

"Night, Lathaar."

"Night, Tarlak, Brug."

The paladin prayed on one knee by the two wounded, his brown hair falling to hide his face as he whispered in the quiet. Finished, he climbed the stairs to sleep.

"It's almost daylight," Tarlak said, turning back to Brug. "Figure we should turn in."

"Go ahead. I can go a day or two without sleep, no problem."

"Aye, but you get grumpy. Go on to bed. This night's been a long one."

"Bah. If you insist."

Tarlak waved at the fireplace. The light dimmed, although the heat from it remained strong. The two trudged up the stairs, leaving the three to sleep.

23

You have forsaken me.

"Leave me," Harruq said. Sweat and blood covered his forehead. Fire raged around him, melting rock and billowing smoke. "I never worshipped you!"

You have forsaken your brother, and you have forsaken me. You turn to Ashhur, who has granted you no power, no wisdom, and no strength. Velixar's fall is a fleeting moment in time. Will you stand beside him when he comes again?

"No," he shouted. The wails of a thousand tormented souls overwhelmed his words. "I love my brother."

You would kill him. You are blind, Harruq Tun. Blind to the path before you. Blind to those who seek to help you. Those who turn against me suffer, half-orc. They suffer greatly.

The tower crumbled to ash. The sky ran with blood, and every star fell. Hordes of the dead marched before him, a single cry on their lips.

"For Qurrah!" they shouted. "For Qurrah! For Qurrah!"

I will hurt you, Harruq Tun. I will ruin all. You betrayed me. Look upon the cost of your betrayal.

The vile voice thundered. The molten earth ran over the dead, burying them. The sky melted, filling the horizon with flame. Only Harruq remained to listen to the cries of his beloved. Aurelia fell into the fire, weeping silently. Tarlak stepped in willingly, tipping his yellow hat as the flesh melted from his bones. Finally, there was Aullienna, who waved at her father.

With a single laugh, she dove in and was consumed.

"Aullienna!" he screamed, horrified as his most precious love disappeared into the raging flow. "Aullienna! Aullienna!" The destruction was complete. Karak's laughter filled the world, and the chant of the dead changed.

For Order! For Order! For Karak and his Chosen!

The fire rose. It burned his arms, his legs, his waist. It flowed in with every breath, charring all that it meant to be him.

"Aullienna!" he shrieked, lunging up from the ground. His arms flailed about in his blindness, each movement intensifying their aches. "Aullienna, don't!"

"Harruq!"

Aurelia wrapped her arms around him and held him still.

"Harruq, it was a dream, just a dream."

He felt her arms and calmed, burying his head into her chest and weeping.

"She was dead," he sobbed. "All of you were dead. Karak wants you, her, and everyone..."

"We won't let that happen," she whispered, stroking his face. "We'll always be here for her. Always."

His sobs faded, and his exhaustion overtook him. He lay back down, glad his wife was at his side. He slept, and this time no dreams came to him.

"What is it, Qurrah?" Tessanna asked. She had been awoken by the screams of her lover. Her kisses had slowly calmed him, chasing away the terror.

"Nothing," he said, sanity returning to his eyes. "I dreamt of Velixar is all. And my brother."

"Go back to sleep," she said. "I was dreaming of dogs eating my heart while worms crawled from my mouth. You whimper like a child." Qurrah chuckled. Tessanna placed her head across his chest, her long hair draping over him like a blanket. Qurrah opened his eyes and stared at the ceiling, unable to shake the horror of the dream. He had been dead, as had his brother. In a demonic haze of smoke and fire, Velixar had mocked him while Karak declared his victory.

"What have we done?" he asked, so softly that Tessanna did not hear. "Have you changed so greatly in the time I was gone?" To him, it had been a few weeks, but to the others, over a year had passed. Perhaps his brother had moved on. Changed. He had a wife and a daughter, after all.

"No," he said. His brother had not changed. He had merely forgotten. The life they had lived, marching at Velixar's side, was but a memory to his brother, one long suppressed.

"I will awaken your anger," he whispered. "I will bring forth the killer you buried. You cannot strike against me, and then deny what we are."

In his silent fury, he found the comfort to sleep.

Harruq awoke to throbbing pain in both his arms. His left felt weak and clumsy, while the right ached like a dagger was lodged to the hilt inside. His next realization, after the pain in his arms, was that he could see again.

Aurelia was gone. A shuffle to his side brought his attention to Haern.

"What are you doing in my bed?" he asked. The idea that he wasn't in his bed followed, and he chuckled, glad that the assassin appeared to be asleep. "Never mind then," he said.

"Did anyone ever tell you your voice is the worst thing to hear in the morning?" Haern mumbled, blinking open a bloodshot eye.

"I take it we're not sparring this morning?"

"No, no sparring. I think I'll pass out again, though."

Harruq struggled into a sitting position, blinking as he looked around the main floor of the tower. Slowly, his groggy mind cleared. He glanced at Haern, seeing his many burns. They were bad, but they appeared to be healing.

"Um, what happened to you?" he asked.

"Your brother happened to me."

"What?"

Haern pulled a pillow over his head. "Ask Tarlak."

The man went back to sleep. Harruq grunted and used his numb arm to push his hefty self to his feet. The contact of his hand against the floor awoke a thousand shocks within. Each one reminded him of what his brother had done.

Needing answers, he wound his way up the stairs for Tarlak's room. He was intercepted halfway there by a very angry priestess.

"What are you doing up?" Delysia asked. "Get your gray butt back downstairs and rest."

"Where's Aurry?" he asked.

"Upstairs with your daughter. I'll get her for you, if you want."

She examined his arms, her mouth locked in a little frown.

"It'll be another day before they're fine," she said, tossing her red hair across one shoulder. "Don't you dare try lifting anything until then. I need to reserve most of my magic for Haern, the poor dear."

"What happened to him?" the half-orc asked, knowing he would not like the answer. "Did Qurrah do that?"

The Cost of Betrayal

"Appears so," the priestess said, letting go of his arms. "Tessanna as well. Ashhur protect us from those two if they decide to repay our kindness." She gave him a wry smile.

Anger bubbled up Harruq's throat. "Tarlak sent him after them, didn't he?"

Delysia crossed her arms and pointed down the stairs.

"I'll bring him to you as well, but get yourself back to your pillows before you hurt yourself...again."

The half-orc reluctantly obeyed. He mulled over the previous days, desperate to understand what had happened. He had struck at his brother, wounded him severely, and then his brother had responded in kind. Now a friend had attempted to take his brother's life. How would Qurrah respond? Would he accept an apology? More importantly, should he even offer one? The sight of the massacred child in the alley, his young eyes frozen in a death gaze, was a haunting one.

"Ugh. Too much thinking," he said, plopping beside Haern.

"Do it silently," came Haern's muffled reply.

Tarlak arrived a few minutes later, just ahead of Aurelia and Delysia.

"How's our wonder-orc?" the wizard asked.

"Loud and annoying."

"Thanks Haern. Seriously, though, your eyes and arms fine?"

Harruq shrugged. "Did you send Haern after Qurrah and Tess?" he asked. Tarlak sat down at the table, sighing.

"Never been one to beat about the bush, eh, Harruq?" the wizard asked.

"Harruq, perhaps this is better to wait for another time," Aurelia said, sliding in beside her husband. Harruq kissed her cheek but disagreed.

"What happened when I was out," he asked.

"I sent Haern to retrieve your brother. He went into the King's Forest and returned hours later looking like a burnt log. End of story."

The half-orc groaned, fighting through his hundred initial reactions. "You had no right to do that," he finally decided on.

"No right?" Tarlak stood, marching over to the wounded half-orc. "No right? Last I remember, he was a wanted fugitive for the city of Veldaren. Last I remember, he has the blood of innocent children on his hands. Last I remember, he had struck down a member of my mercenaries. He may be your brother, Harruq, but you are *my* family, and I do not take kindly to anyone who hurts my kin. Now he has hurt Haern. What did you expect me to do?"

"Just let me deal with him."

"No!" Tarlak knelt down, his face inches from Harruq's. "This is no private matter, not anymore. He is a threat and must be dealt with accordingly. He is too dangerous to leave in the wild."

"He won't hurt any of us," Harruq pleaded. "I didn't mean to hit him. I started our fight, and you sent Haern after him, not the opposite. Just let him be. He will leave us alone."

"You don't know that," Aurelia said.

"Yes, I do. Trust me. I just need to talk to him."

The wizard threw up his hands. He stood and paced with curses on his lips.

"Am I missing all the fun?" Lathaar asked as he came down the stairs still dressed in his bedclothes.

"What do you think we should do?" Tarlak asked him. "Should we hunt for Qurrah, or let him be?"

The paladin shrugged. "We leave him be until he does more harm."

The wizard nearly fell over. Despite the seriousness of the situation, Delysia could not suppress a smile.

"We do what?" he asked.

"Aurelia," Lathaar asked. "Is it alright if I tell them? Good. Qurrah and Tessanna have some sort of magic protecting them from being located. I had Aurelia scry for their location, only to see darkness. Even if we can find them, we'd be marching on their home with them on the defensive. If Tessanna's power is anything like Mira's, it is best to leave them be."

"You're joking," Tarlak fumed. "You have to be joking. Are you telling me you're afraid of that crazy black-eyed little girl?"

"Not afraid," Lathaar said. "But you haven't seen what I've seen."

"And what is that?" The wizard crossed his arms, challenging his friend. "What have you seen that shakes the knees of our most holy defender?"

"Do not confuse fear with wisdom," Lathaar said. "I've seen an ancient demon brought low by the magical barrage of a goddess. I've seen the greatest fire wizard of our time brought to shame by the raging inferno leaving her fingertips. If Tessanna is akin to Mira, her power is awoken by anger. I suggest we not risk unleashing that unless we must. Until they harm again, I would leave them be."

Tarlak frowned in silence. For a brief moment, Lathaar saw the young kid he had first met. Brash, reckless, and with red fuzz in place of a mustache and beard. Even now that recklessness wished out, to demand its way. But Tarlak was a wiser man now. Most of the time.

"This Mira girl really outdid Roand the Flame?" he asked.

"Her fireball was twice the size of his," the paladin said.

"So we'll leave him be?" Harruq asked, daring to hope.

"Yes, for now," Tarlak said, not leaving Lathaar's gaze. "If he's wise, he'll stay gone for a long, long time."

"And if he's not?"

It was Aurelia who asked this. Other than worry for her husband, she had revealed little of her opinion on the matter.

"If he's not wise, then Lathaar might need to fetch that Mira girl to protect us," the wizard said with a chuckle.

No one laughed.

※

Qurrah awoke with the dawn, rising from the warm bed with a ferocious cough. The stolen life had healed much of the sword wound, but the pain and blood remained, clogging his throat. The cold air did little to help. Tessanna stirred, but he kissed her eyes back to sleep. He slipped into Velixar's robes and pulled tight the sash. Xelrak's words haunted the morning air.

It may take time, but he will return. Karak has sworn this to me.

Qurrah cinched the robe tighter. Bracing himself, he opened the door to outside. The chilly air swept around his robe, danced about his legs, and crept its way to his arms and chest. He met it head on, not wishing to disturb Tessanna's slumber. He closed the door behind him.

The earth remained dead all about the home, a gray scar on the orange and red canvas of the forest. Qurrah found comfort in its death.

"I sought you to help my wounded lover," he whispered to a phantom image of his brother he imagined floating along the wind. Frost punctuated his every word. "And now I return, wounded by you."

At least one thing had not changed. He attuned his mind to the darker things in life. He could sense death, and the soul he sought was so strong its pull was like a noose around his neck.

"Karnryk." He whispered the half-orc's name, having never been told it before. The spirit was so desperate to return to life that it was flooding his mind with memories, the way ghosts haunt old homes, dark caves, and the gallows where souls had died. Karnryk should have known better. He had forgotten Qurrah's promise to him.

Karnryk's body was a mess. Something about the cabin scared most animals away, but the carrion eaters were unafraid. Coyotes had consumed his innards. Worms and insects feasted on the remains. His face was puffy, his eyes long gone. To his mild amusement, the corpse's right arm was gone, most likely as a late meal for a scavenger mutt.

He heard a ghostly wail, and the soft touch of fingers pressed against his neck, chilling his blood.

"You are too late to be brought to life," Qurrah whispered to the ghost. "At least, not how you wish. My way, however, does not require freshness of the body."

He spent the next hour carving runes into the dirt surrounding the fetid corpse. Tessanna did not join him. The trials of the past few days had taken their toll, and she slept deep into the morning. That was fine with him. Qurrah preferred torturing in seclusion.

"Drak thun, drak thaye, kaer vrek thal luen," he chanted. *"Kala mar, yund cthular."* They were the words of his teacher, Velixar, and the unnamed Master. The words made him shiver with memory. The runes glowed, the body shrieked, and Karnryk lived once more, if life was the correct word.

"Stand up," Qurrah ordered. Karnryk growled. The first tug-of-war match had already begun, mere seconds after being granted life. Inside his head, Qurrah saw a silver thread linking the two. One end wrapped about Qurrah's skull, the other, Karnryk's throat. The more the warrior pulled, the deeper the ache, but the stronger Qurrah pulled, the less and less will the undead monster kept. In physical strength, Karnryk may have been the greater, but when matched in willpower, he was by far the inferior.

"I said stand," the necromancer shouted. The giant, rotting half-orc lurched to attention. Bits and pieces sloshed off him. Qurrah grabbed his head and forced it downward, placing his other hand over the empty sockets. He cast a spell so the undead thing could see, even though the eyes were long gone. This done, he made sure Karnryk watched the rotting pieces of himself fall.

"How was your stay in the abyss?" the necromancer asked.

The Cost of Betrayal

"I'll kill you," the enslaved being growled back. Qurrah chuckled.

"You did not answer my question."

He sent a mental command to his minion, his will so strong that Karnryk could only obey. He plunged a hand into his ribcage and crushed the remains of his heart. As a rule, undead did not feel pain. Their lungs did not inhale, their hearts did not beat, and their blood was unmoving in their veins. Qurrah, however, had deviated from the original spell. Much of Karnryk's original self had come back from the abyss, and through magical means, retained the sensations of touch, taste, and smell. Most important of all, he had come back able to feel pain.

Qurrah denied him the ability to scream. He would hate to wake up Tessanna.

"You can feel it, can't you?" he asked. His mouth pressed against Karnryk's ear as if whispering sweet words to a lover. "How soft and weak it is? I wonder how many eggs lay inside your flesh. You will find out, in time. Every hatchling will crawl about, blind and rabid for flesh, and they will feast. You will feel every bite. Every burrow. They are in your head, your feet, your chest, even that thing that made you a man before Tessanna mutilated it beyond recognition. Press harder. Mash your heart to pieces. You don't need it, not anymore."

He could feel Karnryk's hatred seething in his mind. He laughed

"A promise is a promise," Qurrah told the living corpse. "And I keep my promises. Tear out your tongue. I hear you clearly enough in my mind."

Without hesitation, Karnryk shoved his hand in his mouth and yanked out his tongue. He held it out to Qurrah as if it were a great offering.

"Throw it to the wolves," the necromancer ordered. "Your jaw next." Tongue and jaw flew into the forest. Karnryk stood erect, his face locked in an enormous hollow smile. Tiny shreds of his tongue hung from a hole above his neck, coated with dried blood. A tiny bug crawled up, poked its head about, and then crawled back. Karnryk felt every skitter of every leg down his windpipe.

"Very good," Qurrah said. "I will come for you tomorrow morning as well, and every morning after, until I am sated. Stand where you are, perfectly still. Enjoy the sensations within you."

The threats ended inside the half-orc's mind. Pleas and bargains flooded in. Karnryk would kill, obey, serve, anything at all, as long as he was spared the ability to feel.

You will make an excellent bodyguard one day, Qurrah told him in his head. *But that time is later. You are not broken yet.*

A single thought and the words ceased. The link between them broke. All Karnryk could do was follow his order, which chained his will greater than that which chained the moon around the world. He stood perfectly still, even when a swarm of flying bugs arrived, swirling down his nostrils and throat to make gluttons of themselves.

<hr />

The bitter aroma of boiling roots greeted him upon entering the cabin.

"Morning lover," Tessanna said, her voice calm and quiet. "I've made us tea to drink. World's getting cold, so I made something hot."

The half-orc ran a hand through her hair before sitting at the tiny table. She retrieved two wood-carved cups from a shelf, pausing to stare at one. A memory of her father sitting by the fire, a knife in one hand and a block of wood in the other, flooded her mind. A shaggy brown beard dirtied his face. Mommy walked by covered in flour. She kissed daddy on the cheek and playfully tugged his beard. The memory was good. Mommy was alive, her mind was one, and father still loved her. A single tear ran down her face. She didn't notice. One cup she placed in front of Qurrah, the other opposite of him. She took the boiling kettle, stirred the insides with a long wooden spoon, and then filled both cups.

"Did you enjoy yourself out there?" Tessanna asked as she placed the little kettle back over the fire.

"He needed to pay for what he did to you," Qurrah said. "And yes, I did enjoy it."

The girl nodded. She sat down, wrapping the cup with her hands and staring into the thick brown liquid. She didn't sip it, not until Qurrah did. It tasted bitter in her mouth, strong and bitter, but it was good.

"Did you pick the roots yourself?" Qurrah asked.

"Yes."

Nothing else. Qurrah accepted this, expecting her to remain silent. For once, something weighed upon her apathetic self beyond the tarnished shreds of her childhood.

The Cost of Betrayal

"I want to see her again," she blurted. Qurrah sipped a bit more of the tea.

"Who?"

"Aullienna loves me," she said. Her hands clenched the side of the table. "But she'll be forced to not love me. They will make her. They will. I won't let them."

"You know they will not let us return to see her," Qurrah said.

"But I have to," she said. Another tear rolled. "They'll ruin her. Not like me. A different way. I must see her again, Qurrah, I must! They love her because she is normal, she is happy. They wouldn't love her if she was like me. They hate me for how I am. They would hate her, too."

"What are you saying, Tessanna?" Qurrah grew alarmed at how white her hands were. She clenched the table so hard her skin scraped off her fingertips.

"I looked in your book," she said, her attitude shifting. She turned shy. "I looked at all the pretty runes that make people go crazy. I saw me in them, Qurrah." She held up her arms. "I saw what I see in me. It will make her like me. They won't love her when she is like me, and then they will give her to us. I can see her again. And I'll never stop loving her, not like they will."

"Show me the runes you saw," Qurrah said, jumping from his seat. Tessanna lazily pointed to their bed, where the tome lay open.

"It's the fourth set down on that page. I even read them aloud. They felt right, just right."

"You read them aloud…but you said you couldn't read?"

Tessanna giggled like mad. "See? They're me. How would I know them if they aren't me?"

Qurrah scanned his eyes over them, instantly recognizing the symbols. They looked very much like those the girl carved in blood across her arms. They were in the final third of the book, and although Qurrah had tested forty forms of insanity, it would have been another hundred before he had reached them.

"You want me to read these to Aullienna?" he asked. Tessanna nodded.

"Please. It won't hurt her. It didn't hurt me."

He felt his gut tighten, and his breath went shallow. "If I do this, Harruq will never forgive me."

"Will he forgive you now? What do you have to lose? He must be punished, Qurrah. He hurt you. It was all you dreamt about last night. Hurting him. Making him angry."

She stood from the table and approached, her eyes livid. Life danced in them, more than he had ever seen.

"You can help us all," she said. "Your brother will learn. The Eschaton will learn. I will have her, and she will love and have me."

"If I cure your mind, I can cure hers as well," Qurrah said, feeling his resolve weaken. "I will do no permanent harm to her. Harruq will forgive me, but first I must be stronger to cure you. I need a spellbook beyond the ones I have been given."

"What is it you need?" Tessanna asked, sliding her body against his. Her hands brushed and caressed.

"Darakken's spellbook," he said. "The paladin knows where it is. He can bring it to me."

"Then let's do it," she whispered, nibbling on his ear. "She will be like me for only a little while, and it's for good, right?"

Qurrah grabbed her wrists and spun, shoving her against the wall. With surprising strength, he pinned her hands above her head. The girl gasped at the sudden force, but it was not of fear, anger, or even surprise.

"You're using me, aren't you?" he said. "You care not for me or my brother. You want their daughter."

"Yes," she moaned. "But you use me as well. And we both like it." He pressed harder against her arms. His chest shoved against hers, pinning her. Her breath quickened, and against his chest, he felt her nipples hardening.

"I would do anything for you," he whispered to her. "Anything. You do not need to play me for it."

"Please," she gasped. "Whatever you want, I'll do it."

He took her there, right against the wall, dwelling in her lust. At her climax, she tore her mouth away from his and shrieked his name, but it was not the name he expected.

"Master," she screamed. "Master! Master!"

He finished shortly after, a bitter feeling in his heart. He knew his role, then, the one he was meant to play. He would play it. Until she needed him as a true lover, an equal, a husband, he would play it, and enjoy every second.

24

Having worms eat his flesh wasn't worse than the abyss, but it was comparable. When night fell a new torture arrived. It came with yellow eyes, patches of missing fur, and a limping gait that explained its desperation. The animal could no longer hunt for food. It would have to do with the carrion it could find, and that night it had found Karnryk.

Qurrah's order was simple: don't move. So he didn't. When the coyote nibbled on his lone hand, he knew a good punch would send the wretched thing running, but knowing and doing were two different things. With a sickening crunch, it tore off a finger and rolled it about its mouth.

Enjoy it, Karnryk thought, lost in a sick delirium. *Chew it good. Maybe even choke. I got plenty for you to eat, you sick little mutt. Think you can eat all of me? My head, too? Scoop my brains out so the gnats won't crawl through the holes in my eyes to feed?*

Crunch went the bones in his hand. It latched on with a feverous grip, yanking until the wrist broke. Tail between its legs, the mongrel ran off with its prize.

When I kill him, it'll be by clubbing him to death with my elbow, he thought. Gods help him, he couldn't even bite, not with his jaw lying twenty feet away in the dirt. His only recourse, his only salvation, was imagining the brutal death of his master. By sword, by foot, by choking, by throttling, smashing his head in a door, burning his face in fire, bleeding him out bit by bit before a stream, everything was good. Every bit of it would be fun. If he had his way, he'd deserve his return to the abyss. He'd take Qurrah with him, hauled over his shoulder to throw him to the demons.

"Something ate your other hand," Qurrah mused the next morning. "A shame. You have no way to wield a sword."

Yes, *such a horrible shame,* came Karnryk's words rudely into his mind. *I can still kick people to death for you, though, you sick bastard.*

Qurrah took a stick from the ground and rammed it through an eye socket.

"Uncalled for," he said. "And unwise. You need a sword hand or you are of no use to me."

Then start searching coyote stomachs, because you're not finding it around here.

Qurrah yanked the stick out and shoved it through the other eye socket, twirling it about for good measure.

"You'll get a new hand," he said. "I've a task for you. Once you've completed it, I'll return you to the abyss. Until then, though..." Qurrah reached into his pocket and pulled out a stale piece of bread. He mashed it in his fingers, scattering crumbs around the rigid warrior's feet. He wadded the rest into the gaping hole that was Karnryk's face.

"That should ensure you plenty of company for the day."

The necromancer trudged back to the cottage, pondering a way to obtain a new sword arm for his slave. Meanwhile, Karnryk silently invented new curses as the first of many flies flew down his throat to investigate the wonderful new smell.

✦

Haern waited until Harruq and Aurelia were upstairs playing with their daughter before slipping into Tarlak's study.

"Afternoon, Haern," the wizard said, not looking up from his bookwork. "So what brings the grand servant of our king to my humble little room? By the way, you've been wandering around the city, haven't you?" He glanced up so his frown would be visible. "Your burns haven't healed. You shouldn't be sleuthing about."

The assassin shrugged. Scars covered his face and hands, although Delysia promised him they would fade. Several fingers were wrapped in bandages. Miraculously enough, his hair had survived mostly intact. Only a small patch near the front had been burned off, so that it appeared he had a receding hairline. Haern combed his blond hair forward best he could to hide it, but it did no good.

"I believe I found where Qurrah is hiding," he said.

"Say again?"

"Karnryk spent a good two months dropping coin for any information about Tessanna," the assassin explained. "He and his cronies vanished weeks ago."

"And not long after Qurrah returned here with Tessanna," Tarlak said, making the connection. "Those wounds to the girl, Karnryk made them."

"Which means Karnryk found them," Haern said, leaning with his hands atop Tarlak's desk. "A few cut-rate thugs knew the girl's father. Evidently, he had a debt to them, gambling of some sort. They followed him to his house, mostly to ensure he couldn't hide if his debts grew out of hand. I've talked with them. There are a few markers, and eventually a path deep enough in the woods. I can track it."

Tarlak folded his hands together and cracked his knuckles.

"I know I must be wrong, but I get the distinct impression you want to go after them again."

Haern grinned. "I've got a score to settle, wouldn't you agree?"

The wizard chuckled. "Hoping you would learn from the first time was foolish of me, wasn't it?"

He stood, closing his book. His hand absently scratched his beard as he stared at the cover, pondering. "Lathaar is right," he said at last. "Until they make a move, it is best to leave them be. I'm glad we know, in case something does happen. For now, let's keep this knowledge between ourselves."

"Quiet in the night," Haern insisted. "There will be no battle. No warning."

"I said no," Tarlak warned. "And they had no warning the first time, either, but you still came back a burned mess."

The assassin's eyes darkened. "They cannot kill me."

"Those marks on your face say differently." The wizard sighed, knowing he had gone too far. "I'm sorry, Haern. I can't risk it. If we take them on, we go together. Right now, I'm keeping my word with Harruq, or he'll never trust me again."

Haern bowed.

"I pray you are right," he whispered, pulling the hood back over his head. "And I pray they accept the uncommon grace they are being given."

With a flutter of gray, he was gone. Tarlak slumped back in his chair and reopened the book.

"I hate being in charge," he muttered.

***

"I have an idea for his hand," Tessanna said one morning after a violent hour of lovemaking.

"My pet's?" Qurrah said, his head nuzzled into her length of hair. The girl laughed at his words.

"Yes, your pet's. We need him to hold a big scary sword right?"

"Right." His breath tickled her neck, and she laughed again.

"I can make him a new hand. One of stone. If you find me a rock, and a fire, I think I can make it. I think."

"That is a lot of thinking for tiny little you," said Qurrah, leaning on his elbow. He shivered as she traced a finger across his naked chest.

"I want to help. I should help you, right? It's the right thing to do?"

"Yes, love," he said. "It is the right thing to do. How large a stone do you need?"

"Big as a fist," she said. "Shouldn't that be obvious?"

The half-orc laughed. "Yes. You're right."

It took him half an hour to find the perfect stone. He pried it from the dirt beside the river. It was smooth and round with a flat bottom. He threw it against a tree twice, just to ensure it could endure a pounding. Only dirt caked off with each collision against the bark. Satisfied, he cleaned it in the river and trekked home.

Tessanna was ready for him. A small fire burned steadily in the dirt. Three small rocks with blood-drawn runes formed a triangle about the fire. Even more blood dripped into the flame, pouring freely from a cut on Tessanna's wrist as she gazed on with glee. When she saw the stone, she beamed.

"Perfect," she said. "Come here. Put it down. I want you to watch."

He set it next to the fire and then glanced at the glyphs on the runes. He recognized the three, but it made no sense. They were symbols usually involved with resurrecting the dead. How would they help with making a hand for his pet?

"Tessanna, how do you know…"

"It'll work," she said, bobbing her head enthusiastically. "Don't ask me how, even though you just did, you naughty boy. I know. Like I know a lot of things."

Without another word, she picked up the stone and placed it in the center of the fire. The burning twigs shoved aside and continued to burn.

"Imagine a hand," she whispered, running her fingers across Qurrah's face to close his eyes. Her voice grew cold and aged. "A hand forged by gods and granted power by things we dare not see. Imagine each vein, pulsing with gold. Imagine its claws, short but strong as steel, their tips stained with the blood of a thousand victims. This hand can wield the mightiest sword and brace the

The Cost of Betrayal

greatest of shields. Imagine it, lover, and I will make it. Let me see, and then you shall see as well."

He did imagine such a hand, its flesh stone, its veins gold, and its thick fingertips red. Her words painted it in his mind sure as a brush on a canvas. He focused on the hand, mesmerized by the strength it possessed. He dimly grew aware that Tessanna was casting a spell, but the haze that enveloped his mind swirled the knowledge away. The hand could have belonged to a deity, he thought, one that made the rock of earth and gave purpose and rhythm to the stones and rivers. A man could die by that hand, and there would be no shame.

"Open your eyes," he heard his lover say. He did. Deep in the fire was the hand. He cried out and stepped back, for it pulsed with a life unworldly. The fingers flexed one by one, even though it ended in a simple stump at the wrist. The flesh was gray and impossibly strong.

"How?" he asked, breathless.

"Someone once had a hand like this," she whispered, soft and quiet. "He was a bad man. Lots of people tried to kill him. When they did, they cut him up in tiny, tiny pieces. Bad people deserved that, they said. So I brought his hand here, and I made it alive. Do you like it Qurrah?"

He nodded, his eyes never leaving the hand.

"What was his name?" he asked. In response, she giggled.

"Jerrick."

Jerrick...

Qurrah laughed. Jerrick Carver, the Cleaver of Newhaven. He had died an age ago, when Ashhur and Karak were but lowly gods warring on the land of Dezrel. Back when Velixar was still alive.

"Run, run, the Cleaver come, you been bad and now you're done," he said. Tessanna gave him a funny look. "A silly rhyme," Qurrah explained. "I thought Jerrick just a myth, a story to scare us as children. Amazing, love. Simply amazing. How will I attach it to Karnryk?"

"Pick it up and put it on," she said, tossing her hair across her shoulder to expose her soft neck. "Pretend you're sliding into me. It'll go just fine."

"I'll remember that," he said, bending down to the still burning fire and retrieving the hand. He felt blood, or some similar fluid, throbbing in the veins. A chill ran through him, and it was a delicious chill. He went to Karnryk.

Bring me a present? asked the voice in his head.

"One you should be proud to bear," he said, holding forth the hand. "Extend your arm."

Karnryk held out his lone arm, the stump a nasty mess of fluids and bone. The necromancer felt a sudden bolt of excitement shoot through his slave when the hand first touched the rotting flesh.

"Wuuuh," Karnryk groaned, his first audible noise in two days.

"It is your hand," Qurrah said, sliding the wrist forward exactly like his lover suggested. Somehow, the bony flesh attached and became firm. "And even in your state, you should know what a tremendous gift this is."

Give me a sword, ordered Karnryk. In response, Qurrah ordered him to his knees.

"I give all commands," the necromancer said. "Nothing has changed. Do not forget your place." He glanced about, trying to remember that chaotic fight that felt years ago, although it had been little less than a month.

"Find your sword," he told him. "Retrieve it and return here. You are allowed to do nothing more."

Karnryk willingly obeyed, returning to the place where he had died. He picked up the mammoth two-handed sword in his one hand, lifting it as if it were a feather. He carried it to Qurrah, who examined his pet and his blade. Curiosity overtook him. He had to see his pet in action.

"Chop down that limb," he said, pointing to a branch hanging low near them. He sensed a bit of magic in the warrior's blade, so he expected little difficulty. A good couple hacks and it would be down. At least, that is what he thought.

When Karnryk lifted up the giant sword and sent it slicing through the wood like it was butter, he realized just how precious a gift he had stumbled upon. "The tree," he said as the branch fell to the ground with a crashing of leaves and sticks. "Cut down the tree."

Without a word, the hulking slave marched over to the trunk. It was easily the width of Karnryk himself. He hefted the sword high above his head and then swung. A great thunder tore through the forest as the blade sunk two feet into the wood before halting.

"Take it out," Qurrah said. Instead his pet ignored him, letting loose a low grunt. His arm flexed, the veins in the hand pulsed gold, and then the sword shoved further and further in, snapping through the final foot. Birds scattered as branches caught on branches and the tree smashed with a whoosh to the ground.

"Tessanna, you goddess," Qurrah said, his voice awestruck.

He might have been scared if he realized just how close his words were to truth.

"Are you sure I cannot go?" Tessanna asked. She sat on the bed, her knees up to her neck with her arms wrapped around them. Her tattered dress covered little of her body.

"I will be fine," Qurrah said, stacking his tome and spellbook into his arms. "Karnryk will provide ample distraction for my purposes."

"But I want to see her," the girl whispered. "Please. I just want to see her."

The half-orc turned and kissed her forehead. He stared into her eyes and promised, just as he had promised many times before.

"You will see her again. I swear it."

He pulled his hood tight over his head, took his whip, and left. Tessanna bitterly stared at the door.

"Qurrah," she said, but the thought had too many endings. She did her best to pass the time. She took her dagger from underneath the bed, moved beside the dying fire, and viciously slashed her arm. Each rune pulsed with blood, and she found strange satisfaction knowing those runes would soon be read aloud to that precious little girl.

"Come, Karnryk," Qurrah said, approaching his pet. "We travel to Veldaren. Should you perform well, I will absolve you of your sins against Tessanna."

I would hate to disappoint, was his reply.

Before they could go, Qurrah needed to cast one last spell. By the time he arrived at Veldaren, the stars would be numerous. Beautiful as they were, he needed them gone. Fear was what he needed. Fear, and chaos. The stars combated both. Tessanna had taught him the words for the spell. The knowledge locked in her brain seemed infinite, yet she used it so sparingly.

The words were simple, at least in terms of magical incantations. He cast the spell with ease. Rolling against the wind, a line of cloud grew across the western horizon. Pleased, Qurrah lowered his arms and let out a sigh of relief.

"We are ready," he said.

The two trudged east in silence. Qurrah had his spells, his whip, and his tome of insanity. Karnryk had his sword and his hand. It was all they needed.

※

"Something is wrong," Aurelia said, sitting up in the bed. The blankets fell to a heap in front of her, revealing the thin silk that covered her body. Beside her, Harruq stirred with an unhappy grunt.

"What is it, baby?" he asked, rubbing her arm with his hand. She turned to him, her eyes wide and her whole body shivering.

"Please, my dreams were dark. Something horrible is coming."

"Just a dream is all," the half-orc mumbled. "Surely you don't…you do, don't you?"

She cast off the blankets and headed for their wardrobe. She let her slinky and unpractical garment fall to the floor, revealing her naked form for a brief moment before she slid on her green dress. It glittered with soft runes and gold trim. She tied a sash about her waist and grabbed her staff, all before Harruq could stumble out of bed.

"Aurry, wait up, what's going on?"

"Your armor," she told him. "Put it on. Now."

Harruq got up, a creeping fear growing in his heart. He had not seen Aurelia this afraid since…well, he wasn't sure he had ever seen her so afraid. He took his black leather armor off the nightstand and began the tedious routine of buckling it on.

"What did you dream?" he asked, his arms reaching behind his back, pulling on strap after strap.

"I saw Tessanna standing over Aullienna," she said, crossing her arms across her chest. "She was killing her with a dagger, but not normal, not…" She turned, tears sparkling in her eyes. "Please. Hurry."

From far down the stairs, they heard a banging on the front door. The sound made Harruq's heart jump.

"That better be coincidence," he said. Not willing to risk it, he strapped on his cloak, buckled his two swords, and rushed down the stairs. Halfway down, he met Tarlak rushing back up. The wizard was dressed in his bed robes and had a funny, pointy hat on his head, topped with what looked like a ball of cotton.

"Get ready we need to…oh, you're ready," he said, giving Harruq a funny look. "How did you know?"

"I didn't," he said. "Aurry got spooked by a dream. What's going on?"

The Cost of Betrayal

"That was a guard from Veldaren," he said, dashing into his room. He grabbed his yellow robes and hat, throwing them on over his bed clothes. "Something's tearing through the town. Tens of guards are already dead. The soldier said they couldn't corner it, couldn't overpower it with numbers. We've been promised a fortune to kill it."

He pulled his hat tight on his head, either not noticing or not caring that is was badly crooked. "Wake up Haern, Lathaar, and Brug. I'll get Delysia. We're moving, now!"

Harruq banged on Haern's door, only to have the fully dressed and armed assassin greet him.

"I heard the knock," was all he said. Lathaar was already awake, his platemail gleaming in the blue light of his swords. Together they roused Brug, who gave Harruq the dirtiest of looks until he heard the reason for his waking.

"Great jumping galoopagots," he said, staggering toward his armor. Harruq glanced at Haern.

"Galoopagots?"

The assassin shrugged.

The entire party massed in the main foyer in less than five minutes, armed and armored.

"Let's go," Tarlak said, seeing all accounted for. "We strike the killing blow and two-thousand gold is ours. Since Lathaar here won't accept any, we're talking a lot of coin split between the rest of us. Oh, and people are dying. That's bad, too."

"What about Aullienna," Aurelia interrupted. "I won't leave her here unguarded."

"She will not be safe with us," Haern whispered.

The wizard rubbed his eyes. "Are you sure we cannot leave her here alone for an hour?"

The elf shook her head, adamant. "I will stay before I leave her."

"But your magic could decide...oh blast it." Tarlak glanced about, his mind frantic. "Brug," he suddenly decided. "Stay and the guard the child."

"Me? I'm no durn babysitter."

Aurelia gave him a pleading look, and it didn't take long for him to melt.

"Please, Brug?" she said. "I will feel much better."

He kicked his foot and caved. "Fine. Just don't have too much fun without me."

With that, the gang headed out into the dark. Rain and wind swept the land.

"The sky was clear when we retired," Aurelia said, her voice shouting above the thunder. Tarlak nodded, feeling his stomach sink.

"Why did you leave Brug behind?" Harruq asked as his wife opened a magical portal to the city.

"Because he's stubborn and cranky, the perfect person to watch her," the wizard shouted. "That, and he's our worst fighter."

The half-orc laughed, but not much. The way his wife had looked when she awoke, he was starting to wonder if he would have preferred the best to remain at his daughter's side. Then the blue portal ripped open, a swirling passage to the city. They all entered, one after another. When Aurelia went in last, the portal swirled closed, its blue light fading. The entrance to the tower fell to darkness.

And in the darkness, something stirred.

25

The portal opened beside the fountain that graced Veldaren's center. The sudden rain had caused the basin to overflow, so the Eschaton stepped out into heavy mud. Already their clothes were soaked to the bone.

"Where is our quarry?" Lathaar asked, glancing every direction.

"When they sent for us, it was in the northern quarter," Tarlak said. "Stay sharp, and look for guards."

Lathaar led the way, a longsword in his right hand, a shortsword in the other. Each one glowed a soft blue-white. The light softened their fears and anxieties, banishing them like they did the darkness. Because of such a beacon, it was not long before a guard in chainmail spotted them and came running.

"Thank Ashhur you're here," the man shouted. His face was bloodied, and he kept wiping the rain from his eyes. "We tried cornering it against the wall, but it blew right through us like we were twigs and straw."

"What is it?" Tarlak asked. "What are we fighting?"

"He's a giant," the guard replied. "Orc blood, and fighting like a crazed demon. Watched him kill twenty like nothing, and took a priest of Ashhur to even make 'em wince."

"Lead us there," Lathaar ordered. The guard bowed.

"Follow me," he shouted. He turned and ran north, following the main road before ducking down a maze of empty streets. The sound of steel against steel rang through the thunder.

"He appeared out of nowhere," the soldier explained, glancing back to make sure they were following. "Don't know how he got in, the gate guards saw nothing, but then… oh shit, that's Darren."

Up ahead, a soldier had staggered toward them, his left arm clutching his chest. His right arm was gone. Their guide ran ahead, shouting his friend's name.

"Wait!" Lathaar shouted, chasing after him. A behemoth in rotting flesh smashed out of the alleyway, a giant sword held in its only hand. The sword swooped in a wide arc, slicing both guards at the waist. They fell, soaking the muddying earth with blood. A thick, guttural roar bellowed from the monster.

"What is that," Delysia asked, her hand over her mouth. Tarlak's eyes narrowed in recognition. Haern clanged his sabers together, remembering his lone encounter long ago with that giant half-orc.

"It's Karnryk," the assassin whispered. "Except he's had his face and arm ripped off..."

"Bring him down," Tarlak ordered. Fire erupted about his hands. "And do it fast."

Karnryk spotted their ensemble, raised his weapon high, and charged. Only Lathaar stood his ground, not fearing the half-orc's giant blade. He had faced larger, and that blade had been consumed in fire and wielded by an ancient demon of the abyss. He crossed his glowing swords into an 'X' and accepted the blow. Energy crackled, and the sound of the collision sundered the air. Lathaar staggered back, his arms numb.

"He hits like a demon," the paladin gasped.

"You would know," Tarlak said. A fireball leapt off his hands, straight for Karnryk's chest. In response, the half-orc put his fist before his face and sucked the magic into his glowing hand.

"That's not good," the wizard said moments before the fireball flew straight back at them. The party scattered as the fire exploded. Haern scooped Aurelia into his arms just before the impact, leaping to a side alley.

"To the tower," Haern whispered to her.

"Why, what is wrong?" she asked.

"Karnryk vanished looking for Tessanna," he explained, glancing back toward the fight. "Can you not see his flesh? He is dead, and imbued with strength unholy. One of the necromancers *commands* him, Aurelia!"

"Aullienna," the elf gasped. Her haunting dream returned in full strength.

"Go," Haern whispered. "Take Harruq if you must." The assassin dashed back into the street. The elf debated, in the end choosing to leave her husband behind. They were acting on a hunch, while the threat in Veldaren was most definitely real. Besides, her magic would do little good. The returned fireball proved that.

She closed her eyes and summoned a portal back to the tower. Her heart in her throat, she stepped through.

"Leave me as a durn babysitter," Brug grumbled, a mug of ale in his hand. He sat at the table, wallowing in the light of a lone torch upon the wall. Five other mugs lay next to him, all empty. "When someone's got to do grunt work, it's always Brug, do this. Brug, do that. Make this, make that. Screw all of ya."

He downed the sixth mug, spilling on his beard about as much as he drank. A burp marked the cup's return to the table.

Knock.

A single rap on the door, but that was all it took. Any semblance of drunkenness vanished from him. Brug stood, a punch dagger in each fist.

"Who's there?" he asked. No voice answered. He approached, low and battle ready. Outside, the wind howled, carrying voices.

Go away, they said, making him shake his head as if to scatter some strange mirage. *Go away, and do not come back. It is not safe. Not safe. Not safe.*

"Shuddup, I ain't no coward," he said. "Whoever's out there, you better have more up your sleeve than that."

"I do," Qurrah suddenly hissed into his ear. Brug whirled, stabbing out, but he found only an illusion to eviscerate. The presence of Qurrah scattered like butterflies made of shadows, each swarming to a separate corner of the room.

"What the abyss?" he said, circling, looking for the intruder. But the intruder wasn't in. Not yet. The doors to the tower burst open. In rushed Qurrah, latching onto the man's wrist. Ice flooded his arm, numbing his entire right side. Brug punched with his other arm. His dagger shattered against some unseen barrier before the half-orc's chest.

"No magical enchantments on your own blades?" Qurrah said. "You idiot."

Brug gasped as Qurrah's other hand clutched his face, his fingers locked tight. Image after image of despair and death swarmed into his mind. His eyes rolled back, he gasped a deep sigh, and then he fell and moved no more.

"Sleep well," Qurrah said. "I have a bedtime story to read."

The half-orc climbed the stairs, a gleaming tome of blood and nightmares in his hands.

"I got him!" Harruq shouted, meeting Karnryk's rush head on. The enchantments on his swords were strong, and his muscles like those of an ox. Like Lathaar, he tried blocking the blow with both swords. Like Lathaar, he flew back, unable to meet such strength head-to-head. A bolt of ice flew from Tarlak, only to be batted away as if it were a pebble.

"Keep him distracted," Haern whispered to them. He lunged straight for the raging undead monster. Karnryk swung his sword in an upward arc, one that would have torn Haern from hip to shoulder. The magic of his ring teleported him behind the warrior, safe from harm. Harruq charged, following the orders of his teacher. He bellowed, lashing out at exposed skin. When the greatsword came swinging in, he dove to safety.

"His head," Lathaar screamed as Haern flew in from behind. "Stab for his head!"

Haern had a different plan in mind. His knees slammed between the half-orc's shoulders, followed by each saber stabbing at the collarbone connected to the lone remaining arm. Karnryk lurched forward, steel biting into his rotted flesh. The assassin pried, feeling muscle tearing and the bone beginning to pop. Karnryk twisted this way and that, like a bull tossing a rider. Twice he slammed his back against a building, splintering wood. Haern dropped after the second hit, all breath blasted from his lungs. One of his sabers remained embedded, while the other fell beside his limp form.

"Haern!" Delysia cried. She dashed over, completely ignoring the behemoth that towered above him. Lathaar chased after, for Karnryk had turned and raised his sword to finish off the dangerous man.

"Elholad!" he cried, sheathing his shortsword and grasping his longsword with both hands. The blue-light flared. The light scattered the darkness. The blade all but vanished, becoming a glowing weapon of holy light.

Lathaar crossed the distance in the single stroke of a lightning bolt. The Elholad intercepted the killing blow. Lathaar's shoulders jarred, his hands ached, but the blade did not break, nor did it falter.

"Get back!" Lathaar screamed, shoving forward one of his hands. Karnryk was undead, and while dark paladins could compel undead to their will, paladins of Ashhur could command their retreat. Lathaar's will was strong, his faith hardened and tested. When the invisible power rolled off him, Karnryk staggered as if slammed by a battering ram.

Lathaar gave him no reprieve. He took to his feet, slashing in with his mystical blade. Karnryk blocked once, twice, each time showering sparks and light throughout the rain. Lightning struck, and in the flicker, he glanced back at the sight of Delysia hunched over the fallen assassin. Healing light enveloped her hands.

"Who is it that commands you wretch?" Lathaar asked, stabbing forward with his Elholad. Karnryk's parry came in late, and the swirling light buried deep into his chest before tearing out the side. A tiny bit of blood leaked to the mud, accompanied by puss and rot. The undead hulk did not relent. Karnryk gurgled something unintelligible and then roared his rage. Their swords clashed as Harruq and Tarlak watched transfixed.

"Should he fall, take up the attack," Tarlak said, the fire of a spell still surrounding his hands. Harruq nodded, waiting for an opening. It appeared he would get none. Lathaar's strokes never slowed, and his skill surpassed Karnryk's. More and more flesh hacked away, including a sizable chunk of the sword arm's elbow. Again, the paladin outstretched his hand and attempted to banish him.

"Be gone from our land!" he cried. Karnryk roared, pain intolerable swarming throughout his mind. Momentarily stunned, he was helpless before the shining white blade that thrust for his head.

The sword struck a wall of pure darkness, accompanied by the sound of steel scraping against stone. Lathaar pulled back, and the others grimaced or swore in fear. Tessanna approached, her hands covered with shadow and her eyes pits of black. Her dress flapped in the wind, her hair clung to her face, and in the dim light she seemed a demoness.

"Oh shit," Tarlak murmured, abandoning his spell and instead preparing a magical shield.

"No kidding," Harruq grumbled, charging the girl as several bolts of shadow flew their way.

⋈

The door crept open with the tiniest of creeks. Although a fierce storm raged outside, calm star-lit sky graced within. A few docile clouds floated across, childlike compared to those that unleashed rain and thunder. The grass was soft against his skin, the wind cool and soothing. Atop her bed, Aullienna squirmed. It seemed even her dreams were speckled with warning.

Qurrah grabbed his tome, his hands covered with sweat. His heart hammered in his ears, yet he could not deny the excitement that flooded his body. For good or ill, he was going to do this. Step after step he took, winding his way up to where the girl slept. The branches creaked. A few leaves rustled. Aullienna startled, and she awoke to see Qurrah standing over her, a smile on his face and a book in his hands.

"Uncle?" she asked, rubbing her eyes. Most would have found it cute, even adorable. Qurrah barely noticed.

"I'm here to read you a bedtime story," the half-orc said.

"Where's mommy?" she asked, turning in bed to look at the dark doorway leading to where Harruq and Aurelia's bed was.

"They are sleeping," Qurrah said. "As should you be. I know your dreams are troubled. Just listen, and I'll send all your fears away."

"I want mommy," she said, shrinking back from his smile. One of her dreams had been of a bear chasing after her, its mouth dripping with honey. Somehow that bear's smile seemed kinder than Qurrah's.

"But mommy's asleep right now," he said, placing thick wads of wax in his ears. "Lay your head down, child."

She did as she was told. Qurrah opened up his tome, marked by a dried leaf to the page where Tessanna had discovered her incantation. His ears blocked, he read aloud the words to break the little girl's mind.

"This way," the man in golden armor said, twenty men behind him. They were all well equipped. Their armor shone in the light of torches, their shields polished and smooth. Their leader carried the standard of Neldar on his shield, and his blade was the finest of the city's smiths. Beside him hurried a priest of Ashhur, his white robes tarnished by rain and mud.

"Do you think they will come, Antonil?" the priest asked, holding a hand up to block the rain.

"Do or don't, we have to find that thing and finish it," the Guard Captain shouted back. "And no devilstorm will provide me excuse should any more die. Can you sense where it went?"

The priest shook his head, his mouth open and gasping for air. "I lost it when he knocked me...hold here. I believe I sense it."

The soldiers waited impatiently as the priest closed his eyes and concentrated. A moment later, the man jerked open his eyes and staggered back as if struck.

"Did you find it?" Antonil asked.

"I...I don't know," the man said. "But I found something." He pointed down a street to their right. "That way. Hurry, and may Ashhur help us all."

They hurried ahead, the squad a fourth of the size it had been a mere hour ago. The undead creature had torn through their ranks, at least sixty were dead by Antonil's count, and he would allow no more. They passed by small homes and closed stores. The normal business of the night had halted. Only killing went unabated. The priest said directions, which they followed without hesitation.

"When you see the creature, charge at once," Antonil shouted back to his men. "We must overwhelm it with numbers, it is our only..."

"Ashhur be with us," the priest said, drawing the Guard Captain's attention back to the front. He halted, his mouth agape. The Eschaton Mercenaries had come, and his heart was thankful, but the battle raging before his eyes defied reason.

A paladin of Ashhur dueled their undead target, matching it blow for blow with his glowing blade. Beside the monster was a girl. Her eyes were dark and her hair wet and clinging to her skin. Magic seemed to explode out of her. A wizard, presumably Tarlak due to the abundance of yellow, did his best to counter and protect against her attacks, but he was sorely pressed. Two others knelt by a house, one a priestess of Ashhur, the other...

"Haern?" Antonil wondered. A bellowing war cry turned his attention to a raging half-orc that seemed incredibly familiar. The half-orc charged the goddess, accepting blows of darkness against his flesh to cross the distance.

"All those with blades, take the creature," Antonil ordered. "Aion, help against the girl."

"I will do my best," the priest said, rushing to the wizard's side. With a communal cry, the guards of Veldaren charged Karnryk, their blades held high.

◈

"You will not interfere," Tessanna shrieked, great spears of shadow leaping from her fingers. Harruq twisted and dodged, but several scraped against his skin as they passed. One wicked spear slashed the side of his cheek, smearing his face with water and blood. He grimaced, swearing to repay her. Not just for the wound. For everything.

"You interfered plenty," Harruq said, jumping over a wall of fire she had summoned and then smashing his blades against her neck. Despite the powerful magic in his swords, she only laughed and accepted the hit. Her legs buckled, but the swords did not pierce flesh. The half-orc shouted out his rage. "You ruined Qurrah! You thrust him into the abyss, you whore!"

"Ruined?" the girl said, the scars on her arms flaring a dull crimson. "Ruined?" She slapped the swords aside and shoved her hands against Harruq's chest. Fire exploded about the armor, the force of it flinging him through the air. He smacked into a house, hitting his head hard. Of course, that wasn't the only hit. The fall to the ground jarred his legs and caused him to bite down on his tongue. Harruq spat blood and glared death at the girl.

"Yeah, ruined!" he cried. A bolt of ice courtesy of Tarlak punctuated his accusation. It struck Tessanna square in the chest, covering her body. The chill in her blood grew worse. Black tendrils danced off her fingers, sweeping aside the next two bolts of ice along with a bolt of fire. They attacked the mage, piercing through his magical warding.

"Not good," the wizard mumbled. His heart ached, he looked to his sister, and then the tendrils hit his flesh. They sizzled and recoiled like a scared viper. Stunned to be alive, the wizard glanced down at his unharmed self, and then to the side, where a priest of Ashhur had joined him.

"Focus on protection," Aion said before casting another spell. A translucent shield appeared between the two casters and Tessanna. Tarlak formed another of his own, doubling the strength.

"Can the half-orc take her if we provide distraction?" Aion asked.

"Ashhur knows," was the wizard's reply.

But her attention was not on them, not then.

"I did not ruin him," she spat to Harruq. "I helped him. I loved him. I love him every night, and it makes him happier." She cast a weakening spell on Harruq, sapping the strength from his muscles. The half-orc felt his energy leaving and fought it how he knew best: pure rage. With a roar, he cast off the curse as if it were a chain about his body. Tarlak fired another bolt of fire, giving Harruq time to cross the distance as she summoned her shield to block the spell.

"He's *not* happy!" Harruq shouted, shoving Condemnation straight for her mouth. The girl ducked, firing a dagger of ice straight into the half-orc's gut. He felt white pain but ignored it. Salvation slammed down, hilt first. His sword cracked as if hitting stone, but he could see he hurt her. The girl collapsed to the ground, a soft moan escaping her lips.

"Are you so blind you can't see it?" he gasped, pulling the long shard of ice out of him. He dropped it to the ground beside her face.

"I...am...not...blind!"

Power rolled out from her like waves on a lake. The half-orc was thrown back against the same building as before. This time he felt the stones give a little as his back smashed into them. And then, of course, came the fall to the ground.

Tarlak hurled several red balls of magic while the priest slashed the air with a golden blade, all traveling unerringly toward Tessanna. The girl stood, her hands quaking and her eyes wide with bits of dark smoke trailing out the corners. She batted the spells aside as if they were nothing.

"How dare you question my love," Tessanna seethed, her voice trembling with power. "You are insects. You are vile. You are wretched and I will show you how wretched you are." Darkness swirled about her in corporeal form. Great wings stretched out her back, made of a dark ethereal substance. Ten feet in the air the wings spread, decorated with black petals that scattered into the air with each beat. The ground before her melted into complete emptiness. The buildings beside her rattled, their very walls shaking.

"Pour every bit of your will into a shield," Aion commanded. Tarlak agreed. Their hands stretched forward as the power of a goddess came streaking forth as pure dark energy focused in one gigantic beam.

❖

Karnryk was feeding off Tessanna's power. It was the only thing that made sense. With the girl's arrival, he had gone on the attack, each blow stronger than the last. Lathaar blocked, his speed easily beyond that of the creature, but the sheer power! Every second, his arms ached a little more. His faith in Ashhur was great, and his Elholad would not break, but his body was an entirely different matter. When the sound of charging men met his ears he smiled for the first time that night.

"Encircle it!" he heard a man shout. Lathaar leapt back as guards of Neldar surrounded his foe, their shields up and their swords ready. A man of honor took position next to him, a grin on his face as well.

"You must be Lathaar," the Guard Captain said.

"My reputation precedes me," the paladin said. Onward rushed Karnryk, ignoring the other men in a desperate lunge at Lathaar. His greatsword cut air as the paladin rolled to the left, lashing out with his sword in one hand. The gleaming white blade tore through Karnryk's calf, shredding bone and rotted muscle. Antonil went the opposite way, using his shield to deflect the sword upward for two quick stabs into the half-orc's gut. Guards charged from behind, hacking away at undead flesh that was rapidly losing volume. Karnryk grunted his anger and spun, but the guards had already retreated.

"It's not too difficult," Antonil shouted, smashing his sword against his shield in an attempt to draw attention his way. "Only one paladin remains, and I'd bet my life that you're him."

"Is that so?" Lathaar countered a swing, chopping off part of Karnryk's nose in the process. He failed to parry the next hit. Desperate, he jerked his body low to avoid decapitation. Antonil did not hesitate. He smashed his shield against Karnryk's waist while hacking at his tree trunk of a leg. The half-orc was unable to strike a killing blow against the off-balance paladin, instead forced to deal with the nuisance at his leg. He rammed his knee beneath the shield, ignoring its sharp bottom tearing into his skin. The blow wrenched Antonil's arm and cracked his head back hard.

Several guards again rushed his back. Karnryk sensed their coming and spun, his sword out in a long arc. He cut two in half and took the arm off a third. Even as their comrades screamed in pain or death, the guards charged in. More and more strikes tore at the rotted flesh. His knees were particularly wounded, and each step caused his entire body to wobble. Two more died, horrible gashes in their chests from the greatsword, but they had fulfilled their goal. As one, Antonil and Lathaar charged.

"Take his knees," Lathaar shouted, lashing out with his sword. Antonil led with his shield, absorbing a direct swing against it. His entire left side of his body screamed in pain as his collarbone broke, but still he ran. Lathaar's sword cut through the left knee, severing the leg from the body. As Karnryk tilted, Antonil swung his sword with all his might. His strike crushed the other kneecap. Like a giant oak, the half-orc fell.

"He is mine," Lathaar yelled. Karnryk's fury had not diminished, but he no longer had height or legs to give his blows strength. One savage block sent the sword back to the ground, exposing the entire body for Lathaar to strike. Holy wrath swarming his hands, he shoved his palm to Karnryk's chest.

"Back to the abyss," he shouted. The rotting flesh melted beneath his hand. Karnryk howled and flailed. Lathaar flipped around his sword. "May Karak welcome you," he said, ramming the tip through the gaping hole where his mouth had been. Rotting flesh melted against its blade. A wave of power surged out of Lathaar, shattering the chain that bound the spirit to the worldly plane. A lone sigh was all there was to signify Karnryk's final death.

Lathaar gasped for air, pulling free his sword. The glow faded. The Elholad returned to earthly steel. The paladin was given no reprieve, for it was then he heard the great cry come from Tessanna. He turned to see her black wings, her empty eyes, and her terrible power. His mind flashed to an image he had seen before, one so similar it horrified him.

"Mira," he gasped, for a brief moment confusing the two. He saw the wizard and priest preparing to defend and knew them doomed.

"No!" he screamed, running toward them. "You can't withstand her!"

Fast as he was, he would not reach them in time. A blur of gray flashed past him, and then the goddess unleashed her onslaught.

◆

Every ounce of his will was in the magical barrier in front of him. Tarlak was a skilled mage, and only once had he fought an opponent that could break his shield. Combined with Aion's, the wizard had every reason to believe they could survive. When that black beam hit their shield, he knew their error. His back arched, his hands flailed about in spasms, and his entire mind turned white with pain. In a distant part of his mind, he felt his shield shattering like glass.

Hands wrapped around his waist. Time seemed slow, and he turned almost lazily to see Haern taking him into one arm. The other arm reached for the priest, but the beam was breaking through, the sound was thunder of demon gods, and the assassin had no choice. He activated the magic of his ring. Tarlak felt a quick sense of distortion. When his mind recovered, he found himself to the side of where he had been. He spun around to look and immediately regretted it.

Aion remained before the great stream of power. His shield shattered, just as Tarlak's had, but there was none there to rescue him. The black power washed over him. It melted his skin. It shattered his bones. It tore his mind asunder, and left only dust where he had been. The stream continued. Several homes exploded into wood, brick and mortar, their occupants ash on the wind.

"No!" he screamed. Beside him, Haern seethed and drew his blades.

"Aion!"

Delysia's cry was like a dagger stabbing Tarlak's gut.

"You are wretched," Tessanna shouted. "You are nothing, nothing to me!"

The Eschaton mercenaries prepared their weapons, be it spells or sword, and faced the dark goddess before them.

26

Aurelia stepped out, her heart sinking. The doors to the tower were splintered and broken. It took little imagination as to why.

"Brug!" she shouted, nearly wrenching an ankle running over the debris. She found him slumped in the middle of the floor, drool on his chin.

"Oh, Brug," she whispered, stroking his face with her hand. She left him there, praying he could be made well. She dashed up the stairs, her staff clutched tightly in her hands. If she met Qurrah, she knew it would come to spells. The elf swore she would be ready.

Had she looked carefully, she would have seen a patch of shadow by the fire deeper than it should have been. She might have even seen a pair of eyes leering out at her with purest contempt. But she did not, so unseen Qurrah slipped out of the tower and into the pouring rain.

At the top of the steps, Aurelia paused, her fears realized in the form of a slightly ajar door. The world silent in her ears, time a forgotten notion, she pushed open the door.

"Aullienna? Baby, are you there?"

From up in her bed Aullienna turned and smiled at her.

"Mommy!"

"Is everything alright?" Aurelia asked, scanning the room as she made her way toward the stairs. "Are you alone?"

"Uncle was here," the little girl beamed. "He read me a story." Aurelia's throat tightened, but she kept a straight face. She climbed the steps two at a time, desperate to hold her daughter.

"He did, did he?"

Aullienna nodded. "Look!"

She held out a small object in her hand. At first, Aurelia did not recognize it, but then it squirmed and raised its silvery tail. It was Qurrah's scorpion, the gift Brug had made for him.

"Put that down, now!"

In response to the elf's shout, it turned, raised its tail, and then buried its stinger into the little girl's wrist.

"Aullienna!"

Aurelia lurched forward, slapping the thing off with the back of her hand. The scorpion fell to the grass and writhed on its back. Aurelia incinerated it with a small bolt of fire before it could right itself. She pulled Aullienna close, her hand tight on her wrist. She turned it upward to see. A trickle of blood marked the sting, but flowing in her veins could be any possible vile poison that scorpions possessed.

"Honey, do you feel alright?" she asked.

Aurelia knelt down, holding her girl's head to command her gaze. Aulliena smiled as if she were completely unaffected.

"Pretty," the little girl said. "Uncle made things pretty."

"Pretty," the elf said. "Is that so? Aullienna, we're going to take you to a priest to get you healed. Come with mommy."

"No!"

The girl suddenly shrieked, and her face turned icy and vile. She clawed at her mother like a captured animal. One of her slender fingernails jabbed against the side of Aurelia's eye, cutting across her pupil.

Tears wet Aurelia's face, and when she blinked, she could see blood.

"What's wrong?" she asked, torn between anger, horror, and confusion. "Baby…"

In response, Aullienna howled like a rabid animal, then turned and leapt off her bed. Aurelia was so stunned she never even dove to stop her. The girl hit the ground on her shoulder and rolled. Aurelia flew after her, crying out her daughter's name. She feared the worst, but Aullienna moaned. The wild bestial nature in which she had acted made Aurelia hesitate before reaching out her arm to her daughter.

"Love, please, I want to help you," she said.

Aullienna looked up from the grass, tears in her eyes.

"I'm scared," the little girl cried. "Please, uncle made me scared."

Aullienna crawled to her mother's lap. Sobbing, she buried her face into her dress. Aurelia stroked her hair, her heart broken.

"I'm scared mommy," she cried. "I'm scared, please help, please, I'm scared, please…"

"Delysia will make you not scared," Aurelia assured her. "I'm going to go get her. Do you want to come with me?"

"Don't!" Aullienna wailed. "Don't, don't leave, don't…"

Then the crying stopped. She fled away from her mother as if she had never met her before. Aurelia reached out a hand, only to watch her shy away.

"What did he do to you," the elf whispered, tears still staining her eyes. She cast a spell over her daughter. At once, the little girl's eyelids drooped, and she yawned long and loud. Curling up like a kitten, she fell asleep atop the illusionary grass. Aurelia took her in her arms and carried her into the separate bedroom. Flowers scattered from the covering as Aurelia placed her daughter's body atop their bed. The elf kissed her cheek, then turned away.

"I'll be right back," she said. A blue portal ripped open in their room. Rain swirled in from the other side, accompanied by cold air that blew her dress and chilled her skin. A single glance back, and then she stepped inside.

Tessanna's first attack was a wave of serrated shadow with a sharp wedge leading. It tore down the street, leaving a great ditch in its wake. Everyone dove aside lest they be torn to pieces. Several of Antonil's soldiers were not so quick. They broke like glass, blood pouring out in great spurts from their mutilated bodies. The other guards she gripped with her mind, assaulting each one with a bleed spell. Blood poured out their eyes, ears, mouths and nostrils. She reveled in their pain, and at the horror that came over the faces of the others.

"They are not worthy of my presence," she mocked.

Haern rushed, beating Lathaar to the girl. He had felt the girl's power firsthand, and knew the quicker he dispatched her, the better. Tessanna laughed at his approach, surrounding herself with a terribly familiar shield of fire.

"And you're not worthy of mine," Haern whispered. He rolled away from a quick blast of dark energy, tucked his legs, and then dove straight for her feet. Although her skin was tough as stone when it came to blades, she was still a frail girl, weighing less than a hundred pounds. Ignoring the biting fire, Haern swept his feet behind her ankles. He grit his teeth at the sudden impact against his shins. Tessanna cried out, the black wings vanishing as she fell.

She struck her fists, and the ground rippled like water. She hovered there as Haern danced for balance, knowing his window to strike was fleeting. Harruq neared, Antonil behind him. The half-orc prepared to hurl one of his swords, but he held it in hand when the assassin bore down on the girl. His sabers stabbed for her neck. The swords struck past her flesh, for the black ethereal wings returned, pushing the girl high into the air. The two collided. He screamed, fire leaping off her frame and onto his face and hands. Still he tried to pull back and stab, only to have her reach up and grab his wrists.

"Now burn," she hissed. Fire tore from her eyes and seared his face. Haern felt his skin bubbling, the flesh rising up and peeling. He tucked his feet, ignored the burning on his face and the sudden heat on his heels, and shoved out of her grasp. He fell, only to be caught in Lathaar's arms. Harruq and Antonil charged to either side of the floating girl, coordinating their attack in a desperate attempt to protect their injured friend. Tessanna righted herself and flapped higher, beyond the reach of their swords.

"Come face us, coward!" Antonil shouted, weakly striking his sword against his shield. Even the slight vibration increased the throbbing from his broken collarbone. Lathaar rushed back to Tarlak and laid Haern on the ground. Prayer on his lips, he placed his glowing hands against the vicious burns across Haern's face.

"Be healed," he whispered, hoping his meager abilities would suffice. Tarlak saw his most trusted friend so severely wounded and decided enough was enough. Tessanna so far refused to lower, instead flapping her black wings higher and higher.

"Time to fall, angel," Tarlak said, pulling out a wand and activating its magic. He had tried to harm her with spells. Now it was time to try the opposite. Tarlak's wand shattered, the powerful magic spent. Waves of anti-magic swarmed over the girl, dispelling all enchantments and effects. Her wings faltered, their magic broken. The fire faded from her flesh, revealing her pale skin and dripping wet hair. With nothing to keep her afloat, she fell, vulnerable and stunned. The two fighters awaited her below, their blades prepared for a killing stroke.

"Do not harm her!"

Antonil turned in surprise to the voice, but Harruq only felt his gut sink ever further. Qurrah had come. A wall of invisible force followed the shout, slamming both of them back. Tessanna hit the ground and gasped in pain. Down the street walked Qurrah, his whip wrapped about his arm in dark flame. His eyes seethed red. Darkness surrounded his other hand, the makings of another spell. A single black tendril shot out, feinted an attack, and then wrapped about Tessanna. He pulled her to him. She collapsed in his arms, sobbing in the rain.

"Qurrah," she said, all her power leaving her. "Qurrah, I'm so sorry, I didn't…"

"We're leaving," he said to her. To the others, he glared death and waited for someone to make a move. He half-expected the Guard Captain, or maybe his brother, but it was Tarlak who struck. A lance of ice flew across the street, the end jagged and impossibly sharp. Clenching his fist, Qurrah created a magical barrier, shattering the projectile. A second and third followed, each one suffering a similar fate. The half-orc chuckled.

"Is that all you can muster?" he asked. Tarlak cracked his knuckles.

"How about this then?" Fire curled inside his hands, growing larger and larger. He glanced to the two fighters, who stood wounded and weak.

Charge him, he thought, hoping they would get the idea. Every bit of power Tarlak poured into the fireball, draining his reservoir of magical energy. It flew from his hands like a giant comet, a great yellow tail trailing after. Air sizzled and smoke billowed. Qurrah took a step, braced his legs, and extended his right arm. The fireball hit the barrier and detonated, swarming over the shield but not crossing. Qurrah shuddered, his mind nearly blanking. He felt his protection cracking. Another spell would surely break it, but the fire was spent. The flame and smoke cleared, and Qurrah gasped for air.

"It is time to go," he said to his lover.

"Into the shadows," Tessanna said, breaking from his arms and running toward the nearest alley. Qurrah turned to follow, but his eye caught movement. Tarlak was on his knees, completely exhausted, and his brother stayed back, confusion evident on his face. The paladin still hovered over the wounded assassin. The Guard Captain, however…

Antonil charged, shield leading. Qurrah lashed out with his whip, taking the man's feet out from under him. The fall jarred his shield. Antonil screamed in pain as he felt the broken pieces of his collarbone grind together. Qurrah turned to leave, but there was one other he had forgotten.

"Ashhur condemn thee!" Delysia shouted, having snuck around and then charged with Antonil. Holy light flashed from her hand, burning his sight like a dagger through each eye. He shrieked, thrusting his fingers forward and unleashing a blast of ice. The priestess struck the building behind her, ice freezing her wrists and chest to the wall. Staggering like a blind man, Qurrah followed his lover's voice.

"Wait," Harruq shouted, breaking out of his paralysis. He rushed after, only to see them step into a dark portal similar to Aurelia's. "Damn it!" he screamed. He slammed a fist against a wall, fuming in mindless anger. "Why? What the abyss did we do?"

"Harruq," he heard his leader call.

The half-orc turned, his swords sagging in his arms. Despite his anger, his guilt overtook him upon seeing his friends. Haern lay on the ground, obviously in pain. Delysia shivered in the rain and ice, her skin pale and her lips blue. He watched Antonil crawl onto his back, gasping for breath while tears streaked his face. And then there were the bloodied bodies of the guards…

"Harruq," Tarlak said again, grabbing his attention. He pointed to where Delysia was stuck to the wall. "Break her free, will you? We need her spells."

"Yeah," Harruq said. He sheathed Condemnation and took Salvation into both hands. He smashed the ice with its hilt, spreading cracks with each blow. Delysia coughed, coming out of her daze.

"Haern," she moaned. "Where's Haern?"

"He's fine," the half-orc said, turning the blade around to slide it underneath the ice. He pulled, dislodging a large chunk. "Take a lot more than that to hurt ol' sneaky. I bet dragons would quake if they knew he was coming to say hello."

"And they would flee in terror from Tessanna," she said, smiling half-heartedly.

"You didn't flee," Harruq said. His hits against the ice grew harder. "You came after them, while I just stood there."

"Harruq…"

The half-orc shook his head, and the comment died on her lips. With most of the ice cracked and broken, he sheathed his sword. The rest he pulled off with his hands, ignoring the biting cold. With a soft cry, she fell forward, clutching him to stand.

"Easy," he said. "Easy. Catch your breath."

"I need to help them," she said, pushing away. He let her go, feeling more helpless than ever before. She staggered toward Haern, only to halt beside Antonil. She said words to him, although he did not hear. Her hands took on the white glow of a healing spell, and three times she cast a spell on his chest. Tarlak checked on her, and then went to Harruq.

"Your brother..." he said, pointing to his sister and his friend. "Your brother did that, along with that Tessanna. Yet you never struck. You watched while my sister nearly killed herself to slow their retreat. You let Lathaar slay the creature. You let Haern burn against the girl. I expect better from you, Harruq. Worlds better."

Lightning flashed, and in its light, Tarlak could see the anger burning inside Harruq's eyes. Good, he thought. Let it burn. Something needed to wake him up. Something needed to force him to see. The wind picked up. Harruq opened his mouth to speak, but then a blue portal tore open behind them. They turned, Harruq realizing for the first time his wife had even left. When the elf dashed through, his words caught in his throat. Her eyes terrified him.

"Harruq!" she shouted, flinging her arms around him. He held her tight. She let his embrace calm her for a second before pushing away. "Qurrah broke into the tower," she said. Her husband's arms tightened around her waist.

"Is Aullienna...?"

"He poisoned her," the elf said. "Please, I need Delysia, she needs to come back!"

"Take me to her," the priestess said, still hunched over Antonil. She gave him a soft kiss on the forehead before standing. Her white robes were covered with mud and water, her hair was soaked to her skin, and exhaustion tainted her face. Somehow she remained regal. "Take me to her, and I will do what I can."

"Thank you," Aurelia said. She glanced back to the portal, which she had kept open. "Please, hurry. I don't know how long she has."

Harruq had heard enough. He dove into the portal. He had to see her. He had to see it for himself. His only thought was simple, plain denial.

He couldn't have. Qurrah. His brother.

He couldn't have.

◈

"Aullienna?" Harruq asked, fighting off a brief wave of disorientation as he rushed up the stairs and entered his bedroom. He saw her on their bed and hurried to her.

"Baby, wake up," he said, shaking her tiny shoulders in his hands. Aurelia's spell broke and her eyes fluttered open.

"I was a flower," she giggled. Harruq sighed. Her skin was fine. Her temperature was normal. A smile was on his daughter's face.

"You were a flower, were you?" he asked. Behind him, he heard Aurelia and Delysia enter. He brushed her cheek with his hand. He would pick her up and show them his brother would never stoop so low as to harm his only daughter. He would show them all was fine, that the chaos in the night was a misunderstanding. But a change hit, so sudden the half-orc never saw it. He only realized when the little girl reached up, grabbed his hand, and sank her teeth into the upper part of his thumb.

He screamed, yanking his hand back. She refused to lessen her grip. Blood spilled across her face, the bed, and his hand as his skin tore underneath her stubborn teeth. He pried her loose and held the bleeding thumb to his chest, gaping at his daughter.

"Aully," the half-orc almost pleaded, tears in his eyes. "Why? Why did you do that?"

Aurelia was at his side, pulling him to her as she looked on.

"I don't know what happened," she said, her voice quivering. "Delysia, it must be a poison. I saw the scorpion sting her."

"Scorpion?" Harruq asked.

"The one Brug made for him."

Harruq pulled away, his temper fuming. "Brug did this? Where is he?"

"Downstairs," the elf said. "He's unconscious. Qurrah did something to him."

Delysia stepped beside them, her eyes on the little girl. Aullienna watched her approach, her legs pulled to her chest, her little white eyes shaking with fear.

"Don't," she said, jerking away from the priestess's gentle hand. "Please. You'll hurt me."

"I won't hurt you," Delysia cooed. "Please. I want to help."

Tears filled Aullienna's eyes, and it broke Harruq's heart that he could not go to her.

"You can't," the little girl said. "You'll make it worse."

Delysia ignored her, whispering another prayer for a healing spell.

"You'll make it worse!" Aullienna shouted, her voice shrill. "Worse, worse, you'll make it worse!"

Delysia shoved her hand forward, the blue-white light pouring out. Aullienna shrieked. She slapped, she kicked, and she dove to the ground, curling into a tiny ball. There she whimpered like an injured dog.

"Whatever it is, I can't cure it," Delysia said to the terrified parents. "We need to take her to Calan. If anyone can save her, he can."

"I'll open us another port-"

She stopped, taking up her staff and preparing to strike. A shadow crawled up the wall. It remained flat against the mossy stone until widening into a perfect visage of Qurrah Tun. Harruq drew his swords, but Aurelia reached out and pushed them down.

"Just a shadow image," she said, eyeing the spell. "What is it you come to tell us, wretch?"

"I seek a trade," Qurrah said. His eyes looked distant and unfocused. "Lathaar knows of a tome I desire, one freed by his defeat of the demon, Darakken. Have him bring this to me and I will hand over the cure for your daughter."

"You bastard," Harruq said. "How could you? How?"

"Harruq?" the image asked, glancing toward the half-orc's general direction. "I mean her no harm. Things will become sane soon, I promise. Everything will return to how it was…how it should be."

The image faded, even as Harruq cursed his name. The three stood silently while Aullienna whimpered.

"To Calan?" Aurelia asked. The other two nodded. She glanced at her daughter and offered a weak smile. "I'm sorry, honey," she said, casting another sleep spell. The whimpering faded. Harruq took her in his arms, his heart aching with pain and anger. A new portal ripped open. They took her to Calan.

❖

Qurrah opened his eyes, the message given. He steadied himself against the wall, furious at his own weakness.

"I should not show you such compassion," he said. "You have grown far too weak."

They were still inside Veldaren, cowering like rats in a wretched slum. Tessanna remained at his side. She huddled in the rain, looking wet and miserable. He remembered the chaos she had sown and felt his anger rise.

"Why did you come?" he said. "You were to remain behind!"

"I didn't want them to find you," she explained. "I had to make sure your pet kept them busy. You had to succeed. You had to."

Qurrah slumped against the building.

"How many did you hurt?" he asked. "How many did you kill?" She turned away, her chin tucked down. Her hair hid her face. "Aullienna was to grant us the tome, Tessanna! Now you've hurt them, nearly killed them! What if they seek vengeance? What if they fear you more than they desire the girl to live?"

"I wanted to help," the girl shrieked, nearly choking with sobs. "Please, you wouldn't let me help, but I want to help! I want to see her one more time!"

The half-orc turned and wrapped his arms around her. He felt her crying into his chest, and his anger broke.

"All is well," he said. "We have not killed any dear to them. They will forgive you, and me. I just need the spellbook. With it, all will be made right."

Tessanna sniffled. "And if they don't give it to us?"

"They will. I know my brother. He would do anything for those he loves."

The girl was not sure if he meant himself or the girl. Perhaps it didn't matter.

"I want to go home," she said.

"As do I. Night and rain will be ending soon. Let us go."

The two slunk off to the western wall, crossing to the other side through a door of shadow. Once again, they retreated to their sanctuary within the King's Forest.

27

"Wake the high priest," Harruq said to the young priest that answered his vicious knockings on the temple doors. The boy paused in indecision. He looked no older than twelve, the lowest of the low in the temple hierarchy. Well, the half-orc had a way with dealing with the lowly.

"I said wake him," Harruq screamed. "My daughter is dying! And if you keep standing here telling me he can't be woken, I will rip the door off and beat you on the head with it."

"I'll go get him," the boy said, flinging the temple doors wide. "Please, just...I'll bring him here. Wait for him, if you please."

"It would please me fine," Harruq said, shoving his way in, "if you show me to his room. I don't have time for this."

The boy glanced at the two girls, his face brightening as he recognized Delysia.

"Oh," he said. "I didn't see you there."

"This is important," the priestess said, doing her best to calm him. "Take us to Calan. I am sure he will understand."

The boy glanced at the half-orc, paled, and then gestured for them to follow. He led them through the entrance, wincing at the water they dripped across the carpets. They veered away from the main altar room, approaching a large oaken door. The boy politely knocked twice. Harruq followed it up with several booming fists of his own.

"That's how you knock to wake someone up," he said. "Now get out of here."

The young priest glanced to Delysia, who gave him an assuring nod. He fled, hoping he had done the right thing. After no commotion from inside, Harruq smashed his fist against the wood a few more times.

"Give an old man time to rise from his bed," came the answering call from within. Harruq stepped back, trying to calm himself. His daughter would be fine. Calan was a powerful priest, at least according to Delysia. Such a man could heal his daughter. Any mortal poison should be within the abilities of such a healer.

At least, he hoped.

The door cracked open, and a haggard, wild-haired Calan opened the door.

"Yes, children?" he asked. Harruq grunted and looked down at his daughter.

"She's been poisoned," he said. "We need you to cure her, now."

"Demands are unnecessary," the man said, brushing his hand across Aullienna's forehead. The half-orc caught a frown, so quick it was as if Calan tried to hide it. His stomach sank. "Bring her inside," Calan said. "Place her on my bed so I may take a look."

He stepped aside so the three could enter. The room was a cramped study filled with tomes, expertly bound and illustrated in archaic lettering. Harruq gently placed his daughter on the bed, his hands lingering on hers. Calan slid between them and knelt. He touched the girl's forehead, closed his eyes in prayer, and began.

For a long while, the three waited, Harruq and Aurelia seeking comfort in each other's arms. Delysia stayed out of the way, her arms crossed, her teeth chattering. Finally, the prayers ended, without any action taken on Calan's part.

"Where's the spell?" Harruq asked. Aurelia tried to shush him but he pushed away her hand. "Don't get up, heal her! Where's the light, the chanting?"

"I can't," Calan said. The ache was evident in his voice, but Harruq pressed on.

"Bullshit, you can, now get on your damn knees and heal her!"

"Harruq," Aurelia shouted.

"She has no poison," Calan said, overpowering her shout with his simple words. "No poison, no curse, no hex, and no spell."

"Then what is wrong with her?" Aurelia asked. "She acted terrified to see me, and other times, she cried like a wild animal."

"I have seen it only once," the high priest said, his left arm searching behind him for his desk to lean upon. When he found it, he slumped back, his face exhausted. "Only once, but I know it well."

"What is it," Harruq asked.

"The girl you brought to me," Calan said. "Tessanna. Their minds are now similar. And just like I cannot heal her, I cannot heal your daughter."

The words pierced them worse than any arrow could.

"But Qurrah said there's a cure," Harruq whispered. "He said he had a cure."

"Then he lied to you," the high priest said. "There is no cure. I do not know how, but her mind has been reshaped. A curse or a hex merely binds and forces a change. A poison is evil in her blood. But this…" He sighed and collapsed into his old rickety chair. "This is beyond me. Beyond anyone."

"What are we to do," Aurelia asked. She felt her husband's arms wrap around her and she clung tightly to him.

"Pray," he said. "Watch her. Hope that in time, she will gain a semblance of her old self. This might be temporary, but I say this only out of hope, not out of reason or wisdom. She is still your daughter, broken mind or not. There will be times she remembers you, and times she loves you. It is your task to love her even when she does not."

"I can't believe this," Harruq said.

"You will in time, my son," Calan said. "It is not the end. Your daughter is alive. Hold to hope."

"Hope," he said. He scooped his daughter into his arms, smiling down at her sleeping face. He didn't know what to think, what to do. He could feel others watching him, and he wanted to appear strong, stronger than the nightmare he was trapped in. Instead, he felt tears run down his face as he spoke in honest anguish.

"At least she's normal when she's sleeping," he said.

They returned to the tower.

They found everyone gathered in the main floor. Haern was propped on pillows beside the fire. Lying on blankets next to him was Brug. His eyes were closed, and he appeared to slumber, a decided improvement over the comatose stare he had possessed earlier. Tarlak sat next to them, chin on his knuckles and lost in thought. Lathaar did his best to comfort the three, bringing drinks, food, and assuring words. When the others arrived, he didn't let any rise from their places.

"Moving is a bad idea," Lathaar warned, crossing his arms. Most of his platemail was gone, but even without it he was an imposing figure. None had the heart to argue with him. Harruq walked through the front door, still carrying Aullienna. He moved like a man drained of life. Aurelia followed, her expression similar. Delysia hurried past, wanting to explain the situation before the two parents had to, but she did not make it in time.

"What happened?" Tarlak asked, sitting up.

"They…" Harruq found a lump in his throat, and no words would come. Aurelia stroked his cheek, looked them in the eye, and said the bare truth.

"Qurrah made her like Tessanna," she said. "He broke her mind and made it like hers."

Despite the burns, despite the pain, despite his near delirium, Haern managed to cough and speak.

"I'll kill him," he said. "I'll kill the bloody bastard."

"Why would he do this?" Tarlak asked, feeling his own hatred growing. "Why would he do such a thing to a beautiful little girl?"

Harruq looked about, wanting a place to put Aullienna down but seeing none. So instead, he placed her in the crack between the blacksmith and the assassin, covering her in both their blankets.

"He wants some spellbook," he said. "Darken or something."

"Darakken," Aurelia said, looking to the paladin. "He said you knew where it was. If we wanted a way to cure Aullienna, you must give it to him."

All waited for Lathaar to speak. When he did, his voice was calm, firm, and unshakable.

"I would give all to make her well, but I will die before I see such a thing in the hands of your brother. I'm sorry, Harruq. The knowledge in that tome is best forgotten."

"It's just a book," the half-orc said. He pointed to his daughter, pleading. "Just a stupid old book. This is my daughter. My *daughter*. How can you say such things?"

"That book has the spells of Karak himself," Tarlak said, holding his head in his hands. "It has incantations that can poison oceans, shake mountains, and summon demons of unimaginable power. With such a book, Qurrah could place Veldaren under siege, assuming he could read it without going mad. Lathaar is right. Qurrah has come close to killing many of us as he is. With the spells of a god at his disposal…"

"I can't believe this," Harruq shouted. "I can't!"

He stormed up the stairs, feeling angry and broken. Aurelia looked around, her beauty marred by her sadness.

"I understand," she whispered. "I do understand."

She went to comfort her husband. Silence followed. There were many things to be said, but none important. Not compared to what had just transpired. It was Haern that ended the horrible quiet, even though his lips cracked and bled.

"I still know where he lives," he whispered.

The Cost of Betrayal

"Not yet," Tarlak said, plopping down beside the fire. "Not with so many of us beaten and broken."

Haern closed his eyes and sighed, knowing the mage was right.

Qurrah tossed and turned, a single sight dominating his dreams. It was of a child laying face down in a pool of his own vomit. Xelrak stood over the child, his hands soaked crimson. He looked like a warrior standing with pride over his victory. When Qurrah awoke, sunlight streaked through the window of the cabin. Tessanna sat next to him, wide-awake.

"You dreamt it too, didn't you?" she asked. The half-orc nodded.

"For his sins I am blamed," he said. "For his conniving I am punished. He has ruined my brother against me."

The half-orc donned his robes and took his whip.

"Don't go," she said. It seemed a meager protest, said as if she thought she were supposed to say it.

"I do not like games," the half-orc said. Then he fell to one side, collapsing against the wall in a sudden spell of weakness. Tessanna rushed to him but he pushed her back.

"Must pay," he mumbled, banging open the door. He rushed out, having not eaten a thing in two days. The girl stood at the entrance, feeling the crisp cold blowing against her skin as she watched her lover trail off into the forest like a possessed being. She watched until he was gone, and then cut herself to pass the time.

Antonil arrived the next day, accompanied by a squad of soldiers. He wore his shield awkwardly, presumably to lessen the pain it caused his wounded arm. Tarlak greeted him at the door, looking worlds better than he had the night before.

"Greetings, our highly esteemed and so dangerously intelligent Guard Captain," the wizard beamed. The dark edges in his eyes added an unintended tinge of sarcasm. "How fares your collarbone?"

"Your sister's magic borders on miracle work," Antonil said. He did not smile. "Do you know where Qurrah has gone?"

"No," Tarlak lied. "I mean, we think we have an idea, but it's not in Veldaren. Out in the wilderness, where he can't harm anyone. Why?"

Antonil sighed. He nodded to his guards, who obediently backed out of listening range. When satisfied, he continued.

"Another child was found butchered, the worst yet. It happened sometime this morning. I thought you told me Qurrah was the Reaper?"

"He is," Tarlak said. His arm shot out, catching the side of the door to steady himself. "I mean, he was…"

Antonil's mouth tightened. "I trusted you, and I still grant you benefit of the doubt. I lost a hundred good men last night, and we were already stretched thin. Whoever you can muster, I need their help."

"We didn't lie to you for the coin," the wizard insisted. "Harruq said he saw Qurrah standing over the dead child with his own two eyes."

"But did he see him kill him?"

Tarlak's silence was answer enough. Antonil gently pressed his good arm against his chest, his way of saluting. "Tell your sister she has my sincerest gratitude."

Tarlak tipped his hat and closed the door. He slumped against it, cursing under his breath.

"Harruq, you fool," he said. "You damn fool."

At the top of the tower, Harruq knelt on the ground, a sweetroll in hand.

"Do you want something to eat?" he asked. Aullienna shook her head, refusing the offered roll. Her entire body quivered in fear. Harruq had seen dogs shake like that, ones that had been beaten, kicked, and abused. No hand had ever struck Aullienna, yet she remained huddled in the corner of the room refusing all attempts to lure her out.

Aurelia took the treat out of her husband's hand and began nibbling on it.

"At least she appears better," the elf said. "Perhaps Calan is wrong."

"Yeah, he seems like he's wrong a lot," the half-orc grumbled, walking away from the corner. He could feel his daughter's eyes lingering on his back. He wondered what she saw. Sure he was big, and he could scare people, but she was his daughter. Not once had he raised his voice in anger to her. Why would she fear him?

In truth, she didn't. She feared the ten-tongued goblin who gibbered nonsense as he offered her a crust of black bread crawling with worms. When the door opened, she shrieked. The god of the

The Cost of Betrayal

goblin had come, his eyes dim yellow, his tongues trailing to the floor. When he spoke, his voice shook the ground.

"Should I leave?" Tarlak asked as Aullienna sobbed and buried her head.

"No, stay," Aurelia said. "She gets like that every now and then. What is it you need?"

The wizard walked in, his hands clasped behind his back. He seemed reluctant to speak. Harruq eyed his pacing for as long as he could stand before putting an end to it.

"Out with it, wizard, before you make me get my swords."

"Another child was killed last night," Tarlak blurted. The two stopped, trying to swallow the news.

"Like before?" Aurelia asked.

"Just like before."

Harruq opened his mouth, and then closed it again. He had no idea how to react. The worst news he had ever heard seemed too good to be true.

"Qurrah wouldn't come back," he said. "There's no reason. He would have left town, gone to wherever he goes in the forest."

"You think someone else killed the children," Aurelia surmised. She stood, her heart a flutter. "You think we wrongly accused Qurrah."

"I struck him first," Harruq said. "Me. All of this was because of me, and it was because I was wrong. You know this now, don't you Tar?"

The wizard turned away, and then the great yellow wizard hat bobbed up and down.

"Yeah I do," Tarlak said. "And that puts a whole new color over this crazy painting. My gut wants us to go after them, kill them if we must, but now?" He sighed.

Harruq approached him, his face reddening.

"You caused this," he said, jamming a finger against the wizard's back. Tarlak spun around, flabbergasted.

"Me?" Tarlak exclaimed. "How is that?"

"You sent Haern after them," he said. "What had happened was between me and him. I was wrong. What I did, I struck first, and I was wrong. He has acted on defense every time, against me, against Haern, and it wasn't Qurrah who attacked us last night, it was Tessanna. I wonder how much control my brother truly has on her."

"You will not blame this on me," Tarlak shouted, matching the half-orc in volume but not height. "Self defense or not, he left you a broken mess. Haern would cut a new smile in any person's throat who did such a thing to a member of my family, regardless who."

"Boys!" Aurelia shouted, drawing both their attentions. "Shut up, right now, or I will polymorph you both into songbirds so at least I will *enjoy* your incessant banter." They quieted, for each could see magic tingling on the edges of her fingers. "Excellent. Whoever's fault this is doesn't matter. A murderer is still loose inside Veldaren, and he needs caught. More importantly, we must decide how we deal with Qurrah. If this is true, the extent of his crimes number only to what he has done to our daughter."

"What he has done is unforgivable," the wizard said.

"I will decide what I can forgive," she said. "And what if he can find a cure? Shall I kill the one person who can save her?" Aurelia pointedly looked to Aullienna and watched her pick at the grass. "Perhaps we should reconsider his offer," she whispered.

"What?" both asked at the same time.

"If this is true, then things are different. We don't know his motivations. We don't know how he will respond if we explain ourselves, or even apologize. There is so much we don't know." She did not say her most nagging thought, the one that had kept her awake all the previous night. She was no fool. She knew why Qurrah wanted the spellbook. He didn't want to just cure Aullienna. He wanted the cure for himself, for Tessanna.

"It is up to Lathaar," the wizard said, storming to the door. "Convince him. But I swear, if you give that tome to Qurrah, it is on your head, not mine."

"I can bear the weight," Aurelia said, her stance firm, regal. "I do not fear such mantles."

"Then try a few of mine," the wizard said. He left in a blur of yellow. Aurelia watched, her anger softening upon his departure. Her true worry showed its face, deep and frightened.

"Do you really think Qurrah might know a way to fix her?" Harruq asked. Aurelia turned to answer him, but it was Aullienna who spoke up, startling them both.

"Uncle lies," she said, rocking back and forth, her large eyes looking at her parents. "But he's hoping. Will you help him, mommy? Help the bad man?"

"Where did you hear that?" Aurelia asked, slowly approaching the girl. "Who told you to say that?"

"The voices," she whispered, giggling. "They whisper, and they're smart."

When Aurelia reached out to stroke her face, she growled and snapped her teeth. The elf let her be.

"There's a lot we don't understand," Harruq said. "And I don't know a single damned thing to do about it."

"I do," Aurelia said.

She pulled him close and held him, each seeking comfort in the other's arms.

28

Under normal circumstances, he would do such deeds after nightfall. His dark robe blended well with the secrecy of the stars, but beneath the unrelenting sun, he drew more curious looks than he preferred. Merchants were wise not to offer him wares. People did their best to skirt his path. Most thought him a priest of Karak. In other cities, other places, they walked openly, even brazenly, but not in Veldaren. Not in the city their god had built. The kings had turned their backs to him. In all of Neldar, the priests of Ashhur claimed dominion. Across the rest of the world the sigil of the lion did not draw ire and curses.

Qurrah found some odd satisfaction in this. Let the city turn its back against what built it and gave it strength and dignity. Just as Karak had made the great wall and castle only to have the city turn away, so too had Harruq betrayed him, forgotten what it was that made him the perfect killer. There were those who fought for the old faith, and Qurrah planned the same. But first, he had to destroy the man who poisoned his brother's mind against him.

"Where are you, Xelrak?" he asked. He tried to see with the darker sight, but the busying commotion of people prevented him. Instead, he reached out with his mind, searching for auras of power. Xelrak was a strong follower of Karak, perhaps stronger than Pelarak and his fellow priests. Not wiser, but stronger. His faith surpassed fanatical. Wherever he was, Qurrah was certain he could find him, and find him sleeping. It was daylight, after all.

He wandered down the street, seeking a moment of solitude. His eyes closed, the jostling noise about him faded for a brief instant. His vision darkened. He could sense Karak's puppet, and his emotions flooded into him. He dreamt of war, of bloodshed, and of purest order brought from the greatest chaos. The man slept to the north. Silken curtains, golden arches, and great oak doors coated with polish flooded his vision.

I found you, Qurrah thought. There in his darkness, someone found him. It was the King of all things where the light held no sway.

He did only what he was meant to do, Karak's voice said. It came cool as the scales of a serpent, poisonous and vile to the mind. Qurrah collapsed to the ground. His mind sought to believe the torrent of whispers, even as his soul shrieked against them.

Only his duty, as will you. No prayers do you offer, but more than a hundred sacrifices you have burnt at my altar. The time is coming. Do not hold back. Slay my servant if you must. His purpose is done. Keep hold your strength, for the confrontation comes, and the chaos of this world will soon be ended in glorious order.

Qurrah scrambled to his feet, sweat covering his hands and face. Many were staring. Others glanced about for guards, although none dared call for one. Crossing a priest of Karak meant death if caught. Furious at interference, even from a god, the half-orc hurried north. Over time, the thump of his heart calmed, his breath lost its ragged edge, and he could think clearly once more.

"I am no pawn of yours," he said. "And I will kill the one who tried to use me as one."

A tall black-iron fence surrounded the robust mansion of some wealthy merchant. It did little to deter him. A shadow enveloped a few bars near the back, turning them to dust. It was daylight, people milled about, and none suspected any trespassers. Two men stood in front of the great oak doors, shortswords hanging from their belts. Across the grass the half-orc brazenly walked to where a smaller house stood like a little brother to a giant. It was meager, bland, and of pathetic quality compared to the garish mansion nearby. From within, Qurrah smelled the sickly-sweet aroma of rotting flesh. He doubted others could detect it.

The half-orc uncoiled his whip, a single thought covering it with crackling fire. He pressed his hand against the door, let dark power flow into it, and then pulled away. The door exploded inward, splintering into great shards that smashed against the back of the single room. Rows of wood and straw beds, three high, filled the place. In one slept a frail man garbed in dirty black robes.

"Rise and shine, precious," the half-orc said. Xelrak gasped, his eyes lurching open. When he saw the half-orc standing over him, his whole body trembled. Qurrah's whip snaked around Xelrak's waist, burning through the flimsy cloth. His muscles tightened. He fought, but the pain was intense. He collapsed to the ground, screaming in agony.

"Did you seek to turn my brother against me?" Qurrah said, stretching his fingers in the shape of a half-moon. Tiny needles of ice shot from his palm, burying into Xelrak's cheeks and throat. One found his eye. His screams grew.

"I will serve," he cried, throwing himself onto his knees so he could bow. The whip only tightened. He tore at it with charred fingers. "You must learn. Karak has set your path!"

"And I refuse to walk it," Qurrah said. Xelrak tried to cast a spell but the whip snapped back, coiled, and then wrapped about his face. His mouth had been open when it did. He tasted oil and leather before his tongue began to cook. Smoke filled his lungs. His eyelids melted away, and the liquid that surrounded his eyes popped and sizzled. His cries were as bubbling oil.

Qurrah let the whip return to his arm. Xelrak collapsed, the pain knocking him unconsciousness. His face was a horrific mess. Bits of skin curled and smoked. Some blood ran down his cheeks, but not much. Even in his slumber, his entire existence was a form of suffering.

"It is a shame the Citadel fell to a wretch such as you," the half-orc said. He spat. "That honor should have gone to a stronger man."

The commotion brought a tired old crone with gray hair and a lizard frown. Qurrah struck her dead with a thought. Her body clumped to the ground in the middle of the doorway.

"We do not have much time," he said, glancing down at the burned man. "It is time you awaken."

He took a chunk of Xelrak's remaining hair in his fist and pulled up his head. With his other hand, he gently sunk his fingertips into the black holes where his eyes had been. Nightmares flooded his mind, invading the blank solitude. Minutes later, Xelrak awoke screaming, first from fear, and then from pain. Qurrah shoved his hand over the man's mouth.

"Silence," he said. "Shut your screams, or I will not kill you. The pain you feel will never leave. Your face is a blackened husk. All those who lay eyes on you will recoil. Karak will not aid you, wretch, only open his arms and await you in death. I will send you to him if you cooperate, is that understood?"

Xelrak bobbed his head up and down, his screams becoming ragged moans.

"I want you to deliver a message to Karak when you see him," the half-orc said. "As the demons spear your flesh, tell them I don't fear his subtle workings. As the fire melts away the flesh on your legs, scream to your god that he may bring his full power against me, and I will not cower, and I will not fail. And when the ravens consume the remains of your tongue, shout, shout to him that I will bring nothing but chaos to this world, splendid chaos, and he is powerless to stop me."

Xelrak's moans grew quiet, exhausted. The pain was too much. In a rare act of mercy, Qurrah pulled out a tiny bit of bone from his pocket, whispered an arcane word, and then sent the man to his master.

"Make sure he gets my message," Qurrah said, dropping the head to the floor, quivering bones lodged in his eye sockets. He left, stepping over the dead woman. No more children would fall victim to the Veldaren Reaper. He had been sent to the fire and the darkness, doomed to look up in torment at the Golden Eternity above, where those he had massacred sung in endless glory.

Even if Qurrah had known, he wouldn't have cared in the slightest. He had his revenge. The hood of his cloak pulled low over his face, he returned to where the most important thing in his life sat in silence and sliced her flesh with her dagger.

The healthy members of the Eschaton returned at dawn, their arms sagging and their eyes dulled with exhaustion. They were granted a welcoming sight at home, for sitting wrapped in blankets by the fire was Brug, downing a mug of ale.

"Hope you all had a great time," he grunted, placing the mug on the floor beside him. "It gets lonely here when the only one to talk to is asleep."

Beside him, Haern chuckled, pulling his own blankets tighter around him. The burns on his face were healing, however slowly. They shone an angry red, with some patches still black and peeling. He could smile with only mild pain, and that he could deal with. Tarlak clapped his hands, pleased with their recovery.

"Welcome back, Brug. Since you're so healthy, we'll put you out there tomorrow night. No slack for the short, as I like to say."

Aurelia and Delysia entered next, each giving him a soft kiss on the cheek. Lathaar came next, casting a grin at Brug. Harruq entered last, his weapons slung over his shoulders and his face sunken.

"We'll find him in time," Tarlak said, slapping his back. He pulled his hand away at the glare he received. The group each made their way upstairs to change out of their wet clothes and armor. Tarlak whipped up a quick breakfast. A simple wave of his hand, and honey-soaked rolls and roasted pork slabs covered the table. Brug and Haern joined him. One by one the others arrived, quiet and solemn in the early morning.

As everyone ate in silence, Lathaar decided it was time to speak.

"I must be leaving soon," he said, drawing many glances his way.

"I thought you wanted to rebuild the Citadel?" Tarlak asked, licking honey off his fingers. "What changed?"

"Nothing has changed," the paladin said. "But the Sanctuary must be warned. Qurrah knows of the book's location and might come looking for it. Others might learn from him, as well."

"You got nothing to fear of Qurrah," Harruq said. The food he ate did little to satisfy the pang in his gut, especially as his brother was spoken of as a villain. "He's done nothing to harm us, any of us. Only Aullienna."

"He cannot heal her," Tarlak said, trying to keep his voice as calm as possible.

"You don't know that," Harruq countered.

"Harruq," Lathaar said, his voice drawing the half-orc's gaze into his unflinching own. "I will speak with them. Calan is a brilliant man, but the clerics of the Sanctuary have helped me with wisdom unparalleled. I do not wish to offer false hope, but there is a chance they will know of a way to restore your daughter's mind."

"And the book?" the half-orc asked.

"It stays," Lathaar said. "I am sorry."

"We are grateful," Aurelia said, taking her husband's hand in hers and squeezing hard enough to hurt.

"Aye," Harruq said. "Grateful."

※

Lathaar decided to leave without sleeping, wanting to cover as many miles as he could before the setting of the sun.

"Your daughter may not have much time if she is to be healed," he explained. "I do not claim wisdom in the ways of magic, but I would rather not risk more than I already have."

Before he left, Lathaar pulled Tarlak aside to talk.

"I will find out more about the girl," he whispered.

"You said that already."

"No. Tessanna. She too closely resembles Mira. The first time I talked with Cleric Keziel, I felt he kept things from me. This time, I will hear the whole truth."

"Godspeed," Tarlak said, hugging his friend.

"Ashhur be with you," Lathaar said.

"Do you want a portal?" Aurelia asked him before he left.

"Can you send me directly to the Sanctuary?" he asked. The elf frowned and shook her head.

"Too far. Is there anywhere closer?"

The paladin thought, then nodded.

"Send me to Haven," he said.

"Very well," Aurelia said. Where the Rigon River ended its divide through Dezrel, it forked, creating a delta filled with rich and fertile land. Amidst this farming paradise was a small town named Haven. A month's travel away, but still closer than the Sanctuary, which nestled amidst mountains on the far southwest corner of the continent. She ripped open a blue portal, kissed his cheek, and joined the rest in waving goodbye. The paladin kissed his fingers and then waved back. He stepped in. The portal closed behind him.

"Good riddance," Harruq said, returning to the tower.

"What's up his butt," Brug asked, glancing back.

"Just leave him be," Tarlak said, sighing.

Aurelia's hand on Brug's shoulder showed she agreed.

Harruq entered his room as if a stranger. He opened the door slow and quiet. A quick scan showed his daughter in the corner, a soft smile on her face. She was carving something in the dirt with her fingers. Her joy appeared honest, and that burned him all the worse. She seemed so normal he almost walked over, took her in his arms, and bounced her on his knee. But he didn't.

"Having fun?" he asked, taking a tentative step forward. Aullienna looked up and smiled, overjoyed to see her father. She stood, scattering her markings with the bottom flap of her dress. She ran across the room, laughing. Harruq knelt, tears already in his eyes. Qurrah's spell had failed, or perhaps merely run its course like a disease. He scooped Aullienna up into the air, smiling although he cried.

"I missed you, daddy," she said, kissing his nose.

"I missed you too, cutie," he said back. Her words melted away his doubts. He returned her kiss on the nose, grinning. His first thought was to hold her forever. His second thought was to call for his wife so she could see. The little girl squirmed in his arms, laughing at something she found hysterical.

"You look funny," she said, swiping at his cheek.

"How's that?" he said.

"Do it again," she cried.

"Hun, do what?"

Her face scrunched, and she pulled back in his arms. "Daddy, I don't like this."

"Like what, Aully? I'm not doing anything."

The girl only squirmed harder, pushing back against his chest. "Stop it daddy, stop it!"

She slapped him, once, the thin nails of her fingers cutting into his gray skin. No blood flowed, but the wound was more severe than a stake to his heart. He set her down, ignoring the marks she made across his hands. Her feet did not support her at first, so she clumped to the grass. With a primal cry, she leapt to one wall. Spinning around, she eyed her father with shaking eyes, bird eyes in the face of the serpent. Her kneels curled to her chest. She hid half her face behind them.

"Stop it," she whispered into the skin of her arms. "Please, daddy, stop it."

He collapsed, his heart breaking. He wanted to die. Shuddering sobs straight from the stomach ripped from his lips.

"Damn you, Qurrah," he said. "Damn you."

Aurelia found him as such: a crying, pitiful sight. Without a word, she knelt beside him, wrapped her arms about his neck, and kissed him. He latched his hands onto her, a drowning man clutching the sides of a boat. He buried his face into her neck, the tomb of her hair about his head the only comfort he could find.

"She was fine," he managed to say. "When I came up, she…she was fine."

"Be glad for it," the elf said, gently stroking the side of his face. The words seemed hollow to her, but they comforted him. Under Aullienna's watchful eyes, the two rocked in the illusionary grass, beneath a blue sky that was a lie, in a peaceful world that did not exist.

After five days, Qurrah decided it was time to receive his answer. He stood behind his home, wincing under the glare of the rising sun. Tessanna sat nearby, running an old brush of her mother's through her great length of black hair. It had been cut only once since her mother's death, a clumsy attempt by her father after the first time he raped her. Despite its length, the hair shimmered with a livid energy in the morning light, washed and well cared for. Qurrah found himself mesmerized by the mystic beauty of his lover. A smile dared grace his lips.

I am so lucky to have you, he thought. So very lucky.

She caught his stare and smiled.

"What are you thinking about, dirty boy?"

"Nothing," he said, turning away. "Nothing at all. Stay silent while I speak with my brother."

She shrugged and resumed brushing. Whispery words slipped off Qurrah's tongue, a simple incantation. In the middle of the Eschaton tower, a shadowy imitation of himself rose from the floor. It stared with dead eyes that saw only the most basic shapes and colors.

"Greetings, Harruq. I trust the past few days have been well."

The abyss has seen happier days. The deep voice rang in his head, coming from nowhere. A second voice spoke, that of the wizard.

It is a shame you aren't here to enjoy them with us. Come, join our breakfast in person. I've got hemlock and poisonberries, special treat just for you.

"You are not witty, wizard, so please do not make me endure any more comments," Qurrah said, his voice sounding far away. "Have you accepted my request?" He listened for his brother, but instead Tarlak spoke again.

You aren't getting the book, butcher. You never will. You've ruined his daughter for nothing. But I'm sure you feel it justified.

Qurrah's forehead sloped downward, narrowing his eyes to slits.

"I do not jest, only I have her cure," he said. "Yet you refuse what I ask?"

I'm sorry brother, he heard Harruq say. *You will never get it. I'm sorry for striking at you. You weren't the Reaper. We know that now. Please, if you are angry, be angry with me. Do not bring my daughter into this. Please. I beg you, as my brother, whatever you wish to do to me, just make her well.*

A strange feeling welled up in his chest, constricting and burning at once. To hear his brother say there was no chance for the book, and such an offer…

Qurrah?

He closed his eyes and turned away, scattering the shadow form into nothingness. He stumbled one way, then another, fingers pressed against his forehead.

You will never get it.

"Why?" he said. "What is it you fear from me?"

I beg you, as my brother...

"Qurrah?" Tessanna asked, seeing the troubled look on her lover's face. "Is something wrong?"

I'm sorry for striking at you.

"I am fine," he said, stumbling for the house. "I just...let me sit for awhile."

He ran to the house, flinging open the door with a burst of magical power that splintered it down the middle. He collapsed into the chair beside the fire, cursing repeatedly. How dare his brother attempt to guilt him? How dare he?

"I don't care if you know now," he said, covering his eyes with his hands. "I do not care! I do this for her, not for myself."

...just make her well...

The thought would not leave. He would do anything in the world for Tessanna. Harruq would do anything in the world for his daughter. Of course he would. So why did he refuse the book? What if they never brought it to him? The half-orc wrenched his head violently side to side. Was it possible? Did Aullienna suffer without reason? Without hope?

"Damn you, Harruq," the half-orc said, burying his head in his hands. "You couldn't let things go as they should. You never can."

So many promises he had made. So many he might never keep.

A floorboard creaked. He glanced up to see Tessanna peering at him with an intolerably shy look on her face.

"When will I get to see Aullienna?" she asked. He glared, so fiercely, so heartlessly, that she stepped back. Tears swelled in her eyes.

"I knew it," she seethed.

She fled from the house. Qurrah gave no chase. He had no words.

29

"Come on," Tarlak said, rising from the table. "We all need a break. Four nights straight searching for our suddenly vanished killer, it is enough to wear anyone out." He glanced to where the shadow form of Qurrah had been. "That sure isn't helping, either."

"What I need is sleep," Harruq said.

"A caravan from Mordeina arrived yesterday," the wizard insisted. "Exotic wines, a few nifty toys, and some new clothes. We can find something for everyone."

"Let's go, Harruq," Aurelia said, nudging her husband in the side. "Or are you afraid of a little shopping?"

"Not much for wine," Brug muttered, "but I'll take a chance for some good old Kerish ale snuck in among the bunch."

"And healing salve for burns," Haern said. He offered everyone a wink. "They actually feel quite fine. Delysia, you're a goddess."

"Only close," the priestess said, blushing.

"Well, you all can go without me," Harruq said. "I'm going to take a long, long nap."

"You don't want to go?" Aurelia asked, looking offended.

"How many times I got to say the word 'nap'?"

"Well, fine," the elf said. "Stay and mope then. I'm going. When do we leave?"

"Right now," Tarlak said. He took out a brown bag tied with a white string at the top. It jingled when he shook it. "And unless any of you get too crazy, I'll be buying."

Haern smiled, and Brug cheered. The mercenaries got up to leave. Only Harruq remaining seated at the table, picking over scraps of his meal. The mercenaries filed out the door, but before she left, Aurelia leaned next to her husband one last time.

"Are you sure you don't want to come?" she asked.

"Someone's got to stay with Aullienna," he said, meeting her eyes briefly.

"Try to cheer up," she said, kissing his cheek. "I always need your strength. I'm not as tough as I look."

He gave her a slight smile and kissed her back.

"I'll try," he said.

"Thank you."

She left to join the others. Harruq waited until the door shut, then stood. He climbed the stairs, one heavy step at a time. Perhaps he was depressed, but he was tired, very tired, and the allure of sleep was a strong one. When he reached the top he paused, took a breath, and stepped inside. Aullienna looked down from her bed, her face devoid of emotion.

"Hey, Aully," he said, dropping his swords to the ground. He unbuckled his armor, casting it carelessly to the grass. He watched her as he placed his hands in a fist and popped his back. "Sure you don't want anything to eat?"

The little girl shook her head, still staring at him.

"That's fine," he said, lumbering to his bed. "I'll be napping. Need anything, just wake me, alright?"

She didn't nod. No surprise, really. He had begun to recognize a few moods. This was her apathetic one. He probably could have stripped naked, set himself on fire, and done a dance before getting a reaction. The half-orc sighed. At least she wasn't screaming or cowering in fear.

"Nighters," he said, sliding under the sheets and burying his head into a pillow. He tossed, he turned, and he groaned and sighed. A few more tosses and turns later, he succumbed. His eyes rolled back, his breathing slowed, and precious sleep came.

Aullienna watched him, strangely intrigued. She recognized him, and some part knew him as a protective and loving figure, but she knew this like she knew that a fall would hurt her, or if she tried to eat the grass in the room it would dissolve into nothing in her mouth. Her interest in the sleeping man passed. Boredom came next. All she could remember was this same, bland room. Grass she could not tear. Sky that was always the same, with nothing to see in the clouds. Wind that was always soft.

She climbed down the stairs from her bed, careful to be silent. She didn't want to wake the sleeping man. When she reached the ground, she paused. The wildness in her eyes ruined an otherwise adorable image of her crouched like a kitten in the grass. When the sleeping man did not move, she crossed over the grass as quick as her tiny legs could go before dashing down the stairs.

She wanted grass that was grass. It didn't make any sense to her, but few things did, lately. She paused in front of Brug's room, where the scattered pieces of armor and weapons looked like a wicked forest where the leaves cut skin and the trunks gleamed in the daylight. The little girl giggled. That was what she wanted. Trees. Leaves. A forest.

When she reached the bottom floor of the tower, Aullienna rushed for the door. She stood on her tippy-toes, her tiny fingers slipping around the handle. She more fell than pulled, but her weight was not enough. Angry, she kicked the door, the obstacle to her freedom. No matter how much she stretched, she could not reach high enough. She was trapped inside the stupid, boring tower.

Suddenly, she heard a rattling sound. The door shook, and then with a loud creak, it opened. Chilly air swirled inside. Aullienna beamed. Smells, true smells, filled her nose. Dew, grass, and in the distance, a forest.

The door opened all the way, spilling sunlight into the room. She squinted to see. Before the door, his red eyes gleaming, his black robes flowing in the wind, stood Velixar.

"Where might you be going?" he asked.

In answer, she put a finger to her mouth and shushed him.

"Sleeping man won't want me to go," she said.

"But you want to go, don't you?" She bobbed her head up and down, fascinated with how the stranger's face kept changing. "I thought so."

He knelt down and put his hands around her. She shivered at his touch.

"Back there is a pretty forest," the man in black said. "It is a special forest. You see, the faeries live there. Do you want to see them?"

"Promise you won't tell the sleeping man?" Aullienna asked.

"I promise. Now go play, and watch for the faeries."

She gave him a shy smile, turned, and then ran around tower. At the sight of the forest, she forgot all about the strange man in black. To her mind, the forest sparkled in purples and reds, a magical place full of adventure. There would be no gibbering goblins in there. Only faeries, beautiful ones with hummingbird wings and sparkling dust marking their trail through the air. She ran, wild, free. Her foot stubbed a rock, and she fell. Her hands scraped against the ground, yet she felt no pain. The forest lost its allure for a brief moment, lost to the mesmerizing view of blood trickling down her palm.

Curious, she licked it. The dirt was nasty, but beneath was a sweet taste that filled her with energy. She ran for the forest.

Harruq awoke with a need he was immediately angry for not dealing with before he lay down to rest. Grumbling, he staggered out of bed and reached for his chamber pot. As he did, he saw the door was open. He stood there, looking at it, as he thought this should alarm him. Why would a door alarm him? It was open. Did that mean something?

"Aullienna," he said, much of the drowsiness leaving him. He looked about the room, calling his daughter's name.

"Aullienna?"

He checked her bed, he checked the corners, he checked underneath everything. She was gone. He screamed her name as he ran down the stairs, all the while telling himself to calm down. The only place she could hurt herself was in Brug's room, and it wasn't like he was dumb enough to leave his...

But of course that door was open too. He looked inside.

"You in here, Aullienna?"

He saw nothing and heard nothing. The mess on the floor looked undisturbed, if that was even detectable in that wreck of a room. He bypassed the other closed doors to the bottom floor. His heart stopped when he saw the main door flung wide open.

"You came and got her," he said, anger flushing into him. "You just came and..."

No. He couldn't believe it. He just couldn't. Perhaps he meant to cure her, if he had even taken her at all. Or maybe she went out on her own. It was possible. Probable. The half-orc bolted outside, immediately wishing he had at least thrown on his cloak. The thin clothing he wore beneath his armor was little comfort against the wind. He looked around the open grass and dirt path leading toward Veldaren. Nothing.

"Where'd you go?" he asked, spinning around. He had no clue how long he'd slept, or how long she had been gone. It could have been minutes. It could have been hours.

"Aullienna!" he screamed, cupping his hands to his mouth. Around the tower he went, scanning all about. When he saw the forest, he felt his stomach churn. If Qurrah had taken her, that was where they were.

"She just wandered in," he said, desperate to believe. "She just wandered in, that's all."

He ran into the forest, repeatedly calling his daughter's name. Harruq's former master watched him run from his hiding place.

"I'm sorry, wayward son," Velixar whispered. "I only do what must be done."

He had spoken those words many times, but for the first time in ages, they felt hollow to him.

The forest was better than she had hoped. Much better. Everything swirled in rainbow colors. The leaves weren't green. They were orange and red and purple, and every other color, except green. That was boring.

Animals wandered by, saying hello as they passed. She said hello back to every one. Mommy and daddy had raised her to be polite, after all. The little girl had no clue how far into the forest she had gone, but that didn't matter. The forest was better than that stupid little room. She never wanted to go back. Never ever.

"Run, kitty kitty," she sang, prancing through the bushes. "Big dog coming, and he's coming for you!"

She fell into leaves, giggling madly. She dragged her arms and legs across the ground, swimming in the colors. She felt so bubbly, so light, that if she jumped high enough she'd just float into the air and fly away. So she tried. Sadly, she fell back into the leaves, banging down on her knee. She wiped the blood onto her hand and kissed it. Kisses made everything better.

"Aullienna!"

She turned, hearing the voice. It was the sleeping man, except now he wasn't sleeping. That meant he wanted to take her back to her room. She ran in the opposite direction of his voice. A new sound met her ears, and she so desperately wanted to see what it was. It was a constant rushing sound. It had to be water. She climbed a log, a mountainous obstacle blocking her path. With a cry of victory, she leapt off. The way was clear. She ran to the noise, beaming at a small stream flowing through her forest of magic.

"I see me!" she said, peering down into the water. She waved hello. Herself waved hello back. Both giggled. Then, deep behind her reflection in the water, she saw lights. They were quick and subtle. Every time she jerked her eyes to see, they were gone. Faeries, she thought. The stranger was right!

She reached into the water to grab them, but her hands were too slow.

"Stop moving," she whined. She reached again, but they zipped deeper. She knelt closer, her concentration complete. A thrill surged through her. She caught one! Aullienna yanked her hand back out, but it was a frog, dull and yellow. It leapt off her hand back to the safety of the water.

Aullienna did not see a frog. She saw a blue pixie beckon after her, leaping into her watery world with a trail of dust tinkling atop the stream. She followed with a smile on her face, for she wished to see the world of faeries.

※

"Where are you?" Harruq cried, doing his best to fight off panic. She could have wandered anywhere. If she got lost, and night came, he'd never...

"Aurelia can find her," he said, remembering her abilities with magical portals. "She could take us right to her."

This calmed him a little. He slowed from a run to a jog, searching for signs of passage. As he charged through some bushes, he found a thick pile of flattened leaves.

"You around here, baby?" he asked, glancing about. He could hear a stream in the distance. Perhaps she was there.

※

Deeper and deeper she went, her eyes open under the water. Much of it was so muddy, so brown, it couldn't be the world of faeries. They had to live beyond, deeper in. She kept swimming, kept pushing, following the twinkling dust that had begun to fade. She cried out for the faerie, her voice a weird echo in her head. The creature did not return to her. Desperate, she hurried faster, into the world of light that she began to see. She swam harder, until the world grew brighter, and she knew she neared the faerie land. She sucked in water, mostly out of instinct. Passing through the dust of the faerie had helped her, she knew. She could breathe water. And so she did, ignoring the retching of her chest, ignoring everything, everything except the twinkling lights that grew forever stronger until they enveloped her very being. The land was golden, the song was eternal, and seeing it, she smiled.

※

Harruq stumbled to the stream, scanning its length. Perhaps she was playing. The water was bound to be cold, but she had done stranger things. He took a few steps, glanced down, and then his world stopped.

Floating face down in the water was his daughter. She twirled in the pull of the stream, her head swaying from side to side. Bits of mud and moss were in her hair. Her hands floated beside her, pale and lifeless. Her entire body moved only with the water.

The half-orc cried out. He plunged into the water, took hold of her shoulders, and yanked her out. He felt her body sink into his arms, her head rolling to one side. Her eyes were open, as was her mouth. Her eyes did not blink. She did not breathe.

"Aully," he pleaded, nearly crushing her against his chest. He brushed a shaking hand across her face, pulling away the hair that stuck to her cheek. "Please, Aully, please no, don't, please, don't…"

He fought the stream, pushing to the shore. Cold water ran down his arms and chest. His eyes lingered on her lips, blue as the sky above. She felt so tiny in his arms, and yet so heavy. A lump in his throat swelled, and his eyes clouded with tears so that he could not look upon her face. He shrieked again, running his arm across his eyes to banish them.

"I'm so sorry," he whispered down to her. "Forgive me. I'm so sorry."

He hugged her. Water spilled from her mouth and across his chest. It was colder than anything he had ever felt before. The world remained frozen. Only he seemed to move at all. He carried her back to the tower, the longest trek he would ever take.

Deep within the forest, Tessanna cried out, grief and horror mixed into one terrible sob.

"What is it?" Qurrah asked, taking her into his arms.

"The girl is dead," she sobbed, clawing at his chest. "I saw it, she's dead. You killed her, you killed her!"

He did not stop her as she dug her nails into his chest so hard that blood flowed. He only held her tight as the shock of what had happened overcame him. He tried to say something, to say anything, but no words would come. They just would not come.

When the mercenaries returned to find the door to the tower open, they knew something was wrong. They set down their bags of trinkets, wine and ale.

"Did Harruq go somewhere?" Tarlak asked. Aurelia shrugged. Fear nagged at her, some nameless worry, so she did not rush up the stairs to check. She cast a divination spell to see her husband in her mind's eye.

She suddenly cried out, startling the rest. She turned and fled out of the tower. Tarlak and the others followed, so surprised it took them a moment to realize she had even left. Around the tower Aurelia went, running for the forest as fast as her elven grace allowed. Staggering out from the trees came her husband, their daughter in his arms.

"Harruq!" she cried, flying over the grass. Her husband looked up at her, his eyes lifeless. She saw that look and knew. She did not need words, she did not need to see the way Aullienna's arms hung lifeless beside her, or how her neck slumped in an unnatural way. She knew. She stopped running, her hands going up to cover her mouth, squelching a moan.

The half-orc stumbled. Tears streamed down his face. Less than ten feet away, he fell to his knees and cradled the girl to his chest.

"She's dead," he said, and then the sobbing came. It erupted from the center of him, great and powerful. He tried to speak, to say something, but he could not. Aurelia knelt before him, her slender fingers caressing her daughter's face.

"How?" she managed to ask.

"She drowned," he said, fighting for control. He placed her on the grass in front of him, unable to bear the weight any longer. The rest of the mercenaries came running, falling silent at the sight. Tarlak's face flushed the deepest red. Delysia let out a startled cry before turning away. Harruq stood, looked to his wife, and then took her in his arms. He needed her. More than ever, he needed her. The two embraced, each quietly crying.

At last he could cry no more, for an easier feeling, one he knew well, overcame Harruq.

"He killed her," he said. Aurelia gave no reaction, so he said it again. The words made him better somehow. "He killed her." He pulled back, looked her in the eye, and said it one more time. "He killed her."

"Don't go," she said, but he already was. He marched past the others, heading for where his armor and swords lay scattered across the bedroom floor.

"Where are you going?" Haern dared ask.

"I'm going to kill him," Harruq turned and screamed. "I'm going to make him pay."

"We need to talk," Tarlak said. Harruq ignored him. He rushed for the tower, putting his daughter behind him. He could bear that image no more. He heard his wife call his name but he fought against it. Sorrow was for another time. Vengeance was now.

Then she took his wrist in her hands. He whirled around, fury raging in his eyes. Aurelia did not back down, even as the pain filled her face.

"Please, don't go," she pleaded. "I need you. Please."

"He killed my daughter!" he shouted.

"She was my daughter too," she said. A tear ran down past her nose and fell to the ground. "Can't you see? She was *our* daughter."

He nodded. More tears came to his eyes.

"I just, Aurry, I…" The anger melted away. His grief lost its razor-edge, fading down to a constant throb.

"We need to build a pyre," she said. Harruq nodded and sighed. His shoulders sagged.

"I'll make one out back," he said. "I guess tonight we'll…we…"

"We'll give her body back to nature," Aurelia said, trying to be strong. "Her soul has moved on. The pyre will make her as she was."

"She'll never be as she was," Harruq said. To this Aurelia only clutched him tighter. The cold wind blew, the couple mourning amidst it as deep in the woods two more lovers suffered much the same.

30

Scattered among the forest of metal within Brug's room was a great, hulking axe. One side was enormously thick, the edge sharpened to a lumberjack's point. Harruq retrieved it, grunting at the weight in his hands. It weighed more than Aullienna. He didn't know why, but that fact irritated him. He jammed it down on a broken chestplate, frowning as it punched a giant triangular dent across the middle.

"Good enough," he said. They were the last words he spoke for the next three hours. His breathing ragged, and still wearing the thin sweaty clothes from the morning, he approached the forest. He knew the others watched him. This irritated him even more. The first tree he reached became his victim. Into the air the axe went, lifted high, both hands gripping the far bottom of the handle. When it swung, it swung with anger, with pain. The first bite drawn, he settled in for the rest.

The tree, a spindly, stubborn thing that had lost its leaves early, was just about to fall when Brug appeared.

"Thought someone should show you how to cut a tree properly," he said, trying to sound callous, unimpressed, or bored. Harruq did not respond, nor did he move out of the way to let the smaller man move in with his thicker axe. So instead, Brug stood by and watched as the tree came tumbling down.

They needed logs, so Harruq began cutting off the branches and placing them in a large pile. Some were just tiny, while others were enormous chunks with many warts and growths. Meanwhile, Brug cut the tree into quarters, hefting the axe high above his head before crashing it down.

Haern arrived then, his hood removed. He knew kindling was needed, so he had retrieved a small hatchet from the tower. The smaller branches he trimmed and smoothed. The larger ones he hacked into smaller pieces. This he did while Harruq split the quarters into more manageable chunks, which Brug took wordlessly. With one great swing, he cut them into perfect sized logs.

With a polite nod to the half-orc, Tarlak arrived. Bearing no axe or hatchet, he instead took the branches to the place where the pyre would burn. Then he came for the logs, carrying them three at a time back toward the tower. He could have used a levitation spell to carry them, but he did not. Without sweat and toil, his help would be meaningless. The two women accepted his gifts with thanks given only in their eyes. It was their duty to prepare the pyre. It would be smaller than normal, much smaller. A web of the thinner twigs and branches formed the center, to give easy life to the fire. Surrounding it went the bigger logs, like a wall protecting a scattered bird nest. One or two thick logs went in the center for support, and then more twigs, branches, even dry leaves, all packed atop everything. They placed more logs around the sides as sweat ran down their necks.

When the pyre neared completion, Aurelia told Tarlak to bring them no more. He nodded, dreading the act. He didn't want to speak. The silence and backbreaking work had done much to mask the grief that made them toil. A bond formed out of tragedy would soon be broken. His words would break it.

"We're done here," the wizard told them, crossing his arms to pull his yellow robe tighter across his chest. A large pile of wood remained to be taken, but they left it abandoned. Harruq plopped the head of his axe to the ground and leaned on the handle.

"You sure?" he asked.

Tarlak nodded. "Yes. I'm sure."

The four left the woods. It was still the afternoon, but the days had grown shorter. The sun was already speeding its way toward the horizon. The orange light would soon be gone. Come nightfall, the fire would be lit.

Seeing the pyre filled Harruq's eyes with tears and ripped apart his heart. It looked like an altar, one he would sacrifice his daughter upon. To what god would she go? What purpose? He imagined his own body lying atop of it, his flesh burning in the fire. He would bear it willingly, gladly, if it would bring life back to the water-filled lungs of his daughter. Still, despite all this, the pyre was beautiful. It was made out of love, and all things made this way are beautiful, to those who have the eyes to see it.

He hugged his wife and kissed her forehead.

"Well done," he said. His voice cracked.

"Help me move her body," she said.

"Alright. Let me get her."

She seemed so peaceful, lying on her back with her eyes closed. Just like a nap, he thought. Never mind how blue her lips were, or how pale her skin had become. Just napping.

The weight of her in his arms was greater than he remembered. He held her away from his body, as if her very touch would set fire to his flesh. He walked slowly, a thief approaching the gallows. Her small frame fit snug atop the pyre. Crisscrossing twigs surrounded the very top, and if he stepped back just far enough, he couldn't see her.

"What do we do until nightfall?" he asked his wife.

"We make our fire," Delysia answered, touching his arm.

It was an Eschaton tradition, not an elven one, the business about the fire. Several years before, one of their original members, a wily rogue named Senke, had died in a pointless brawl in a tavern. They had buried him in one of Veldaren's cemeteries, but they felt it appropriate to honor him in a way all their own. From this came the bonfire. Delysia, Tarlak, Brug and Haern all found an object of theirs, something valuable, and tossed it into a bonfire.

"Why must it be something so valuable?" Aurelia asked as it was explained to her.

"We had lost something dear that day," Tarlak said. "But it was nothing that belonged to us. I threw my first spellbook into that fire. The hassle, the cost, and the annoyances to regain the knowledge I lost took a mere five months. Before that, I had thought it something I could never live without." The wizard sighed. "It put things into perspective. Any possession is a possession. Senke was so much more, as was your daughter."

They piled a few of the remaining logs that Tarlak had brought back next to the pyre and soaked them with oil. The wizard used a tiny spark, just a little magic, to get it burning. Haern was the first to go. He tossed his gray hood upon the flame.

"It is about time the scum feared my real face," he said, watching it burn as if losing a part of him.

Brug was next.

He pulled out a pouch, shaking it a couple times so everyone could hear the rattle. Yanking the string open with a quivering hand, he spilled out four precious emeralds onto his open palm.

"I was going to make her a necklace," he said, smiling briefly. "You know, for her birthday."

He sniffed. Out went his hand, sprinkling the four into the flame.

"Probably would have been an ugly necklace," he muttered, staring at his feet.

Delysia removed a small gold pendant from around her neck, one shaped in the outline of a mountain.

"I'm sure Ashhur knows you mean no disrespect," Tarlak said as she tossed it upon the fire.

"He'd better."

Tarlak's laughter was forced, and did not last long. Into his pocket went his hand, coming out with a single scroll. He read its words, the scroll in one hand, his staff in the other. At the end, the scroll shriveled, and a great shimmer went across the staff. This done, he let it fall into the fire.

"Had to make sure it would actually burn," he chuckled.

It was Harruq's turn. He sighed, unfolding the bundle in his hands. It was the cape Delysia had made him for his wedding.

"Always thought I looked good in it," he said. He felt his wife wrap an arm around him, and it gave him the strength he needed. He folded it into the fire, careful not to let it drop flat and snuff the flame. The fine material caught and burned. Aurelia looked around to the others, and then removed a thin silk cloth wrapped around her gift. It was a bouquet of flowers.

"Harruq gave me these a long time ago," she said, looking at them lovingly. "I've kept them alive. I don't know why I did, even then. But I don't need to know anymore."

She threw them into the fire. They were consumed. In silence, the group stood. They watched the flickering of the flame, enjoying the warmth and loathing the meaning.

"I don't think I should be giving a eulogy," Tarlak said. He glanced around, tucked his arms, untucked them, and then continued. "But someone should say something, and it always seems to be me that does. So I'll do it again."

He turned to the parents, their arms wrapped about each other's waists for support.

"I've never been around a baby," he said. "Never. The crying, the feeding, the constant yelling at you to take care of her, Ashhur spare me such a fate. But we loved her here. I was hoping one day she might grow up and, well, learn a little from me. I wanted to show her a thing or two, and be there when she cast her first spell. I've never had a student, but I'm sure she would have been a great one. I know you two loved her, more than us. My hurt, I'm sure it pales, but it's there, and Ashhur help me should such a day as this come to my heart. But to Ashhur she has gone. He has always said the lives of children belong to him, and to each one he will open his arms and embrace. If Ashhur grants me the same welcome, the first person I'll ask to see is that little brown-haired girl, to see how she's grown. To see…"

He stopped to swallow, and then stared into the fire.

"Thank you," Harruq said. "For everything."

"We owe you two for all of it," Delysia said. "For the time we had with her, on behalf of us all, thank you."

Two tears, running twin paths down each cheek, lined Aurelia's smile.

"You're welcome," she said.

"It's dark enough," the wizard said. "It's time."

Harruq demanded the task be his. He dipped a branch halfway into the fire, letting it heat and burn for several minutes until it was solidly lit. His heart in his throat, he turned to the pyre. The rest of the Eschaton surrounded it, their faces somber. He wiped his sniffling nose on his other sleeve and then, slowly, reluctantly, lit the fence of twigs lining the outer rim of the pyre. As it caught, he stared at the face of his daughter. The feeling was surreal, but he knew whatever it was that had made his daughter able to love, to feel, to cling to his leg and look up with an emotion purer than anything in the world, was gone from that body. For the first time, he saw her truly dead.

He dropped the branch into the fire, put his arm around Aurelia's waist, and stood straight. He watched the pyre burn. He felt his wife's head rest against his shoulder, and the wetness there he knew was tears. All about, the others watched in silence. Brighter and brighter the fire grew. Smoke poured up, first light, and then a heavy billowing shield, protecting him from the sight of that little angel, chubbier than most elven girls, taller, her skin soft and her smile innocent and wonderful, being consumed by the fire. No animals sounded in the newly come night, and it seemed even the stars watched in sorrow at that small flicker of flame.

Harruq swore upon the pyre to avenge the loss of his daughter. He hated the bitter feeling welling within, but he could not deny it, only succumb and feed the entity. Under red visions of rage, he imagined killing his brother, ramming his sword through his

The Cost of Betrayal

forehead, shoving every shred of pain he felt into a crimson blade drenched with blood. Vengeance. Gods help him, it was all that gave him comfort.

But for the first time the images broke, unable to stand beneath their horrid weight. He was not a monster. He was not what Qurrah thought he was. He leaned his neck atop Aurelia's head, their arms holding each other tight as they swayed in the heat of the pyre. In his heart, he cast aside his vengeance.

"It's all right," he whispered. Aurelia did not know to whom he spoke. "It's all right. We'll be all right. Everything will be all right."

She turned away from the fire and buried her face into his neck.

They stood before the flame for more than an hour. At last, Tarlak put a hand on their shoulders and led them back to the tower for the rest they so desperately needed. Delysia went as well, preparing their bed and doing her best to remove bits and things of Aullienna's before they arrived.

Brug and Haern, side by side in the orange light, held their solemn stand.

"What kind of man can kill another's daughter?" Haern whispered to the pyre. "What kind of monster?"

"It doesn't take a monster," Brug whispered back. "It's the act that makes you one."

From his pocket, Haern pulled out the green ribbon he had offered Aullienna on the day of her birth. On it was the vow of the Eschaton to protect her. Haern dropped it into the fire, wondering how he had so miserably failed such a vow. Brug saw and clapped the assassin on the back. They left without another word. Unwatched, the ribbon burned and blackened until nothing but ash remained of the love that had made it.

Qurrah Tun stood below the star-filled sky, his body a motionless statue, his arms out at his sides and his legs stiff. His neck ached, and his clenched fists trembled with each ragged breath he took.

He wept, the stars his only witness.

31

Qurrah slept outside, shivering as the chill sank into his bones. He was a cold, blue-lipped, and miserable. Even when shame overwhelmed his tears, he could not enter the cabin. He knew Tessanna awaited him, probably needing his arms... Or did she? He never knew with her. Never. So out in the dirt he huddled, his penance for hurting the girl she loved.

He thought of his days as a child, huddled against his brother for warmth in the slums of Veldaren. Now he had no brother to comfort him. If anything, Harruq would greet him with drawn swords instead of open arms.

"Go ahead," Qurrah said to a phantom Harruq, clenching his jaw to stop the chattering. "Condemn me if you want."

He drifted in and out of sleep, slowly growing aware of a slight rain. His robes were pitiful protection against it. The cabin tempted his mind, flitting in and out of his self-pity. Guilt rooted him firm. He dreamt, just a little. A spider hung above his head, dangling by a silver-glinted thread. Eight eyes sparkled violet, and from its fanged mouth he heard words but did not understand.

He awoke to the touch of feminine fingers against his arm. He kept his eyes closed as Tessanna knelt beside him, curling her arms about his waist. She pressed her body against his, her face nestling into the nape of his neck. She said nothing. Neither did he. Her warmth was not great, but it was enough. His great convulsions slowed to constant trembling. Together they rode out the cold suffering they shared.

The damned persistent sun ripped open Qurrah's eyelids with its light. Water rimmed his eyeballs, so he turned away and buried his face into his arm. A cold wind blew against his back, and he realized his lover was not with him. A burning stirred within his turmoil, one he must obey. He had to make sure nothing changed. Despite his broken promise, despite his grotesque error, he had to know something remained stable.

He stood and shook the dirt from his hair. Inside the cabin, Tessanna sat beside the fire, shivering in wet clothing. She glanced up at him, her face ragged and tired.

"Sleep well?" she asked.

He pulled her to her feet. Off went her wet rags she called a dress. When she started to protest, he rammed his mouth against hers. His clothes went next. She was like a doll, weightless, obedient. He threw her against a wall, her hands pinned behind her back. His tongue and teeth nipped and flitted across her neck.

"Am I still who I was?" he hissed into her ear.

"You always will be," she said, her bottom lip trembling. "Always."

It should have been enough, but anger stirred where there had once been guilt. He took her on their bed, his motions seeming of vengeance rather than love, but she cried out just the same.

Once he had dressed, Qurrah sought solitude in the forest. Tessanna gave him time before joining him. Despite the cold, she ventured naked from the cabin. Qurrah glanced back, his heart fluttering at the sight. Every curve, every tender touch of her skin, was beyond human. If not for the way her ribs showed when she walked, or how thin her arms sometimes looked, she would have been flawless.

He knelt at the edge of the dead wildlife. When she approached, he kept his eyes low and his words quiet.

"Do you blame me?" he asked her.

"Part of me does," she said. "But I think it's more Aurelia's fault, and your brother's. I have to. Otherwise, I would kill you, and I don't want to do that. What do you think they'll do?"

"Harruq will want blood," he said, standing. "And the others will seek the same, even if he does not."

"Can they find us?"

"In time. Even if they must search the entire forest."

She glanced over at him, a shy look on her face.

"What are, what are we going to do when they show up?" The half-orc turned away, and in his silence, she found the answer. "We can go," she said, the idea offered reluctantly, almost in embarrassment. "Let's just go. We don't have to stay."

"Yes, we do." A bird dared sing a happy tone, and he struck it dead with a wave of his hand. Tessanna watched with idle curiosity as the rigid lump of feathers fell.

"But why?" she asked.

"Because I will not run," he said, so softly that the girl had to strain to hear.

"Why not?"

"Because then Harruq will be right."

"Right about what?"

He turned on her, a dark anger smoking underneath the brown of his eyes.

"Everything."

Tessanna's apathy rose to match his anger. "Fine. What do you want me to do?"

Qurrah walked to where the dead bird lay. A quick mutter of magic syllables and the hollow bones tore out from beneath the soft feathers. They swirled around the half-orc's hand, so tiny.

"I must face Harruq," he said, watching their flight. One by one, he flung them against a tree. "The others are yours. Kill them."

He returned to the cabin for warmth but the fire had died. His frail body shook underneath the blankets of his bed, but still the pleasant feel of heat eluded him. He shivered and shivered. When Tessanna offered to join him, he turned her away. Spurned, sat before the dead fire. A single slit across the end of her forefinger sent blood dripping down. Her soft breath blew against the drops. When they touched the wood, they flickered with flame, growing hotter and hotter with each successive drop. By the time a great fire roared, Qurrah had fallen into slumber.

Tessanna did not mind. She sucked on her bleeding finger, a look of pure hatred blanketing her face as she watched her lover sleep. She did not move, nor did her look change, until she saw his body stir, and then apathy grabbed the anger and locked it away.

Haern snuck into their room, just as he had so often to awaken Harruq for sparring. But this time he did not seek swordplay.

"Wake up," he said, nudging the half-orc.

"What is it?" Harruq asked, rolling toward him. His eyes were wide-awake and bloodshot. The assassin felt a pang of guilt as he wondered how little the half-orc had slept that night.

"I know where your brother hides," he whispered.

"Not now, Haern," Aurelia pleaded from the other side of the bed.

"How do you know?" Harruq said, propping himself up with an elbow.

"That does not matter. We must not let them have time to slip away. You deserve vengeance, and I will help give it to you."

The half-orc flung off the blankets and put his feet on the cold floor. He shuffled about, grabbing armor and swords. Aurelia sat up, not caring that only the flimsiest of fabrics protected her skin from Haern's eyes.

"What are you going to do," she asked. "Run off on your own?"

"If I have to," Harruq said, struggling against the buckles of his chestpiece.

"Leave," she said to Haern. The assassin bowed and did as he was told. When he was gone, the elf left the bed and took her husband's hands in her own, halting his preparations.

"I have to do this," he said to her.

"But you don't have to do it alone," she said. Harruq pulled against her hands, expecting her to release, but she held on, something in her stronger than he realized. "Not alone," she said, a quick movement of her hands releasing his grip and unbuckling his armor so that it slid to the ground. "And not yet."

She pulled him back to the bed and held him close. His hands did not wander, and she did not desire it. Together, they huddled against the coming trials, enjoying the last moments of darkness before the illusionary dawn rose above the ivy walls, matching the rise of the sun outside.

"I don't know what to do," Harruq said as morning came.

"What do you mean?"

"How do I prove him wrong? How do I show him I am not the killer he claims, when the only right path I see is him dying by my hands?"

She stroked his face.

"Do what you think is right. Just don't do it alone." At last, she let him go. "All of us," she said, sliding her green dress over her body. "That is how it should be."

"If you say so."

When they came down for breakfast, food was ready, and not surprisingly, all were dressed for battle. Brug grumbled from beneath his platemail, sharpening one of his punch daggers. Tarlak had no staff, but a spellbook lay on the table beside his plate. Haern wore his cloaks, his twin sabers hidden beneath their fabric. Even Delysia seemed regal and dangerous, her white dress so clean and bright it hurt the eyes. The golden mountain on her chest shimmered with angry power.

Out of everyone, only Harruq lacked his armor and did not carry his weapons.

"Well, didn't expect that," Tarlak said, tearing a strip of bacon in half and shoving it into his mouth. "Grab something to eat, ol' buddy, and then get ready. We have a job to do."

"Of course," he said, flustered by the sight of so many ready to risk their lives for him. His appetite was greater than he expected. He devoured the entire plate put before him, plus some of Aurelia's. When finished, he dashed up the stairs and returned with his oiled black leather armor strapped tight across his body. Salvation and Condemnation swung from his hips. The others saw him ready and rose from the table.

One by one, they filed out the door. Tarlak pulled the half-orc aside, away from the others, and talked in a quiet tone.

"Are you sure you can do this?" he asked. The half-orc nodded, remembering that tortured moment when he had yanked Aullienna's body from the cold water.

"Yeah, I think so."

"Good." The wizard patted his shoulder. "Then let's get to it."

Qurrah dragged himself out of bed, his shoulders hunched as if carrying a greater weight than his frail body could handle. He kissed Tessanna's forehead, ignoring the way her eyes stared numbly past him. He flipped through his spellbook, glancing over lines he had read hundreds of times.

"They are almost here," Tessanna said, the words intoned as if she were informing him that the sky was cloudy.

"I know," the half-orc said. He took his whip and let it wrap around his arm. "Can you cast spells to protect me?"

The girl nodded, her back still to him. "I can make you safe for awhile. His swords are strong. The medallion makes them stronger. Qurrah?"

"Yes, Tessanna?"

"Promise you won't be mad?"

"What is it?"

"I don't *want* to kill them. But I will. I thought you should know that."

The words were spoken with a calm, dead voice. Ghosts carried more passion, more life. The half-orc gently rocked his head up and down, knowing that the fire lived underneath, ready to burst forth to wreck and burn.

"I love you," he said.

"So you say," she said. She finally glanced back to him. There was no smile on her face. No sarcasm. Her words bit deep. He opened his spellbook, closed it, opened it again, and then sighed.

"How do we end this?" he suddenly asked. "How do we end this right?"

Tessanna looked at him, her eyes aching with sorrow. "I don't think we can," she said.

Qurrah nodded. He opened the cabin door.

"We must prepare," he said, stepping outside. Tessanna followed him out, proud and beautiful and sad.

32

The Eschaton arrived.

There was no immediate burst of combat. Spells did not flare. Swords stayed sheathed. Haern remained back, told to wait until an opportune moment. Harruq walked ahead, wishing to speak alone with his brother one last time. He entered the clearing surrounding the cabin, his blood chilled at the feeling of death that hung palpable in the air. Nothing good has happened in this place, he thought.

Qurrah and Tessanna waited for him. They stood dressed, anxious, and uncertain. Harruq looked at his brother, seeing for the first time how he had aged. His skin had grown paler. His hair hung dirty past his shoulders. His eyes scared even him. Intensity beyond words. Fire. His entire body seemed to be dying, its life drained into those all-seeing orbs.

"Hello, Qurrah," he said, the words sending the butterflies in his stomach careening into a thousand different flights.

"Hello, brother," Qurrah said. He gestured to the swords sheathed at his side. "Do you plan to use them?"

"I do," he answered.

"I know of your daughter."

"I hoped you would."

Harruq waited, wishing to hear his next words. If they were of repentance, guilt, horror, even regret no matter how insincere, he would have stayed his hands.

"We were fools to think our actions would not come back to haunt us," Qurrah said. "But they have. Will you accept their message, or will you try to kill me?"

Harruq drew his swords. "I am different than you."

"You are a monster. A killer. One of the greatest."

"I said I am different!"

The rest of the Eschaton approached, preparing blade and magic.

"No," Qurrah said, sadness creeping into his voice. "If you were different, then you would not be here. You would not be so ready to kill. You are the same as I, only weaker, and the truth is painful to see."

The rage built inside Harruq, a fire fueled by hate and revenge. He turned to Tarlak, who waited a step behind.

"Do it," he told him.

Fire surrounded Tarlak's hands, mirroring the heat that burned in Harruq's chest. Great arcs of electricity crackled from Aurelia's palms. As one, the mages sent their attacks forward, on either side of the charging half-orc. Tessanna cried out in shock, for both blasts were aimed straight for her. She brought up a shield, holding back the attacks with her pure magical strength. Qurrah let free his whip, and with a single crack, the clearing became chaos.

Harruq's eyes swam red. He saw his brother in a vision of blood and water, wet hair and breathless lungs. He saw his daughter, and through her, he saw the need to finish things, to end it all. No longer was this frail thing of black robes and dying skin his brother. A thing to be murdered, that was all. His last murder.

Qurrah lashed the whip at his legs, but it was too predictable to be a surprise. Harruq swept the flaring leather away with his swords. The necromancer struck again, drawing a black line across the flesh of Harruq's left arm. He accepted the pain willingly. A few bits of bone flew from a pouch on Qurrah's hip. Arms up to protect his eyes, Harruq barreled forward, closing the last bit of distance between them.

What should have been an easy kill, a stab into his unprotected brother's stomach, turned horribly wrong. Qurrah stood his ground, eyes rolled back in his head as he cast a spell. Condemnation rammed against his robe and recoiled. Swirling darkness leapt from the robe, bleeding into the blade and up the hilt. When it touched his hand, every nerve went white. His hand clenched achingly tight, a death grip, so that his muscles bulged and his forearms shook.

When he pulled back the blade, the darkness retreated as if it never were. The contraction of his muscles loosened. With no other plan, no other ideas, Harruq shoved his other sword at a crease between his brother's ribs. Again the numbing pain and the excruciating tear of every muscle stretching beyond its limits. It took all his strength to pull the swords back and break contact with the horrid spell. Harruq gasped, his arms exhausted from only two swings.

Qurrah finished his spell.

Invisible irons attached to every part of Harruq's body. His armor felt thrice its normal weight. His swords felt thick and unwieldy. He swung, but the attack was like that of a dream, connecting with the force of a feather. It clacked against Qurrah's side, and then came the damned darkness, pouring into his flesh. Salvation fell to the ground.

"As much as you have trained, you are still a child with knives," the necromancer said. He lashed with his whip. Harruq's reaction was half of its finely honed speed, his hands lagging behind each blow. Fire and leather scarred his face, his hands, and his throat. Blood seeped down his neck to his armor.

"Damn you," Harruq said. The sounds of battle roared around them. Fire, wind, and ice crashed and exploded everywhere, but to their eyes, they saw no death. They saw no other battle. The two were in their world, and none but the gods could interfere. Harruq cut at his brother, each stroke hitting like a stick against the trunk of a tree. He held the sword with both hands, needing every bit of strength, but now the darkness leaked from the weapon to both arms. The pain alone finally caused the sword to fall limp from his hands. As Harruq knelt and reached for it, he felt fire wrap around his neck. The smell of burning flesh filled his nostrils.

"You shouldn't have come here," Qurrah said, yanking the whip tight. Harruq pulled at the fire, ignoring the horrid pain in his fingers and palms. What breath he could draw was clouded with smoke and the bitter taste of his own charred self. Colorful dots swirled before his eyes. Desperate, he let go of the stubborn end of the whip, instead grabbing the middle of the length. The fire roared greater, his bare hands nearly blackened, but his strength, no matter how reduced by curse it was, was still greater than his brother's. One fierce yank and the handle flew from Qurrah's hand. The fire died, the whip slackened, and Harruq gasped in air.

Qurrah did not give him time to recover. He whispered the words of a spell, and then glared at the stubborn remembrance of his past life that refused to die.

"*Hemorrhage,*" he hissed.

A feeling of blood and pressure filled Harruq's chest. He slammed a fist against his breast, roaring in defiance to the magic. He felt blood slip from his flesh, and he knew somewhere beneath his armor a laceration had opened, but the eruption lacked power.

"Best you got?" Harruq said.

"Forgive my pity," Qurrah said. "And my foolishness for trying to spare you pain."

He began to cast as the warrior took up his weapons and staggered forward. Both swords rammed into Qurrah's throat, ricocheting to either side of his neck. The brief contact prevented too much of the dark armor from slipping into his arms, but his muscles were already weakened. Harruq let out a cry, both swords falling back to the ground. He felt a hand close about his face. He saw his brother through the gaps of his fingers. Qurrah looked back, his eyes unforgiving. Merciless.

Two things happened then. First, the contact spread the dark of Qurrah's enchantment from the flesh of his hand to the flesh of Harruq's face. Second, the spell the necromancer cast filled all he touched with chilling cold, a river of it pouring from his palm into the beaten half-orc's forehead. The pain of the darkness was a thousand biting wolves. His face twisted and contorted, contracting into a horrible visage of pain. The cold flooded his mind, numbing his entire being. Thoughts grew hazy. Images replaced conscious thought. He knew he had to move. He had to fight. Aullienna deserved no less.

He swung both arms like they were tree trunks. They knocked Qurrah's hand aside, breaking both spells. Harruq gasped, feeling his mind returning, but not just his mind. His rage. He forced his fingers to close around the hilts of his swords. He wasn't sure if he could feel them or not, but it didn't matter. Staggering to his feet, he bellowed a mindless, strengthening roar.

"Pitiful," Qurrah said, reaching for his bag of bones. "Just pitiful."

When the twin spells of fire and lightning hit her shield, Tessanna flinched, feeling her energy draining away to protect her vulnerable flesh. She saw Harruq charge, a brief lashing of whip, but then she could watch no more. Another dual blast ripped through the air. She outstretched her fingers, the translucent shield appearing once more. Two fireballs detonated, flames licking the edges her curved barrier. As the smoke died, there came Brug, dressed in full platemail.

"Get away," she said, moving her hand in a slapping motion. An invisible force slammed Brug to the side, his flight ending against the trunk of a tree. Someone shouted his name, she didn't know who.

"Push me," she cried, shattering a bolt of ice into shards with lightning, halting another fireball with a globe of black that swallowed it whole. "Higher! Higher!"

Her pulse quickened when she saw a familiar shape shoot out of the woods. Gray cloaks trailed behind, whipping in a chaotic pattern. Light glinted off drawn sabers. The watcher had come to play.

"Do you miss my fire?" she asked, another slapping motion deflecting the magically summoned boulders aside to crash into the cabin. She heard the splintering of logs and the destruction of her childhood home, but she felt no loss. It was just rotted wood. Darkness ringing the edges of her fingers, she greeted the assassin in her own special way.

Black chains reached up from the ground, writhing like snakes. They wrapped around Haern as he leapt. They pulled him down, cracking his chin as he landed with a thud. More black chains tore upward, wrapping around the assassin's helpless body. A sickly rattle echoed from them as he struggled.

"I got you, Haern," Tarlak said, casting one of his few spells designed to dispel magic from an area. The darkness wavered. The chains' strength faded as they turned white and pale. Aurelia tore a chunk of earth into the air, blocking Tessanna's path.

The earth exploded outward, forming a door for the girl to walk through. She approached Haern, who shook off the last of the chains and readied his blades.

"I asked a question," she said as burning flames enveloped her flesh. "Did you miss my fire?"

"Sorry sweetie," Haern said, his hand reaching into a pocket beneath his cloaks. "I'm tired of being your torch."

His hand flipped forward, hurling a small blue sapphire. It hit with a thud against Tessanna's forehead, an insignificant thing. The magic inside it, however, was massive. White light flared out in a sphere, washing over her. Every trace of her fire died. Her skin exposed, Haern charged, saber tips eager to claim an eye.

Furious at the banishment of her fire, she looked at Haern and snarled. The noise reached tremendous levels, and within it, power. The assassin flew back, sound and wind battering him senseless. A lightning bolt shot past his head, only to be deflected off Tessanna's hand and sent careening wild. The girl clapped her hands together, the black of her eyes pushing away all traces of white within them.

Her fingernails went dark. Her flesh lost what little trace of color it had.

Unsure of what spell she was casting, and not caring to see the results, Tarlak followed his gut. He tried a new tactic, using a similar spell Aurelia had used to control the earth. Instead of forming a protective wall, he ripped a few large chunks directly underneath Tessanna. The first and largest smashed her hands and chin on its ascent. The girl moaned, her teeth snapping down on her tongue. Another section of earth flew into the air, spinning her in a sideways cartwheel. She landed on her shoulder. Blood spewed from her mouth as she cried out in pain.

Blue light danced on Aurelia's fingers, and then shards of ice flew from them, growing larger in rapid succession. Tessanna rolled, warding her body with her arms. Most pieces missed, but one jagged lance tore through her palm. It forced apart bone and puncturing out the other side. The skin between her two middle fingers tore halfway to her wrist.

She did not cry. She did not scream. She rolled to her knees, flipped her long hair away from her face, and laughed.

"It feels beautifully alive," she said, holding out her hand so that the blood dripped onto her dress.

"Then this'll feel like a picnic," Brug said, having snuck up unnoticed behind her despite his noisy platemail. He jammed his right hand forward, the blade aiming for her heart. The girl heard his voice and twirled to the side. The dagger shredded her dress and nicked a rib. His desire to speak ruined him. Tessanna ducked, her eyes alight with fire. She smashed her healthy palm to the ground. A dome of shimmering violet surrounded them. Both mages tried to punch through with spells, but they were unable to penetrate. Haern slashed once with his saber. The metal bounced back, a healthy shock accompanied the swing. Brug was beyond their help.

"You penetrated me," Tessanna said, laughing. Just a happy girl, laughing as fire burned her eyes. Brug dove, both hands punching at blurring speeds. Despite his speed, his strength, and his armor, he still only attacked with plain non-magical metal. Tessanna made a strange triangular shape with the fingers of her healthy hand. An invisible force smashed him back. He stuck for a moment to the inside of the violet dome, shivering as electricity jolted through his body. When he fell, smoke wafted from the open parts of his armor.

"Brug!" a female voice shouted. Tessanna glanced up to see Delysia emerge from hiding behind a tree. The crazed girl smiled at her.

"I missed you," Tessanna said, drawing out her dagger. So often it had cut her own flesh, but many men had been on the receiving end of it as well. The girl stalked toward him, her dagger ready.

"She should be watching," Tessanna said as she hunched down like an animal. "It makes this better."

She lunged, snarling like a panther. Brug's arms felt dead to him. He tried to defend himself, but his hands refused to move. He screamed once, when the dagger punched through the crease between his shoulder and his arm. Blood spilled. Tessanna licked the blade as the others watched in horror.

"Not as sweet as her," she giggled. "But it'll do."

She shoved her dagger with all her strength. Brug kept his mouth shut, refusing to cry out. His thoughts dwindled briefly on the project he had just begun, an amazing sword that would have granted him prestige among those of his craft. He was only half done, but it was stunning. His last thought was of that sturdy blade before the dagger punched through his eye and sent him to the life beyond.

The others trembled with rage and grief as she pulled the dagger out, an eyeball pierced halfway up the blade. She pressed it off with her tongue as she giggled. She held up her torn hand to Aurelia, the ice shard still lodge deeply within. Its blue color was now a deep purple from the blood that soaked into it.

"A present for a present," she said, throwing her dagger at the elf. It broke through the violet dome, shattering the cage that had sealed Brug to his death. The dagger landed by Aurelia's feet, bounced twice, and then finally came to a rest pointed toward her like an arrow. Aurelia's hands shook, and she was unsure if she could calm them enough to cast another spell. Beside her, Tarlak removed his hat and let it fall to the ground.

"Hold nothing back," he said, his pain muffled behind his anger.

"I won't."

As one, they unleashed their greatest spells. A solid beam of pure magic tore from Aurelia, white brilliance, a magical flood. Tarlak shook as a stream of acid erupted from his hands. The two attacks hit the girl simultaneously. Both braced themselves, each of the attacks able to continue as long as they poured their strength into

The Cost of Betrayal

them. They expected Tessanna to raise a shield to protect herself, but she did no such thing. With open arms, she accepted the attacks.

The acid bubbled over her skin, hissing and burning. Aurelia's white beam struck her in the chest, much of it spilling past her small frame. This, too, she endured. Her tattered dress burned away, as did her flesh. Her stomach crunched inward. Bits of her ribs poked through the exposed flesh.

And yet, she laughed. Both streams ended, neither mage able to focus them any longer. Haern streaked in, hoping for surprise after the torrent of spells. Tessanna sensed his approach without ever looking. She pointed her maimed hand at him and extended her fingers to their fullest. Black tendrils shot forth. They cut Haern's flesh, tore at his cloaks, and slammed him to the dirt.

"Thank you," she said to all of them. Her tattered dress fell from her body. She looked like a dead aberration, her ribs showing and her chest horribly burned. Yet her eyes and hair shimmered with life they did not understand. Tessanna spread her arms, and from her back grew ethereal wings. She turned her eyes to the sky, a robe of purest black flowing over her naked body. When she spoke, the death in her voice chilled them where they stood.

"You cannot harm a goddess," she said, bolts of shadow growing around her hands. She threw them like pebbles, dozens of the swelling meteors. Haern, unable to dodge due to the tendrils that still bit into his skin, screamed under the assault. Each one bruised like a brick, and then the magic seeped in, igniting every nerve with pain. Tarlak, Aurelia, and even Delysia summoned what shielding they could, but the torrent was great, and their own beings weakened. Two hit Tarlak square in the chest, sapping his breath. One hit Aurelia's hand, numbing her fingers. Poor Delysia felt one punch through her shield and crash against her throat. She fell to the ground, gasping for breath that refused to come.

"You're no goddess," Haern said, squirming away from his biting prison.

She tried to kill him for his insolence. Her blade of darkness sliced off a chunk of his hair but drew no blood. It went on to fell two trees before dissipating. The assassin lunged, hurling a saber as he did. The weapon hit her and bounced off. She tried to grab him but he twirled, avoiding her touch, and then slashed at her neck. He felt grim satisfaction as it pierced flesh. Tessanna shrieked, the wail of an injured banshee. Blood flowed down her neck.

"*Be gone!*" she screamed. The command flung him through the air. Three more bolts of shadow followed. When he smacked into the upper branches of a tree, the bolts pummeled his chest. He fell to the dirt, moaning.

Tessanna glared at him, her good hand pressed against the wound. Blood, her blood, poured over her fingers and onto her shimmering black dress. Delysia rushed to Haern's side, tears on her face and healing light pouring from her hands.

"For a goddess, you bleed nicely," Tarlak said, preparing another spell. His head ached. His temples throbbed. Beside him, Aurelia seemed to be suffering similar problems. She looked unsteady on her feet as she loosed an arcing net of lightning. The silver-white swirled around Tessanna's body, causing no damage. Tarlak tried another fireball, but she prematurely detonated it with a spell of her own.

"I do this for Aullienna," Tessanna said before chanting words of a spell. A wave of shadows rolled toward them. Within the wave they saw stars, nebulas, and galaxies that they had no name for. Then the blackness hit, and all they knew was pain. Delysia lost her concentration, her healing spell dying on her lips. Tarlak fell to his knees, his mind spinning. Aurelia managed to stand, the darkness parting before her as if out of respect. When the wave passed, the elf looked at Tessanna with an expression that fueled the dark goddess's anger: pity.

⚜

Before Qurrah could draw any bones from his bag, Harruq slashed it open, spilling a chalky white pile to the dirt. Nonplussed, Qurrah enchanted all of them into a giant barrage of ribs, teeth, and fingers. Harruq crossed his arms and endured. The bones could bruise, even draw blood, but they could not do serious damage unless they found his eyes, mouth, or throat. The half-orc took a blind step forward, then another. He felt his brother's hand latch onto his wrist, and again a thieving, draining sensation flooded him. He gave it no time to feed. Both swords whipped around, slashing away the wrist. Harruq looked down, fascinated by what he saw.

"Your armor is gone," Harruq said, lifting Condemnation so that Qurrah could see a single, scarlet drop of blood fall from the keen edge. Qurrah glanced to his arm, where a thin cut marred his pale skin. For once, fear rounded the edges of the necromancer's eyes.

"You will not dare strike," Qurrah said, firing off a spell. A bolt of shadow leapt from his fingers, thudding into Harruq's chest like a hammer. Ribs snapped. Before he could move, a second followed, striking his shoulder. For an agonizing moment, he thought the bones there would crack and break, the pain was so intense. They did not, and his anger grew with each new source of pain. Not desiring a third blow, he leapt forward, his head leading. The top of his skull rammed into Qurrah's chest, knocking the air out of another spell.

Harruq tried an awkward cut as they both fell. The blade sliced just below the knee. No pain or darkness flooded into his hand. No solid stone greeted his blade. Just soft, bleeding flesh. Qurrah rolled back and pushed away, needing distance from those cursed swords. He put his weight on the cut leg, which buckled from its wound. He hobbled on the other. Harruq hefted his bulk from the dirt, glaring death. A bolt of lightning flashed over his head, from which of the three casters, he did not know. The glare hurt his eyes and disorientated his vision. In a haze of black, Qurrah turned to face his brother.

"You are a killer," Qurrah said, reaching a hand into a hidden pocket of his robe. "You prove me right with every cut."

"Just one last time," Harruq said.

He charged. Qurrah's hand streaked victoriously from the pocket, scattering a great white mist of bones he had laboriously prepared. A single word by the necromancer and they grew rigid in the air. Harruq tried to slam through. The hovering bits tore into the flesh of his face and hands. When his chest hit the bulk of it, he gasped in pain. Blood poured down, coloring the powder red. His strength sapped, he fell back, landing hard on one elbow. He heard another pop, his collarbone.

"Yes, brother," Qurrah mocked, dark energy covering his hands. "Just one last time."

"You wanted to see her again, didn't you?" Aurelia asked.

"You kept her from me," Tessanna seethed. The elf shook her head, as if things suddenly made sense to her.

"It was your idea, wasn't it? You wanted to make Aullienna's mind like yours?"

"She was mine to love," the girl said, her hands shaking. "Mine."

"You know it, don't you," Aurelia said. Tears wanted to run down her face, but she was too exhausted to cry. "It was you that killed her. You killed what you loved…but you've always done that, haven't you?"

Tessanna's face froze. Her anger and confusion spun out of control. She could think of no action that seemed right. She wanted to kneel and cry. She wanted to tear the elf into shreds. She wanted to flee. She wanted to beg for forgiveness. She wanted to die.

So she did nothing.

Harruq tried to move, tried to lift his swords, but his arms refused. Another spell would come, and he would be helpless before it. Although he had dealt death so often, he felt overwhelmingly unprepared. He closed his eyes, terror in every fiber. Dimly, he felt regret knowing he would never feel the soft silk of Aurelia's hair through his fingers again.

He thought of Aullienna smiling up at him as she bounced on his knee.

No, he thought. No.

He rammed his heel against Qurrah's cut knee. The necromancer screamed. Blood ran down his leg. He staggered back, struggling to regain his balance on his one good leg. Harruq clutched his swords with renewed strength. His anger fought against the curse. He would not fail. He would not betray Aullienna.

He closed the distance between them, slashing with both blades. Qurrah more fell than dove away, but it was enough. Salvation tore through the robes and across his chest, the wound too shallow to do more than spray blood across the glowing blade. His good leg pushed him back to his feet. He ran, knowing his brother followed with legs that pumped with life and vigor Qurrah had not known since birth. Suddenly a great force pressed into his back, and then he was flying. A tree stopped him.

The collision blacked out his vision. He lay slumped, his arms out as if he were embracing the trunk. His breath wheezed in a most pitiful way. He clutched the bark with his fingers and pushed himself around, refusing to die with a blade in his back like a coward.

"Will you kill me," Qurrah asked, a strange leer spreading across his face.

"Yes," Harruq said. He stabbed Salvation to the ground. Both hands closed around the hilt of Condemnation. He looked upon his brother, beaten and bloodied. A great welt swelled across his forehead. Blood surrounded his irises. The sound of his breath, labored and weak, brought him back to the days when Qurrah was a scrawny child unable to defend himself. A child that had looked to him for protection.

And now he looked to him with eyes begging for death.

In her frozen chaos, Tessanna turned, yearning for her lover. She saw him there, propped against the tree. Harruq towered over him. The others followed her gaze. Every soul there watched. Every soul waited.

"I was right," Qurrah said. "Kill me. Let me die knowing that one truth."

"I'm sorry," Harruq said. His sword hesitated. His arms shook. His lips trembled. From his gut bellowed a roar, filled with anguish, hate, pain, and love. He slammed his blade deep into the trunk of the tree. It drew no blood. It took no life.

Condemnation missed.

"I'm sorry," Harruq said, gasping out the words. "But I can't."

"You fool," Tarlak said, his heart sinking.

Tessanna shrieked, a cry Harruq knew well. It was the same sound he had made upon finding his daughter. A thick bolt of lightning struck the side of his chest, plowing him away from the beaten Qurrah. He did not resist, every muscle in his body slack. The goddess ran to her lover, her ethereal wings fading away like smoke. Qurrah rose, took a weak step forward, and collapsed into her arms. Tessanna's dark robe faded away. Naked and wounded, she struggled to hold what little weight the half-orc had. She saw his bruises. She felt the wet blood spilling on her. He tried to speak, but it was an inane hiss to her ears.

"Aullienna loved you!" Aurelia shouted. Her magical strength was gone. It was the only attack she could make. Tessanna shrieked back at her, the sound like the cry an alley cat. She turned, waved her arms, and then a black portal ripped into the air. She carried her lover inside, desperate to flee the damning words of the elf. With a hiss of air, the portal closed, one final crack signifying its disappearance.

The brief silence that came after was shocking. Aurelia rushed to her husband, crying out his name. She knelt down at his side, his bruised body covered with blood.

"I'm so sorry," he grunted before passing out.

"Oh, Harruq," she said, brushing a hand across his face. She laid her head on his chest and listened to the beat of his heart.

Tarlak went to his sister. She was sobbing over Haern, pouring healing spell after healing spell into his beaten body. The wizard took her hands and pulled her to a stand so he could embrace her.

"He'll be fine," he whispered into her ear. "Give him time. He'll be fine."

"I have to help him," Delysia sobbed. "I can't let him, not like Brug, not like…"

Tarlak shushed her. She buried her head in his shoulder and cried silently. He closed his eyes and rocked side-to-side, thinking a thousand deaths he would not mind befalling Qurrah Tun.

They turned to look at Brug's still body. Tarlak left her to go to him. He knelt down and closed the eyelids. When the vacant eye refused to stay shut, he tilted the helmet to cover it, but only after he kissed the man's forehead.

"Keep a drink ready for me," he said, standing. His eyes turned to the half-orc, still in his wife's arms.

"You idiot," the wizard said, unable to convey the weight of everything, but that was close. Close enough to matter. "You damn, fucking idiot."

33

They made another pyre using the leftover wood cut the day before. The mood was no less somber. Their hearts torn, the four watched the body consumed by fire.

"Will we chase them?" Haern asked. He looked healthier, Delysia's healing spells doing much to cure the many bruises the shadow bolts had left. Before he answered, Tarlak looked over at the half-orc, who stood with his wife's arms around him. His arm was in a sling and his face and neck a burnt mess.

"No," he said at last. "We've lost too many. Let them come to us. I will not send any more to die."

"Will he leave us be?"

Tarlak cast a ring Brug had made for him onto the fire. "Only Ashhur knows," he said. "But I pray that he does."

Harruq watched the body burn, the comfort of his wife meager compared to the guilt he now carried. Two lives had come to repay the debt of the countless he had massacred. Two lives he could have spared. Worse, Qurrah remained free with his demon girl at his side.

The fire swayed to one side, dancing in the wind. He wondered if his brother felt guilt for his actions. Just the previous night, he had sworn death, and yet he could not see it through. What did that mean? He had spared his brother's life and done what his conscience had demanded in that brutal second where he almost plunged the blade into flesh. Try as he might, he could not convince himself he had done the right thing. He had been a coward. Or a fool. Or a failure.

"Was I wrong?" he whispered.

"What was that?" Aurelia asked, glancing up at him. He only shook his head.

"Nothing."

He stayed out later than the rest, watching until the fire died deep in the night. At its last flicker, he wished to whatever god that might exist, that might listen, to have that day back over again.

No god answered, not in a way he knew how to listen for. Alone he stood, feeling forsaken by the world. A cold wind blew against his skin, a sign that winter was coming early.

Against that same wind, Qurrah and Tessanna huddled without fire or blanket for warmth. The girl shivered naked, her thin body nestled into his robes. Neither had been able to find sleep.

"She wasn't right," Tessanna muttered, unable to stand the voices that echoed incessantly in her head.

"Right about what?" Qurrah asked. The girl opened her mouth to answer, but could not say it. So instead, she asked, "What will we do?"

The half-orc pulled her closer, burying his face into her hair to hide his few stubborn tears.

"I have broken too many promises. I will keep the rest. I will go west and claim Darakken's spellbook as my own. I will heal your mind. It is the one promise I can still keep."

"Can I come?" she asked, his robe clutched tight in her hands. "I do not want to be alone. Please, take me with you."

In answer, Qurrah lifted her face and kissed her. Together, they shared their warmth against the biting wind. When he looked to the stars, his mind thought only of his brother, and of how he had veered his blade at the last moment when he should have buried it to the hilt in his forehead.

It was in this Qurrah found something to cling to, some hope within the madness of the day. His brother still loved him. Comforted, he curled closer to Tessanna and endured the long, dreary night.

The Cost of Betrayal

A Note from the Author:

First of all, if you've made it this far, I want to say thanks. You're two stories in, with three more to go. Plenty of fun is in store for the brothers Tun, and I hope you're as excited as I am in continuing the next book.

So why am I yammering instead of typing 'The End' and letting you get back to your to-be-read list? There's a lot of good books waiting for you, and that's exactly while I'm still writing. You spent time reading my book, and on my part, that is a huge thrill. That's all I want, really. I've got this huge story begging to be told, and I'm doing my best to tell it, but these characters don't really *live* until they've got a reader.

I'm just a crackpot, self-publishing these works on every avenue I can find. In this, I am certainly not alone. If you enjoyed this novel, or at least thought it was worth your time and hard-earned money, then do me a favor: write a review. I don't care if it's a single sentence or a longwinded mini-novel (sort of like this little note, eh?). I know I'm asking a lot, but help others find me. Give me a bad review even, if you feel that I deserve it. I'm still writing, I'm still telling stories, and sometimes a stern word telling you your faults will do better than a thousand pages praising you to the sky.

Not that I don't mind hearing some praise every now and then.

So again, thanks for reading. I hope you enjoyed my story. A special thanks to Mrs. Patterson, Mrs. Borushaski, and Dr. Brown. They were my Creative Writing teachers throughout High School and College, and I owe them more than they could possibly know.

Questions? Comments? Call me a fool, make a request, or just plain say 'hi': send me an email at ddalglish@yahoo.com. I promise you, I'll respond to every single one, and be thrilled every time.

Also, in case you liked the cover art, it was by an awesome guy named Peter Ortiz. You can find more of his work at http://standalone-complex.deviantart.com/.

Thanks so much,

David Dalglish

Printed in Great Britain
by Amazon